Les Misérables

Volume II: Cosette

Les Misérables

Volume II: Cosette

Victor Hugo

MINT EDITIONS

Les Misérables was first published in 1862.

This edition published by Mint Editions 2021.

ISBN 9781513263465 | E-ISBN 9781513264011

Published by Mint Editions®

 MINT EDITIONS

minteditionsbooks.com

Publishing Director: Jennifer Newens
Design & Production: Rachel Lopez Metzger
Project Manager: Micaela Clark
Translated by: Isabel F. Hapgood
Typesetting: Westchester Publishing Services

Les Misérables Volume I: Fantine P|9781513267449
E|9781513272443
Les Misérables Volume III: Marius P|9781513279787
E|9781513284804
Les Misérables Volume IV: The Idyll in the Rue Plumet and the
Epic in the Rue St. Denis P| 9781513279794 E|9781513284811
Les Misérables Volume V: Jean Valjean P|9781513284811
E|9781513284828

Contents

BOOK FIRST
WATERLOO

I

What is Met with on the Way from Nivelles

L ast year (1861), on a beautiful May morning, a traveller, the person who is telling this story, was coming from Nivelles, and directing his course towards La Hulpe. He was on foot. He was pursuing a broad paved road, which undulated between two rows of trees, over the hills which succeed each other, raise the road and let it fall again, and produce something in the nature of enormous waves.

He had passed Lillois and Bois-Seigneur-Isaac. In the west he perceived the slate-roofed tower of Braine-l'Alleud, which has the form of a reversed vase. He had just left behind a wood upon an eminence; and at the angle of the crossroad, by the side of a sort of mouldy gibbet bearing the inscription *Ancient Barrier No. 4*, a public house, bearing on its front this sign: *At the Four Winds* (Aux Quatre Vents). *Échabeau, Private Café*.

A quarter of a league further on, he arrived at the bottom of a little valley, where there is water which passes beneath an arch made through the embankment of the road. The clump of sparsely planted but very green trees, which fills the valley on one side of the road, is dispersed over the meadows on the other, and disappears gracefully and as in order in the direction of Braine-l'Alleud.

On the right, close to the road, was an inn, with a four-wheeled cart at the door, a large bundle of hop-poles, a plough, a heap of dried brushwood near a flourishing hedge, lime smoking in a square hole, and a ladder suspended along an old penthouse with straw partitions. A young girl was weeding in a field, where a huge yellow poster, probably of some outside spectacle, such as a parish festival, was fluttering in the wind. At one corner of the inn, beside a pool in which a flotilla of ducks was navigating, a badly paved path plunged into the bushes. The wayfarer struck into this.

After traversing a hundred paces, skirting a wall of the fifteenth century, surmounted by a pointed gable, with bricks set in contrast, he found himself before a large door of arched stone, with a rectilinear impost, in the sombre style of Louis XIV, flanked by two flat medallions.

A severe façade rose above this door; a wall, perpendicular to the façade, almost touched the door, and flanked it with an abrupt right angle. In the meadow before the door lay three harrows, through which, in disorder, grew all the flowers of May. The door was closed. The two decrepit leaves which barred it were ornamented with an old rusty knocker.

The sun was charming; the branches had that soft shivering of May, which seems to proceed rather from the nests than from the wind. A brave little bird, probably a lover, was carolling in a distracted manner in a large tree.

The wayfarer bent over and examined a rather large circular excavation, resembling the hollow of a sphere, in the stone on the left, at the foot of the pier of the door.

At this moment the leaves of the door parted, and a peasant woman emerged.

She saw the wayfarer, and perceived what he was looking at.

"It was a French cannon-ball which made that," she said to him. And she added:—

"That which you see there, higher up in the door, near a nail, is the hole of a big iron bullet as large as an egg. The bullet did not pierce the wood."

"What is the name of this place?" inquired the wayfarer.

"Hougomont," said the peasant woman.

The traveller straightened himself up. He walked on a few paces, and went off to look over the tops of the hedges. On the horizon through the trees, he perceived a sort of little elevation, and on this elevation something which at that distance resembled a lion.

He was on the battle-field of Waterloo.

II

HOUGOMONT

Hougomont,—this was a funereal spot, the beginning of the obstacle, the first resistance, which that great wood-cutter of Europe, called Napoleon, encountered at Waterloo, the first knot under the blows of his axe.

It was a château; it is no longer anything but a farm. For the antiquary, Hougomont is *Hugomons*. This manor was built by Hugo, Sire of Somerel, the same who endowed the sixth chaplaincy of the Abbey of Villiers.

The traveller pushed open the door, elbowed an ancient calash under the porch, and entered the courtyard.

The first thing which struck him in this paddock was a door of the sixteenth century, which here simulates an arcade, everything else having fallen prostrate around it. A monumental aspect often has its birth in ruin. In a wall near the arcade opens another arched door, of the time of Henry IV, permitting a glimpse of the trees of an orchard; beside this door, a manure-hole, some pickaxes, some shovels, some carts, an old well, with its flagstone and its iron reel, a chicken jumping, and a turkey spreading its tail, a chapel surmounted by a small bell-tower, a blossoming pear-tree trained in espalier against the wall of the chapel— behold the court, the conquest of which was one of Napoleon's dreams. This corner of earth, could he but have seized it, would, perhaps, have given him the world likewise. Chickens are scattering its dust abroad with their beaks. A growl is audible; it is a huge dog, who shows his teeth and replaces the English.

The English behaved admirably there. Cooke's four companies of guards there held out for seven hours against the fury of an army.

Hougomont viewed on the map, as a geometrical plan, comprising buildings and enclosures, presents a sort of irregular rectangle, one angle of which is nicked out. It is this angle which contains the southern door, guarded by this wall, which commands it only a gun's length away. Hougomont has two doors,—the southern door, that of the château; and the northern door, belonging to the farm. Napoleon sent his brother Jérôme against Hougomont; the divisions of Foy, Guilleminot, and Bachelu hurled themselves against it; nearly the entire corps of Reille was employed against it, and miscarried; Kellermann's balls were exhausted on this heroic section of wall. Bauduin's brigade was not strong enough to force Hougomont on the north, and the brigade of Soye could not do more than effect the beginning of a breach on the south, but without taking it.

The farm buildings border the courtyard on the south. A bit of the north door, broken by the French, hangs suspended to the wall. It consists of four planks nailed to two cross-beams, on which the scars of the attack are visible.

The northern door, which was beaten in by the French, and which has had a piece applied to it to replace the panel suspended on the wall, stands half-open at the bottom of the paddock; it is cut squarely in the wall, built of stone below, of brick above which closes in the courtyard on the north. It is a simple door for carts, such as exist in all farms, with the two large leaves made of rustic planks: beyond lie the meadows. The dispute over this entrance was furious. For a long time, all sorts of imprints of bloody hands were visible on the door-posts. It was there that Bauduin was killed.

The storm of the combat still lingers in this courtyard; its horror is visible there; the confusion of the fray was petrified there; it lives and it dies there; it was only yesterday. The walls are in the death agony, the stones fall; the breaches cry aloud; the holes are wounds; the drooping, quivering trees seem to be making an effort to flee.

This courtyard was more built up in 1815 than it is to-day. Buildings which have since been pulled down then formed redans and angles.

The English barricaded themselves there; the French made their way in, but could not stand their ground. Beside the chapel, one wing of the château, the only ruin now remaining of the manor of Hougomont, rises in a crumbling state,—disembowelled, one might say. The château served for a dungeon, the chapel for a block-house. There men exterminated each other. The French, fired on from every point,—from behind the walls, from the summits of the garrets, from the depths of the cellars, through all the casements, through all the air-holes, through every crack in the stones,—fetched fagots and set fire to walls and men; the reply to the grape-shot was a conflagration.

In the ruined wing, through windows garnished with bars of iron, the dismantled chambers of the main building of brick are visible; the English guards were in ambush in these rooms; the spiral of the staircase, cracked from the ground floor to the very roof, appears like the inside of a broken shell. The staircase has two stories; the English, besieged on the staircase, and massed on its upper steps, had cut off the lower steps. These consisted of large slabs of blue stone, which form a heap among the nettles. Half a score of steps still cling to the wall; on the first is cut the figure of a trident. These inaccessible steps are solid in their niches. All the rest resembles a jaw which has been denuded of its teeth. There are two old trees there: one is dead; the other is wounded at its base, and is clothed with verdure in April. Since 1815 it has taken to growing through the staircase.

A massacre took place in the chapel. The interior, which has recovered its calm, is singular. The mass has not been said there since the carnage. Nevertheless, the altar has been left there—an altar of unpolished wood, placed against a background of roughhewn stone. Four whitewashed walls, a door opposite the altar, two small arched windows; over the door a large wooden crucifix, below the crucifix a square air-hole stopped up with a bundle of hay; on the ground, in one corner, an old window-frame with the glass all broken to pieces—such is the chapel. Near the altar there is nailed up a wooden statue of Saint Anne, of the fifteenth century; the head of the infant Jesus has been carried off by a large ball. The French, who were masters of the chapel for a moment, and were then dislodged, set fire to it. The flames filled this building; it was a perfect furnace; the door was burned, the floor was burned, the wooden Christ was not burned. The fire preyed upon his feet, of which only the blackened stumps are now to be seen; then it stopped,—a miracle, according to the assertion of the people of the neighborhood. The infant Jesus, decapitated, was less fortunate than the Christ.

The walls are covered with inscriptions. Near the feet of Christ this name is to be read: *Henquinez*. Then these others: *Conde de Rio Maior Marques y Marquesa de Almagro (Habana)*. There are French names with exclamation points,—a sign of wrath. The wall was freshly whitewashed in 1849. The nations insulted each other there.

It was at the door of this chapel that the corpse was picked up which held an axe in its hand; this corpse was Sub-Lieutenant Legros.

On emerging from the chapel, a well is visible on the left. There are two in this courtyard. One inquires, Why is there no bucket and pulley to this? It is because water is no longer drawn there. Why is water not drawn there? Because it is full of skeletons.

The last person who drew water from the well was named Guillaume van Kylsom. He was a peasant who lived at Hougomont, and was gardener there. On the 18th of June, 1815, his family fled and concealed themselves in the woods.

The forest surrounding the Abbey of Villiers sheltered these unfortunate people who had been scattered abroad, for many days and nights. There are at this day certain traces recognizable, such as old boles of burned trees, which mark the site of these poor bivouacs trembling in the depths of the thickets.

Guillaume van Kylsom remained at Hougomont, "to guard the château," and concealed himself in the cellar. The English discovered him there. They tore him from his hiding-place, and the combatants forced this frightened man to serve them, by administering blows with the flats of their swords. They were thirsty; this Guillaume brought them water. It was from this well that he drew it. Many drank there their last draught. This well where drank so many of the dead was destined to die itself.

After the engagement, they were in haste to bury the dead bodies. Death has a fashion of harassing victory, and she causes the pest to follow glory. The typhus is a concomitant of triumph. This well was deep, and it was turned into a sepulchre. Three hundred dead bodies were cast into it. With too much haste perhaps. Were they all dead? Legend says they were not. It seems that on the night succeeding the interment, feeble voices were heard calling from the well.

This well is isolated in the middle of the courtyard. Three walls, part stone, part brick, and simulating a small, square tower, and folded like the leaves of a screen, surround it on all sides. The fourth side is open. It is there that the water was drawn. The wall at the bottom has a sort of shapeless loophole, possibly the hole made by a shell. This little tower had a platform, of which only the beams remain. The iron supports of the well on the right form a cross. On leaning over, the eye is lost in a deep cylinder of brick which is filled with a heaped-up mass of shadows. The base of the walls all about the well is concealed in a growth of nettles.

This well has not in front of it that large blue slab which forms the table for all wells in Belgium. The slab has here been replaced by a cross-beam, against which lean five or six shapeless fragments of knotty and petrified wood which resemble huge bones. There is no longer either pail, chain, or pulley; but there is still the stone basin which served the overflow. The rain-water collects there, and from time to time a bird of the neighboring forests comes thither to drink, and then flies away. One house in this ruin, the farmhouse, is still inhabited. The door of this house opens on the courtyard. Upon this door, beside a pretty Gothic lock-plate, there is an iron handle with trefoils placed slanting. At the moment when the Hanoverian lieutenant, Wilda, grasped this handle in order to take refuge in the farm, a French sapper hewed off his hand with an axe.

The family who occupy the house had for their grandfather Guillaume van Kylsom, the old gardener, dead long since. A woman with gray hair said to us: "I was there. I was three years old. My sister, who was older, was terrified and wept. They carried us off to the woods. I went there in my mother's arms. We glued our ears to the earth to hear. I imitated the cannon, and went *boum! boum!*"

A door opening from the courtyard on the left led into the orchard, so we were told. The orchard is terrible.

It is in three parts; one might almost say, in three acts. The first part is a garden, the second is an orchard, the third is a wood. These three parts have a common enclosure: on the side of the entrance, the buildings of the château and the farm; on the left, a hedge; on the right, a wall; and at the end, a wall. The wall on the right is of brick, the wall at the bottom is of stone. One enters the garden first. It slopes downwards, is planted with gooseberry bushes, choked with a wild growth of vegetation, and terminated by a monumental terrace of cut stone, with balustrade with a double curve.

It was a seignorial garden in the first French style which preceded Le Nôtre; to-day it is ruins and briars. The pilasters are surmounted by globes which resemble cannon-balls of stone. Forty-three balusters can still be counted on their sockets; the rest lie prostrate in the grass. Almost all bear scratches of bullets. One broken baluster is placed on the pediment like a fractured leg.

It was in this garden, further down than the orchard, that six light-infantry men of the 1st, having made their way thither, and being unable to escape, hunted down and caught like bears in their dens, accepted the combat with two Hanoverian companies, one of which was armed with carbines. The Hanoverians lined this balustrade and fired from above. The infantry men, replying from below, six against two hundred, intrepid and with no shelter save the currant-bushes, took a quarter of an hour to die.

One mounts a few steps and passes from the garden into the orchard, properly speaking. There, within the limits of those few square fathoms, fifteen hundred men fell in less than an hour. The wall seems ready to renew the combat. Thirty-eight loopholes, pierced by the English at irregular heights, are there still. In front of the sixth are placed two English tombs of granite. There are loopholes only in the south wall, as the principal attack came from that quarter. The wall is hidden on the outside by a tall hedge; the French came up, thinking that they had to deal only with a hedge, crossed it, and found the wall both an obstacle and an ambuscade, with the English guards behind it, the thirty-eight loopholes firing at once a shower of grape-shot and balls, and Soye's brigade was broken against it. Thus Waterloo began.

Nevertheless, the orchard was taken. As they had no ladders, the French scaled it with their nails. They fought hand to hand amid the trees. All this grass has been soaked in blood. A battalion of Nassau, seven hundred strong, was overwhelmed there. The outside of the wall, against which Kellermann's two batteries were trained, is gnawed by grape-shot.

This orchard is sentient, like others, in the month of May. It has its buttercups and its daisies; the grass is tall there; the cart-horses browse there; cords of hair, on which linen is drying, traverse the spaces between the trees and force the passer-by to bend his head; one walks over this uncultivated land, and one's foot dives into mole-holes. In the middle of the grass one observes an uprooted tree-bole which lies there all verdant. Major Blackmann leaned against it to die. Beneath a great tree in the neighborhood fell the German general, Duplat, descended from a French family which fled on the revocation of the Edict of Nantes. An aged and falling apple-tree leans far over to one side, its wound dressed with a bandage of straw and of clayey loam. Nearly all the apple-trees are falling with age. There is not one which has not had its bullet or its biscayan. The skeletons of dead trees abound in this orchard. Crows fly through their branches, and at the end of it is a wood full of violets.

Bauduin killed, Foy wounded, conflagration, massacre, carnage, a rivulet formed of English blood, French blood, German blood mingled in fury, a well crammed with corpses, the regiment of Nassau and the regiment of Brunswick destroyed, Duplat killed, Blackmann killed, the English Guards mutilated, twenty French battalions, besides the forty from Reille's corps, decimated, three thousand men in that hovel of Hougomont alone cut down, slashed to pieces, shot, burned, with their throats cut,—and all this so that a peasant can say to-day to the traveller: *Monsieur, give me three francs, and if you like, I will explain to you the affair of Waterloo!*

III

The Eighteenth of June, 1815

L et us turn back,—that is one of the story-teller's rights,—and put ourselves once more in the year 1815, and even a little earlier than the epoch when the action narrated in the first part of this book took place.

If it had not rained in the night between the 17th and the 18th of June, 1815, the fate of Europe would have been different. A few drops of water, more or less, decided the downfall of Napoleon. All that Providence required in order to make Waterloo the end of Austerlitz was a little more rain, and a cloud traversing the sky out of season sufficed to make a world crumble.

The battle of Waterloo could not be begun until half-past eleven o'clock, and that gave Blücher time to come up. Why? Because the ground was wet. The artillery had to wait until it became a little firmer before they could manœuvre.

Napoleon was an artillery officer, and felt the effects of this. The foundation of this wonderful captain was the man who, in the report to the Directory on Aboukir, said: *Such a one of our balls killed six men*. All his plans of battle were arranged for projectiles. The key to his victory was to make the artillery converge on one point. He treated the strategy of the hostile general like a citadel, and made a breach in it. He overwhelmed the weak point with grape-shot; he joined and dissolved battles with cannon. There was something of the sharpshooter in his genius. To beat in squares, to pulverize regiments, to break lines, to crush and disperse masses,—for him everything lay in this, to strike, strike, strike incessantly,—and he intrusted this task to the cannon-ball. A redoubtable method, and one which, united with genius, rendered this gloomy athlete of the pugilism of war invincible for the space of fifteen years.

On the 18th of June, 1815, he relied all the more on his artillery, because he had numbers on his side. Wellington had only one hundred and fifty-nine mouths of fire; Napoleon had two hundred and forty.

Suppose the soil dry, and the artillery capable of moving, the action would have begun at six o'clock in the morning. The battle would have been won and ended at two o'clock, three hours before the change of fortune in favor of the Prussians. What amount of blame attaches to Napoleon for the loss of this battle? Is the shipwreck due to the pilot?

Was it the evident physical decline of Napoleon that complicated this epoch by an inward diminution of force? Had the twenty years of war worn out the blade as it had worn the scabbard, the soul as well as the body? Did the veteran make himself disastrously felt in the leader? In a word, was this genius, as many historians of note have thought, suffering from an eclipse? Did he go into a frenzy in order to disguise his weakened powers from himself? Did he begin to waver under the delusion of a breath of adventure? Had he become—a grave matter in a general—unconscious of peril? Is there an age, in this class of material great men, who may be called the giants of action, when genius grows short-sighted? Old age has no hold on the geniuses of the ideal; for the Dantes and Michael Angelos to grow old is to grow in greatness; is it to grow less for the Hannibals and the Bonapartes? Had Napoleon lost the direct sense of victory? Had he reached the point where he could no longer recognize the reef, could no longer divine the snare, no longer discern the crumbling brink of abysses? Had he lost his power of scenting out catastrophes? He who had in former days known all the roads to triumph, and who, from the summit of his chariot of lightning, pointed them out with a sovereign finger, had he now reached that state of sinister amazement when he could lead his tumultuous legions harnessed to it, to the precipice? Was he seized at the age of forty-six with a supreme madness? Was that titanic charioteer of destiny no longer anything more than an immense dare-devil?

We do not think so.

His plan of battle was, by the confession of all, a masterpiece. To go straight to the centre of the Allies' line, to make a breach in the enemy, to cut them in two, to drive the British half back on Hal, and the Prussian half on Tongres, to make two shattered fragments of Wellington and Blücher, to carry Mont-Saint-Jean, to seize Brussels, to hurl the German into the Rhine, and the Englishman into the sea. All this was contained in that battle, according to Napoleon. Afterwards people would see.

Of course, we do not here pretend to furnish a history of the battle of Waterloo; one of the scenes of the foundation of the story which we are relating is connected with this battle, but this history is not our subject; this history, moreover, has been finished, and finished in a masterly manner, from one point of view by Napoleon, and from another point of view by a whole pleiad of historians.

As for us, we leave the historians at loggerheads; we are but a distant witness, a passer-by on the plain, a seeker bending over that soil all made of human flesh, taking appearances for realities, perchance; we have no right to oppose, in the name of science, a collection of facts which contain illusions, no doubt; we possess neither military practice nor strategic ability which authorize a system; in our opinion, a chain of accidents dominated the two leaders at Waterloo; and when it becomes a question of destiny, that mysterious culprit, we judge like that ingenious judge, the populace.

IV

A

Those persons who wish to gain a clear idea of the battle of Waterloo have only to place, mentally, on the ground, a capital A. The left limb of the A is the road to Nivelles, the right limb is the road to Genappe, the tie of the A is the hollow road to Ohain from Braine-l'Alleud. The top of the A is Mont-Saint-Jean, where Wellington is; the lower left tip is Hougomont, where Reille is stationed with Jérôme Bonaparte; the right tip is the Belle-Alliance, where Napoleon was. At the centre of this chord is the precise point where the final word of the battle was pronounced. It was there that the lion has been placed, the involuntary symbol of the supreme heroism of the Imperial Guard.

The triangle included in the top of the A, between the two limbs and the tie, is the plateau of Mont-Saint-Jean. The dispute over this plateau constituted the whole battle. The wings of the two armies extended to the right and left of the two roads to Genappe and Nivelles; d'Erlon facing Picton, Reille facing Hill.

Behind the tip of the A, behind the plateau of Mont-Saint-Jean, is the forest of Soignes.

As for the plain itself, let the reader picture to himself a vast undulating sweep of ground; each rise commands the next rise, and all the undulations mount towards Mont-Saint-Jean, and there end in the forest.

Two hostile troops on a field of battle are two wrestlers. It is a question of seizing the opponent round the waist. The one seeks to trip up the other. They clutch at everything: a bush is a point of support; an angle of the wall offers them a rest to the shoulder; for the lack of a hovel under whose cover they can draw up, a regiment yields its ground; an unevenness in the ground, a chance turn in the landscape, a cross-path encountered at the right moment, a grove, a ravine, can stay the heel of that colossus which is called an army, and prevent its retreat. He who quits the field is beaten; hence the necessity devolving on the responsible leader, of examining the most insignificant clump of trees, and of studying deeply the slightest relief in the ground.

The two generals had attentively studied the plain of Mont-Saint-Jean, now called the plain of Waterloo. In the preceding year, Wellington, with the sagacity of foresight, had examined it as the possible seat of a great battle. Upon this spot, and for this duel, on the 18th of June, Wellington had the good post, Napoleon the bad post. The English army was stationed above, the French army below.

It is almost superfluous here to sketch the appearance of Napoleon on horseback, glass in hand, upon the heights of Rossomme, at daybreak, on June 18, 1815. All the world has seen him before we can show him. That calm profile under the little three-cornered hat of the school of Brienne, that green uniform, the white revers concealing the star of the Legion of Honor, his great coat hiding his epaulets, the corner of red ribbon peeping from beneath his vest, his leather trousers, the white horse with the saddle-cloth of purple velvet bearing on the corners crowned N's and eagles, Hessian boots over silk stockings, silver spurs, the sword of Marengo,—that whole figure of the last of the Cæsars is present to all imaginations, saluted with acclamations by some, severely regarded by others.

That figure stood for a long time wholly in the light; this arose from a certain legendary dimness evolved by the majority of heroes, and which always veils the truth for a longer or shorter time; but to-day history and daylight have arrived.

That light called history is pitiless; it possesses this peculiar and divine quality, that, pure light as it is, and precisely because it is wholly light, it often casts a shadow in places where people had hitherto beheld rays; from the same man it constructs two different phantoms, and the one attacks the other and executes justice on it, and the shadows of the despot contend with the brilliancy of the leader. Hence arises a truer measure in the definitive judgments of nations. Babylon violated lessens Alexander, Rome enchained lessens Cæsar, Jerusalem murdered lessens Titus, tyranny follows the tyrant. It is a misfortune for a man to leave behind him the night which bears his form.

V

The Quid Obscurum of Battles

Every one is acquainted with the first phase of this battle; a beginning which was troubled, uncertain, hesitating, menacing to both armies, but still more so for the English than for the French.

It had rained all night, the earth had been cut up by the downpour, the water had accumulated here and there in the hollows of the plain as if in casks; at some points the gear of the artillery carriages was buried up to the axles, the circingles of the horses were dripping with liquid mud. If the wheat and rye trampled down by this cohort of transports on the march had not filled in the ruts and strewn a litter beneath the wheels, all movement, particularly in the valleys, in the direction of Papelotte would have been impossible.

The affair began late. Napoleon, as we have already explained, was in the habit of keeping all his artillery well in hand, like a pistol, aiming it now at one point, now at another, of the battle; and it had been his wish to wait until the horse batteries could move and gallop freely. In order to do that it was necessary that the sun should come out and dry the soil. But the sun did not make its appearance. It was no longer the rendezvous of Austerlitz. When the first cannon was fired, the English general, Colville, looked at his watch, and noted that it was thirty-five minutes past eleven.

The action was begun furiously, with more fury, perhaps, than the Emperor would have wished, by the left wing of the French resting on Hougomont. At the same time Napoleon attacked the centre by hurling Quiot's brigade on La Haie-Sainte, and Ney pushed forward the right wing of the French against the left wing of the English, which rested on Papelotte.

The attack on Hougomont was something of a feint; the plan was to draw Wellington thither, and to make him swerve to the left. This plan would have succeeded if the four companies of the English guards and the brave Belgians of Perponcher's division had not held the position solidly, and Wellington, instead of massing his troops there, could confine himself to despatching thither, as reinforcements, only four more companies of guards and one battalion from Brunswick.

The attack of the right wing of the French on Papelotte was calculated, in fact, to overthrow the English left, to cut off the road to Brussels, to bar the passage against possible Prussians, to force Mont-Saint-Jean, to turn Wellington back on Hougomont, thence on Braine-l'Alleud, thence on Hal; nothing easier. With the exception of a few incidents this attack succeeded. Papelotte was taken; La Haie-Sainte was carried.

A detail to be noted. There was in the English infantry, particularly in Kempt's brigade, a great many raw recruits. These young soldiers were valiant in the presence of our redoubtable infantry; their inexperience extricated them intrepidly from the dilemma; they performed particularly excellent service as skirmishers: the soldier skirmisher, left somewhat to himself, becomes, so to speak, his own general. These recruits displayed some of the French ingenuity and fury. This novice of an infantry had dash. This displeased Wellington.

After the taking of La Haie-Sainte the battle wavered.

There is in this day an obscure interval, from midday to four o'clock; the middle portion of this battle is almost indistinct, and participates in the sombreness of the hand-to-hand conflict. Twilight reigns over it. We perceive vast fluctuations in that fog, a dizzy mirage, paraphernalia of war almost unknown to-day, pendant colbacks, floating sabre-taches, cross-belts, cartridge-boxes for grenades, hussar dolmans, red boots with a thousand wrinkles, heavy shakos garlanded with torsades, the almost black infantry of Brunswick mingled with the scarlet infantry of England, the English soldiers with great, white circular pads on the slopes of their shoulders for epaulets, the Hanoverian light-horse with their oblong casques of leather, with brass hands and red horse-tails, the Scotch with their bare knees and plaids, the great white gaiters of our grenadiers; pictures, not strategic lines—what Salvator Rosa requires, not what is suited to the needs of Gribeauval.

A certain amount of tempest is always mingled with a battle. *Quid obscurum, quid divinum*. Each historian traces, to some extent, the particular feature which pleases him amid this pell-mell. Whatever may be the combinations of the generals, the shock of armed masses has an incalculable ebb. During the action the plans of the two leaders enter into each other and become mutually thrown out of shape. Such a point of the field of battle devours more combatants than such another, just as more or less spongy soils soak up more or less quickly the water which is poured on them. It becomes necessary to pour out more soldiers than one would like; a series of expenditures which are the unforeseen. The line of battle waves and undulates like a thread, the trails of blood gush illogically, the fronts of the armies waver, the regiments form capes and gulfs as they enter and withdraw; all these reefs are continually moving in front of each other. Where the infantry stood the artillery arrives, the cavalry rushes in where the artillery was, the battalions are like smoke. There was something there; seek it. It has disappeared; the open spots change place, the sombre folds advance and retreat, a sort of wind from the sepulchre pushes forward, hurls back, distends, and disperses these tragic multitudes. What is a fray? an oscillation? The immobility of a mathematical plan expresses a minute, not a day. In order to depict a battle, there is required one of those powerful painters who have chaos in their brushes. Rembrandt is better than Vandermeulen; Vandermeulen, exact at noon, lies at three o'clock. Geometry is deceptive; the hurricane alone is trustworthy. That is what confers on Folard the right to contradict Polybius. Let us add, that there is a certain instant when the battle degenerates into a combat, becomes specialized, and disperses into innumerable detailed feats, which, to borrow the expression of Napoleon himself, "belong rather to the biography of the regiments than to the history of the army." The historian has, in this case, the evident right to sum up the whole. He cannot do more than seize the principal outlines of the struggle, and it is not given to any one narrator, however conscientious he may be, to fix, absolutely, the form of that horrible cloud which is called a battle.

This, which is true of all great armed encounters, is particularly applicable to Waterloo.

Nevertheless, at a certain moment in the afternoon the battle came to a point.

VI

Four O'clock in the Afternoon

Towards four o'clock the condition of the English army was serious. The Prince of Orange was in command of the centre, Hill of the right wing, Picton of the left wing. The Prince of Orange, desperate and intrepid, shouted to the Hollando-Belgians: "Nassau! Brunswick! Never retreat!" Hill, having been weakened, had come up to the support of Wellington; Picton was dead. At the very moment when the English had captured from the French the flag of the 105th of the line, the French had killed the English general, Picton, with a bullet through the head. The battle had, for Wellington, two bases of action, Hougomont and La Haie-Sainte; Hougomont still held out, but was on fire; La Haie-Sainte was taken. Of the German battalion which defended it, only forty-two men survived; all the officers, except five, were either dead or captured. Three thousand combatants had been massacred in that barn. A sergeant of the English Guards, the foremost boxer in England, reputed invulnerable by his companions, had been killed there by a little French drummer-boy. Baring had been dislodged, Alten put to the sword. Many flags had been lost, one from Alten's division, and one from the battalion of Lunenburg, carried by a prince of the house of Deux-Ponts. The Scotch Grays no longer existed; Ponsonby's great dragoons had been hacked to pieces. That valiant cavalry had bent beneath the lancers of Bro and beneath the cuirassiers of Travers; out of twelve hundred horses, six hundred remained; out of three lieutenant-colonels, two lay on the earth,—Hamilton wounded, Mater slain. Ponsonby had fallen, riddled by seven lance-thrusts. Gordon was dead. Marsh was dead. Two divisions, the fifth and the sixth, had been annihilated.

Hougomont injured, La Haie-Sainte taken, there now existed but one rallying-point, the centre. That point still held firm. Wellington reinforced it. He summoned thither Hill, who was at Merle-Braine; he summoned Chassé, who was at Braine-l'Alleud.

The centre of the English army, rather concave, very dense, and very compact, was strongly posted. It occupied the plateau of Mont-Saint-Jean, having behind it the village, and in front of it the slope, which was tolerably steep then. It rested on that stout stone dwelling which at that time belonged to the domain of Nivelles, and which marks the intersection of the roads—a pile of the sixteenth century, and so robust that the cannon-balls rebounded from it without injuring it. All about the plateau the English had cut the hedges here and there, made embrasures in the hawthorn-trees, thrust the throat of a cannon between two branches, embattled the shrubs. There artillery was ambushed in the brushwood. This punic labor, incontestably authorized by war, which permits traps, was so well done, that Haxo, who had been despatched by the Emperor at nine o'clock in the morning to reconnoitre the enemy's batteries, had discovered nothing of it, and had returned and reported to Napoleon that there were no obstacles except the two barricades which barred the road to Nivelles and to Genappe. It was at the season when the grain is tall; on the edge of the plateau a battalion of Kempt's brigade, the 95th, armed with carabines, was concealed in the tall wheat.

Thus assured and buttressed, the centre of the Anglo-Dutch army was well posted. The peril of this position lay in the forest of Soignes, then adjoining the field of battle, and intersected by the ponds of Groenendael and Boitsfort. An army could not retreat thither without dissolving; the regiments would have broken up immediately there. The artillery would have been lost among the morasses. The retreat, according to many a man versed in the art,—though it is disputed by others,—would have been a disorganized flight.

To this centre, Wellington added one of Chassé's brigades taken from the right wing, and one of Wincke's brigades taken from the left wing, plus Clinton's division. To his English, to the regiments of Halkett, to the brigades of Mitchell, to the guards of Maitland, he gave as reinforcements and aids, the infantry of Brunswick, Nassau's contingent, Kielmansegg's Hanoverians, and Ompteda's Germans. This placed twenty-six battalions under his hand. *The right wing*, as Charras says, *was thrown back on the centre*. An enormous battery was masked by sacks of earth at the spot where there now stands what is called the "Museum of Waterloo." Besides this, Wellington had, behind a rise in the ground, Somerset's Dragoon Guards, fourteen hundred horse strong. It was the remaining half of the justly celebrated English cavalry. Ponsonby destroyed, Somerset remained.

The battery, which, if completed, would have been almost a redoubt, was ranged behind a very low garden wall, backed up with a coating of bags of sand and a large slope of earth. This work was not finished; there had been no time to make a palisade for it.

Wellington, uneasy but impassive, was on horseback, and there remained the whole day in the same attitude, a little in advance of the old mill of Mont-Saint-Jean, which is still in existence, beneath an elm, which an Englishman, an enthusiastic vandal, purchased later on for two hundred francs, cut down, and carried off. Wellington was coldly heroic. The bullets rained about him. His aide-de-camp, Gordon, fell at his side. Lord Hill, pointing to a shell which had burst, said to him: "My lord, what are your orders in case you are killed?" "To do like me," replied Wellington. To Clinton he said laconically, "To hold this spot to the last man." The day was evidently turning out ill. Wellington shouted to his old companions of Talavera, of Vittoria, of Salamanca: "Boys, can retreat be thought of? Think of old England!"

Towards four o'clock, the English line drew back. Suddenly nothing was visible on the crest of the plateau except the artillery and the sharpshooters; the rest had disappeared: the regiments, dislodged by the shells and the French bullets, retreated into the bottom, now intersected by the back road of the farm of Mont-Saint-Jean; a retrograde movement took place, the English front hid itself, Wellington drew back. "The beginning of retreat!" cried Napoleon.

VII

Napoleon in a Good Humor

The Emperor, though ill and discommoded on horseback by a local trouble, had never been in a better humor than on that day. His impenetrability had been smiling ever since the morning. On the 18th of June, that profound soul masked by marble beamed blindly. The man who had been gloomy at Austerlitz was gay at Waterloo. The greatest favorites of destiny make mistakes. Our joys are composed of shadow. The supreme smile is God's alone.

Ridet Cæsar, Pompeius flebit, said the legionaries of the Fulminatrix Legion. Pompey was not destined to weep on that occasion, but it is certain that Cæsar laughed. While exploring on horseback at one o'clock on the preceding night, in storm and rain, in company with Bertrand, the communes in the neighborhood of Rossomme, satisfied at the sight of the long line of the English camp-fires illuminating the whole horizon from Frischemont to Braine-l'Alleud, it had seemed to him that fate, to whom he had assigned a day on the field of Waterloo, was exact to the appointment; he stopped his horse, and remained for some time motionless, gazing at the lightning and listening to the thunder; and this fatalist was heard to cast into the darkness this mysterious saying, "We are in accord." Napoleon was mistaken. They were no longer in accord.

He took not a moment for sleep; every instant of that night was marked by a joy for him. He traversed the line of the principal outposts, halting here and there to talk to the sentinels. At half-past two, near the wood of Hougomont, he heard the tread of a column on the march; he thought at the moment that it was a retreat on the part of Wellington. He said: "It is the rear-guard of the English getting under way for the purpose of decamping. I will take prisoners the six thousand English who have just arrived at Ostend." He conversed expansively; he regained the animation which he had shown at his landing on the first of March, when he pointed out to the Grand-Marshal the enthusiastic peasant of the Gulf Juan, and cried, "Well, Bertrand, here is a reinforcement already!" On the night of the 17th to the 18th of June he rallied Wellington. "That little Englishman needs a lesson," said

Napoleon. The rain redoubled in violence; the thunder rolled while the Emperor was speaking.

At half-past three o'clock in the morning, he lost one illusion; officers who had been despatched to reconnoitre announced to him that the enemy was not making any movement. Nothing was stirring; not a bivouac-fire had been extinguished; the English army was asleep. The silence on earth was profound; the only noise was in the heavens. At four o'clock, a peasant was brought in to him by the scouts; this peasant had served as guide to a brigade of English cavalry, probably Vivian's brigade, which was on its way to take up a position in the village of Ohain, at the extreme left. At five o'clock, two Belgian deserters reported to him that they had just quitted their regiment, and that the English army was ready for battle. "So much the better!" exclaimed Napoleon. "I prefer to overthrow them rather than to drive them back."

In the morning he dismounted in the mud on the slope which forms an angle with the Plancenoit road, had a kitchen table and a peasant's chair brought to him from the farm of Rossomme, seated himself, with a truss of straw for a carpet, and spread out on the table the chart of the battle-field, saying to Soult as he did so, "A pretty checker-board."

In consequence of the rains during the night, the transports of provisions, embedded in the soft roads, had not been able to arrive by morning; the soldiers had had no sleep; they were wet and fasting. This did not prevent Napoleon from exclaiming cheerfully to Ney, "We have ninety chances out of a hundred." At eight o'clock the Emperor's breakfast was brought to him. He invited many generals to it. During breakfast, it was said that Wellington had been to a ball two nights before, in Brussels, at the Duchess of Richmond's; and Soult, a rough man of war, with a face of an archbishop, said, "The ball takes place to-day." The Emperor jested with Ney, who said, "Wellington will not be so simple as to wait for Your Majesty." That was his way, however. "He was fond of jesting," says Fleury de Chaboulon. "A merry humor was at the foundation of his character," says Gourgaud. "He abounded in pleasantries, which were more peculiar than witty," says Benjamin Constant. These gayeties of a giant are worthy of insistence. It was he who called his grenadiers "his grumblers"; he pinched their ears; he pulled their moustaches. "The Emperor did nothing but play pranks on us," is the remark of one of them. During the mysterious trip from the island of Elba to France, on the 27th of February, on the open sea, the French brig of war, *Le Zéphyr*, having encountered the brig *L'Inconstant*, on which Napoleon was concealed, and having asked the news of Napoleon from *L'Inconstant*, the Emperor, who still wore in his hat the white and amaranthine cockade sown with bees, which he had adopted at the isle of Elba, laughingly seized the speaking-trumpet, and answered for himself, "The Emperor is well." A man who laughs like that is on familiar terms with events. Napoleon indulged in many fits of this laughter during the breakfast at Waterloo. After breakfast he meditated for a quarter of an hour; then two generals seated themselves on the truss of straw, pen in hand and their paper on their knees, and the Emperor dictated to them the order of battle.

At nine o'clock, at the instant when the French army, ranged in echelons and set in motion in five columns, had deployed—the divisions in two lines, the artillery between the brigades, the music at their head; as they beat the march, with rolls on the drums and the blasts of trumpets, mighty, vast, joyous, a sea of casques, of sabres, and of bayonets on the horizon, the Emperor was touched, and twice exclaimed, "Magnificent! Magnificent!"

Between nine o'clock and half-past ten the whole army, incredible as it may appear, had taken up its position and ranged itself in six lines, forming, to repeat the Emperor's expression, "the figure of six V's." A few moments after the formation of the battle-array, in the midst of that profound silence, like that which heralds the beginning of a storm, which precedes engagements, the Emperor tapped Haxo on the shoulder, as he beheld the three batteries of twelve-pounders, detached by his orders from the corps of Erlon, Reille, and Lobau, and destined to begin the action by taking Mont-Saint-Jean, which was situated at the intersection of the Nivelles and the Genappe roads, and said to him, "There are four and twenty handsome maids, General."

Sure of the issue, he encouraged with a smile, as they passed before him, the company of sappers of the first corps, which he had appointed to barricade Mont-Saint-Jean as soon as the village should be carried. All this serenity had been traversed by but a single word of haughty pity; perceiving on his left, at a spot where there now stands a large tomb, those admirable Scotch Grays, with their superb horses, massing themselves, he said, "It is a pity."

Then he mounted his horse, advanced beyond Rossomme, and selected for his post of observation a contracted elevation of turf to the right of the road from Genappe to Brussels, which was his second station during the battle. The third station, the one adopted at seven o'clock in the evening, between La Belle-Alliance and La Haie-Sainte, is formidable; it is a rather elevated knoll, which still exists, and behind which the guard was massed on a slope of the plain. Around this knoll the balls rebounded from the pavements of the road, up to Napoleon himself. As at Brienne, he had over his head the shriek of the bullets and of the heavy artillery. Mouldy cannon-balls, old sword-blades, and shapeless projectiles, eaten up with rust, were picked up at the spot where his horse's feet stood. *Scabra rubigine.* A few years ago, a shell of sixty pounds, still charged, and with its fuse broken off level with the bomb, was unearthed. It was at this last post that the Emperor said to his guide, Lacoste, a hostile and terrified peasant, who was attached to the saddle of a hussar, and who turned round at every discharge of canister and tried to hide behind Napoleon: "Fool, it is shameful! You'll get yourself killed with a ball in the back." He who writes these lines has himself found, in the friable soil of this knoll, on turning over the sand, the remains of the neck of a bomb, disintegrated, by the oxidization of six and forty years, and old fragments of iron which parted like elder-twigs between the fingers.

Every one is aware that the variously inclined undulations of the plains, where the engagement between Napoleon and Wellington took place, are no longer what they were on June 18, 1815. By taking from this mournful field the wherewithal to make a monument to it, its real relief has been taken away, and history, disconcerted, no longer finds her bearings there. It has been disfigured for the sake of glorifying it. Wellington, when he beheld Waterloo once more, two years later, exclaimed, "They have altered my field of battle!" Where the great pyramid of earth, surmounted by the lion, rises to-day, there was a hillock which descended in an easy slope towards the Nivelles road, but which was almost an escarpment on the side of the highway to Genappe. The elevation of this escarpment can still be measured by the height of the two knolls of the two great sepulchres which enclose the road from Genappe to Brussels: one, the English tomb, is on the left; the other, the German tomb, is on the right. There is no French tomb. The whole of that plain is a sepulchre for France. Thanks to the thousands upon thousands of cartloads of earth employed in the hillock one hundred and fifty feet in height and half a mile in circumference, the plateau of Mont-Saint-Jean is now accessible by an easy slope. On the day of battle, particularly on the side of La Haie-Sainte, it was abrupt and difficult of approach. The slope there is so steep that the English cannon could not see the farm, situated in the bottom of the valley, which was the centre of the combat. On the 18th of June, 1815, the rains had still farther increased this acclivity, the mud complicated the problem of the ascent, and the men not only slipped back, but stuck fast in the mire. Along the crest of the plateau ran a sort of trench whose presence it was impossible for the distant observer to divine.

What was this trench? Let us explain. Braine-l'Alleud is a Belgian village; Ohain is another. These villages, both of them concealed in curves of the landscape, are connected by a road about a league and a half in length, which traverses the plain along its undulating level, and often enters and buries itself in the hills like a furrow, which makes a ravine of this road in some places. In 1815, as at the present day, this road cut the crest of the plateau of Mont-Saint-Jean between the two highways from Genappe and Nivelles; only, it is now on a level with the plain; it was then a hollow way. Its two slopes have been appropriated for the monumental hillock. This road was, and still is, a trench throughout the greater portion of its course; a hollow trench, sometimes a dozen feet in depth, and whose banks, being too steep, crumbled away here and there, particularly in winter, under driving rains. Accidents happened here. The road was so narrow at the Braine-l'Alleud entrance that a passer-by was crushed by a cart, as is proved by a stone cross which stands near the cemetery, and which gives the name of the dead, *Monsieur Bernard Debrye, Merchant of Brussels*, and the date of the accident, *February, 1637*. It was so deep on the table-land of Mont-Saint-Jean that a peasant, Mathieu Nicaise, was crushed there, in 1783, by a slide from the slope, as is stated on another stone cross, the top of which has disappeared in the process of clearing the ground, but whose overturned pedestal is still visible on the grassy slope to the left of the highway between La Haie-Sainte and the farm of Mont-Saint-Jean.

On the day of battle, this hollow road whose existence was in no way indicated, bordering the crest of Mont-Saint-Jean, a trench at the summit of the escarpment, a rut concealed in the soil, was invisible; that is to say, terrible.

VIII

The Emperor puts a Question to the Guide Lacoste

S o, on the morning of Waterloo, Napoleon was content.

He was right; the plan of battle conceived by him was, as we have seen, really admirable.

The battle once begun, its very various changes,—the resistance of Hougomont; the tenacity of La Haie-Sainte; the killing of Bauduin; the disabling of Foy; the unexpected wall against which Soye's brigade was shattered; Guilleminot's fatal heedlessness when he had neither petard nor powder sacks; the miring of the batteries; the fifteen unescorted pieces overwhelmed in a hollow way by Uxbridge; the small effect of the bombs falling in the English lines, and there embedding themselves in the rain-soaked soil, and only succeeding in producing volcanoes of mud, so that the canister was turned into a splash; the uselessness of Piré's demonstration on Braine-l'Alleud; all that cavalry, fifteen squadrons, almost exterminated; the right wing of the English badly alarmed, the left wing badly cut into; Ney's strange mistake in massing, instead of echelonning the four divisions of the first corps; men delivered over to grape-shot, arranged in ranks twenty-seven deep and with a frontage of two hundred; the frightful holes made in these masses by the cannon-balls; attacking columns disorganized; the side-battery suddenly unmasked on their flank; Bourgeois, Donzelot, and Durutte compromised; Quiot repulsed; Lieutenant Vieux, that Hercules graduated at the Polytechnic School, wounded at the moment when he was beating in with an axe the door of La Haie-Sainte under the downright fire of the English barricade which barred the angle of the road from Genappe to Brussels; Marcognet's division caught between the infantry and the cavalry, shot down at the very muzzle of the guns amid the grain by Best and Pack, put to the sword by Ponsonby; his battery of seven pieces spiked; the Prince of Saxe-Weimar holding and guarding, in spite of the Comte d'Erlon, both Frischemont and Smohain; the flag of the 105th taken, the flag of the 45th captured; that black Prussian hussar stopped by runners of the flying column of three hundred light cavalry on the scout between Wavre and Plancenoit; the alarming things that had been said by prisoners; Grouchy's delay; fifteen hundred men killed in the orchard of Hougomont in less than an hour; eighteen hundred men overthrown in a still shorter time about La Haie-Sainte,—all these stormy incidents passing like the clouds of battle before Napoleon, had hardly troubled his gaze and had not overshadowed that face of imperial certainty. Napoleon was accustomed to gaze steadily at war; he never added up the heart-rending details, cipher by cipher; ciphers mattered little to him, provided that they furnished the total—victory; he was not alarmed if the beginnings did go astray, since he thought himself the master and the possessor at the end; he knew how to wait, supposing himself to be out of the question, and he treated destiny as his equal: he seemed to say to fate, Thou wilt not dare.

Composed half of light and half of shadow, Napoleon thought himself protected in good and tolerated in evil. He had, or thought that he had, a connivance, one might almost say a complicity, of events in his favor, which was equivalent to the invulnerability of antiquity.

Nevertheless, when one has Bérésina, Leipzig, and Fontainebleau behind one, it seems as though one might distrust Waterloo. A mysterious frown becomes perceptible in the depths of the heavens.

At the moment when Wellington retreated, Napoleon shuddered. He suddenly beheld the table-land of Mont-Saint-Jean cleared, and the van of the English army disappear. It was rallying, but hiding itself. The Emperor half rose in his stirrups. The lightning of victory flashed from his eyes.

Wellington, driven into a corner at the forest of Soignes and destroyed—that was the definitive conquest of England by France; it was Crécy, Poitiers, Malplaquet, and Ramillies avenged. The man of Marengo was wiping out Agincourt.

So the Emperor, meditating on this terrible turn of fortune, swept his glass for the last time over all the points of the field of battle. His guard, standing behind him with grounded arms, watched him from below with a sort of religion. He pondered; he examined the slopes, noted the declivities, scrutinized the clumps of trees, the square of rye, the path; he seemed to be counting each bush. He gazed with some intentness at the English barricades of the two highways,—two large abatis of trees, that on the road to Genappe above La Haie-Sainte, armed with two cannon, the only ones out of all the English artillery which commanded the extremity of the field of battle, and that on the road to Nivelles where gleamed the Dutch bayonets of Chassé's brigade. Near this barricade he observed the old chapel of Saint Nicholas, painted white, which stands at the angle of the crossroad near Braine-l'Alleud; he bent down and spoke in a low voice to the guide Lacoste. The guide made a negative sign with his head, which was probably perfidious.

The Emperor straightened himself up and fell to thinking.

Wellington had drawn back.

All that remained to do was to complete this retreat by crushing him.

Napoleon turning round abruptly, despatched an express at full speed to Paris to announce that the battle was won.

Napoleon was one of those geniuses from whom thunder darts.

He had just found his clap of thunder.

He gave orders to Milhaud's cuirassiers to carry the table-land of Mont-Saint-Jean.

IX

THE UNEXPECTED

There were three thousand five hundred of them. They formed a front a quarter of a league in extent. They were giant men, on colossal horses. There were six and twenty squadrons of them; and they had behind them to support them Lefebvre-Desnouettes's division,— the one hundred and six picked gendarmes, the light cavalry of the Guard, eleven hundred and ninety-seven men, and the lancers of the guard of eight hundred and eighty lances. They wore casques without horse-tails, and cuirasses of beaten iron, with horse-pistols in their holsters, and long sabre-swords. That morning the whole army had admired them, when, at nine o'clock, with braying of trumpets and all the music playing "Let us watch o'er the Safety of the Empire," they had come in a solid column, with one of their batteries on their flank, another in their centre, and deployed in two ranks between the roads to Genappe and Frischemont, and taken up their position for battle in that powerful second line, so cleverly arranged by Napoleon, which, having on its extreme left Kellermann's cuirassiers and on its extreme right Milhaud's cuirassiers, had, so to speak, two wings of iron.

Aide-de-camp Bernard carried them the Emperor's orders. Ney drew his sword and placed himself at their head. The enormous squadrons were set in motion.

Then a formidable spectacle was seen.

All their cavalry, with upraised swords, standards and trumpets flung to the breeze, formed in columns by divisions, descended, by a simultaneous movement and like one man, with the precision of a brazen battering-ram which is effecting a breach, the hill of La Belle Alliance, plunged into the terrible depths in which so many men had already fallen, disappeared there in the smoke, then emerging from that shadow, reappeared on the other side of the valley, still compact and in close ranks, mounting at a full trot, through a storm of grape-shot which burst upon them, the terrible muddy slope of the table-land of Mont-Saint-Jean. They ascended, grave, threatening, imperturbable; in the intervals between the musketry and the artillery, their colossal trampling was audible. Being two divisions, there were two columns of them; Wathier's division held the right, Delort's division was on the left. It seemed as though two immense adders of steel were to be seen crawling towards the crest of the table-land. It traversed the battle like a prodigy.

Nothing like it had been seen since the taking of the great redoubt of the Muskowa by the heavy cavalry; Murat was lacking here, but Ney was again present. It seemed as though that mass had become a monster and had but one soul. Each column undulated and swelled like the ring of a polyp. They could be seen through a vast cloud of smoke which was rent here and there. A confusion of helmets, of cries, of sabres, a stormy heaving of the cruppers of horses amid the cannons and the flourish of trumpets, a terrible and disciplined tumult; over all, the cuirasses like the scales on the hydra.

These narrations seemed to belong to another age. Something parallel to this vision appeared, no doubt, in the ancient Orphic epics, which told of the centaurs, the old hippanthropes, those Titans with human heads and equestrian chests who scaled Olympus at a gallop, horrible, invulnerable, sublime—gods and beasts.

Odd numerical coincidence,—twenty-six battalions rode to meet twenty-six battalions. Behind the crest of the plateau, in the shadow of the masked battery, the English infantry, formed into thirteen squares, two battalions to the square, in two lines, with seven in the first line, six in the second, the stocks of their guns to their shoulders, taking aim at that which was on the point of appearing, waited, calm, mute, motionless. They did not see the cuirassiers, and the cuirassiers did not see them. They listened to the rise of this flood of men. They heard the swelling noise of three thousand horse, the alternate and symmetrical tramp of their hoofs at full trot, the jingling of the cuirasses, the clang of the sabres and a sort of grand and savage breathing. There ensued a most terrible silence; then, all at once, a long file of uplifted arms, brandishing sabres, appeared above the crest, and casques, trumpets, and standards, and three thousand heads with gray moustaches, shouting, "Vive l'Empereur!" All this cavalry debouched on the plateau, and it was like the appearance of an earthquake.

All at once, a tragic incident; on the English left, on our right, the head of the column of cuirassiers reared up with a frightful clamor. On arriving at the culminating point of the crest, ungovernable, utterly given over to fury and their course of extermination of the squares and cannon, the cuirassiers had just caught sight of a trench,—a trench between them and the English. It was the hollow road of Ohain.

It was a terrible moment. The ravine was there, unexpected, yawning, directly under the horses' feet, two fathoms deep between its double slopes; the second file pushed the first into it, and the third pushed on the second; the horses reared and fell backward, landed on their haunches, slid down, all four feet in the air, crushing and overwhelming the riders; and there being no means of retreat,—the whole column being no longer anything more than a projectile,—the force which had been acquired to crush the English crushed the French; the inexorable ravine could only yield when filled; horses and riders rolled there pell-mell, grinding each other, forming but one mass of flesh in this gulf: when this trench was full of living men, the rest marched over them and passed on. Almost a third of Dubois's brigade fell into that abyss.

This began the loss of the battle.

A local tradition, which evidently exaggerates matters, says that two thousand horses and fifteen hundred men were buried in the hollow road of Ohain. This figure probably comprises all the other corpses which were flung into this ravine the day after the combat.

Let us note in passing that it was Dubois's sorely tried brigade which, an hour previously, making a charge to one side, had captured the flag of the Lunenburg battalion.

Napoleon, before giving the order for this charge of Milhaud's cuirassiers, had scrutinized the ground, but had not been able to see that hollow road, which did not even form a wrinkle on the surface of the plateau. Warned, nevertheless, and put on the alert by the little white chapel which marks its angle of junction with the Nivelles highway, he had probably put a question as to the possibility of an obstacle, to the guide Lacoste. The guide had answered No. We might almost affirm that Napoleon's catastrophe originated in that sign of a peasant's head.

Other fatalities were destined to arise.

Was it possible that Napoleon should have won that battle? We answer No. Why? Because of Wellington? Because of Blücher? No. Because of God.

Bonaparte victor at Waterloo; that does not come within the law of the nineteenth century. Another series of facts was in preparation, in which there was no longer any room for Napoleon. The ill will of events had declared itself long before.

It was time that this vast man should fall.

The excessive weight of this man in human destiny disturbed the balance. This individual alone counted for more than a universal group. These plethoras of all human vitality concentrated in a single head; the world mounting to the brain of one man,—this would be mortal to civilization were it to last. The moment had arrived for the incorruptible and supreme equity to alter its plan. Probably the principles and the elements, on which the regular gravitations of the moral, as of the material, world depend, had complained. Smoking blood, over-filled cemeteries, mothers in tears,— these are formidable pleaders. When the earth is suffering from too heavy a burden, there are mysterious groanings of the shades, to which the abyss lends an ear.

Napoleon had been denounced in the infinite and his fall had been decided on.

He embarrassed God.

Waterloo is not a battle; it is a change of front on the part of the Universe.

X

The Plateau of Mont-Saint-Jean

The battery was unmasked at the same moment with the ravine.

Sixty cannons and the thirteen squares darted lightning point-blank on the cuirassiers. The intrepid General Delort made the military salute to the English battery.

The whole of the flying artillery of the English had re-entered the squares at a gallop. The cuirassiers had not had even the time for a halt. The disaster of the hollow road had decimated, but not discouraged them. They belonged to that class of men who, when diminished in number, increase in courage.

Wathier's column alone had suffered in the disaster; Delort's column, which Ney had deflected to the left, as though he had a presentiment of an ambush, had arrived whole.

The cuirassiers hurled themselves on the English squares.

At full speed, with bridles loose, swords in their teeth, pistols in fist,—such was the attack.

There are moments in battles in which the soul hardens the man until the soldier is changed into a statue, and when all this flesh turns into granite. The English battalions, desperately assaulted, did not stir.

Then it was terrible.

All the faces of the English squares were attacked at once. A frenzied whirl enveloped them. That cold infantry remained impassive. The first rank knelt and received the cuirassiers on their bayonets, the second ranks shot them down; behind the second rank the cannoneers charged their guns, the front of the square parted, permitted the passage of an eruption of grape-shot, and closed again. The cuirassiers replied by crushing them. Their great horses reared, strode across the ranks, leaped over the bayonets and fell, gigantic, in the midst of these four living wells. The cannon-balls ploughed furrows in these cuirassiers; the cuirassiers made breaches in the squares. Files of men disappeared, ground to dust under the horses. The bayonets plunged into the bellies of these centaurs; hence a hideousness of wounds which has probably never been seen anywhere else. The squares, wasted by this mad cavalry, closed up their ranks without flinching. Inexhaustible in the matter of grape-shot, they created explosions in their assailants' midst. The form of this combat was monstrous. These squares were no longer battalions, they were craters; those cuirassiers were no longer cavalry, they were a tempest. Each square was a volcano attacked by a cloud; lava contended with lightning.

The square on the extreme right, the most exposed of all, being in the air, was almost annihilated at the very first shock. It was formed of the 75th regiment of Highlanders. The bagpipe-player in the centre dropped his melancholy eyes, filled with the reflections of the forests and the lakes, in profound inattention, while men were being exterminated around him, and seated on a drum, with his pibroch under his arm, played the Highland airs. These Scotchmen died thinking of Ben Lothian, as did the Greeks recalling Argos. The sword of a cuirassier, which hewed down the bagpipes and the arm which bore it, put an end to the song by killing the singer.

The cuirassiers, relatively few in number, and still further diminished by the catastrophe of the ravine, had almost the whole English army against them, but they multiplied themselves so that each man of them was equal to ten. Nevertheless, some Hanoverian battalions yielded. Wellington perceived it, and thought of his cavalry. Had Napoleon at that same moment thought of his infantry, he would have won the battle. This forgetfulness was his great and fatal mistake.

All at once, the cuirassiers, who had been the assailants, found themselves assailed. The English cavalry was at their back. Before them two squares, behind them Somerset; Somerset meant fourteen hundred dragoons of the guard. On the right, Somerset had Dornberg with the German light-horse, and on his left, Trip with the Belgian carabineers; the cuirassiers attacked on the flank and in front, before and in the rear, by infantry and cavalry, had to face all sides. What mattered it to them? They were a whirlwind. Their valor was something indescribable.

In addition to this, they had behind them the battery, which was still thundering. It was necessary that it should be so, or they could never have been wounded in the back. One of their cuirasses, pierced on the shoulder by a ball from a biscayan, is in the collection of the Waterloo Museum.

For such Frenchmen nothing less than such Englishmen was needed. It was no longer a hand-to-hand conflict; it was a shadow, a fury, a dizzy transport of souls and courage, a hurricane of lightning swords. In an instant the fourteen hundred dragoon guards numbered only eight hundred. Fuller, their lieutenant-colonel, fell dead. Ney rushed up with the lancers and Lefebvre-Desnouettes's light-horse. The plateau of Mont-Saint-Jean was captured, recaptured, captured again. The cuirassiers quitted the cavalry to return to the infantry; or, to put it more exactly, the whole of that formidable rout collared each other without releasing the other. The squares still held firm.

There were a dozen assaults. Ney had four horses killed under him. Half the cuirassiers remained on the plateau. This conflict lasted two hours.

The English army was profoundly shaken. There is no doubt that, had they not been enfeebled in their first shock by the disaster of the hollow road the cuirassiers would have overwhelmed the centre and decided the victory. This extraordinary cavalry petrified Clinton, who had seen Talavera and Badajoz. Wellington, three-quarters vanquished, admired heroically. He said in an undertone, "Sublime!"

The cuirassiers annihilated seven squares out of thirteen, took or spiked sixty pieces of ordnance, and captured from the English regiments six flags, which three cuirassiers and three chasseurs of the Guard bore to the Emperor, in front of the farm of La Belle Alliance.

Wellington's situation had grown worse. This strange battle was like a duel between two raging, wounded men, each of whom, still fighting and still resisting, is expending all his blood.

Which of the two will be the first to fall?

The conflict on the plateau continued.

What had become of the cuirassiers? No one could have told. One thing is certain, that on the day after the battle, a cuirassier and his horse were found dead among the woodwork of the scales for vehicles at Mont-Saint-Jean, at the very point where the four roads from Nivelles, Genappe, La Hulpe, and Brussels meet and intersect each other. This horseman had pierced the English lines. One of the men who picked up the body still lives at Mont-Saint-Jean. His name is Dehaze. He was eighteen years old at that time.

Wellington felt that he was yielding. The crisis was at hand.

The cuirassiers had not succeeded, since the centre was not broken through. As every one was in possession of the plateau, no one held it, and in fact it remained, to a great extent, with the English. Wellington held the village and the culminating plain; Ney had only the crest and the slope. They seemed rooted in that fatal soil on both sides.

But the weakening of the English seemed irremediable. The bleeding of that army was horrible. Kempt, on the left wing, demanded reinforcements. "There are none," replied Wellington; "he must let himself be killed!" Almost at that same moment, a singular coincidence which paints the exhaustion of the two armies, Ney demanded infantry from Napoleon, and Napoleon exclaimed, "Infantry! Where does he expect me to get it? Does he think I can make it?"

Nevertheless, the English army was in the worse case of the two. The furious onsets of those great squadrons with cuirasses of iron and breasts of steel had ground the infantry to nothing. A few men clustered round a flag marked the post of a regiment; such and such a battalion was commanded only by a captain or a lieutenant; Alten's division, already so roughly handled at La Haie-Sainte, was almost destroyed; the intrepid Belgians of Van Kluze's brigade strewed the rye-fields all along the Nivelles road; hardly anything was left of those Dutch grenadiers, who, intermingled with Spaniards in our ranks in 1811, fought against Wellington; and who, in 1815, rallied to the English standard, fought against Napoleon. The loss in officers was considerable. Lord Uxbridge, who had his leg buried on the following day, had his knee shattered. If, on the French side, in that tussle of the cuirassiers, Delort, l'Héritier, Colbert, Dnop, Travers, and Blancard were disabled, on the side of the English there was Alten wounded, Barne wounded, Delancey killed, Van Meeren killed, Ompteda killed, the whole of Wellington's staff decimated, and England had the worse of it in that bloody scale. The second regiment of foot-guards had lost five lieutenant-colonels, four captains, and three ensigns; the first battalion of the 30th infantry had lost 24 officers and 1,200 soldiers; the 79th Highlanders had lost 24 officers wounded, 18 officers killed, 450 soldiers killed. The Hanoverian hussars of Cumberland, a whole regiment, with Colonel Hacke at its head, who was destined to be tried later on and cashiered, had turned bridle in the presence of the fray, and had fled to the forest of Soignes, sowing defeat all the way to Brussels. The transports, ammunition-wagons, the baggage-wagons, the wagons filled with wounded, on perceiving that the French were gaining ground and approaching the forest, rushed headlong thither. The Dutch, mowed down by the French cavalry, cried, "Alarm!" From Vert-Coucou to Groenendael, for a distance of nearly two leagues in the direction of Brussels, according to the testimony of eye-witnesses who are still alive, the roads were encumbered with fugitives. This panic was such that it attacked the Prince de Condé at Mechlin, and Louis XVIII at Ghent. With the exception of the feeble reserve echelonned behind the ambulance established at the farm of Mont-Saint-Jean, and of Vivian's and Vandeleur's brigades, which flanked the left wing, Wellington had no cavalry left. A number of batteries lay unhorsed. These facts are attested by Siborne; and Pringle, exaggerating the disaster, goes so far as to say that the Anglo-Dutch army was reduced to thirty-four thousand men. The Iron Duke remained calm, but his lips blanched. Vincent, the Austrian commissioner, Alava, the Spanish commissioner, who were present at the battle in the English staff, thought the Duke lost. At five o'clock Wellington drew out his watch, and he was heard to murmur these sinister words, "Blücher, or night!"

It was at about that moment that a distant line of bayonets gleamed on the heights in the direction of Frischemont.

Here comes the change of face in this giant drama.

XI

A Bad Guide to Napoleon;
A Good Guide to Bülow

The painful surprise of Napoleon is well known. Grouchy hoped for, Blücher arriving. Death instead of life.

Fate has these turns; the throne of the world was expected; it was Saint Helena that was seen.

If the little shepherd who served as guide to Bülow, Blücher's lieutenant, had advised him to debouch from the forest above Frischemont, instead of below Plancenoit, the form of the nineteenth century might, perhaps, have been different. Napoleon would have won the battle of Waterloo. By any other route than that below Plancenoit, the Prussian army would have come out upon a ravine impassable for artillery, and Bülow would not have arrived.

Now the Prussian general, Muffling, declares that one hour's delay, and Blücher would not have found Wellington on his feet. "The battle was lost."

It was time that Bülow should arrive, as will be seen. He had, moreover, been very much delayed. He had bivouacked at Dion-le-Mont, and had set out at daybreak; but the roads were impassable, and his divisions stuck fast in the mire. The ruts were up to the hubs of the cannons. Moreover, he had been obliged to pass the Dyle on the narrow bridge of Wavre; the street leading to the bridge had been fired by the French, so the caissons and ammunition-wagons could not pass between two rows of burning houses, and had been obliged to wait until the conflagration was extinguished. It was midday before Bülow's vanguard had been able to reach Chapelle-Saint-Lambert.

Had the action been begun two hours earlier, it would have been over at four o'clock, and Blücher would have fallen on the battle won by Napoleon. Such are these immense risks proportioned to an infinite which we cannot comprehend.

The Emperor had been the first, as early as midday, to descry with his field-glass, on the extreme horizon, something which had attracted his attention. He had said, "I see yonder a cloud, which seems to me to be troops." Then he asked the Duc de Dalmatie, "Soult, what do you see in the direction of Chapelle-Saint-Lambert?" The marshal, levelling his glass, answered, "Four or five thousand men, Sire; evidently Grouchy." But it remained motionless in the mist. All the glasses of the staff had studied "the cloud" pointed out by the Emperor. Some said: "It is trees." The truth is, that the cloud did not move. The Emperor detached Domon's division of light cavalry to reconnoitre in that quarter.

Bülow had not moved, in fact. His vanguard was very feeble, and could accomplish nothing. He was obliged to wait for the body of the army corps, and he had received orders to concentrate his forces before entering into line; but at five o'clock, perceiving Wellington's peril, Blücher ordered Bülow to attack, and uttered these remarkable words: "We must give air to the English army."

A little later, the divisions of Losthin, Hiller, Hacke, and Ryssel deployed before Lobau's corps, the cavalry of Prince William of Prussia debouched from the forest of Paris, Plancenoit was in flames, and the Prussian cannon-balls began to rain even upon the ranks of the guard in reserve behind Napoleon.

XII

The Guard

Every one knows the rest,—the irruption of a third army; the battle broken to pieces; eighty-six mouths of fire thundering simultaneously; Pirch the first coming up with Bülow; Zieten's cavalry led by Blücher in person, the French driven back; Marcognet swept from the plateau of Ohain; Durutte dislodged from Papelotte; Donzelot and Quiot retreating; Lobau caught on the flank; a fresh battle precipitating itself on our dismantled regiments at nightfall; the whole English line resuming the offensive and thrust forward; the gigantic breach made in the French army; the English grape-shot and the Prussian grape-shot aiding each other; the extermination; disaster in front; disaster on the flank; the Guard entering the line in the midst of this terrible crumbling of all things.

Conscious that they were about to die, they shouted, "Vive l'Empereur!" History records nothing more touching than that agony bursting forth in acclamations.

The sky had been overcast all day long. All of a sudden, at that very moment,—it was eight o'clock in the evening—the clouds on the horizon parted, and allowed the grand and sinister glow of the setting sun to pass through, athwart the elms on the Nivelles road. They had seen it rise at Austerlitz.

Each battalion of the Guard was commanded by a general for this final catastrophe. Friant, Michel, Roguet, Harlet, Mallet, Poret de Morvan, were there. When the tall caps of the grenadiers of the Guard, with their large plaques bearing the eagle appeared, symmetrical, in line, tranquil, in the midst of that combat, the enemy felt a respect for France; they thought they beheld twenty victories entering the field of battle, with wings outspread, and those who were the conquerors, believing themselves to be vanquished, retreated; but Wellington shouted, "Up, Guards, and aim straight!" The red regiment of English guards, lying flat behind the hedges, sprang up, a cloud of grape-shot riddled the tricolored flag and whistled round our eagles; all hurled themselves forwards, and the final carnage began. In the darkness, the Imperial Guard felt the army losing ground around it, and in the vast shock of the rout it heard the desperate flight which had taken the place of the "Vive l'Empereur!" and, with flight behind it, it continued to advance, more crushed, losing more men at every step that it took. There were none who hesitated, no timid men in its ranks. The soldier in that troop was as much of a hero as the general. Not a man was missing in that suicide.

Ney, bewildered, great with all the grandeur of accepted death, offered himself to all blows in that tempest. He had his fifth horse killed under him there. Perspiring, his eyes aflame, foaming at the mouth, with uniform unbuttoned, one of his epaulets half cut off by a sword-stroke from a horseguard, his plaque with the great eagle dented by a bullet; bleeding, bemired, magnificent, a broken sword in his hand, he said, "Come and see how a Marshal of France dies on the field of battle!" But in vain; he did not die. He was haggard and angry. At Drouet d'Erlon he hurled this question, "Are you not going to get yourself killed?" In the midst of all that artillery engaged in crushing a handful of men, he shouted: "So there is nothing for me! Oh! I should like to have all these English bullets enter my bowels!" Unhappy man, thou wert reserved for French bullets!

XIII

The Catastrophe

The rout behind the Guard was melancholy.

The army yielded suddenly on all sides at once,—Hougomont, La Haie-Sainte, Papelotte, Plancenoit. The cry "Treachery!" was followed by a cry of "Save yourselves who can!" An army which is disbanding is like a thaw. All yields, splits, cracks, floats, rolls, falls, jostles, hastens, is precipitated. The disintegration is unprecedented. Ney borrows a horse, leaps upon it, and without hat, cravat, or sword, places himself across the Brussels road, stopping both English and French. He strives to detain the army, he recalls it to its duty, he insults it, he clings to the rout. He is overwhelmed. The soldiers fly from him, shouting, "Long live Marshal Ney!" Two of Durutte's regiments go and come in affright as though tossed back and forth between the swords of the Uhlans and the fusillade of the brigades of Kempt, Best, Pack, and Rylandt; the worst of hand-to-hand conflicts is the defeat; friends kill each other in order to escape; squadrons and battalions break and disperse against each other, like the tremendous foam of battle. Lobau at one extremity, and Reille at the other, are drawn into the tide. In vain does Napoleon erect walls from what is left to him of his Guard; in vain does he expend in a last effort his last serviceable squadrons. Quiot retreats before Vivian, Kellermann before Vandeleur, Lobau before Bülow, Morand before Pirch, Domon and Subervic before Prince William of Prussia; Guyot, who led the Emperor's squadrons to the charge, falls beneath the feet of the English dragoons. Napoleon gallops past the line of fugitives, harangues, urges, threatens, entreats them. All the mouths which in the morning had shouted, "Long live the Emperor!" remain gaping; they hardly recognize him. The Prussian cavalry, newly arrived, dashes forwards, flies, hews, slashes, kills, exterminates. Horses lash out, the cannons flee; the soldiers of the artillery-train unharness the caissons and use the horses to make their escape; transports overturned, with all four wheels in the air, clog the road and occasion massacres. Men are crushed, trampled down, others walk over the dead and the living. Arms are lost. A dizzy multitude fills the roads, the paths, the bridges, the plains, the hills, the valleys, the woods, encumbered by this invasion of forty thousand men. Shouts despair, knapsacks and guns flung among the rye, passages forced at the point of the sword, no more comrades, no more officers, no more generals, an inexpressible terror. Zieten putting France to the sword at its leisure. Lions converted into goats. Such was the flight.

At Genappe, an effort was made to wheel about, to present a battle front, to draw up in line. Lobau rallied three hundred men. The entrance to the village was barricaded, but at the first volley of Prussian canister, all took to flight again, and Lobau was taken. That volley of grape-shot can be seen to-day imprinted on the ancient gable of a brick building on the right of the road at a few minutes' distance before you enter Genappe. The Prussians threw themselves into Genappe, furious, no doubt, that they were not more entirely the conquerors. The pursuit was stupendous. Blücher ordered extermination. Roguet had set the lugubrious example of threatening with death any French grenadier who should bring him a Prussian prisoner. Blücher outdid Roguet. Duhesme, the general of the Young Guard, hemmed in at the doorway of an inn at Genappe, surrendered his sword to a huzzar of death, who took the sword and slew the prisoner. The victory was completed by the assassination of the vanquished. Let us inflict punishment, since we are history: old Blücher disgraced himself. This ferocity put the finishing touch to the disaster. The desperate route traversed Genappe, traversed Quatre-Bras, traversed Gosselies, traversed Frasnes, traversed Charleroi, traversed Thuin, and only halted at the frontier. Alas! and who, then, was fleeing in that manner? The Grand Army.

This vertigo, this terror, this downfall into ruin of the loftiest bravery which ever astounded history,—is that causeless? No. The shadow of an enormous right is projected athwart Waterloo. It is the day of destiny. The force which is mightier than man produced that day. Hence the terrified wrinkle of those brows; hence all those great souls surrendering their swords. Those who had conquered Europe have fallen prone on the earth, with nothing left to say nor to do, feeling the present shadow of a terrible presence. *Hoc erat in fatis.* That day the perspective of the human race underwent a change. Waterloo is the hinge of the nineteenth century. The disappearance of the great man was necessary to the advent of the great century. Some one, a person to whom one replies not, took the responsibility on himself. The panic of heroes can be explained. In the battle of Waterloo there is something more than a cloud, there is something of the meteor. God has passed by.

At nightfall, in a meadow near Genappe, Bernard and Bertrand seized by the skirt of his coat and detained a man, haggard, pensive, sinister, gloomy, who, dragged to that point by the current of the rout, had just dismounted, had passed the bridle of his horse over his arm, and with wild eye was returning alone to Waterloo. It was Napoleon, the immense somnambulist of this dream which had crumbled, essaying once more to advance.

XIV

The Last Square

S everal squares of the Guard, motionless amid this stream of the defeat, as rocks in running water, held their own until night. Night came, death also; they awaited that double shadow, and, invincible, allowed themselves to be enveloped therein. Each regiment, isolated from the rest, and having no bond with the army, now shattered in every part, died alone. They had taken up position for this final action, some on the heights of Rossomme, others on the plain of Mont-Saint-Jean. There, abandoned, vanquished, terrible, those gloomy squares endured their death-throes in formidable fashion. Ulm, Wagram, Jena, Friedland, died with them.

At twilight, towards nine o'clock in the evening, one of them was left at the foot of the plateau of Mont-Saint-Jean. In that fatal valley, at the foot of that declivity which the cuirassiers had ascended, now inundated by the masses of the English, under the converging fires of the victorious hostile cavalry, under a frightful density of projectiles, this square fought on. It was commanded by an obscure officer named Cambronne. At each discharge, the square diminished and replied. It replied to the grape-shot with a fusillade, continually contracting its four walls. The fugitives pausing breathless for a moment in the distance, listened in the darkness to that gloomy and ever-decreasing thunder.

When this legion had been reduced to a handful, when nothing was left of their flag but a rag, when their guns, the bullets all gone, were no longer anything but clubs, when the heap of corpses was larger than the group of survivors, there reigned among the conquerors, around those men dying so sublimely, a sort of sacred terror, and the English artillery, taking breath, became silent. This furnished a sort of respite. These combatants had around them something in the nature of a swarm of spectres, silhouettes of men on horseback, the black profiles of cannon, the white sky viewed through wheels and gun-carriages, the colossal death's-head, which the heroes saw constantly through the smoke, in the depths of the battle, advanced upon them and gazed at them. Through the shades of twilight they could hear the pieces being loaded; the matches all lighted, like the eyes of tigers at night, formed a circle round their heads; all the lintstocks of the English batteries approached the cannons, and then, with emotion, holding the supreme moment suspended above these men, an English general, Colville according to some, Maitland according to others, shouted to them, "Surrender, brave Frenchmen!" Cambronne replied, "——."

XV

CAMBRONNE

If any French reader object to having his susceptibilities offended, one would have to refrain from repeating in his presence what is perhaps the finest reply that a Frenchman ever made. This would enjoin us from consigning something sublime to History.

At our own risk and peril, let us violate this injunction.

Now, then, among those giants there was one Titan,—Cambronne.

To make that reply and then perish, what could be grander? For being willing to die is the same as to die; and it was not this man's fault if he survived after he was shot.

The winner of the battle of Waterloo was not Napoleon, who was put to flight; nor Wellington, giving way at four o'clock, in despair at five; nor Blücher, who took no part in the engagement. The winner of Waterloo was Cambronne.

To thunder forth such a reply at the lightning-flash that kills you is to conquer!

Thus to answer the Catastrophe, thus to speak to Fate, to give this pedestal to the future lion, to hurl such a challenge to the midnight rainstorm, to the treacherous wall of Hougomont, to the sunken road of Ohain, to Grouchy's delay, to Blücher's arrival, to be Irony itself in the tomb, to act so as to stand upright though fallen, to drown in two syllables the European coalition, to offer kings privies which the Cæsars once knew, to make the lowest of words the most lofty by entwining with it the glory of France, insolently to end Waterloo with Mardigras, to finish Leonidas with Rabellais, to set the crown on this victory by a word impossible to speak, to lose the field and preserve history, to have the laugh on your side after such a carnage,—this is immense!

It was an insult such as a thunder-cloud might hurl! It reaches the grandeur of Æschylus!

Cambronne's reply produces the effect of a violent break. 'Tis like the breaking of a heart under a weight of scorn. 'Tis the overflow of agony bursting forth. Who conquered? Wellington? No! Had it not been for Blücher, he was lost. Was it Blücher? No! If Wellington had not begun, Blücher could not have finished. This Cambronne, this man spending his last hour, this unknown soldier, this infinitesimal of war, realizes that here is a falsehood, a falsehood in a catastrophe, and so doubly agonizing; and at the moment when his rage is bursting forth because of it, he is offered this mockery,—life! How could he restrain himself? Yonder are all the kings of Europe, the general's flushed with victory, the Jupiter's darting thunderbolts; they have a hundred thousand victorious soldiers, and back of the hundred thousand a million; their cannon stand with yawning mouths, the match is lighted; they grind down under their heels the Imperial guards, and the grand army; they have just crushed Napoleon, and only Cambronne remains,—only this earthworm is left to protest. He will protest. Then he seeks for the appropriate word as one seeks for a sword. His mouth froths, and the froth is the word. In face of this mean and mighty victory, in face of this victory which counts none victorious, this desperate soldier stands erect. He grants its overwhelming immensity, but he establishes its triviality; and he does more than spit upon it. Borne down by numbers, by superior force, by brute matter, he finds in his soul an expression: *"Excrément!"* We repeat it,—to use that word, to do thus, to invent such an expression, is to be the conqueror!

The spirit of mighty days at that portentous moment made its descent on that unknown man. Cambronne invents the word for Waterloo as Rouget invents the "Marseillaise," under the visitation of a breath from on high. An emanation from the divine whirlwind leaps forth and comes sweeping over these men, and they shake, and one of them sings the song supreme, and the other utters the frightful cry.

This challenge of titanic scorn Cambronne hurls not only at Europe in the name of the Empire,—that would be a trifle: he hurls it at the past in the name of the Revolution. It is heard, and Cambronne is recognized as possessed by the ancient spirit of the Titans. Danton seems to be speaking! Kléber seems to be bellowing!

At that word from Cambronne, the English voice responded, "Fire!" The batteries flamed, the hill trembled, from all those brazen mouths belched a last terrible gush of grape-shot; a vast volume of smoke, vaguely white in the light of the rising moon, rolled out, and when the smoke dispersed, there was no longer anything there. That formidable remnant had been annihilated; the Guard was dead. The four walls of the living redoubt lay prone, and hardly was there discernible, here and there, even a quiver in the bodies; it was thus that the French legions, greater than the Roman legions, expired on

Mont-Saint-Jean, on the soil watered with rain and blood, amid the gloomy grain, on the spot where nowadays Joseph, who drives the post-wagon from Nivelles, passes whistling, and cheerfully whipping up his horse at four o'clock in the morning.

XVI

Quot Libras in Duce?

The battle of Waterloo is an enigma. It is as obscure to those who won it as to those who lost it. For Napoleon it was a panic; Blücher sees nothing in it but fire; Wellington understands nothing in regard to it. Look at the reports. The bulletins are confused, the commentaries involved. Some stammer, others lisp. Jomini divides the battle of Waterloo into four moments; Muffling cuts it up into three changes; Charras alone, though we hold another judgment than his on some points, seized with his haughty glance the characteristic outlines of that catastrophe of human genius in conflict with divine chance. All the other historians suffer from being somewhat dazzled, and in this dazzled state they fumble about. It was a day of lightning brilliancy; in fact, a crumbling of the military monarchy which, to the vast stupefaction of kings, drew all the kingdoms after it—the fall of force, the defeat of war.

In this event, stamped with superhuman necessity, the part played by men amounts to nothing.

If we take Waterloo from Wellington and Blücher, do we thereby deprive England and Germany of anything? No. Neither that illustrious England nor that august Germany enter into the problem of Waterloo. Thank Heaven, nations are great, independently of the lugubrious feats of the sword. Neither England, nor Germany, nor France is contained in a scabbard. At this epoch when Waterloo is only a clashing of swords, above Blücher, Germany has Schiller; above Wellington, England has Byron. A vast dawn of ideas is the peculiarity of our century, and in that aurora England and Germany have a magnificent radiance. They are majestic because they think. The elevation of level which they contribute to civilization is intrinsic with them; it proceeds from themselves and not from an accident. The aggrandizement which they have brought to the nineteenth century has not Waterloo as its source. It is only barbarous peoples who undergo rapid growth after a victory. That is the temporary vanity of torrents swelled by a storm. Civilized people, especially in our day, are neither elevated nor abased by the good or bad fortune of a captain. Their specific gravity in the human species results from something more than a combat. Their honor, thank God!

their dignity, their intelligence, their genius, are not numbers which those gamblers, heroes and conquerors, can put in the lottery of battles. Often a battle is lost and progress is conquered. There is less glory and more liberty. The drum holds its peace; reason takes the word. It is a game in which he who loses wins. Let us, therefore, speak of Waterloo coldly from both sides. Let us render to chance that which is due to chance, and to God that which is due to God. What is Waterloo? A victory? No. The winning number in the lottery.

The quine won by Europe, paid by France.

It was not worthwhile to place a lion there.

Waterloo, moreover, is the strangest encounter in history. Napoleon and Wellington. They are not enemies; they are opposites. Never did God, who is fond of antitheses, make a more striking contrast, a more extraordinary comparison. On one side, precision, foresight, geometry, prudence, an assured retreat, reserves spared, with an obstinate coolness, an imperturbable method, strategy, which takes advantage of the ground, tactics, which preserve the equilibrium of battalions, carnage, executed according to rule, war regulated, watch in hand, nothing voluntarily left to chance, the ancient classic courage, absolute regularity; on the other, intuition, divination, military oddity, superhuman instinct, a flaming glance, an indescribable something which gazes like an eagle, and which strikes like the lightning, a prodigious art in disdainful impetuosity, all the mysteries of a profound soul, associated with destiny; the stream, the plain, the forest, the hill, summoned, and in a manner, forced to obey, the despot going even so far as to tyrannize over the field of battle; faith in a star mingled with strategic science, elevating but perturbing it. Wellington was the Barême of war; Napoleon was its Michael Angelo; and on this occasion, genius was vanquished by calculation. On both sides some one was awaited. It was the exact calculator who succeeded. Napoleon was waiting for Grouchy; he did not come. Wellington expected Blücher; he came.

Wellington is classic war taking its revenge. Bonaparte, at his dawning, had encountered him in Italy, and beaten him superbly. The old owl had fled before the young vulture. The old tactics had been not only struck as by lightning, but disgraced. Who was that Corsican of six and twenty? What signified that splendid ignoramus, who, with everything against him, nothing in his favor, without provisions, without ammunition, without cannon, without shoes, almost without an army, with a mere handful of men against masses, hurled himself on Europe combined, and absurdly won victories in the impossible? Whence had issued that fulminating convict, who almost without taking breath, and with the same set of combatants in hand, pulverized, one after the other, the five armies of the emperor of Germany, upsetting Beaulieu on Alvinzi, Wurmser on Beaulieu, Mélas on Wurmser, Mack on Mélas? Who was this novice in war with the effrontery of a luminary? The academical military school excommunicated him, and as it lost its footing; hence, the implacable rancor of the old Cæsarism against the new; of the regular sword against the flaming sword; and of the exchequer against genius. On the 18th of June, 1815, that rancor had the last word, and beneath Lodi, Montebello, Montenotte, Mantua, Arcola, it wrote: Waterloo. A triumph of the mediocres which is sweet to the majority. Destiny consented to this irony. In his decline, Napoleon found Wurmser, the younger, again in front of him.

In fact, to get Wurmser, it sufficed to blanch the hair of Wellington.

Waterloo is a battle of the first order, won by a captain of the second.

That which must be admired in the battle of Waterloo, is England; the English firmness, the English resolution, the English blood; the superb thing about England there, no offence to her, was herself. It was not her captain; it was her army.

Wellington, oddly ungrateful, declares in a letter to Lord Bathurst, that his army, the army which fought on the 18th of June, 1815, was a "detestable army." What does that sombre intermingling of bones buried beneath the furrows of Waterloo think of that?

England has been too modest in the matter of Wellington. To make Wellington so great is to belittle England. Wellington is nothing but a hero like many another. Those Scotch Grays, those Horse Guards, those regiments of Maitland and of Mitchell, that infantry of Pack and Kempt, that cavalry of Ponsonby and Somerset, those Highlanders playing the pibroch under the shower of grape-shot, those battalions of Rylandt, those utterly raw recruits, who hardly knew how to handle a musket holding their own against Essling's and Rivoli's old troops,—that is what was grand. Wellington was tenacious; in that lay his merit, and we are not seeking to lessen it: but the least of his foot-soldiers and of his cavalry would have been as solid as he. The iron soldier is worth as much as the Iron Duke. As for us, all our glorification goes to the English soldier, to the English army, to the English people. If trophy there be, it is to England that the trophy is due. The column of Waterloo would be more just, if, instead of the figure of a man, it bore on high the statue of a people.

But this great England will be angry at what we are saying here. She still cherishes, after her own 1688 and our 1789, the feudal illusion. She believes in heredity and hierarchy. This people, surpassed by none in power and glory, regards itself as a nation, and not as a people. And as a people, it willingly subordinates itself and takes a lord for its head. As a workman, it allows itself to be disdained; as a soldier, it allows itself to be flogged.

It will be remembered, that at the battle of Inkermann a sergeant who had, it appears, saved the army, could not be mentioned by Lord Paglan, as the English military hierarchy does not permit any hero below the grade of an officer to be mentioned in the reports.

That which we admire above all, in an encounter of the nature of Waterloo, is the marvellous cleverness of chance. A nocturnal rain, the wall of Hougomont, the hollow road of Ohain, Grouchy deaf to the cannon, Napoleon's guide deceiving him, Bülow's guide enlightening him,—the whole of this cataclysm is wonderfully conducted.

On the whole, let us say it plainly, it was more of a massacre than of a battle at Waterloo.

Of all pitched battles, Waterloo is the one which has the smallest front for such a number of combatants. Napoleon three-quarters of a league; Wellington, half a league; seventy-two thousand combatants on each side. From this denseness the carnage arose.

The following calculation has been made, and the following proportion established: Loss of men: at Austerlitz, French, fourteen per cent; Russians, thirty per cent; Austrians, forty-four per cent. At Wagram, French, thirteen per cent; Austrians, fourteen. At the Moskowa, French, thirty-seven per cent; Russians, forty-four. At Bautzen, French, thirteen per cent; Russians and Prussians, fourteen. At Waterloo, French, fifty-six per cent; the Allies, thirty-one. Total for Waterloo, forty-one per cent; one hundred and forty-four thousand combatants; sixty thousand dead.

To-day the field of Waterloo has the calm which belongs to the earth, the impassive support of man, and it resembles all plains.

At night, moreover, a sort of visionary mist arises from it; and if a traveller strolls there, if he listens, if he watches, if he dreams like Virgil in the fatal plains of Philippi, the hallucination of the catastrophe takes possession of him. The frightful 18th of June lives again; the false monumental hillock disappears, the lion vanishes in air, the battle-field resumes its reality, lines of infantry undulate over the plain, furious gallops traverse the horizon; the frightened dreamer beholds the flash of sabres, the gleam of bayonets, the flare of bombs, the tremendous interchange of thunders; he hears, as it were, the death rattle in the depths of a tomb, the vague clamor of the battle phantom; those shadows are grenadiers, those lights are cuirassiers; that skeleton Napoleon, that other skeleton is Wellington; all this no longer exists, and yet it clashes together and combats still; and the ravines are empurpled, and the trees quiver, and there is fury even in the clouds and in the shadows; all those terrible heights, Hougomont, Mont-Saint-Jean, Frischemont, Papelotte, Plancenoit, appear confusedly crowned with whirlwinds of spectres engaged in exterminating each other.

XVII

Is Waterloo to be Considered Good?

There exists a very respectable liberal school which does not hate Waterloo. We do not belong to it. To us, Waterloo is but the stupefied date of liberty. That such an eagle should emerge from such an egg is certainly unexpected.

If one places one's self at the culminating point of view of the question, Waterloo is intentionally a counter-revolutionary victory. It is Europe against France; it is Petersburg, Berlin, and Vienna against Paris; it is the *statu quo* against the initiative; it is the 14th of July, 1789, attacked through the 20th of March, 1815; it is the monarchies clearing the decks in opposition to the indomitable French rioting. The final extinction of that vast people which had been in eruption for twenty-six years—such was the dream. The solidarity of the Brunswicks, the Nassaus, the Romanoffs, the Hohenzollerns, the Hapsburgs with the Bourbons. Waterloo bears divine right on its crupper. It is true, that the Empire having been despotic, the kingdom by the natural reaction of things, was forced to be liberal, and that a constitutional order was the unwilling result of Waterloo, to the great regret of the conquerors. It is because revolution cannot be really conquered, and that being providential and absolutely fatal, it is always cropping up afresh: before Waterloo, in Bonaparte overthrowing the old thrones; after Waterloo, in Louis XVIII granting and conforming to the charter. Bonaparte places a postilion on the throne of Naples, and a sergeant on the throne of Sweden, employing inequality to demonstrate equality; Louis XVIII at Saint-Ouen countersigns the declaration of the rights of man. If you wish to gain an idea of what revolution is, call it Progress; and if you wish to acquire an idea of the nature of progress, call it To-morrow. To-morrow fulfils its work irresistibly, and it is already fulfilling it to-day. It always reaches its goal strangely. It employs Wellington to make of Foy, who was only a soldier, an orator. Foy falls at Hougomont and rises again in the tribune. Thus does progress proceed. There is no such thing as a bad tool for that workman. It does not become disconcerted, but adjusts to its divine work the man who has bestridden the Alps, and the good old tottering invalid of Father Élysée. It makes use of the gouty man as well as of the conqueror; of the conqueror without, of the gouty man within. Waterloo, by cutting short the demolition of European thrones by the sword, had no other effect than to cause the revolutionary work to be continued in another direction. The slashers have finished; it was the turn of the thinkers. The century that Waterloo was intended to arrest has pursued its march. That sinister victory was vanquished by liberty.

In short, and incontestably, that which triumphed at Waterloo; that which smiled in Wellington's rear; that which brought him all the marshals' staffs of Europe, including, it is said, the staff of a marshal of France; that which joyously trundled the barrows full of bones to erect the knoll of the lion; that which triumphantly inscribed on that pedestal the date "*June* 18, 1815"; that which encouraged Blücher, as he put the flying army to the sword; that which, from the heights of the plateau of Mont-Saint-Jean, hovered over France as over its prey, was the counter-revolution. It was the counter-revolution which murmured that infamous word "dismemberment." On arriving in Paris, it beheld the crater close at hand; it felt those ashes which scorched its feet, and it changed its mind; it returned to the stammer of a charter.

Let us behold in Waterloo only that which is in Waterloo. Of intentional liberty there is none. The counter-revolution was involuntarily liberal, in the same manner as, by a corresponding phenomenon, Napoleon was involuntarily revolutionary. On the 18th of June, 1815, the mounted Robespierre was hurled from his saddle.

XVIII

A Recrudescence of Divine Right

End of the dictatorship. A whole European system crumbled away. The Empire sank into a gloom which resembled that of the Roman world as it expired. Again we behold the abyss, as in the days of the barbarians; only the barbarism of 1815, which must be called by its pet name of the counter-revolution, was not long breathed, soon fell to panting, and halted short. The Empire was bewept,—let us acknowledge the fact,—and bewept by heroic eyes. If glory lies in the sword converted into a sceptre, the Empire had been glory in person. It had diffused over the earth all the light which tyranny can give—a sombre light. We will say more; an obscure light. Compared to the true daylight, it is night. This disappearance of night produces the effect of an eclipse.

Louis XVIII re-entered Paris. The circling dances of the 8th of July effaced the enthusiasms of the 20th of March. The Corsican became the antithesis of the Bearnese. The flag on the dome of the Tuileries was white. The exile reigned. Hartwell's pine table took its place in front of the fleur-de-lys-strewn throne of Louis XIV. Bouvines and Fontenoy were mentioned as though they had taken place on the preceding day, Austerlitz having become antiquated. The altar and the throne fraternized majestically. One of the most undisputed forms of the health of society in the nineteenth century was established over France, and over the continent. Europe adopted the white cockade. Trestaillon was celebrated. The device *non pluribus impar* reappeared on the stone rays representing a sun upon the front of the barracks on the Quai d'Orsay. Where there had been an Imperial Guard, there was now a red house. The Arc du Carrousel, all laden with badly borne victories, thrown out of its element among these novelties, a little ashamed, it may be, of Marengo and Arcola, extricated itself from its predicament with the statue of the Duc d'Angoulême. The cemetery of the Madeleine, a terrible pauper's grave in 1793, was covered with jasper and marble, since the bones of Louis XVI and Marie Antoinette lay in that dust.

In the moat of Vincennes a sepulchral shaft sprang from the earth, recalling the fact that the Duc d'Enghien had perished in the very month when Napoleon was crowned. Pope Pius VII, who had performed the coronation very near this death, tranquilly bestowed his blessing on the fall as he had bestowed it on the elevation. At Schoenbrunn there was a little shadow, aged four, whom it was seditious to call the King of Rome. And these things took place, and the kings resumed their thrones, and the master of Europe was put in a cage, and the old regime became the new regime, and all the shadows and all the light of the earth changed place, because, on the afternoon of a certain summer's day, a shepherd said to a Prussian in the forest, "Go this way, and not that!"

This 1815 was a sort of lugubrious April. Ancient unhealthy and poisonous realities were covered with new appearances. A lie wedded 1789; the right divine was masked under a charter; fictions became constitutional; prejudices, superstitions and mental reservations, with Article 14 in the heart, were varnished over with liberalism. It was the serpent's change of skin.

Man had been rendered both greater and smaller by Napoleon. Under this reign of splendid matter, the ideal had received the strange name of ideology! It is a grave imprudence in a great man to turn the future into derision. The populace, however, that food for cannon which is so fond of the cannoneer, sought him with its glance. Where is he? What is he doing? "Napoleon is dead," said a passer-by to a veteran of Marengo and Waterloo. "He dead!" cried the soldier; "you don't know him." Imagination distrusted this man, even when overthrown. The depths of Europe were full of darkness after Waterloo. Something enormous remained long empty through Napoleon's disappearance.

The kings placed themselves in this void. Ancient Europe profited by it to undertake reforms. There was a Holy Alliance; *Belle-Alliance*, Beautiful Alliance, the fatal field of Waterloo had said in advance.

In presence and in face of that antique Europe reconstructed, the features of a new France were sketched out. The future, which the Emperor had rallied, made its entry. On its brow it bore the star, Liberty. The glowing eyes of all young generations were turned on it. Singular fact! people were, at one and the same time, in love with the future, Liberty, and the past, Napoleon. Defeat had rendered the vanquished greater. Bonaparte fallen seemed more lofty than Napoleon erect. Those who had triumphed were alarmed. England had him guarded by Hudson Lowe, and France had him watched by Montchenu. His folded arms became a source of uneasiness to thrones. Alexander called him "my sleeplessness." This terror was the result of the quantity of revolution which was contained in him. That is what explains and excuses Bonapartist liberalism. This phantom caused the old world to tremble. The kings reigned, but ill at their ease, with the rock of Saint Helena on the horizon.

While Napoleon was passing through the death struggle at Longwood, the sixty thousand men who had fallen on the field of Waterloo were quietly rotting, and something of their peace was shed abroad over the world. The Congress of Vienna made the treaties in 1815, and Europe called this the Restoration.

This is what Waterloo was.

But what matters it to the Infinite? all that tempest, all that cloud, that war, then that peace? All that darkness did not trouble for a moment the light of that immense Eye before which a grub skipping from one blade of grass to another equals the eagle soaring from belfry to belfry on the towers of Notre Dame.

XIX

The Battle-Field at Night

Let us return—it is a necessity in this book—to that fatal battle-field. On the 18th of June the moon was full. Its light favored Blücher's ferocious pursuit, betrayed the traces of the fugitives, delivered up that disastrous mass to the eager Prussian cavalry, and aided the massacre. Such tragic favors of the night do occur sometimes during catastrophes.

After the last cannon-shot had been fired, the plain of Mont-Saint-Jean remained deserted.

The English occupied the encampment of the French; it is the usual sign of victory to sleep in the bed of the vanquished. They established their bivouac beyond Rossomme. The Prussians, let loose on the retreating rout, pushed forward. Wellington went to the village of Waterloo to draw up his report to Lord Bathurst.

If ever the *sic vos non vobis* was applicable, it certainly is to that village of Waterloo. Waterloo took no part, and lay half a league from the scene of action. Mont-Saint-Jean was cannonaded, Hougomont was burned, La Haie-Sainte was taken by assault, Papelotte was burned, Plancenoit was burned, La Belle-Alliance beheld the embrace of the two conquerors; these names are hardly known, and Waterloo, which worked not in the battle, bears off all the honor.

We are not of the number of those who flatter war; when the occasion presents itself, we tell the truth about it. War has frightful beauties which we have not concealed; it has also, we acknowledge, some hideous features. One of the most surprising is the prompt stripping of the bodies of the dead after the victory. The dawn which follows a battle always rises on naked corpses.

Who does this? Who thus soils the triumph? What hideous, furtive hand is that which is slipped into the pocket of victory? What pickpockets are they who ply their trade in the rear of glory? Some philosophers—Voltaire among the number—affirm that it is precisely those persons who have made the glory. It is the same men, they say; there is no relief corps; those who are erect pillage those who are prone on the earth. The hero of the day is the vampire of the night. One has assuredly the right, after all, to strip a corpse a bit when one is the author of that corpse. For our own part, we do not think so; it seems to us impossible that the same hand should pluck laurels and purloin the shoes from a dead man.

One thing is certain, which is, that generally after conquerors follow thieves. But let us leave the soldier, especially the contemporary soldier, out of the question.

Every army has a rear-guard, and it is that which must be blamed. Bat-like creatures, half brigands and lackeys; all the sorts of vespertillos that that twilight called war engenders; wearers of uniforms, who take no part in the fighting; pretended invalids; formidable limpers; interloping sutlers, trotting along in little carts, sometimes accompanied by their wives, and stealing things which they sell again; beggars offering themselves as guides to officers; soldiers' servants; marauders; armies on the march in days gone by,—we are not speaking of the present,—dragged all this behind them, so that in the special language they are called "stragglers." No army, no nation, was responsible for those beings; they spoke Italian and followed the Germans, then spoke French and followed the English. It was by one of these wretches, a Spanish straggler who spoke French, that the Marquis of Fervacques, deceived by his Picard jargon, and taking him for one of our own men, was traitorously slain and robbed on the battle-field itself, in the course of the night which followed the victory of Cerisoles. The rascal sprang from this marauding. The detestable maxim, *Live on the enemy!* produced this leprosy, which a strict discipline alone could heal. There are reputations which are deceptive; one does not always know why certain generals, great in other directions, have been so popular. Turenne was adored by his soldiers because he tolerated pillage; evil permitted constitutes part of goodness. Turenne was so good that he allowed the Palatinate to be delivered over to fire and blood. The marauders in the train of an army were more or less in number, according as the chief was more or less severe. Hoche and Marceau had no stragglers; Wellington had few, and we do him the justice to mention it.

Nevertheless, on the night from the 18th to the 19th of June, the dead were robbed. Wellington was rigid; he gave orders that any one caught in the act should be shot; but rapine is tenacious. The marauders stole in one corner of the battlefield while others were being shot in another.

The moon was sinister over this plain.

Towards midnight, a man was prowling about, or rather, climbing in the direction of the hollow road of Ohain. To all appearance he was one of those whom we have just described,—neither English nor French, neither peasant nor soldier, less a man than a ghoul attracted by the scent of the dead bodies having theft for his victory, and come to rifle Waterloo. He was clad in a blouse that was something like a great coat; he was uneasy and audacious; he walked forwards and gazed behind him. Who was this man? The night probably knew more of him than the day. He had no sack, but evidently he had large pockets under his coat. From time to time he halted, scrutinized the plain around him as though to see whether he were observed, bent over abruptly, disturbed something silent and motionless on the ground, then rose and fled. His sliding motion, his attitudes, his mysterious and rapid gestures, caused him to resemble those twilight larvæ which haunt ruins, and which ancient Norman legends call the Alleurs.

Certain nocturnal wading birds produce these silhouettes among the marshes.

A glance capable of piercing all that mist deeply would have perceived at some distance a sort of little sutler's wagon with a fluted wicker hood, harnessed to a famished nag which was cropping the grass across its bit as it halted, hidden, as it were, behind the hovel which adjoins the highway to Nivelles, at the angle of the road from Mont-Saint-Jean to Braine l'Alleud; and in the wagon, a sort of woman seated on coffers and packages. Perhaps there was some connection between that wagon and that prowler.

The darkness was serene. Not a cloud in the zenith. What matters it if the earth be red! the moon remains white; these are the indifferences of the sky. In the fields, branches of trees broken by grape-shot, but not fallen, upheld by their bark, swayed gently in the breeze of night. A breath, almost a respiration, moved the shrubbery. Quivers which resembled the departure of souls ran through the grass.

In the distance the coming and going of patrols and the general rounds of the English camp were audible.

Hougomont and La Haie-Sainte continued to burn, forming, one in the west, the other in the east, two great flames which were joined by the cordon of bivouac fires of the English, like a necklace of rubies with two carbuncles at the extremities, as they extended in an immense semicircle over the hills along the horizon.

We have described the catastrophe of the road of Ohain. The heart is terrified at the thought of what that death must have been to so many brave men.

If there is anything terrible, if there exists a reality which surpasses dreams, it is this: to live, to see the sun; to be in full possession of virile force; to possess health and joy; to laugh valiantly; to rush towards a glory which one sees dazzling in front of one; to feel in one's breast lungs which breathe, a heart which beats, a will which reasons; to speak, think, hope, love; to have a mother, to have a wife, to have children; to have the light—and all at once, in the space of a shout, in less than a minute, to sink into an abyss; to fall, to roll, to crush, to be crushed; to see ears of wheat, flowers, leaves, branches; not to be able to catch hold of anything; to feel one's sword useless, men beneath one, horses on top of one; to struggle in vain, since one's bones have been broken by some kick in the darkness; to feel a heel which makes one's eyes start from their sockets; to bite horses' shoes in one's rage; to stifle, to yell, to writhe; to be beneath, and to say to one's self, "But just a little while ago I was a living man!"

There, where that lamentable disaster had uttered its death-rattle, all was silence now. The edges of the hollow road were encumbered with horses and riders, inextricably heaped up. Terrible entanglement! There was no longer any slope, for the corpses had levelled the road with the plain, and reached the brim like a well-filled bushel of barley. A heap of dead bodies in the upper part, a river of blood in the lower part—such was that road on the evening of the 18th of June, 1815. The blood ran even to the Nivelles highway, and there overflowed in a large pool in front of the abatis of trees which barred the way, at a spot which is still pointed out.

It will be remembered that it was at the opposite point, in the direction of the Genappe road, that the destruction of the cuirassiers had taken place. The thickness of the layer of bodies was proportioned to the depth of the hollow road. Towards the middle, at the point where it became level, where Delort's division had passed, the layer of corpses was thinner.

The nocturnal prowler whom we have just shown to the reader was going in that direction. He was searching that vast tomb. He gazed about. He passed the dead in some sort of hideous review. He walked with his feet in the blood.

All at once he paused.

A few paces in front of him, in the hollow road, at the point where the pile of dead came to an end, an open hand, illumined by the moon, projected from beneath that heap of men. That hand had on its finger something sparkling, which was a ring of gold.

The man bent over, remained in a crouching attitude for a moment, and when he rose there was no longer a ring on the hand.

He did not precisely rise; he remained in a stooping and frightened attitude, with his back turned to the heap of dead, scanning the horizon on his knees, with the whole upper portion of his body supported on his two forefingers, which rested on the earth, and his head peering above the edge of the hollow road. The jackal's four paws suit some actions.

Then coming to a decision, he rose to his feet.

At that moment, he gave a terrible start. He felt some one clutch him from behind.

He wheeled round; it was the open hand, which had closed, and had seized the skirt of his coat.

An honest man would have been terrified; this man burst into a laugh.

"Come," said he, "it's only a dead body. I prefer a spook to a gendarme."

But the hand weakened and released him. Effort is quickly exhausted in the grave.

"Well now," said the prowler, "is that dead fellow alive? Let's see."

He bent down again, fumbled among the heap, pushed aside everything that was in his way, seized the hand, grasped the arm, freed the head, pulled out the body, and a few moments later he was dragging the lifeless, or at least the unconscious, man, through the shadows of hollow road. He was a cuirassier, an officer, and even an officer of considerable rank; a large gold epaulette peeped from beneath the cuirass; this officer no longer possessed a helmet. A furious sword-cut had scarred his face, where nothing was discernible but blood.

However, he did not appear to have any broken limbs, and, by some happy chance, if that word is permissible here, the dead had been vaulted above him in such a manner as to preserve him from being crushed. His eyes were still closed.

On his cuirass he wore the silver cross of the Legion of Honor.

The prowler tore off this cross, which disappeared into one of the gulfs which he had beneath his great coat.

Then he felt of the officer's fob, discovered a watch there, and took possession of it. Next he searched his waistcoat, found a purse and pocketed it.

When he had arrived at this stage of succor which he was administering to this dying man, the officer opened his eyes.

"Thanks," he said feebly.

The abruptness of the movements of the man who was manipulating him, the freshness of the night, the air which he could inhale freely, had roused him from his lethargy.

The prowler made no reply. He raised his head. A sound of footsteps was audible in the plain; some patrol was probably approaching.

The officer murmured, for the death agony was still in his voice:—

"Who won the battle?"

"The English," answered the prowler.

The officer went on:—

"Look in my pockets; you will find a watch and a purse. Take them."

It was already done.

The prowler executed the required feint, and said:—

"There is nothing there."

"I have been robbed," said the officer; "I am sorry for that. You should have had them."

The steps of the patrol became more and more distinct.

"Some one is coming," said the prowler, with the movement of a man who is taking his departure.

The officer raised his arm feebly, and detained him.

"You have saved my life. Who are you?"

The prowler answered rapidly, and in a low voice:—

"Like yourself, I belonged to the French army. I must leave you. If they were to catch me, they would shoot me. I have saved your life. Now get out of the scrape yourself."

"What is your rank?"

"Sergeant."

"What is your name?"

"Thénardier."

"I shall not forget that name," said the officer; "and do you remember mine. My name is Pontmercy."

BOOK SECOND
THE SHIP ORION

I

NUMBER 24,601 BECOMES NUMBER 9,430

Jean Valjean had been recaptured.

The reader will be grateful to us if we pass rapidly over the sad details. We will confine ourselves to transcribing two paragraphs published by the journals of that day, a few months after the surprising events which had taken place at M. sur M.

These articles are rather summary. It must be remembered, that at that epoch the *Gazette des Tribunaux* was not yet in existence.

We borrow the first from the *Drapeau Blanc*. It bears the date of July 25, 1823.

An arrondissement of the Pas de Calais has just been the theatre of an event quite out of the ordinary course. A man, who was a stranger in the Department, and who bore the name of M. Madeleine, had, thanks to the new methods, resuscitated some years ago an ancient local industry, the manufacture of jet and of black glass trinkets. He had made his fortune in the business, and that of the arrondissement as well, we will admit. He had been appointed mayor, in recognition of his services. The police discovered that M. Madeleine was no other than an ex-convict who had broken his ban, condemned in 1796 for theft, and named Jean Valjean. Jean Valjean has been recommitted to prison. It appears that previous to his arrest he had succeeded in withdrawing from the hands of M. Laffitte, a sum of over half a million which he had lodged there, and which he had, moreover, and by perfectly legitimate means, acquired in his business. No one has been able to discover where Jean Valjean has concealed this money since his return to prison at Toulon.

The second article, which enters a little more into detail, is an extract from the *Journal de Paris*, of the same date.

A former convict, who had been liberated, named Jean Valjean, has just appeared before the Court of Assizes of the Var, under circumstances calculated to attract attention. This wretch had succeeded in escaping the vigilance of the police, he had changed his name, and had succeeded in getting himself appointed mayor of one of our small northern towns; in this town he had established a considerable commerce. He has at last been unmasked and arrested, thanks to the indefatigable zeal of the public prosecutor. He had for his concubine a woman of the town, who died of a shock at the moment of his arrest. This scoundrel, who is endowed with Herculean strength, found means to escape; but three or four days after his flight the police laid their hands on him once more, in Paris itself, at the very moment when he was entering one of those little vehicles which run between the capital and the village of Montfermeil (Seine-et-Oise). He is said to have profited by this interval of three or four days of liberty, to withdraw a considerable sum deposited by him with one of our leading bankers. This sum has been estimated at six or seven hundred thousand francs. If the indictment is to be trusted, he has hidden it in some place known to himself alone, and it has not been possible to lay hands on it. However that may be, the said Jean Valjean has just been brought before the Assizes of the Department of the Var as accused of highway robbery accompanied with violence, about eight years ago, on the person of one of those honest children who, as the patriarch of Ferney has said, in immortal verse,

> ". . . Arrive from Savoy every year,
> And who, with gentle hands, do clear
> Those long canals choked up with soot."

This bandit refused to defend himself. It was proved by the skilful and eloquent representative of the public prosecutor, that the theft was committed in complicity with others, and that Jean Valjean was a member of a band of robbers in the south. Jean Valjean was pronounced guilty and was condemned to the death penalty in consequence. This criminal refused to lodge an appeal. The king, in his inexhaustible clemency, has deigned to commute his penalty to that of penal servitude for life. Jean Valjean was immediately taken to the prison at Toulon.

The reader has not forgotten that Jean Valjean had religious habits at M. sur M. Some papers, among others the *Constitutional*, presented this commutation as a triumph of the priestly party.

Jean Valjean changed his number in the galleys. He was called 9,430.

However, and we will mention it at once in order that we may not be obliged to recur to the subject, the prosperity of M. sur M. vanished with M. Madeleine; all that he had foreseen during his night of fever and hesitation was realized; lacking him, there actually was *a soul lacking*. After this fall, there took place at M. sur M. that egotistical division of great existences which have fallen, that fatal dismemberment of flourishing things which is accomplished every day, obscurely, in the human community, and which history has noted only once, because it occurred after the death of Alexander. Lieutenants are crowned kings; superintendents improvise manufacturers out of themselves. Envious rivalries arose. M. Madeleine's vast workshops were shut; his buildings fell to ruin, his workmen were scattered. Some of them quitted the country, others abandoned the trade. Thenceforth, everything was done on a small scale, instead of on a grand scale; for lucre instead of the general good. There was no longer a centre; everywhere there was competition and animosity. M. Madeleine had reigned over all and directed all. No sooner had he fallen, than each pulled things to himself; the spirit of combat succeeded to the spirit of organization, bitterness to cordiality, hatred of one another to the benevolence of the founder towards all; the threads which M. Madeleine had set were tangled and broken, the methods were adulterated, the products were debased, confidence was killed; the market diminished, for lack of orders; salaries were reduced, the workshops stood still, bankruptcy arrived. And then there was nothing more for the poor. All had vanished.

The state itself perceived that some one had been crushed somewhere. Less than four years after the judgment of the Court of Assizes establishing the identity of Jean Valjean and M. Madeleine, for the benefit of the galleys, the cost of collecting taxes had doubled in the arrondissement of M. sur M.; and M. de Villèle called attention to the fact in the rostrum, in the month of February, 1827.

II

In which the Reader will Peruse Two Verses, which are of the Devil's Composition, Possibly

Before proceeding further, it will be to the purpose to narrate in some detail, a singular occurrence which took place at about the same epoch, in Montfermeil, and which is not lacking in coincidence with certain conjectures of the indictment.

There exists in the region of Montfermeil a very ancient superstition, which is all the more curious and all the more precious, because a popular superstition in the vicinity of Paris is like an aloe in Siberia. We are among those who respect everything which is in the nature of a rare plant. Here, then, is the superstition of Montfermeil: it is thought that the devil, from time immemorial, has selected the forest as a hiding-place for his treasures. Goodwives affirm that it is no rarity to encounter at nightfall, in secluded nooks of the forest, a black man with the air of a carter or a wood-chopper, wearing wooden shoes, clad in trousers and a blouse of linen, and recognizable by the fact, that, instead of a cap or hat, he has two immense horns on his head. This ought, in fact, to render him recognizable. This man is habitually engaged in digging a hole. There are three ways of profiting by such an encounter. The first is to approach the man and speak to him. Then it is seen that the man is simply a peasant, that he appears black because it is nightfall; that he is not digging any hole whatever, but is cutting grass for his cows, and that what had been taken for horns is nothing but a dung-fork which he is carrying on his back, and whose teeth, thanks to the perspective of evening, seemed to spring from his head. The man returns home and dies within the week. The second way is to watch him, to wait until he has dug his hole, until he has filled it and has gone away; then to run with great speed to the trench, to open it once more and to seize the "treasure" which the black man has necessarily placed there. In this case one dies within the month. Finally, the last method is not to speak to the black man, not to look at him, and to flee at the best speed of one's legs. One then dies within the year.

As all three methods are attended with their special inconveniences, the second, which at all events, presents some advantages, among others that of possessing a treasure, if only for a month, is the one most generally adopted. So bold men, who are tempted by every chance, have quite frequently, as we are assured, opened the holes excavated by the black man, and tried to rob the devil. The success of the operation appears to be but moderate. At least, if the tradition is to be believed, and in particular the two enigmatical lines in barbarous Latin, which an evil Norman monk, a bit of a sorcerer, named Tryphon has left on this subject. This Tryphon is buried at the Abbey of Saint-Georges de Bocherville, near Rouen, and toads spawn on his grave.

Accordingly, enormous efforts are made. Such trenches are ordinarily extremely deep; a man sweats, digs, toils all night—for it must be done at night; he wets his shirt, burns out his candle, breaks his mattock, and when he arrives at the bottom of the hole, when he lays his hand on the "treasure," what does he find? What is the devil's treasure? A sou, sometimes a crown-piece, a stone, a skeleton, a bleeding body, sometimes a spectre folded in four like a sheet of paper in a portfolio, sometimes nothing. This is what Tryphon's verses seem to announce to the indiscreet and curious:—

"Fodit, et in fossa thesauros condit opaca,
As, nummas, lapides, cadaver, simulacra, nihilque."

It seems that in our day there is sometimes found a powder-horn with bullets, sometimes an old pack of cards greasy and worn, which has evidently served the devil. Tryphon does not record these two finds, since Tryphon lived in the twelfth century, and since the devil does not appear to have had the wit to invent powder before Roger Bacon's time, and cards before the time of Charles VI.

Moreover, if one plays at cards, one is sure to lose all that one possesses! and as for the powder in the horn, it possesses the property of making your gun burst in your face.

Now, a very short time after the epoch when it seemed to the prosecuting attorney that the liberated convict Jean Valjean during his flight of several days had been prowling around Montfermeil, it was remarked in that village that a certain old road-laborer, named Boulatruelle, had "peculiar ways" in the forest. People thereabouts thought they knew that this Boulatruelle had been in the galleys. He was subjected to certain police supervision, and, as he could find work nowhere, the administration employed him at reduced rates as a road-mender on the crossroad from Gagny to Lagny.

This Boulatruelle was a man who was viewed with disfavor by the inhabitants of the district as too respectful, too humble, too prompt in removing his cap to every one, and trembling and smiling in the presence of the gendarmes,—probably affiliated to robber bands, they said; suspected of lying in ambush at verge of copses at nightfall. The only thing in his favor was that he was a drunkard.

This is what people thought they had noticed:—

Of late, Boulatruelle had taken to quitting his task of stone-breaking and care of the road at a very early hour, and to betaking himself to the forest with his pickaxe. He was encountered towards evening in the most deserted clearings, in the wildest thickets; and he had the appearance of being in search of something, and sometimes he was digging holes. The goodwives who passed took him at first for Beelzebub; then they recognized Boulatruelle, and were not in the least reassured thereby. These encounters seemed to cause Boulatruelle a lively displeasure. It was evident that he sought to hide, and that there was some mystery in what he was doing.

It was said in the village: "It is clear that the devil has appeared. Boulatruelle has seen him, and is on the search. In sooth, he is cunning enough to pocket Lucifer's hoard."

The Voltairians added, "Will Boulatruelle catch the devil, or will the devil catch Boulatruelle?" The old women made a great many signs of the cross.

In the meantime, Boulatruelle's manœuvres in the forest ceased; and he resumed his regular occupation of roadmending; and people gossiped of something else.

Some persons, however, were still curious, surmising that in all this there was probably no fabulous treasure of the legends, but some fine windfall of a more serious and palpable sort than the devil's bank-bills, and that the road-mender had half discovered the secret. The most "puzzled" were the schoolmaster and Thénardier, the proprietor of the tavern, who was everybody's friend, and had not disdained to ally himself with Boulatruelle.

"He has been in the galleys," said Thénardier. "Eh! Good God! no one knows who has been there or will be there."

One evening the schoolmaster affirmed that in former times the law would have instituted an inquiry as to what Boulatruelle did in the forest, and that the latter would have been forced to speak, and that he would have been put to the torture in case of need, and that Boulatruelle would not have resisted the water test, for example. "Let us put him to the wine test," said Thénardier.

They made an effort, and got the old road-mender to drinking. Boulatruelle drank an enormous amount, but said very little. He combined with admirable art, and in masterly proportions, the thirst of a gormandizer with the discretion of a judge. Nevertheless, by dint of returning to the charge and of comparing and putting together the few obscure words which he did allow to escape him, this is what Thénardier and the schoolmaster imagined that they had made out:—

One morning, when Boulatruelle was on his way to his work, at daybreak, he had been surprised to see, at a nook of the forest in the underbrush, a shovel and a pickaxe, *concealed, as one might say*.

However, he might have supposed that they were probably the shovel and pick of Father Six-Fours, the water-carrier, and would have thought no more about it. But, on the evening of that day, he saw, without being seen himself, as he was hidden by a large tree, "a person who did not belong in those parts, and whom he, Boulatruelle, knew well," directing his steps towards the densest part of the wood. Translation by Thénardier: *A comrade of the galleys*. Boulatruelle obstinately refused to reveal his name. This person carried a package—something square, like a large box or a small trunk. Surprise on the part of Boulatruelle. However, it was only after the expiration of seven or eight minutes that the idea of following that "person" had occurred to him. But it was too late; the person was already in the thicket, night had descended, and Boulatruelle had not been able to catch up with him. Then he had adopted the course of watching for him at the edge of the woods. "It was moonlight." Two or three hours later, Boulatruelle had seen this person emerge from the brushwood, carrying no longer the coffer, but a shovel and pick. Boulatruelle had allowed the person to pass, and had not dreamed of accosting him, because he said to himself that the other man was three times as strong as he was, and armed with a pickaxe, and that he would probably knock him over the head on recognizing him, and on perceiving that he was recognized. Touching effusion of two old comrades on meeting again. But the shovel and pick had served as a ray of light to Boulatruelle; he had hastened to the thicket in the morning, and had found neither shovel nor pick. From this he had drawn the inference that this person, once in the forest, had dug a hole with his pick, buried the coffer, and reclosed the hole with his shovel. Now, the coffer was too small to contain a body; therefore it contained money. Hence his researches. Boulatruelle had explored, sounded, searched the entire forest and the thicket, and had dug wherever the earth appeared to him to have been recently turned up. In vain.

He had "ferreted out" nothing. No one in Montfermeil thought any more about it. There were only a few brave gossips, who said, "You may be certain that the mender on the Gagny road did not take all that trouble for nothing; he was sure that the devil had come."

III

The Ankle-Chain must have Undergone a Certain Preparatory Manipulation to be thus Broken with a Blow from a Hammer

Towards the end of October, in that same year, 1823, the inhabitants of Toulon beheld the entry into their port, after heavy weather, and for the purpose of repairing some damages, of the ship *Orion*, which was employed later at Brest as a school-ship, and which then formed a part of the Mediterranean squadron.

This vessel, battered as it was,—for the sea had handled it roughly,—produced a fine effect as it entered the roads. It flew some colors which procured for it the regulation salute of eleven guns, which it returned, shot for shot; total, twenty-two. It has been calculated that what with salvos, royal and military politenesses, courteous exchanges of uproar, signals of etiquette, formalities of roadsteads and citadels, sunrises and sunsets, saluted every day by all fortresses and all ships of war, openings and closings of ports, etc., the civilized world, discharged all over the earth, in the course of four and twenty hours, one hundred and fifty thousand useless shots. At six francs the shot, that comes to nine hundred thousand francs a day, three hundred millions a year, which vanish in smoke. This is a mere detail. All this time the poor were dying of hunger.

The year 1823 was what the Restoration called "the epoch of the Spanish war."

This war contained many events in one, and a quantity of peculiarities. A grand family affair for the house of Bourbon; the branch of France succoring and protecting the branch of Madrid, that is to say, performing an act devolving on the elder; an apparent return to our national traditions, complicated by servitude and by subjection to the cabinets of the North; M. le Duc d'Angoulême, surnamed by the liberal sheets *the hero of Andujar*, compressing in a triumphal attitude that was somewhat contradicted by his peaceable air, the ancient and very powerful terrorism of the Holy Office at variance with the chimerical terrorism of the liberals; the *sansculottes* resuscitated, to the great terror of dowagers, under the name of *descamisados*; monarchy opposing an obstacle to progress described as anarchy; the theories of '89 roughly interrupted in the sap; a European halt, called to the French idea, which was making the tour of the world; beside the son of France as generalissimo, the Prince de Carignan, afterwards Charles Albert, enrolling himself in that crusade of kings against people as a volunteer, with grenadier epaulets of red worsted; the soldiers of the Empire setting out on a fresh campaign, but aged, saddened, after eight years of repose, and under the white cockade; the tricolored standard waved abroad by a heroic handful of Frenchmen, as the white standard had been thirty years earlier at Coblentz; monks mingled with our troops; the spirit of liberty and of novelty brought to its senses by bayonets; principles slaughtered by cannonades; France undoing by her arms that which she had done by her mind; in addition to this, hostile leaders sold, soldiers hesitating, cities besieged by millions; no military perils, and yet possible explosions, as in every mine which is surprised and invaded; but little bloodshed, little honor won, shame for some, glory for no one. Such was this war, made by the princes descended from Louis XIV, and conducted by generals who had been under Napoleon. Its sad fate was to recall neither the grand war nor grand politics.

Some feats of arms were serious; the taking of the Trocadéro, among others, was a fine military action; but after all, we repeat, the trumpets of this war give back a cracked sound, the whole effect was suspicious; history approves of France for making a difficulty about accepting this false triumph. It seemed evident that certain Spanish officers charged with resistance yielded too easily; the idea of corruption was connected with the victory; it appears as though generals and not battles had been won, and the conquering soldier returned humiliated. A debasing war, in short, in which the *Bank of France* could be read in the folds of the flag.

Soldiers of the war of 1808, on whom Saragossa had fallen in formidable ruin, frowned in 1823 at the easy surrender of citadels, and began to regret Palafox. It is the nature of France to prefer to have Rostopchine rather than Ballesteros in front of her.

From a still more serious point of view, and one which it is also proper to insist upon here, this war, which wounded the military spirit of France, enraged the democratic spirit. It was an enterprise of enthralment. In that campaign, the object of the French soldier, the son of democracy, was the conquest of a yoke for others. A hideous contradiction. France is made to arouse the soul of nations, not to stifle it. All the revolutions of Europe since 1792 are the French Revolution: liberty darts rays from France. That is a solar fact. Blind is he who will not see! It was Bonaparte who said it.

The war of 1823, an outrage on the generous Spanish nation, was then, at the same time, an outrage on the French Revolution. It was France who committed this monstrous violence; by foul means, for, with the exception of wars of liberation, everything that armies do is by foul means. The words *passive obedience* indicate this. An army is a strange masterpiece of combination where force results from an enormous sum of impotence. Thus is war, made by humanity against humanity, despite humanity, explained.

As for the Bourbons, the war of 1823 was fatal to them. They took it for a success. They did not perceive the danger that lies in having an idea slain to order. They went astray, in their innocence, to such a degree that they introduced the immense enfeeblement of a crime into their establishment as an element of strength. The spirit of the ambush entered into their politics. 1830 had its germ in 1823. The Spanish campaign became in their counsels an argument for force and for adventures by right Divine. France, having re-established *el rey netto* in Spain, might well have re-established the absolute king at home. They fell into the alarming error of taking the obedience of the soldier for the consent of the nation. Such confidence is the ruin of thrones. It is not permitted to fall asleep, either in the shadow of a machineel tree, nor in the shadow of an army.

Let us return to the ship *Orion*.

During the operations of the army commanded by the prince generalissimo, a squadron had been cruising in the Mediterranean. We have just stated that the *Orion* belonged to this fleet, and that accidents of the sea had brought it into port at Toulon.

The presence of a vessel of war in a port has something about it which attracts and engages a crowd. It is because it is great, and the crowd loves what is great.

A ship of the line is one of the most magnificent combinations of the genius of man with the powers of nature.

A ship of the line is composed, at the same time, of the heaviest and the lightest of possible matter, for it deals at one and the same time with three forms of substance,—solid, liquid, and fluid,—and it must do battle with all three. It has eleven claws of iron with which to seize the granite on the bottom of the sea, and more wings and more antennæ than winged insects, to catch the wind in the clouds. Its breath pours out through its hundred and twenty cannons as through enormous trumpets, and replies proudly to the thunder. The ocean seeks to lead it astray in the alarming sameness of its billows, but the vessel has its soul, its compass, which counsels it and always shows it the north. In the blackest nights, its lanterns supply the place of the stars. Thus, against the wind, it has its cordage and its canvas; against the water, wood; against the rocks, its iron, brass, and lead; against the shadows, its light; against immensity, a needle.

If one wishes to form an idea of all those gigantic proportions which, taken as a whole, constitute the ship of the line, one has only to enter one of the six-story covered construction stocks, in the ports of Brest or Toulon. The vessels in process of construction are under a bell-glass there, as it were. This colossal beam is a yard; that great column of wood which stretches out on the earth as far as the eye can reach is the main-mast. Taking it from its root in the stocks to its tip in the clouds, it is sixty fathoms long, and its diameter at its base is three feet. The English main-mast rises to a height of two hundred and seventeen feet above the water-line. The navy of our fathers employed cables, ours employs chains. The simple pile of chains on a ship of a hundred guns is four feet high, twenty feet in breadth, and eight feet in depth. And how much wood is required to make this ship? Three thousand cubic metres. It is a floating forest.

And moreover, let this be borne in mind, it is only a question here of the military vessel of forty years ago, of the simple sailing-vessel; steam, then in its infancy, has since added new miracles to that prodigy which is called a war vessel. At the present time, for example, the mixed vessel with a screw is a surprising machine, propelled by three thousand square metres of canvas and by an engine of two thousand five hundred horse-power.

Not to mention these new marvels, the ancient vessel of Christopher Columbus and of De Ruyter is one of the masterpieces of man. It is as inexhaustible in force as is the Infinite in gales; it stores up the wind in its sails, it is precise in the immense vagueness of the billows, it floats, and it reigns.

There comes an hour, nevertheless, when the gale breaks that sixty-foot yard like a straw, when the wind bends that mast four hundred feet tall, when that anchor, which weighs tens of thousands, is twisted in the jaws of the waves like a fisherman's hook in the jaws of a pike, when those monstrous cannons utter plaintive and futile roars, which the hurricane bears forth into the void and into night, when all that power and all that majesty are engulfed in a power and majesty which are superior.

Every time that immense force is displayed to culminate in an immense feebleness it affords men food for thought. Hence in the ports curious people abound around these marvellous machines of war and of navigation, without being able to explain perfectly to themselves why. Every day, accordingly, from morning until night, the quays, sluices, and the jetties of the port of Toulon were covered with a multitude of idlers and loungers, as they say in Paris, whose business consisted in staring at the *Orion*.

The *Orion* was a ship that had been ailing for a long time; in the course of its previous cruises thick layers of barnacles had collected on its keel to such a degree as to deprive it of half its speed; it had gone into the dry dock the year before this, in order to have the barnacles scraped off, then it had put to sea again; but this cleaning had affected the bolts of the keel: in the neighborhood of the Balearic Isles the sides had been strained and had opened; and, as the plating in those days was not of sheet iron, the vessel had sprung a leak. A violent equinoctial gale had come up, which had first staved in a grating and a porthole on the larboard side, and damaged the foretop-gallant-shrouds; in consequence of these injuries, the *Orion* had run back to Toulon.

It anchored near the Arsenal; it was fully equipped, and repairs were begun. The hull had received no damage on the starboard, but some of the planks had been unnailed here and there, according to custom, to permit of air entering the hold.

One morning the crowd which was gazing at it witnessed an accident.

THE CREW WAS BUSY BENDING the sails; the topman, who had to take the upper corner of the main-top-sail on the starboard, lost his balance; he was seen to waver; the multitude thronging the Arsenal quay uttered a cry; the man's head overbalanced his body; the man fell around the yard, with his hands outstretched towards the abyss; on his way he seized the footrope, first with one hand, then with the other, and remained hanging from it: the sea lay below him at a dizzy depth; the shock of his fall had imparted to the foot-rope a violent swinging motion; the man swayed back and forth at the end of that rope, like a stone in a sling.

It was incurring a frightful risk to go to his assistance; not one of the sailors, all fishermen of the coast, recently levied for the service, dared to attempt it. In the meantime, the unfortunate topman was losing his strength; his anguish could not be discerned on his face, but his exhaustion was visible in every limb; his arms were contracted in horrible twitchings; every effort which he made to re-ascend served but to augment the oscillations of the foot-rope; he did not shout, for fear of exhausting his strength. All were awaiting the minute when he should release his hold on the rope, and, from instant to instant, heads were turned aside that his fall might not be seen. There are moments when a bit of rope, a pole, the branch of a tree, is life itself, and it is a terrible thing to see a living being detach himself from it and fall like a ripe fruit.

All at once a man was seen climbing into the rigging with the agility of a tiger-cat; this man was dressed in red; he was a convict; he wore a green cap; he was a life convict. On arriving on a level with the top, a gust of wind carried away his cap, and allowed a perfectly white head to be seen: he was not a young man.

A convict employed on board with a detachment from the galleys had, in fact, at the very first instant, hastened to the officer of the watch, and, in the midst of the consternation and the hesitation of the crew, while all the sailors were trembling and drawing back, he had asked the officer's permission to risk his life to save the topman; at an affirmative sign from the officer he had broken the chain riveted to his ankle with one blow of a hammer, then he had caught up a rope, and had dashed into the rigging: no one noticed, at the instant, with what ease that chain had been broken; it was only later on that the incident was recalled.

In a twinkling he was on the yard; he paused for a few seconds and appeared to be measuring it with his eye; these seconds, during which the breeze swayed the topman at the extremity of a thread, seemed centuries to those who were looking on. At last, the convict raised his eyes to heaven and advanced a step: the crowd drew a long breath. He was seen to run out along the yard: on arriving at the point, he fastened the rope which he had brought to it, and allowed the other end to hang down, then he began to descend the rope, hand over hand, and then,— and the anguish was indescribable,—instead of one man suspended over the gulf, there were two.

One would have said it was a spider coming to seize a fly, only here the spider brought life, not death. Ten thousand glances were fastened on this group; not a cry, not a word; the same tremor contracted every brow; all mouths held their breath as though they feared to add the slightest puff to the wind which was swaying the two unfortunate men.

In the meantime, the convict had succeeded in lowering himself to a position near the sailor. It was high time; one minute more, and the exhausted and despairing man would have allowed himself to fall into the abyss. The convict had moored him securely with the cord to which he clung with one hand, while he was working with the other. At last, he was seen to climb back on the yard, and to drag the sailor up after him; he held him there a moment to allow him to recover his strength, then he grasped him in his arms and carried him, walking on the yard himself to the cap, and from there to the main-top, where he left him in the hands of his comrades.

At that moment the crowd broke into applause: old convict-sergeants among them wept, and women embraced each other on the quay, and all voices were heard to cry with a sort of tender rage, "Pardon for that man!"

He, in the meantime, had immediately begun to make his descent to rejoin his detachment. In order to reach them the more speedily, he dropped into the rigging, and ran along one of the lower yards; all eyes were following him. At a certain moment fear assailed them; whether it was that he was fatigued, or that his head turned, they thought they saw him hesitate and stagger. All at once the crowd uttered a loud shout: the convict had fallen into the sea.

The fall was perilous. The frigate *Algésiras* was anchored alongside the *Orion*, and the poor convict had fallen between the two vessels: it was to be feared that he would slip under one or the other of them. Four men flung themselves hastily into a boat; the crowd cheered them on; anxiety again took possession of all souls; the man had not risen to the surface; he had disappeared in the sea without leaving a ripple, as though he had fallen into a cask of oil: they sounded, they dived. In vain. The search was continued until the evening: they did not even find the body.

On the following day the Toulon newspaper printed these lines:—

"Nov. 17, 1823. Yesterday, a convict belonging to the detachment on board of the *Orion*, on his return from rendering assistance to a sailor, fell into the sea and was drowned. The body has not yet been found; it is supposed that it is entangled among the piles of the Arsenal point: this man was committed under the number 9,430, and his name was Jean Valjean."

BOOK THIRD

ACCOMPLISHMENT OF THE PROMISE
MADE TO THE DEAD WOMAN

I

THE WATER QUESTION AT MONTFERMEIL

Montfermeil is situated between Livry and Chelles, on the southern edge of that lofty table-land which separates the Ourcq from the Marne. At the present day it is a tolerably large town, ornamented all the year through with plaster villas, and on Sundays with beaming bourgeois. In 1823 there were at Montfermeil neither so many white houses nor so many well-satisfied citizens: it was only a village in the forest. Some pleasure-houses of the last century were to be met with there, to be sure, which were recognizable by their grand air, their balconies in twisted iron, and their long windows, whose tiny panes cast all sorts of varying shades of green on the white of the closed shutters; but Montfermeil was nonetheless a village. Retired cloth-merchants and rusticating attorneys had not discovered it as yet; it was a peaceful and charming place, which was not on the road to anywhere: there people lived, and cheaply, that peasant rustic life which is so bounteous and so easy; only, water was rare there, on account of the elevation of the plateau.

It was necessary to fetch it from a considerable distance; the end of the village towards Gagny drew its water from the magnificent ponds which exist in the woods there. The other end, which surrounds the church and which lies in the direction of Chelles, found drinking-water only at a little spring half-way down the slope, near the road to Chelles, about a quarter of an hour from Montfermeil.

Thus each household found it hard work to keep supplied with water. The large houses, the aristocracy, of which the Thénardier tavern formed a part, paid half a farthing a bucketful to a man who made a business of it, and who earned about eight sous a day in his enterprise of supplying Montfermeil with water; but this good man only worked until seven o'clock in the evening in summer, and five in winter; and night once come and the shutters on the ground floor once closed, he who had no water to drink went to fetch it for himself or did without it.

This constituted the terror of the poor creature whom the reader has probably not forgotten,—little Cosette. It will be remembered that Cosette was useful to the Thénardiers in two ways: they made the mother pay them, and they made the child serve them. So when the mother ceased to pay altogether, the reason for which we have read in preceding chapters, the Thénardiers kept Cosette. She took the place of a servant in their house. In this capacity she it was who ran to fetch water when it was required. So the child, who was greatly terrified at the idea of going to the spring at night, took great care that water should never be lacking in the house.

Christmas of the year 1823 was particularly brilliant at Montfermeil. The beginning of the winter had been mild; there had been neither snow nor frost up to that time. Some mountebanks from Paris had obtained permission of the mayor to erect their booths in the principal street of the village, and a band of itinerant merchants, under protection of the same tolerance, had constructed their stalls on the Church Square, and even extended them into Boulanger Alley, where, as the reader will perhaps remember, the Thénardiers' hostelry was situated. These people filled the inns and drinking-shops, and communicated to that tranquil little district a noisy and joyous life. In order to play the part of a faithful historian, we ought even to add that, among the curiosities displayed in the square, there was a menagerie, in which frightful clowns, clad in rags and coming no one knew whence, exhibited to the peasants of Montfermeil in 1823 one of those horrible Brazilian vultures, such as our Royal Museum did not possess until 1845, and which have a tricolored cockade for an eye. I believe that naturalists call this bird Caracara Polyborus; it belongs to the order of the Apicides, and to the family of the vultures. Some good old Bonapartist soldiers, who had retired to the village, went to see this creature with great devotion. The mountebanks gave out that the tricolored cockade was a unique phenomenon made by God expressly for their menagerie.

On Christmas eve itself, a number of men, carters, and peddlers, were seated at table, drinking and smoking around four or five candles in the public room of Thénardier's hostelry. This room resembled all drinking-shop rooms,—tables, pewter jugs, bottles, drinkers, smokers; but little light and a great deal of noise. The date of the year 1823 was indicated, nevertheless, by two objects which were then fashionable in the bourgeois class: to wit, a kaleidoscope and a lamp of ribbed tin. The female Thénardier was attending to the supper, which was roasting in front of a clear fire; her husband was drinking with his customers and talking politics.

Besides political conversations which had for their principal subjects the Spanish war and M. le Duc d'Angoulême, strictly local parentheses, like the following, were audible amid the uproar:—

"About Nanterre and Suresnes the vines have flourished greatly. When ten pieces were reckoned on there have been twelve. They have yielded a great deal of juice under the press." "But the grapes cannot be ripe?" "In those parts the grapes should not be ripe; the wine turns oily as soon as spring comes." "Then it is very thin wine?" "There are wines poorer even than these. The grapes must be gathered while green." Etc.

Or a miller would call out:—

"Are we responsible for what is in the sacks? We find in them a quantity of small seed which we cannot sift out, and which we are obliged to send through the mill-stones; there are tares, fennel, vetches, hempseed, fox-tail, and a host of other weeds, not to mention pebbles, which abound in certain wheat, especially in Breton wheat. I am not fond of grinding Breton wheat, any more than long-sawyers like to saw beams with nails in them. You can judge of the bad dust that makes in grinding. And then people complain of the flour. They are in the wrong. The flour is no fault of ours."

In a space between two windows a mower, who was seated at table with a landed proprietor who was fixing on a price for some meadow work to be performed in the spring, was saying:—

"It does no harm to have the grass wet. It cuts better. Dew is a good thing, sir. It makes no difference with that grass. Your grass is young and very hard to cut still. It's terribly tender. It yields before the iron." Etc.

Cosette was in her usual place, seated on the cross-bar of the kitchen table near the chimney. She was in rags; her bare feet were thrust into wooden shoes, and by the firelight she was engaged in knitting woollen stockings destined for the young Thénardiers. A very young kitten was playing about among the chairs. Laughter and chatter were audible in the adjoining room, from two fresh children's voices: it was Éponine and Azelma.

In the chimney-corner a cat-o'-nine-tails was hanging on a nail.

At intervals the cry of a very young child, which was somewhere in the house, rang through the noise of the dram-shop. It was a little boy who had been born to the Thénardiers during one of the preceding winters,—"she did not know why," she said, "the result of the cold,"— and who was a little more than three years old. The mother had nursed him, but she did not love him. When the persistent clamor of the brat became too annoying, "Your son is squalling," Thénardier would say; "do go and see what he wants." "Bah!" the mother would reply, "he bothers me." And the neglected child continued to shriek in the dark.

II

Two Complete Portraits

So far in this book the Thénardiers have been viewed only in profile; the moment has arrived for making the circuit of this couple, and considering it under all its aspects.

Thénardier had just passed his fiftieth birthday; Madame Thénardier was approaching her forties, which is equivalent to fifty in a woman; so that there existed a balance of age between husband and wife.

Our readers have possibly preserved some recollection of this Thénardier woman, ever since her first appearance,—tall, blond, red, fat, angular, square, enormous, and agile; she belonged, as we have said, to the race of those colossal wild women, who contort themselves at fairs with paving-stones hanging from their hair. She did everything about the house,—made the beds, did the washing, the cooking, and everything else. Cosette was her only servant; a mouse in the service of an elephant. Everything trembled at the sound of her voice,—window panes, furniture, and people. Her big face, dotted with red blotches, presented the appearance of a skimmer. She had a beard. She was an ideal market-porter dressed in woman's clothes. She swore splendidly; she boasted of being able to crack a nut with one blow of her fist. Except for the romances which she had read, and which made the affected lady peep through the ogress at times, in a very queer way, the idea would never have occurred to any one to say of her, "That is a woman." This Thénardier female was like the product of a wench engrafted on a fishwife. When one heard her speak, one said, "That is a gendarme"; when one saw her drink, one said, "That is a carter"; when one saw her handle Cosette, one said, "That is the hangman." One of her teeth projected when her face was in repose.

Thénardier was a small, thin, pale, angular, bony, feeble man, who had a sickly air and who was wonderfully healthy. His cunning began here; he smiled habitually, by way of precaution, and was almost polite to everybody, even to the beggar to whom he refused half a farthing. He had the glance of a pole-cat and the bearing of a man of letters. He greatly resembled the portraits of the Abbé Delille. His coquetry consisted in drinking with the carters. No one had ever succeeded in rendering him drunk. He smoked a big pipe. He wore a blouse, and under his blouse an old black coat. He made pretensions to literature and to materialism. There were certain names which he often pronounced to support whatever things he might be saying,—Voltaire, Raynal, Parny, and, singularly enough, Saint Augustine. He declared that he had "a system." In addition, he was a great swindler. A *filousophe* (philosophe), a scientific thief. The species does exist. It will be remembered that he pretended to have served in the army; he was in the habit of relating with exuberance, how, being a sergeant in the 6th or the 9th light something or other, at Waterloo, he had alone, and in the presence of a squadron of death-dealing hussars, covered with his body and saved from death, in the midst of the grape-shot, "a general, who had been dangerously wounded." Thence arose for his wall the flaring sign, and for his inn the name which it bore in the neighborhood, of "the cabaret of the Sergeant of Waterloo." He was a liberal, a classic, and a Bonapartist. He had subscribed for the Champ d'Asile. It was said in the village that he had studied for the priesthood.

We believe that he had simply studied in Holland for an inn-keeper. This rascal of composite order was, in all probability, some Fleming from Lille, in Flanders, a Frenchman in Paris, a Belgian at Brussels, being comfortably astride of both frontiers. As for his prowess at Waterloo, the reader is already acquainted with that. It will be perceived that he exaggerated it a trifle. Ebb and flow, wandering, adventure, was the leven of his existence; a tattered conscience entails a fragmentary life, and, apparently at the stormy epoch of June 18, 1815, Thénardier belonged to that variety of marauding sutlers of which we have spoken, beating about the country, selling to some, stealing from others, and travelling like a family man, with wife and children, in a rickety cart, in the rear of troops on the march, with an instinct for always attaching himself to the victorious army. This campaign ended, and having, as he said, "some quibus," he had come to Montfermeil and set up an inn there.

This *quibus*, composed of purses and watches, of gold rings and silver crosses, gathered in harvest-time in furrows sown with corpses, did not amount to a large total, and did not carry this sutler turned eating-house-keeper very far.

Thénardier had that peculiar rectilinear something about his gestures which, accompanied by an oath, recalls the barracks, and by a sign of the cross, the seminary. He was a fine talker. He allowed it to be thought that he was an educated man. Nevertheless, the schoolmaster had noticed that he pronounced improperly.

He composed the travellers' tariff card in a superior manner, but practised eyes sometimes spied out orthographical errors in it. Thénardier was cunning, greedy, slothful, and clever. He did not disdain his servants, which caused his wife to dispense with them. This giantess was jealous. It seemed to her that that thin and yellow little man must be an object coveted by all.

Thénardier, who was, above all, an astute and well-balanced man, was a scamp of a temperate sort. This is the worst species; hypocrisy enters into it.

It is not that Thénardier was not, on occasion, capable of wrath to quite the same degree as his wife; but this was very rare, and at such times, since he was enraged with the human race in general, as he bore within him a deep furnace of hatred. And since he was one of those people who are continually avenging their wrongs, who accuse everything that passes before them of everything which has befallen them, and who are always ready to cast upon the first person who comes to hand, as a legitimate grievance, the sum total of the deceptions, the bankruptcies, and the calamities of their lives,—when all this leaven was stirred up in him and boiled forth from his mouth and eyes, he was terrible. Woe to the person who came under his wrath at such a time!

In addition to his other qualities, Thénardier was attentive and penetrating, silent or talkative, according to circumstances, and always highly intelligent. He had something of the look of sailors, who are accustomed to screw up their eyes to gaze through marine glasses. Thénardier was a statesman.

Every newcomer who entered the tavern said, on catching sight of Madame Thénardier, "There is the master of the house." A mistake. She was not even the mistress. The husband was both master and mistress. She worked; he created. He directed everything by a sort of invisible and constant magnetic action. A word was sufficient for him, sometimes a sign; the mastodon obeyed. Thénardier was a sort of special and sovereign being in Madame Thénardier's eyes, though she did not thoroughly realize it. She was possessed of virtues after her own kind; if she had ever had a disagreement as to any detail with "Monsieur Thénardier,"—which was an inadmissible hypothesis, by the way,—she would not have blamed her husband in public on any subject whatever. She would never have committed "before strangers" that mistake so often committed by women, and which is called in parliamentary language, "exposing the crown." Although their concord had only evil as its result, there was contemplation in Madame Thénardier's submission to her husband. That mountain of noise and of flesh moved under the little finger of that frail despot. Viewed on its dwarfed and grotesque side, this was that grand and universal thing, the adoration of mind by matter; for certain ugly features have a cause in the very depths of eternal beauty. There was an unknown quantity about Thénardier; hence the absolute empire of the man over that woman. At certain moments she beheld him like a lighted candle; at others she felt him like a claw.

This woman was a formidable creature who loved no one except her children, and who did not fear any one except her husband. She was a mother because she was mammiferous. But her maternity stopped short with her daughters, and, as we shall see, did not extend to boys. The man had but one thought,—how to enrich himself.

He did not succeed in this. A theatre worthy of this great talent was lacking. Thénardier was ruining himself at Montfermeil, if ruin is possible to zero; in Switzerland or in the Pyrenees this penniless scamp would have become a millionaire; but an inn-keeper must browse where fate has hitched him.

It will be understood that the word *inn-keeper* is here employed in a restricted sense, and does not extend to an entire class.

In this same year, 1823, Thénardier was burdened with about fifteen hundred francs' worth of petty debts, and this rendered him anxious.

Whatever may have been the obstinate injustice of destiny in this case, Thénardier was one of those men who understand best, with the most profundity and in the most modern fashion, that thing which is a virtue among barbarous peoples and an object of merchandise among civilized peoples,—hospitality. Besides, he was an admirable poacher, and quoted for his skill in shooting. He had a certain cold and tranquil laugh, which was particularly dangerous.

His theories as a landlord sometimes burst forth in lightning flashes. He had professional aphorisms, which he inserted into his wife's mind. "The duty of the inn-keeper," he said to her one day, violently, and in a low voice, "is to sell to the first comer, stews, repose, light, fire, dirty sheets, a servant, lice, and a smile; to stop passers-by, to empty small purses, and to honestly lighten heavy ones; to shelter travelling families respectfully: to shave the man, to pluck the woman, to pick the child clean; to quote the window open, the window shut, the chimney-corner, the armchair, the chair, the ottoman, the stool, the feather-bed, the mattress and the truss of straw; to know how much the shadow uses up the mirror, and to put a price on it; and, by five hundred thousand devils, to make the traveller pay for everything, even for the flies which his dog eats!"

This man and this woman were ruse and rage wedded—a hideous and terrible team.

While the husband pondered and combined, Madame Thénardier thought not of absent creditors, took no heed of yesterday nor of to-morrow, and lived in a fit of anger, all in a minute.

Such were these two beings. Cosette was between them, subjected to their double pressure, like a creature who is at the same time being ground up in a mill and pulled to pieces with pincers. The man and the woman each had a different method: Cosette was overwhelmed with blows—this was the woman's; she went barefooted in winter—that was the man's doing.

Cosette ran upstairs and down, washed, swept, rubbed, dusted, ran, fluttered about, panted, moved heavy articles, and weak as she was, did the coarse work. There was no mercy for her; a fierce mistress and venomous master. The Thénardier hostelry was like a spider's web, in which Cosette had been caught, and where she lay trembling. The ideal of oppression was realized by this sinister household. It was something like the fly serving the spiders.

The poor child passively held her peace.

What takes place within these souls when they have but just quitted God, find themselves thus, at the very dawn of life, very small and in the midst of men all naked!

III

Men must have Wine, and Horses must have Water

Four new travellers had arrived.

Cosette was meditating sadly; for, although she was only eight years old, she had already suffered so much that she reflected with the lugubrious air of an old woman. Her eye was black in consequence of a blow from Madame Thénardier's fist, which caused the latter to remark from time to time, "How ugly she is with her fist-blow on her eye!"

Cosette was thinking that it was dark, very dark, that the pitchers and caraffes in the chambers of the travellers who had arrived must have been filled and that there was no more water in the cistern.

She was somewhat reassured because no one in the Thénardier establishment drank much water. Thirsty people were never lacking there; but their thirst was of the sort which applies to the jug rather than to the pitcher. Any one who had asked for a glass of water among all those glasses of wine would have appeared a savage to all these men. But there came a moment when the child trembled; Madame Thénardier raised the cover of a stew-pan which was boiling on the stove, then seized a glass and briskly approached the cistern. She turned the faucet; the child had raised her head and was following all the woman's movements. A thin stream of water trickled from the faucet, and half filled the glass. "Well," said she, "there is no more water!" A momentary silence ensued. The child did not breathe.

"Bah!" resumed Madame Thénardier, examining the half-filled glass, "this will be enough."

Cosette applied herself to her work once more, but for a quarter of an hour she felt her heart leaping in her bosom like a big snow-flake.

She counted the minutes that passed in this manner, and wished it were the next morning.

From time to time one of the drinkers looked into the street, and exclaimed, "It's as black as an oven!" or, "One must needs be a cat to go about the streets without a lantern at this hour!" And Cosette trembled.

All at once one of the pedlers who lodged in the hostelry entered, and said in a harsh voice:—

"My horse has not been watered."

"Yes, it has," said Madame Thénardier.

"I tell you that it has not," retorted the pedler.

Cosette had emerged from under the table.

"Oh, yes, sir!" said she, "the horse has had a drink; he drank out of a bucket, a whole bucketful, and it was I who took the water to him, and I spoke to him."

It was not true; Cosette lied.

"There's a brat as big as my fist who tells lies as big as the house," exclaimed the pedler. "I tell you that he has not been watered, you little jade! He has a way of blowing when he has had no water, which I know well."

Cosette persisted, and added in a voice rendered hoarse with anguish, and which was hardly audible:—

"And he drank heartily."

"Come," said the pedler, in a rage, "this won't do at all, let my horse be watered, and let that be the end of it!"

Cosette crept under the table again.

"In truth, that is fair!" said Madame Thénardier, "if the beast has not been watered, it must be."

Then glancing about her:—

"Well, now! Where's that other beast?"

She bent down and discovered Cosette cowering at the other end of the table, almost under the drinkers' feet.

"Are you coming?" shrieked Madame Thénardier.

Cosette crawled out of the sort of hole in which she had hidden herself. The Thénardier resumed:—

"Mademoiselle Dog-lack-name, go and water that horse."

"But, Madame," said Cosette, feebly, "there is no water."

The Thénardier threw the street door wide open:—

"Well, go and get some, then!"

Cosette dropped her head, and went for an empty bucket which stood near the chimney-corner.

This bucket was bigger than she was, and the child could have set down in it at her ease.

The Thénardier returned to her stove, and tasted what was in the stewpan, with a wooden spoon, grumbling the while:—

"There's plenty in the spring. There never was such a malicious creature as that. I think I should have done better to strain my onions."

Then she rummaged in a drawer which contained sous, pepper, and shallots.

"See here, Mam'selle Toad," she added, "on your way back, you will get a big loaf from the baker. Here's a fifteen-sou piece."

Cosette had a little pocket on one side of her apron; she took the coin without saying a word, and put it in that pocket.

Then she stood motionless, bucket in hand, the open door before her. She seemed to be waiting for some one to come to her rescue.

"Get along with you!" screamed the Thénardier.

Cosette went out. The door closed behind her.

IV

ENTRANCE ON THE SCENE OF A DOLL

The line of open-air booths starting at the church, extended, as the reader will remember, as far as the hostelry of the Thénardiers. These booths were all illuminated, because the citizens would soon pass on their way to the midnight mass, with candles burning in paper funnels, which, as the schoolmaster, then seated at the table at the Thénardiers' observed, produced "a magical effect." In compensation, not a star was visible in the sky.

The last of these stalls, established precisely opposite the Thénardiers' door, was a toy-shop all glittering with tinsel, glass, and magnificent objects of tin. In the first row, and far forwards, the merchant had placed on a background of white napkins, an immense doll, nearly two feet high, who was dressed in a robe of pink crepe, with gold wheat-ears on her head, which had real hair and enamel eyes. All that day, this marvel had been displayed to the wonderment of all passers-by under ten years of age, without a mother being found in Montfermeil sufficiently rich or sufficiently extravagant to give it to her child. Éponine and Azelma had passed hours in contemplating it, and Cosette herself had ventured to cast a glance at it, on the sly, it is true.

At the moment when Cosette emerged, bucket in hand, melancholy and overcome as she was, she could not refrain from lifting her eyes to that wonderful doll, towards *the lady*, as she called it. The poor child paused in amazement. She had not yet beheld that doll close to. The whole shop seemed a palace to her: the doll was not a doll; it was a vision. It was joy, splendor, riches, happiness, which appeared in a sort of chimerical halo to that unhappy little being so profoundly engulfed in gloomy and chilly misery. With the sad and innocent sagacity of childhood, Cosette measured the abyss which separated her from that doll. She said to herself that one must be a queen, or at least a princess, to have a "thing" like that. She gazed at that beautiful pink dress, that beautiful smooth hair, and she thought, "How happy that doll must be!" She could not take her eyes from that fantastic stall. The more she looked, the more dazzled she grew. She thought she was gazing at paradise. There were other dolls behind the large one, which seemed to her to be fairies and genii. The merchant, who was pacing back and forth in front of his shop, produced on her somewhat the effect of being the Eternal Father.

In this adoration she forgot everything, even the errand with which she was charged.

All at once the Thénardier's coarse voice recalled her to reality: "What, you silly jade! you have not gone? Wait! I'll give it to you! I want to know what you are doing there! Get along, you little monster!"

The Thénardier had cast a glance into the street, and had caught sight of Cosette in her ecstasy.

Cosette fled, dragging her pail, and taking the longest strides of which she was capable.

V

The Little One All Alone

As the Thénardier hostelry was in that part of the village which is near the church, it was to the spring in the forest in the direction of Chelles that Cosette was obliged to go for her water.

She did not glance at the display of a single other merchant. So long as she was in Boulanger Lane and in the neighborhood of the church, the lighted stalls illuminated the road; but soon the last light from the last stall vanished. The poor child found herself in the dark. She plunged into it. Only, as a certain emotion overcame her, she made as much motion as possible with the handle of the bucket as she walked along. This made a noise which afforded her company.

The further she went, the denser the darkness became. There was no one in the streets. However, she did encounter a woman, who turned around on seeing her, and stood still, muttering between her teeth: "Where can that child be going? Is it a werewolf child?" Then the woman recognized Cosette. "Well," said she, "it's the Lark!"

In this manner Cosette traversed the labyrinth of tortuous and deserted streets which terminate in the village of Montfermeil on the side of Chelles. So long as she had the houses or even the walls only on both sides of her path, she proceeded with tolerable boldness. From time to time she caught the flicker of a candle through the crack of a shutter—this was light and life; there were people there, and it reassured her. But in proportion as she advanced, her pace slackened mechanically, as it were. When she had passed the corner of the last house, Cosette paused. It had been hard to advance further than the last stall; it became impossible to proceed further than the last house. She set her bucket on the ground, thrust her hand into her hair, and began slowly to scratch her head,—a gesture peculiar to children when terrified and undecided what to do. It was no longer Montfermeil; it was the open fields. Black and desert space was before her. She gazed in despair at that darkness, where there was no longer any one, where there were beasts, where there were spectres, possibly. She took a good look, and heard the beasts walking on the grass, and she distinctly saw spectres moving in the trees. Then she seized her bucket again; fear had lent her audacity. "Bah!" said she; "I will tell him that there was no more water!" And she resolutely re-entered Montfermeil.

Hardly had she gone a hundred paces when she paused and began to scratch her head again. Now it was the Thénardier who appeared to her, with her hideous, hyena mouth, and wrath flashing in her eyes. The child cast a melancholy glance before her and behind her. What was she to do? What was to become of her? Where was she to go? In front of her was the spectre of the Thénardier; behind her all the phantoms of the night and of the forest. It was before the Thénardier that she recoiled. She resumed her path to the spring, and began to run. She emerged from the village, she entered the forest at a run, no longer looking at or listening to anything. She only paused in her course when her breath failed her; but she did not halt in her advance. She went straight before her in desperation.

As she ran she felt like crying.

The nocturnal quivering of the forest surrounded her completely.

She no longer thought, she no longer saw. The immensity of night was facing this tiny creature. On the one hand, all shadow; on the other, an atom.

It was only seven or eight minutes' walk from the edge of the woods to the spring. Cosette knew the way, through having gone over it many times in daylight. Strange to say, she did not get lost. A remnant of instinct guided her vaguely. But she did not turn her eyes either to right or to left, for fear of seeing things in the branches and in the brushwood. In this manner she reached the spring.

It was a narrow, natural basin, hollowed out by the water in a clayey soil, about two feet deep, surrounded with moss and with those tall, crimped grasses which are called Henry IV's frills, and paved with several large stones. A brook ran out of it, with a tranquil little noise.

Cosette did not take time to breathe. It was very dark, but she was in the habit of coming to this spring. She felt with her left hand in the dark for a young oak which leaned over the spring, and which usually served to support her, found one of its branches, clung to it, bent down, and plunged the bucket in the water. She was in a state of such violent excitement that her strength was trebled. While thus bent over, she did not notice that the pocket of her apron had emptied itself into the spring. The fifteen-sou piece fell into the water. Cosette neither saw nor heard it fall. She drew out the bucket nearly full, and set it on the grass.

That done, she perceived that she was worn out with fatigue. She would have liked to set out again at once, but the effort required to fill the bucket had been such that she found it impossible to take a step. She was forced to sit down. She dropped on the grass, and remained crouching there.

She shut her eyes; then she opened them again, without knowing why, but because she could not do otherwise. The agitated water in the bucket beside her was describing circles which resembled tin serpents.

Overhead the sky was covered with vast black clouds, which were like masses of smoke. The tragic mask of shadow seemed to bend vaguely over the child.

Jupiter was setting in the depths.

The child stared with bewildered eyes at this great star, with which she was unfamiliar, and which terrified her. The planet was, in fact, very near the horizon and was traversing a dense layer of mist which imparted to it a horrible ruddy hue. The mist, gloomily empurpled, magnified the star. One would have called it a luminous wound.

A cold wind was blowing from the plain. The forest was dark, not a leaf was moving; there were none of the vague, fresh gleams of summertide. Great boughs uplifted themselves in frightful wise. Slender and misshapen bushes whistled in the clearings. The tall grasses undulated like eels under the north wind. The nettles seemed to twist long arms furnished with claws in search of prey. Some bits of dry heather, tossed by the breeze, flew rapidly by, and had the air of fleeing in terror before something which was coming after. On all sides there were lugubrious stretches.

The darkness was bewildering. Man requires light. Whoever buries himself in the opposite of day feels his heart contract. When the eye sees black, the heart sees trouble. In an eclipse in the night, in the sooty opacity, there is anxiety even for the stoutest of hearts. No one walks alone in the forest at night without trembling. Shadows and trees— two formidable densities. A chimerical reality appears in the indistinct depths. The inconceivable is outlined a few paces distant from you with a spectral clearness. One beholds floating, either in space or in one's own brain, one knows not what vague and intangible thing, like the dreams of sleeping flowers. There are fierce attitudes on the horizon. One inhales the effluvia of the great black void. One is afraid to glance behind him, yet desirous of doing so. The cavities of night, things grown haggard, taciturn profiles which vanish when one advances, obscure dishevelments, irritated tufts, livid pools, the lugubrious reflected in the funereal, the sepulchral immensity of silence, unknown but possible beings, bendings of mysterious branches, alarming torsos of trees, long handfuls of quivering plants,—against all this one has no protection. There is no hardihood which does not shudder and which does not feel the vicinity of anguish. One is conscious of something hideous, as though one's soul were becoming amalgamated with the darkness. This penetration of the shadows is indescribably sinister in the case of a child.

Forests are apocalypses, and the beating of the wings of a tiny soul produces a sound of agony beneath their monstrous vault.

Without understanding her sensations, Cosette was conscious that she was seized upon by that black enormity of nature; it was no longer terror alone which was gaining possession of her; it was something more terrible even than terror; she shivered. There are no words to express the strangeness of that shiver which chilled her to the very bottom of her heart; her eye grew wild; she thought she felt that she should not be able to refrain from returning there at the same hour on the morrow.

Then, by a sort of instinct, she began to count aloud, one, two, three, four, and so on up to ten, in order to escape from that singular state which she did not understand, but which terrified her, and, when she had finished, she began again; this restored her to a true perception of the things about her. Her hands, which she had wet in drawing the water, felt cold; she rose; her terror, a natural and unconquerable terror, had returned: she had but one thought now,—to flee at full speed through the forest, across the fields to the houses, to the windows, to the lighted candles. Her glance fell upon the water which stood before her; such was the fright which the Thénardier inspired in her, that she dared not flee without that bucket of water: she seized the handle with both hands; she could hardly lift the pail.

In this manner she advanced a dozen paces, but the bucket was full; it was heavy; she was forced to set it on the ground once more. She took breath for an instant, then lifted the handle of the bucket again, and resumed her march, proceeding a little further this time, but again she was obliged to pause. After some seconds of repose she set out again. She walked bent forward, with drooping head, like an old woman; the weight of the bucket strained and stiffened her thin arms. The iron handle completed the benumbing and freezing of her wet and tiny hands; she was forced to halt from time to time, and each time that she did so, the cold water which splashed from the pail fell on her bare legs. This took place in the depths of a forest, at night, in winter, far from all human sight; she was a child of eight: no one but God saw that sad thing at the moment.

And her mother, no doubt, alas!

For there are things that make the dead open their eyes in their graves.

She panted with a sort of painful rattle; sobs contracted her throat, but she dared not weep, so afraid was she of the Thénardier, even at a distance: it was her custom to imagine the Thénardier always present.

However, she could not make much headway in that manner, and she went on very slowly. In spite of diminishing the length of her stops, and of walking as long as possible between them, she reflected with anguish that it would take her more than an hour to return to Montfermeil in this manner, and that the Thénardier would beat her. This anguish was mingled with her terror at being alone in the woods at night; she was worn out with fatigue, and had not yet emerged from the forest. On arriving near an old chestnut-tree with which she was acquainted, made a last halt, longer than the rest, in order that she might get well rested; then she summoned up all her strength, picked up her bucket again, and courageously resumed her march, but the poor little desperate creature could not refrain from crying, "O my God! my God!"

At that moment she suddenly became conscious that her bucket no longer weighed anything at all: a hand, which seemed to her enormous, had just seized the handle, and lifted it vigorously. She raised her head. A large black form, straight and erect, was walking beside her through the darkness; it was a man who had come up behind her, and whose approach she had not heard. This man, without uttering a word, had seized the handle of the bucket which she was carrying.

There are instincts for all the encounters of life.

The child was not afraid.

VI

WHICH POSSIBLY PROVES
BOULATRUELLE'S INTELLIGENCE

On the afternoon of that same Christmas Day, 1823, a man had walked for rather a long time in the most deserted part of the Boulevard de l'Hôpital in Paris. This man had the air of a person who is seeking lodgings, and he seemed to halt, by preference, at the most modest houses on that dilapidated border of the faubourg Saint-Marceau.

We shall see further on that this man had, in fact, hired a chamber in that isolated quarter.

This man, in his attire, as in all his person, realized the type of what may be called the well-bred mendicant,—extreme wretchedness combined with extreme cleanliness. This is a very rare mixture which inspires intelligent hearts with that double respect which one feels for the man who is very poor, and for the man who is very worthy. He wore a very old and very well brushed round hat; a coarse coat, worn perfectly threadbare, of an ochre yellow, a color that was not in the least eccentric at that epoch; a large waistcoat with pockets of a venerable cut; black breeches, worn gray at the knee, stockings of black worsted; and thick shoes with copper buckles. He would have been pronounced a preceptor in some good family, returned from the emigration. He would have been taken for more than sixty years of age, from his perfectly white hair, his wrinkled brow, his livid lips, and his countenance, where everything breathed depression and weariness of life. Judging from his firm tread, from the singular vigor which stamped all his movements, he would have hardly been thought fifty. The wrinkles on his brow were well placed, and would have disposed in his favor any one who observed him attentively. His lip contracted with a strange fold which seemed severe, and which was humble. There was in the depth of his glance an indescribable melancholy serenity. In his left hand he carried a little bundle tied up in a handkerchief; in his right he leaned on a sort of a cudgel, cut from some hedge. This stick had been carefully trimmed, and had an air that was not too threatening; the most had been made of its knots, and it had received a coral-like head, made from red wax: it was a cudgel, and it seemed to be a cane.

There are but few passers-by on that boulevard, particularly in the winter. The man seemed to avoid them rather than to seek them, but this without any affectation.

At that epoch, King Louis XVIII went nearly every day to Choisy-le-Roi: it was one of his favorite excursions. Towards two o'clock, almost invariably, the royal carriage and cavalcade was seen to pass at full speed along the Boulevard de l'Hôpital.

This served in lieu of a watch or clock to the poor women of the quarter who said, "It is two o'clock; there he is returning to the Tuileries."

And some rushed forward, and others drew up in line, for a passing king always creates a tumult; besides, the appearance and disappearance of Louis XVIII produced a certain effect in the streets of Paris. It was rapid but majestic. This impotent king had a taste for a fast gallop; as he was not able to walk, he wished to run: that cripple would gladly have had himself drawn by the lightning. He passed, pacific and severe, in the midst of naked swords. His massive couch, all covered with gilding, with great branches of lilies painted on the panels, thundered noisily along. There was hardly time to cast a glance upon it. In the rear angle on the right there was visible on tufted cushions of white satin a large, firm, and ruddy face, a brow freshly powdered *à l'oiseau royal*, a proud, hard, crafty eye, the smile of an educated man, two great epaulets with bullion fringe floating over a bourgeois coat, the Golden Fleece, the cross of Saint Louis, the cross of the Legion of Honor, the silver plaque of the Saint-Esprit, a huge belly, and a wide blue ribbon: it was the king. Outside of Paris, he held his hat decked with white ostrich plumes on his knees enwrapped in high English gaiters; when he re-entered the city, he put on his hat and saluted rarely; he stared coldly at the people, and they returned it in kind. When he appeared for the first time in the Saint-Marceau quarter, the whole success which he produced is contained in this remark of an inhabitant of the faubourg to his comrade, "That big fellow yonder is the government."

This infallible passage of the king at the same hour was, therefore, the daily event of the Boulevard de l'Hôpital.

The promenader in the yellow coat evidently did not belong in the quarter, and probably did not belong in Paris, for he was ignorant as to this detail. When, at two o'clock, the royal carriage, surrounded by a squadron of the body-guard all covered with silver lace, debouched on the boulevard, after having made the turn of the Salpêtrière, he appeared surprised and almost alarmed. There was no one but himself in this cross-lane. He drew up hastily behind the corner of the wall of an enclosure, though this did not prevent M. le Duc de Havré from spying him out.

M. le Duc de Havré, as captain of the guard on duty that day, was seated in the carriage, opposite the king. He said to his Majesty, "Yonder is an evil-looking man." Members of the police, who were clearing the king's route, took equal note of him: one of them received an order to follow him. But the man plunged into the deserted little streets of the faubourg, and as twilight was beginning to fall, the agent lost trace of him, as is stated in a report addressed that same evening to M. le Comte d'Anglès, Minister of State, Prefect of Police.

When the man in the yellow coat had thrown the agent off his track, he redoubled his pace, not without turning round many a time to assure himself that he was not being followed. At a quarter-past four, that is to say, when night was fully come, he passed in front of the theatre of the Porte Saint-Martin, where *The Two Convicts* was being played that day. This poster, illuminated by the theatre lanterns, struck him; for, although he was walking rapidly, he halted to read it. An instant later he was in the blind alley of La Planchette, and he entered the *Plat d'Etain* (the Pewter Platter), where the office of the coach for Lagny was then situated. This coach set out at half-past four. The horses were harnessed, and the travellers, summoned by the coachman, were hastily climbing the lofty iron ladder of the vehicle.

The man inquired:—

"Have you a place?"

"Only one—beside me on the box," said the coachman.

"I will take it."

"Climb up."

Nevertheless, before setting out, the coachman cast a glance at the traveller's shabby dress, at the diminutive size of his bundle, and made him pay his fare.

"Are you going as far as Lagny?" demanded the coachman.

"Yes," said the man.

The traveller paid to Lagny.

They started. When they had passed the barrier, the coachman tried to enter into conversation, but the traveller only replied in monosyllables. The coachman took to whistling and swearing at his horses.

The coachman wrapped himself up in his cloak. It was cold. The man did not appear to be thinking of that. Thus they passed Gournay and Neuilly-sur-Marne.

Towards six o'clock in the evening they reached Chelles. The coachman drew up in front of the carters' inn installed in the ancient buildings of the Royal Abbey, to give his horses a breathing spell.

"I get down here," said the man.

He took his bundle and his cudgel and jumped down from the vehicle.

An instant later he had disappeared.

He did not enter the inn.

When the coach set out for Lagny a few minutes later, it did not encounter him in the principal street of Chelles.

The coachman turned to the inside travellers.

"There," said he, "is a man who does not belong here, for I do not know him. He had not the air of owning a sou, but he does not consider money; he pays to Lagny, and he goes only as far as Chelles. It is night; all the houses are shut; he does not enter the inn, and he is not to be found. So he has dived through the earth."

The man had not plunged into the earth, but he had gone with great strides through the dark, down the principal street of Chelles, then he had turned to the right before reaching the church, into the crossroad leading to Montfermeil, like a person who was acquainted with the country and had been there before.

He followed this road rapidly. At the spot where it is intersected by the ancient tree-bordered road which runs from Gagny to Lagny, he heard people coming. He concealed himself precipitately in a ditch, and there waited until the passers-by were at a distance. The precaution was nearly superfluous, however; for, as we have already said, it was a very dark December night. Not more than two or three stars were visible in the sky.

It is at this point that the ascent of hill begins. The man did not return to the road to Montfermeil; he struck across the fields to the right, and entered the forest with long strides.

Once in the forest he slackened his pace, and began a careful examination of all the trees, advancing, step by step, as though seeking and following a mysterious road known to himself alone. There came a moment when he appeared to lose himself, and he paused in indecision. At last he arrived, by dint of feeling his way inch by inch, at a clearing where there was a great heap of whitish stones. He stepped up briskly to these stones, and examined them attentively through the mists of night, as though he were passing them in review. A large tree, covered with those excrescences which are the warts of vegetation, stood a few paces distant from the pile of stones. He went up to this tree and passed his hand over the bark of the trunk, as though seeking to recognize and count all the warts.

Opposite this tree, which was an ash, there was a chestnut-tree, suffering from a peeling of the bark, to which a band of zinc had been nailed by way of dressing. He raised himself on tiptoe and touched this band of zinc.

Then he trod about for awhile on the ground comprised in the space between the tree and the heap of stones, like a person who is trying to assure himself that the soil has not recently been disturbed.

That done, he took his bearings, and resumed his march through the forest.

It was the man who had just met Cosette.

As he walked through the thicket in the direction of Montfermeil, he had espied that tiny shadow moving with a groan, depositing a burden on the ground, then taking it up and setting out again. He drew near, and perceived that it was a very young child, laden with an enormous bucket of water. Then he approached the child, and silently grasped the handle of the bucket.

VII

Cosette Side by Side with the Stranger in the Dark

Cosette, as we have said, was not frightened.

The man accosted her. He spoke in a voice that was grave and almost bass.

"My child, what you are carrying is very heavy for you."

Cosette raised her head and replied:—

"Yes, sir."

"Give it to me," said the man; "I will carry it for you."

Cosette let go of the bucket-handle. The man walked along beside her.

"It really is very heavy," he muttered between his teeth. Then he added:—

"How old are you, little one?"

"Eight, sir."

"And have you come from far like this?"

"From the spring in the forest."

"Are you going far?"

"A good quarter of an hour's walk from here."

The man said nothing for a moment; then he remarked abruptly:—

"So you have no mother."

"I don't know," answered the child.

Before the man had time to speak again, she added:—

"I don't think so. Other people have mothers. I have none."

And after a silence she went on:—

"I think that I never had any."

The man halted; he set the bucket on the ground, bent down and placed both hands on the child's shoulders, making an effort to look at her and to see her face in the dark.

Cosette's thin and sickly face was vaguely outlined by the livid light in the sky.

"What is your name?" said the man.

"Cosette."

The man seemed to have received an electric shock. He looked at her once more; then he removed his hands from Cosette's shoulders, seized the bucket, and set out again.

After a moment he inquired:—

"Where do you live, little one?"

"At Montfermeil, if you know where that is."

"That is where we are going?"

"Yes, sir."

He paused; then began again:—

"Who sent you at such an hour to get water in the forest?"

"It was Madame Thénardier."

The man resumed, in a voice which he strove to render indifferent, but in which there was, nevertheless, a singular tremor:—

"What does your Madame Thénardier do?"

"She is my mistress," said the child. "She keeps the inn."

"The inn?" said the man. "Well, I am going to lodge there to-night. Show me the way."

"We are on the way there," said the child.

The man walked tolerably fast. Cosette followed him without difficulty. She no longer felt any fatigue. From time to time she raised her eyes towards the man, with a sort of tranquillity and an indescribable confidence. She had never been taught to turn to Providence and to pray; nevertheless, she felt within her something which resembled hope and joy, and which mounted towards heaven.

Several minutes elapsed. The man resumed:—

"Is there no servant in Madame Thénardier's house?"

"No, sir."

"Are you alone there?"

"Yes, sir."

Another pause ensued. Cosette lifted up her voice:—

"That is to say, there are two little girls."

"What little girls?"

"Ponine and Zelma."

This was the way the child simplified the romantic names so dear to the female Thénardier.

"Who are Ponine and Zelma?"

"They are Madame Thénardier's young ladies; her daughters, as you would say."

"And what do those girls do?"

"Oh!" said the child, "they have beautiful dolls; things with gold in them, all full of affairs. They play; they amuse themselves."

"All day long?"

"Yes, sir."

"And you?"

"I? I work."

"All day long?"

The child raised her great eyes, in which hung a tear, which was not visible because of the darkness, and replied gently:—

"Yes, sir."

After an interval of silence she went on:—

"Sometimes, when I have finished my work and they let me, I amuse myself, too."

"How do you amuse yourself?"

"In the best way I can. They let me alone; but I have not many playthings. Ponine and Zelma will not let me play with their dolls. I have only a little lead sword, no longer than that."

The child held up her tiny finger.

"And it will not cut?"

"Yes, sir," said the child; "it cuts salad and the heads of flies."

They reached the village. Cosette guided the stranger through the streets. They passed the bakeshop, but Cosette did not think of the bread which she had been ordered to fetch. The man had ceased to ply her with questions, and now preserved a gloomy silence.

When they had left the church behind them, the man, on perceiving all the open-air booths, asked Cosette:—

"So there is a fair going on here?"

"No, sir; it is Christmas."

As they approached the tavern, Cosette timidly touched his arm:—

"Monsieur?"

"What, my child?"

"We are quite near the house."

"Well?"

"Will you let me take my bucket now?"

"Why?"

"If Madame sees that some one has carried it for me, she will beat me."

The man handed her the bucket. An instant later they were at the tavern door.

VIII

The Unpleasantness of Receiving into One's House a Poor Man who May be a Rich Man

Cosette could not refrain from casting a sidelong glance at the big doll, which was still displayed at the toy-merchant's; then she knocked. The door opened. The Thénardier appeared with a candle in her hand.

"Ah! so it's you, you little wretch! good mercy, but you've taken your time! The hussy has been amusing herself!"

"Madame," said Cosette, trembling all over, "here's a gentleman who wants a lodging."

The Thénardier speedily replaced her gruff air by her amiable grimace, a change of aspect common to tavern-keepers, and eagerly sought the newcomer with her eyes.

"This is the gentleman?" said she.

"Yes, Madame," replied the man, raising his hand to his hat.

Wealthy travellers are not so polite. This gesture, and an inspection of the stranger's costume and baggage, which the Thénardier passed in review with one glance, caused the amiable grimace to vanish, and the gruff mien to reappear. She resumed dryly:—

"Enter, my good man."

The "good man" entered. The Thénardier cast a second glance at him, paid particular attention to his frock-coat, which was absolutely threadbare, and to his hat, which was a little battered, and, tossing her head, wrinkling her nose, and screwing up her eyes, she consulted her husband, who was still drinking with the carters. The husband replied by that imperceptible movement of the forefinger, which, backed up by an inflation of the lips, signifies in such cases: A regular beggar. Thereupon, the Thénardier exclaimed:—

"Ah! see here, my good man; I am very sorry, but I have no room left."

"Put me where you like," said the man; "in the attic, in the stable. I will pay as though I occupied a room."

"Forty sous."

"Forty sous; agreed."

VICTOR HUGO

"Very well, then!"

"Forty sous!" said a carter, in a low tone, to the Thénardier woman; "why, the charge is only twenty sous!"

"It is forty in his case," retorted the Thénardier, in the same tone. "I don't lodge poor folks for less."

"That's true," added her husband, gently; "it ruins a house to have such people in it."

In the meantime, the man, laying his bundle and his cudgel on a bench, had seated himself at a table, on which Cosette made haste to place a bottle of wine and a glass. The merchant who had demanded the bucket of water took it to his horse himself. Cosette resumed her place under the kitchen table, and her knitting.

The man, who had barely moistened his lips in the wine which he had poured out for himself, observed the child with peculiar attention.

Cosette was ugly. If she had been happy, she might have been pretty. We have already given a sketch of that sombre little figure. Cosette was thin and pale; she was nearly eight years old, but she seemed to be hardly six. Her large eyes, sunken in a sort of shadow, were almost put out with weeping. The corners of her mouth had that curve of habitual anguish which is seen in condemned persons and desperately sick people. Her hands were, as her mother had divined, "ruined with chilblains." The fire which illuminated her at that moment brought into relief all the angles of her bones, and rendered her thinness frightfully apparent. As she was always shivering, she had acquired the habit of pressing her knees one against the other. Her entire clothing was but a rag which would have inspired pity in summer, and which inspired horror in winter. All she had on was hole-ridden linen, not a scrap of woollen. Her skin was visible here and there and everywhere black and blue spots could be descried, which marked the places where the Thénardier woman had touched her. Her naked legs were thin and red. The hollows in her neck were enough to make one weep. This child's whole person, her mien, her attitude, the sound of her voice, the intervals which she allowed to elapse between one word and the next, her glance, her silence, her slightest gesture, expressed and betrayed one sole idea,—fear.

Fear was diffused all over her; she was covered with it, so to speak; fear drew her elbows close to her hips, withdrew her heels under her petticoat, made her occupy as little space as possible, allowed her only the breath that was absolutely necessary, and had become what might be called the habit of her body, admitting of no possible variation except an increase. In the depths of her eyes there was an astonished nook where terror lurked.

Her fear was such, that on her arrival, wet as she was, Cosette did not dare to approach the fire and dry herself, but sat silently down to her work again.

The expression in the glance of that child of eight years was habitually so gloomy, and at times so tragic, that it seemed at certain moments as though she were on the verge of becoming an idiot or a demon.

As we have stated, she had never known what it is to pray; she had never set foot in a church. "Have I the time?" said the Thénardier.

The man in the yellow coat never took his eyes from Cosette.

All at once, the Thénardier exclaimed:—

"By the way, where's that bread?"

Cosette, according to her custom whenever the Thénardier uplifted her voice, emerged with great haste from beneath the table.

She had completely forgotten the bread. She had recourse to the expedient of children who live in a constant state of fear. She lied.

"Madame, the baker's shop was shut."

"You should have knocked."

"I did knock, Madame."

"Well?"

"He did not open the door."

"I'll find out to-morrow whether that is true," said the Thénardier; "and if you are telling me a lie, I'll lead you a pretty dance. In the meantime, give me back my fifteen-sou piece."

Cosette plunged her hand into the pocket of her apron, and turned green. The fifteen-sou piece was not there.

"Ah, come now," said Madame Thénardier, "did you hear me?"

Cosette turned her pocket inside out; there was nothing in it. What could have become of that money? The unhappy little creature could not find a word to say. She was petrified.

"Have you lost that fifteen-sou piece?" screamed the Thénardier, hoarsely, "or do you want to rob me of it?"

At the same time, she stretched out her arm towards the cat-o'-nine-tails which hung on a nail in the chimney-corner.

This formidable gesture restored to Cosette sufficient strength to shriek:—

"Mercy, Madame, Madame! I will not do so any more!"

The Thénardier took down the whip.

In the meantime, the man in the yellow coat had been fumbling in the fob of his waistcoat, without any one having noticed his movements. Besides, the other travellers were drinking or playing cards, and were not paying attention to anything.

Cosette contracted herself into a ball, with anguish, within the angle of the chimney, endeavoring to gather up and conceal her poor half-nude limbs. The Thénardier raised her arm.

"Pardon me, Madame," said the man, "but just now I caught sight of something which had fallen from this little one's apron pocket, and rolled aside. Perhaps this is it."

At the same time he bent down and seemed to be searching on the floor for a moment.

"Exactly; here it is," he went on, straightening himself up.

And he held out a silver coin to the Thénardier.

"Yes, that's it," said she.

It was not it, for it was a twenty-sou piece; but the Thénardier found it to her advantage. She put the coin in her pocket, and confined herself to casting a fierce glance at the child, accompanied with the remark, "Don't let this ever happen again!"

Cosette returned to what the Thénardier called "her kennel," and her large eyes, which were riveted on the traveller, began to take on an expression such as they had never worn before. Thus far it was only an innocent amazement, but a sort of stupefied confidence was mingled with it.

"By the way, would you like some supper?" the Thénardier inquired of the traveller.

He made no reply. He appeared to be absorbed in thought.

"What sort of a man is that?" she muttered between her teeth. "He's some frightfully poor wretch. He hasn't a sou to pay for a supper. Will he even pay me for his lodging? It's very lucky, all the same, that it did not occur to him to steal the money that was on the floor."

In the meantime, a door had opened, and Éponine and Azelma entered.

They were two really pretty little girls, more bourgeois than peasant in looks, and very charming; the one with shining chestnut tresses, the other with long black braids hanging down her back, both vivacious, neat, plump, rosy, and healthy, and a delight to the eye. They were warmly clad, but with so much maternal art that the thickness of the stuffs did not detract from the coquetry of arrangement. There was a hint of winter, though the springtime was not wholly effaced. Light emanated from these two little beings. Besides this, they were on the throne. In their toilettes, in their gayety, in the noise which they made, there was sovereignty. When they entered, the Thénardier said to them in a grumbling tone which was full of adoration, "Ah! there you are, you children!"

Then drawing them, one after the other to her knees, smoothing their hair, tying their ribbons afresh, and then releasing them with that gentle manner of shaking off which is peculiar to mothers, she exclaimed, "What frights they are!"

They went and seated themselves in the chimney-corner. They had a doll, which they turned over and over on their knees with all sorts of joyous chatter. From time to time Cosette raised her eyes from her knitting, and watched their play with a melancholy air.

Éponine and Azelma did not look at Cosette. She was the same as a dog to them. These three little girls did not yet reckon up four and twenty years between them, but they already represented the whole society of man; envy on the one side, disdain on the other.

The doll of the Thénardier sisters was very much faded, very old, and much broken; but it seemed nonetheless admirable to Cosette, who had never had a doll in her life, *a real doll*, to make use of the expression which all children will understand.

All at once, the Thénardier, who had been going back and forth in the room, perceived that Cosette's mind was distracted, and that, instead of working, she was paying attention to the little ones at their play.

"Ah! I've caught you at it!" she cried. "So that's the way you work! I'll make you work to the tune of the whip; that I will."

The stranger turned to the Thénardier, without quitting his chair.

"Bah, Madame," he said, with an almost timid air, "let her play!"

Such a wish expressed by a traveller who had eaten a slice of mutton and had drunk a couple of bottles of wine with his supper, and who had not the air of being frightfully poor, would have been equivalent to an order. But that a man with such a hat should permit himself such a desire, and that a man with such a coat should permit himself to have a will, was something which Madame Thénardier did not intend to tolerate. She retorted with acrimony:—

"She must work, since she eats. I don't feed her to do nothing."

"What is she making?" went on the stranger, in a gentle voice which contrasted strangely with his beggarly garments and his porter's shoulders.

The Thénardier deigned to reply:—

"Stockings, if you please. Stockings for my little girls, who have none, so to speak, and who are absolutely barefoot just now."

The man looked at Cosette's poor little red feet, and continued:—

"When will she have finished this pair of stockings?"

"She has at least three or four good days' work on them still, the lazy creature!"

"And how much will that pair of stockings be worth when she has finished them?"

The Thénardier cast a glance of disdain on him.

"Thirty sous at least."

"Will you sell them for five francs?" went on the man.

"Good heavens!" exclaimed a carter who was listening, with a loud laugh; "five francs! the deuce, I should think so! five balls!"

Thénardier thought it time to strike in.

"Yes, sir; if such is your fancy, you will be allowed to have that pair of stockings for five francs. We can refuse nothing to travellers."

"You must pay on the spot," said the Thénardier, in her curt and peremptory fashion.

"I will buy that pair of stockings," replied the man, "and," he added, drawing a five-franc piece from his pocket, and laying it on the table, "I will pay for them."

Then he turned to Cosette.

"Now I own your work; play, my child."

The carter was so much touched by the five-franc piece, that he abandoned his glass and hastened up.

"But it's true!" he cried, examining it. "A real hind wheel! and not counterfeit!"

Thénardier approached and silently put the coin in his pocket.

The Thénardier had no reply to make. She bit her lips, and her face assumed an expression of hatred.

In the meantime, Cosette was trembling. She ventured to ask:—

"Is it true, Madame? May I play?"

"Play!" said the Thénardier, in a terrible voice.

"Thanks, Madame," said Cosette.

And while her mouth thanked the Thénardier, her whole little soul thanked the traveller.

Thénardier had resumed his drinking; his wife whispered in his ear:—

"Who can this yellow man be?"

"I have seen millionaires with coats like that," replied Thénardier, in a sovereign manner.

Cosette had dropped her knitting, but had not left her seat. Cosette always moved as little as possible. She picked up some old rags and her little lead sword from a box behind her.

Éponine and Azelma paid no attention to what was going on. They had just executed a very important operation; they had just got hold of the cat. They had thrown their doll on the ground, and Éponine, who was the elder, was swathing the little cat, in spite of its mewing and its contortions, in a quantity of clothes and red and blue scraps. While performing this serious and difficult work she was saying to her sister in that sweet and adorable language of children, whose grace, like the splendor of the butterfly's wing, vanishes when one essays to fix it fast.

"You see, sister, this doll is more amusing than the other. She twists, she cries, she is warm. See, sister, let us play with her. She shall be my little girl. I will be a lady. I will come to see you, and you shall look at her. Gradually, you will perceive her whiskers, and that will surprise you. And then you will see her ears, and then you will see her tail and it will amaze you. And you will say to me, 'Ah! Mon Dieu!' and I will say to you: 'Yes, Madame, it is my little girl. Little girls are made like that just at present.'"

Azelma listened admiringly to Éponine.

In the meantime, the drinkers had begun to sing an obscene song, and to laugh at it until the ceiling shook. Thénardier accompanied and encouraged them.

As birds make nests out of everything, so children make a doll out of anything which comes to hand. While Éponine and Azelma were bundling up the cat, Cosette, on her side, had dressed up her sword. That done, she laid it in her arms, and sang to it softly, to lull it to sleep.

The doll is one of the most imperious needs and, at the same time, one of the most charming instincts of feminine childhood. To care for, to clothe, to deck, to dress, to undress, to redress, to teach, scold a little, to rock, to dandle, to lull to sleep, to imagine that something is some one,—therein lies the whole woman's future. While dreaming and chattering, making tiny outfits, and baby clothes, while sewing little gowns, and corsages and bodices, the child grows into a young girl, the young girl into a big girl, the big girl into a woman. The first child is the continuation of the last doll.

A little girl without a doll is almost as unhappy, and quite as impossible, as a woman without children.

So Cosette had made herself a doll out of the sword.

Madame Thénardier approached *the yellow man*; "My husband is right," she thought; "perhaps it is M. Laffitte; there are such queer rich men!"

She came and set her elbows on the table.

"Monsieur," said she. At this word, *Monsieur*, the man turned; up to that time, the Thénardier had addressed him only as *brave homme* or *bonhomme*.

"You see, sir," she pursued, assuming a sweetish air that was even more repulsive to behold than her fierce mien, "I am willing that the child should play; I do not oppose it, but it is good for once, because you are generous. You see, she has nothing; she must needs work."

"Then this child is not yours?" demanded the man.

"Oh! mon Dieu! no, sir! she is a little beggar whom we have taken in through charity; a sort of imbecile child. She must have water on the brain; she has a large head, as you see. We do what we can for her, for we are not rich; we have written in vain to her native place, and have received no reply these six months. It must be that her mother is dead."

"Ah!" said the man, and fell into his reverie once more.

"Her mother didn't amount to much," added the Thénardier; "she abandoned her child."

During the whole of this conversation Cosette, as though warned by some instinct that she was under discussion, had not taken her eyes from the Thénardier's face; she listened vaguely; she caught a few words here and there.

Meanwhile, the drinkers, all three-quarters intoxicated, were repeating their unclean refrain with redoubled gayety; it was a highly spiced and wanton song, in which the Virgin and the infant Jesus were introduced. The Thénardier went off to take part in the shouts of laughter. Cosette, from her post under the table, gazed at the fire, which was reflected from her fixed eyes. She had begun to rock the sort of baby which she had made, and, as she rocked it, she sang in a low voice, "My mother is dead! my mother is dead! my mother is dead!"

On being urged afresh by the hostess, the yellow man, "the millionaire," consented at last to take supper.

"What does Monsieur wish?"

"Bread and cheese," said the man.

"Decidedly, he is a beggar" thought Madame Thénardier.

The drunken men were still singing their song, and the child under the table was singing hers.

All at once, Cosette paused; she had just turned round and caught sight of the little Thénardiers' doll, which they had abandoned for the cat and had left on the floor a few paces from the kitchen table.

Then she dropped the swaddled sword, which only half met her needs, and cast her eyes slowly round the room. Madame Thénardier was whispering to her husband and counting over some money; Ponine and Zelma were playing with the cat; the travellers were eating or drinking or singing; not a glance was fixed on her. She had not a moment to lose; she crept out from under the table on her hands and knees, made sure once more that no one was watching her; then she slipped quickly up to the doll and seized it. An instant later she was in her place again, seated motionless, and only turned so as to cast a shadow on the doll which she held in her arms. The happiness of playing with a doll was so rare for her that it contained all the violence of voluptuousness.

No one had seen her, except the traveller, who was slowly devouring his meagre supper.

This joy lasted about a quarter of an hour.

But with all the precautions that Cosette had taken she did not perceive that one of the doll's legs stuck out and that the fire on the hearth lighted it up very vividly. That pink and shining foot, projecting from the shadow, suddenly struck the eye of Azelma, who said to Éponine, "Look! sister."

The two little girls paused in stupefaction; Cosette had dared to take their doll!

Éponine rose, and, without releasing the cat, she ran to her mother, and began to tug at her skirt.

"Let me alone!" said her mother; "what do you want?"

"Mother," said the child, "look there!"

And she pointed to Cosette.

Cosette, absorbed in the ecstasies of possession, no longer saw or heard anything.

Madame Thénardier's countenance assumed that peculiar expression which is composed of the terrible mingled with the trifles of life, and which has caused this style of woman to be named *Megaeras*.

On this occasion, wounded pride exasperated her wrath still further. Cosette had overstepped all bounds; Cosette had laid violent hands on the doll belonging to "these young ladies." A czarina who should see a muzhik trying on her imperial son's blue ribbon would wear no other face.

She shrieked in a voice rendered hoarse with indignation:—

"Cosette!"

Cosette started as though the earth had trembled beneath her; she turned round.

"Cosette!" repeated the Thénardier.

Cosette took the doll and laid it gently on the floor with a sort of veneration, mingled with despair; then, without taking her eyes from it, she clasped her hands, and, what is terrible to relate of a child of that age, she wrung them; then—not one of the emotions of the day, neither the trip to the forest, nor the weight of the bucket of water, nor the loss of the money, nor the sight of the whip, nor even the sad words which she had heard Madame Thénardier utter had been able to wring this from her—she wept; she burst out sobbing.

Meanwhile, the traveller had risen to his feet.

"What is the matter?" he said to the Thénardier.

"Don't you see?" said the Thénardier, pointing to the *corpus delicti* which lay at Cosette's feet.

"Well, what of it?" resumed the man.

"That beggar," replied the Thénardier, "has permitted herself to touch the children's doll!"

"All this noise for that!" said the man; "well, what if she did play with that doll?"

"She touched it with her dirty hands!" pursued the Thénardier, "with her frightful hands!"

Here Cosette redoubled her sobs.

"Will you stop your noise?" screamed the Thénardier.

The man went straight to the street door, opened it, and stepped out.

As soon as he had gone, the Thénardier profited by his absence to give Cosette a hearty kick under the table, which made the child utter loud cries.

The door opened again, the man reappeared; he carried in both hands the fabulous doll which we have mentioned, and which all the village brats had been staring at ever since the morning, and he set it upright in front of Cosette, saying:—

"Here; this is for you."

It must be supposed that in the course of the hour and more which he had spent there he had taken confused notice through his reverie of that toy shop, lighted up by fire-pots and candles so splendidly that it was visible like an illumination through the window of the drinking-shop.

Cosette raised her eyes; she gazed at the man approaching her with that doll as she might have gazed at the sun; she heard the unprecedented words, "It is for you"; she stared at him; she stared at the doll; then she slowly retreated, and hid herself at the extreme end, under the table in a corner of the wall.

She no longer cried; she no longer wept; she had the appearance of no longer daring to breathe.

The Thénardier, Éponine, and Azelma were like statues also; the very drinkers had paused; a solemn silence reigned through the whole room.

Madame Thénardier, petrified and mute, recommenced her conjectures: "Who is that old fellow? Is he a poor man? Is he a millionaire? Perhaps he is both; that is to say, a thief."

The face of the male Thénardier presented that expressive fold which accentuates the human countenance whenever the dominant instinct appears there in all its bestial force. The tavern-keeper stared alternately at the doll and at the traveller; he seemed to be scenting out the man, as he would have scented out a bag of money. This did not last longer than the space of a flash of lightning. He stepped up to his wife and said to her in a low voice:—

"That machine costs at least thirty francs. No nonsense. Down on your belly before that man!"

Gross natures have this in common with *naïve* natures, that they possess no transition state.

"Well, Cosette," said the Thénardier, in a voice that strove to be sweet, and which was composed of the bitter honey of malicious women, "aren't you going to take your doll?"

Cosette ventured to emerge from her hole.

"The gentleman has given you a doll, my little Cosette," said Thénardier, with a caressing air. "Take it; it is yours."

Cosette gazed at the marvellous doll in a sort of terror. Her face was still flooded with tears, but her eyes began to fill, like the sky at daybreak, with strange beams of joy. What she felt at that moment was a little like what she would have felt if she had been abruptly told, "Little one, you are the Queen of France."

It seemed to her that if she touched that doll, lightning would dart from it.

VICTOR HUGO

This was true, up to a certain point, for she said to herself that the Thénardier would scold and beat her.

Nevertheless, the attraction carried the day. She ended by drawing near and murmuring timidly as she turned towards Madame Thénardier:—

"May I, Madame?"

No words can render that air, at once despairing, terrified, and ecstatic.

"Pardi!" cried the Thénardier, "it is yours. The gentleman has given it to you."

"Truly, sir?" said Cosette. "Is it true? Is the 'lady' mine?"

The stranger's eyes seemed to be full of tears. He appeared to have reached that point of emotion where a man does not speak for fear lest he should weep. He nodded to Cosette, and placed the "lady's" hand in her tiny hand.

Cosette hastily withdrew her hand, as though that of the "lady" scorched her, and began to stare at the floor. We are forced to add that at that moment she stuck out her tongue immoderately. All at once she wheeled round and seized the doll in a transport.

"I shall call her Catherine," she said.

It was an odd moment when Cosette's rags met and clasped the ribbons and fresh pink muslins of the doll.

"Madame," she resumed, "may I put her on a chair?"

"Yes, my child," replied the Thénardier.

It was now the turn of Éponine and Azelma to gaze at Cosette with envy.

Cosette placed Catherine on a chair, then seated herself on the floor in front of her, and remained motionless, without uttering a word, in an attitude of contemplation.

"Play, Cosette," said the stranger.

"Oh! I am playing," returned the child.

This stranger, this unknown individual, who had the air of a visit which Providence was making on Cosette, was the person whom the Thénardier hated worse than any one in the world at that moment. However, it was necessary to control herself. Habituated as she was to dissimulation through endeavoring to copy her husband in all his actions, these emotions were more than she could endure. She made haste to send her daughters to bed, then she asked the man's *permission* to send Cosette off also; "for she has worked hard all day," she added with a maternal air. Cosette went off to bed, carrying Catherine in her arms.

From time to time the Thénardier went to the other end of the room where her husband was, to *relieve her soul*, as she said. She exchanged with her husband words which were all the more furious because she dared not utter them aloud.

"Old beast! What has he got in his belly, to come and upset us in this manner! To want that little monster to play! to give away forty-franc dolls to a jade that I would sell for forty sous, so I would! A little more and he will be saying *Your Majesty* to her, as though to the Duchesse de Berry! Is there any sense in it? Is he mad, then, that mysterious old fellow?"

"Why! it is perfectly simple," replied Thénardier, "if that amuses him! It amuses you to have the little one work; it amuses him to have her play. He's all right. A traveller can do what he pleases when he pays for it. If the old fellow is a philanthropist, what is that to you? If he is an imbecile, it does not concern you. What are you worrying for, so long as he has money?"

The language of a master, and the reasoning of an innkeeper, neither of which admitted of any reply.

The man had placed his elbows on the table, and resumed his thoughtful attitude. All the other travellers, both pedlers and carters, had withdrawn a little, and had ceased singing. They were staring at him from a distance, with a sort of respectful awe. This poorly dressed man, who drew "hind-wheels" from his pocket with so much ease, and who lavished gigantic dolls on dirty little brats in wooden shoes, was certainly a magnificent fellow, and one to be feared.

Many hours passed. The midnight mass was over, the chimes had ceased, the drinkers had taken their departure, the drinking-shop was closed, the public room was deserted, the fire extinct, the stranger still remained in the same place and the same attitude. From time to time he changed the elbow on which he leaned. That was all; but he had not said a word since Cosette had left the room.

The Thénardiers alone, out of politeness and curiosity, had remained in the room.

"Is he going to pass the night in that fashion?" grumbled the Thénardier. When two o'clock in the morning struck, she declared herself vanquished, and said to her husband, "I'm going to bed. Do as you like." Her husband seated himself at a table in the corner, lighted a candle, and began to read the *Courrier Français*.

A good hour passed thus. The worthy inn-keeper had perused the *Courrier Français* at least three times, from the date of the number to the printer's name. The stranger did not stir.

Thénardier fidgeted, coughed, spit, blew his nose, and creaked his chair. Not a movement on the man's part. "Is he asleep?" thought Thénardier. The man was not asleep, but nothing could arouse him.

At last Thénardier took off his cap, stepped gently up to him, and ventured to say:—

"Is not Monsieur going to his repose?"

Not going to bed would have seemed to him excessive and familiar. *To repose* smacked of luxury and respect. These words possess the mysterious and admirable property of swelling the bill on the following day. A chamber where one *sleeps* costs twenty sous; a chamber in which one *reposes* costs twenty francs.

"Well!" said the stranger, "you are right. Where is your stable?"

"Sir!" exclaimed Thénardier, with a smile, "I will conduct you, sir."

He took the candle; the man picked up his bundle and cudgel, and Thénardier conducted him to a chamber on the first floor, which was of rare splendor, all furnished in mahogany, with a low bedstead, curtained with red calico.

"What is this?" said the traveller.

"It is really our bridal chamber," said the tavern-keeper. "My wife and I occupy another. This is only entered three or four times a year."

"I should have liked the stable quite as well," said the man, abruptly.

Thénardier pretended not to hear this unamiable remark.

He lighted two perfectly fresh wax candles which figured on the chimney-piece. A very good fire was flickering on the hearth.

On the chimney-piece, under a glass globe, stood a woman's head-dress in silver wire and orange flowers.

"And what is this?" resumed the stranger.

"That, sir," said Thénardier, "is my wife's wedding bonnet."

The traveller surveyed the object with a glance which seemed to say, "There really was a time, then, when that monster was a maiden?"

Thénardier lied, however. When he had leased this paltry building for the purpose of converting it into a tavern, he had found this chamber decorated in just this manner, and had purchased the furniture and obtained the orange flowers at second hand, with the idea that this would cast a graceful shadow on "his spouse," and would result in what the English call respectability for his house.

When the traveller turned round, the host had disappeared. Thénardier had withdrawn discreetly, without venturing to wish him a good night, as he did not wish to treat with disrespectful cordiality a man whom he proposed to fleece royally the following morning.

The inn-keeper retired to his room. His wife was in bed, but she was not asleep. When she heard her husband's step she turned over and said to him:—

"Do you know, I'm going to turn Cosette out of doors to-morrow."

Thénardier replied coldly:—

"How you do go on!"

They exchanged no further words, and a few moments later their candle was extinguished.

As for the traveller, he had deposited his cudgel and his bundle in a corner. The landlord once gone, he threw himself into an armchair and remained for some time buried in thought. Then he removed his shoes, took one of the two candles, blew out the other, opened the door, and quitted the room, gazing about him like a person who is in search of something. He traversed a corridor and came upon a staircase. There he heard a very faint and gentle sound like the breathing of a child. He followed this sound, and came to a sort of triangular recess built under the staircase, or rather formed by the staircase itself. This recess was nothing else than the space under the steps. There, in the midst of all sorts of old papers and potsherds, among dust and spiders' webs, was a bed—if one can call by the name of bed a straw pallet so full of holes as to display the straw, and a coverlet so tattered as to show the pallet. No sheets. This was placed on the floor.

In this bed Cosette was sleeping.

The man approached and gazed down upon her.

Cosette was in a profound sleep; she was fully dressed. In the winter she did not undress, in order that she might not be so cold.

Against her breast was pressed the doll, whose large eyes, wide open, glittered in the dark. From time to time she gave vent to a deep sigh as though she were on the point of waking, and she strained the doll almost convulsively in her arms. Beside her bed there was only one of her wooden shoes.

A door which stood open near Cosette's pallet permitted a view of a rather large, dark room. The stranger stepped into it. At the further extremity, through a glass door, he saw two small, very white beds. They belonged to Éponine and Azelma. Behind these beds, and half hidden, stood an uncurtained wicker cradle, in which the little boy who had cried all the evening lay asleep.

The stranger conjectured that this chamber connected with that of the Thénardier pair. He was on the point of retreating when his eye fell upon the fireplace—one of those vast tavern chimneys where there is always so little fire when there is any fire at all, and which are so cold to look at. There was no fire in this one, there was not even ashes; but there was something which attracted the stranger's gaze, nevertheless. It was two tiny children's shoes, coquettish in shape and unequal in size. The traveller recalled the graceful and immemorial custom in accordance with which children place their shoes in the chimney on Christmas eve, there to await in the darkness some sparkling gift from their good fairy. Éponine and Azelma had taken care not to omit this, and each of them had set one of her shoes on the hearth.

The traveller bent over them.

The fairy, that is to say, their mother, had already paid her visit, and in each he saw a brand-new and shining ten-sou piece.

The man straightened himself up, and was on the point of withdrawing, when far in, in the darkest corner of the hearth, he caught sight of another object. He looked at it, and recognized a wooden shoe, a frightful shoe of the coarsest description, half dilapidated and all covered with ashes and dried mud. It was Cosette's sabot. Cosette, with that touching trust of childhood, which can always be deceived yet never discouraged, had placed her shoe on the hearth-stone also.

Hope in a child who has never known anything but despair is a sweet and touching thing.

There was nothing in this wooden shoe.

The stranger fumbled in his waistcoat, bent over and placed a louis d'or in Cosette's shoe.

Then he regained his own chamber with the stealthy tread of a wolf.

IX

Thénardier and his Manœuvres

On the following morning, two hours at least before day-break, Thénardier, seated beside a candle in the public room of the tavern, pen in hand, was making out the bill for the traveller with the yellow coat.

His wife, standing beside him, and half bent over him, was following him with her eyes. They exchanged not a word. On the one hand, there was profound meditation, on the other, the religious admiration with which one watches the birth and development of a marvel of the human mind. A noise was audible in the house; it was the Lark sweeping the stairs.

After the lapse of a good quarter of an hour, and some erasures, Thénardier produced the following masterpiece:—

Bill of the Gentleman in No. 1.

Supper	3 francs.
Chamber	10 ”
Candle	5 ”
Fire	4 ”
Service	1 ”
Total	23 francs.

Service was written *servisse*.

"Twenty-three francs!" cried the woman, with an enthusiasm which was mingled with some hesitation.

Like all great artists, Thénardier was dissatisfied.

"Peuh!" he exclaimed.

It was the accent of Castlereagh auditing France's bill at the Congress of Vienna.

"Monsieur Thénardier, you are right; he certainly owes that," murmured the wife, who was thinking of the doll bestowed on Cosette in the presence of her daughters. "It is just, but it is too much. He will not pay it."

Thénardier laughed coldly, as usual, and said:—

"He will pay."

This laugh was the supreme assertion of certainty and authority. That which was asserted in this manner must needs be so. His wife did not insist.

She set about arranging the table; her husband paced the room. A moment later he added:—

"I owe full fifteen hundred francs!"

He went and seated himself in the chimney-corner, meditating, with his feet among the warm ashes.

"Ah! by the way," resumed his wife, "you don't forget that I'm going to turn Cosette out of doors to-day? The monster! She breaks my heart with that doll of hers! I'd rather marry Louis XVIII than keep her another day in the house!"

Thénardier lighted his pipe, and replied between two puffs:—

"You will hand that bill to the man."

Then he went out.

Hardly had he left the room when the traveller entered.

Thénardier instantly reappeared behind him and remained motionless in the half-open door, visible only to his wife.

The yellow man carried his bundle and his cudgel in his hand.

"Up so early?" said Madame Thénardier; "is Monsieur leaving us already?"

As she spoke thus, she was twisting the bill about in her hands with an embarrassed air, and making creases in it with her nails. Her hard face presented a shade which was not habitual with it,—timidity and scruples.

To present such a bill to a man who had so completely the air "of a poor wretch" seemed difficult to her.

The traveller appeared to be preoccupied and absent-minded. He replied:—

"Yes, Madame, I am going."

"So Monsieur has no business in Montfermeil?"

"No, I was passing through. That is all. What do I owe you, Madame," he added.

The Thénardier silently handed him the folded bill.

The man unfolded the paper and glanced at it; but his thoughts were evidently elsewhere.

"Madame," he resumed, "is business good here in Montfermeil?"

"So so, Monsieur," replied the Thénardier, stupefied at not witnessing another sort of explosion.

She continued, in a dreary and lamentable tone:—

"Oh! Monsieur, times are so hard! and then, we have so few bourgeois in the neighborhood! All the people are poor, you see. If we had not, now and then, some rich and generous travellers like Monsieur, we should not get along at all. We have so many expenses. Just see, that child is costing us our very eyes."

"What child?"

"Why, the little one, you know! Cosette—the Lark, as she is called hereabouts!"

"Ah!" said the man.

She went on:—

"How stupid these peasants are with their nicknames! She has more the air of a bat than of a lark. You see, sir, we do not ask charity, and we cannot bestow it. We earn nothing and we have to pay out a great deal. The license, the imposts, the door and window tax, the hundredths! Monsieur is aware that the government demands a terrible deal of money. And then, I have my daughters. I have no need to bring up other people's children."

The man resumed, in that voice which he strove to render indifferent, and in which there lingered a tremor:—

"What if one were to rid you of her?"

"Who? Cosette?"

"Yes."

The landlady's red and violent face brightened up hideously.

"Ah! sir, my dear sir, take her, keep her, lead her off, carry her away, sugar her, stuff her with truffles, drink her, eat her, and the blessings of the good holy Virgin and of all the saints of paradise be upon you!"

"Agreed."

"Really! You will take her away?"

"I will take her away."

"Immediately?"

"Immediately. Call the child."

"Cosette!" screamed the Thénardier.

"In the meantime," pursued the man, "I will pay you what I owe you. How much is it?"

He cast a glance on the bill, and could not restrain a start of surprise:—

"Twenty-three francs!"

He looked at the landlady, and repeated:—

"Twenty-three francs?"

There was in the enunciation of these words, thus repeated, an accent between an exclamation and an interrogation point.

The Thénardier had had time to prepare herself for the shock. She replied, with assurance:—

"Good gracious, yes, sir, it is twenty-three francs."

The stranger laid five five-franc pieces on the table.

"Go and get the child," said he.

At that moment Thénardier advanced to the middle of the room, and said:—

"Monsieur owes twenty-six sous."

"Twenty-six sous!" exclaimed his wife.

"Twenty sous for the chamber," resumed Thénardier, coldly, "and six sous for his supper. As for the child, I must discuss that matter a little with the gentleman. Leave us, wife."

Madame Thénardier was dazzled as with the shock caused by unexpected lightning flashes of talent. She was conscious that a great actor was making his entrance on the stage, uttered not a word in reply, and left the room.

As soon as they were alone, Thénardier offered the traveller a chair. The traveller seated himself; Thénardier remained standing, and his face assumed a singular expression of good-fellowship and simplicity.

"Sir," said he, "what I have to say to you is this, that I adore that child."

The stranger gazed intently at him.

"What child?"

Thénardier continued:—

"How strange it is, one grows attached. What money is that? Take back your hundred-sou piece. I adore the child."

"Whom do you mean?" demanded the stranger.

"Eh! our little Cosette! Are you not intending to take her away from us? Well, I speak frankly; as true as you are an honest man, I will not consent to it. I shall miss that child. I saw her first when she was a tiny thing. It is true that she costs us money; it is true that she has her faults; it is true that we are not rich; it is true that I have paid out over four hundred francs for drugs for just one of her illnesses! But one must do something for the good God's sake. She has neither father nor mother. I have brought her up. I have bread enough for her and for myself. In truth, I think a great deal of that child. You understand, one conceives an affection for a person; I am a good sort of a beast, I am; I do not reason; I love that little girl; my wife is quick-tempered, but she loves her also. You see, she is just the same as our own child. I want to keep her to babble about the house."

The stranger kept his eye intently fixed on Thénardier. The latter continued:—

"Excuse me, sir, but one does not give away one's child to a passer-by, like that. I am right, am I not? Still, I don't say—you are rich; you have the air of a very good man,—if it were for her happiness. But one must find out that. You understand: suppose that I were to let her go and to sacrifice myself, I should like to know what becomes of her; I should not wish to lose sight of her; I should like to know with whom she is living, so that I could go to see her from time to time; so that she may know that her good foster-father is alive, that he is watching over her. In short, there are things which are not possible. I do not even know your name. If you were to take her away, I should say: 'Well, and the Lark, what has become of her?' One must, at least, see some petty scrap of paper, some trifle in the way of a passport, you know!"

The stranger, still surveying him with that gaze which penetrates, as the saying goes, to the very depths of the conscience, replied in a grave, firm voice:—

"Monsieur Thénardier, one does not require a passport to travel five leagues from Paris. If I take Cosette away, I shall take her away, and that is the end of the matter. You will not know my name, you will not know my residence, you will not know where she is; and my intention is that she shall never set eyes on you again so long as she lives. I break the thread which binds her foot, and she departs. Does that suit you? Yes or no?"

Since geniuses, like demons, recognize the presence of a superior God by certain signs, Thénardier comprehended that he had to deal with a very strong person. It was like an intuition; he comprehended it with his clear and sagacious promptitude. While drinking with the carters, smoking, and singing coarse songs on the preceding evening, he had devoted the whole of the time to observing the stranger, watching him like a cat, and studying him like a mathematician. He had watched him, both on his own account, for the pleasure of the thing, and through instinct, and had spied upon him as though he had been paid for so doing. Not a movement, not a gesture, on the part of the man in the yellow great-coat had escaped him. Even before the stranger had so clearly manifested his interest in Cosette, Thénardier had divined his purpose. He had caught the old man's deep glances returning constantly to the child. Who was this man? Why this interest? Why this hideous costume, when he had so much money in his purse? Questions which he put to himself without being able to solve them, and which irritated him. He had pondered it all night long. He could not be Cosette's father. Was he her grandfather? Then why not make himself known at once? When one has a right, one asserts it. This man evidently had no right over Cosette. What was it, then? Thénardier lost himself in conjectures. He caught glimpses of everything, but he saw nothing. Be that as it may, on entering into conversation with the man, sure that there was some secret in the case, that the latter had some interest in remaining in the shadow, he felt himself strong; when he perceived from the stranger's clear and firm retort, that this mysterious personage was mysterious in so simple a way, he became conscious that he was weak. He had expected nothing of the sort. His conjectures were put to the rout. He rallied his ideas. He weighed everything in the space of a second. Thénardier was one of those men who take in a situation at a glance. He decided that the moment had arrived for proceeding straightforward, and quickly at that. He did as great leaders do at the decisive moment, which they know that they alone recognize; he abruptly unmasked his batteries.

"Sir," said he, "I am in need of fifteen hundred francs."

The stranger took from his side pocket an old pocketbook of black leather, opened it, drew out three bank-bills, which he laid on the table. Then he placed his large thumb on the notes and said to the inn-keeper:—

"Go and fetch Cosette."

While this was taking place, what had Cosette been doing?

On waking up, Cosette had run to get her shoe. In it she had found the gold piece. It was not a Napoleon; it was one of those perfectly new twenty-franc pieces of the Restoration, on whose effigy the little Prussian queue had replaced the laurel wreath. Cosette was dazzled. Her destiny began to intoxicate her. She did not know what a gold piece was; she had never seen one; she hid it quickly in her pocket, as though she had stolen it. Still, she felt that it really was hers; she guessed whence her gift had come, but the joy which she experienced was full of fear. She was happy; above all she was stupefied. Such magnificent and beautiful things did not appear real. The doll frightened her, the gold piece frightened her. She trembled vaguely in the presence of this magnificence. The stranger alone did not frighten her. On the contrary, he reassured her. Ever since the preceding evening, amid all her amazement, even in her sleep, she had been thinking in her little childish mind of that man who seemed to be so poor and so sad, and who was so rich and so kind. Everything had changed for her since she had met that good man in the forest. Cosette, less happy than the most insignificant swallow of heaven, had never known what it was to take refuge under a mother's shadow and under a wing. For the last five years, that is to say, as far back as her memory ran, the poor child had shivered and trembled. She had always been exposed completely naked to the sharp wind of adversity; now it seemed to her she was clothed. Formerly her soul had seemed cold, now it was warm. Cosette was no longer afraid of the Thénardier. She was no longer alone; there was some one there.

She hastily set about her regular morning duties. That louis, which she had about her, in the very apron pocket whence the fifteen-sou piece had fallen on the night before, distracted her thoughts. She dared not touch it, but she spent five minutes in gazing at it, with her tongue hanging out, if the truth must be told. As she swept the staircase, she paused, remained standing there motionless, forgetful of her broom and of the entire universe, occupied in gazing at that star which was blazing at the bottom of her pocket.

It was during one of these periods of contemplation that the Thénardier joined her. She had gone in search of Cosette at her husband's orders. What was quite unprecedented, she neither struck her nor said an insulting word to her.

"Cosette," she said, almost gently, "come immediately."

An instant later Cosette entered the public room.

The stranger took up the bundle which he had brought and untied it. This bundle contained a little woollen gown, an apron, a fustian bodice, a kerchief, a petticoat, woollen stockings, shoes—a complete outfit for a girl of seven years. All was black.

"My child," said the man, "take these, and go and dress yourself quickly."

Daylight was appearing when those of the inhabitants of Montfermeil who had begun to open their doors beheld a poorly clad old man leading a little girl dressed in mourning, and carrying a pink doll in her arms, pass along the road to Paris. They were going in the direction of Livry.

It was our man and Cosette.

No one knew the man; as Cosette was no longer in rags, many did not recognize her. Cosette was going away. With whom? She did not know. Whither? She knew not. All that she understood was that she was leaving the Thénardier tavern behind her. No one had thought of bidding her farewell, nor had she thought of taking leave of any one. She was leaving that hated and hating house.

Poor, gentle creature, whose heart had been repressed up to that hour!

Cosette walked along gravely, with her large eyes wide open, and gazing at the sky. She had put her louis in the pocket of her new apron. From time to time, she bent down and glanced at it; then she looked at the good man. She felt something as though she were beside the good God.

X

He who Seeks to Better himself May Render his Situation Worse

Madame Thénardier had allowed her husband to have his own way, as was her wont. She had expected great results. When the man and Cosette had taken their departure, Thénardier allowed a full quarter of an hour to elapse; then he took her aside and showed her the fifteen hundred francs.

"Is that all?" said she.

It was the first time since they had set up housekeeping that she had dared to criticise one of the master's acts.

The blow told.

"You are right, in sooth," said he; "I am a fool. Give me my hat."

He folded up the three bank-bills, thrust them into his pocket, and ran out in all haste; but he made a mistake and turned to the right first. Some neighbors, of whom he made inquiries, put him on the track again; the Lark and the man had been seen going in the direction of Livry. He followed these hints, walking with great strides, and talking to himself the while:—

"That man is evidently a million dressed in yellow, and I am an animal. First he gave twenty sous, then five francs, then fifty francs, then fifteen hundred francs, all with equal readiness. He would have given fifteen thousand francs. But I shall overtake him."

And then, that bundle of clothes prepared beforehand for the child; all that was singular; many mysteries lay concealed under it. One does not let mysteries out of one's hand when one has once grasped them. The secrets of the wealthy are sponges of gold; one must know how to subject them to pressure. All these thoughts whirled through his brain. "I am an animal," said he.

When one leaves Montfermeil and reaches the turn which the road takes that runs to Livry, it can be seen stretching out before one to a great distance across the plateau. On arriving there, he calculated that he ought to be able to see the old man and the child. He looked as far as his vision reached, and saw nothing. He made fresh inquiries, but he had wasted time. Some passers-by informed him that the man and child of whom he was in search had gone towards the forest in the direction of Gagny. He hastened in that direction.

They were far in advance of him; but a child walks slowly, and he walked fast; and then, he was well acquainted with the country.

All at once he paused and dealt himself a blow on his forehead like a man who has forgotten some essential point and who is ready to retrace his steps.

"I ought to have taken my gun," said he to himself.

Thénardier was one of those double natures which sometimes pass through our midst without our being aware of the fact, and who disappear without our finding them out, because destiny has only exhibited one side of them. It is the fate of many men to live thus half submerged. In a calm and even situation, Thénardier possessed all that is required to make—we will not say to be—what people have agreed to call an honest trader, a good bourgeois. At the same time certain circumstances being given, certain shocks arriving to bring his under-nature to the surface, he had all the requisites for a blackguard. He was a shopkeeper in whom there was some taint of the monster. Satan must have occasionally crouched down in some corner of the hovel in which Thénardier dwelt, and have fallen a-dreaming in the presence of this hideous masterpiece.

After a momentary hesitation:—

"Bah!" he thought; "they will have time to make their escape."

And he pursued his road, walking rapidly straight ahead, and with almost an air of certainty, with the sagacity of a fox scenting a covey of partridges.

In truth, when he had passed the ponds and had traversed in an oblique direction the large clearing which lies on the right of the Avenue de Bellevue, and reached that turf alley which nearly makes the circuit of the hill, and covers the arch of the ancient aqueduct of the Abbey of Chelles, he caught sight, over the top of the brushwood, of the hat on which he had already erected so many conjectures; it was that man's hat. The brushwood was not high. Thénardier recognized the fact that the man and Cosette were sitting there. The child could not be seen on account of her small size, but the head of her doll was visible.

Thénardier was not mistaken. The man was sitting there, and letting Cosette get somewhat rested. The inn-keeper walked round the brushwood and presented himself abruptly to the eyes of those whom he was in search of.

"Pardon, excuse me, sir," he said, quite breathless, "but here are your fifteen hundred francs."

So saying, he handed the stranger the three bank-bills.

The man raised his eyes.

"What is the meaning of this?"

Thénardier replied respectfully:—

"It means, sir, that I shall take back Cosette."

Cosette shuddered, and pressed close to the old man.

He replied, gazing to the very bottom of Thénardier's eyes the while, and enunciating every syllable distinctly:—

"You are go-ing to take back Co-sette?"

"Yes, sir, I am. I will tell you; I have considered the matter. In fact, I have not the right to give her to you. I am an honest man, you see; this child does not belong to me; she belongs to her mother. It was her mother who confided her to me; I can only resign her to her mother. You will say to me, 'But her mother is dead.' Good; in that case I can only give the child up to the person who shall bring me a writing, signed by her mother, to the effect that I am to hand the child over to the person therein mentioned; that is clear."

The man, without making any reply, fumbled in his pocket, and Thénardier beheld the pocket-book of bank-bills make its appearance once more.

The tavern-keeper shivered with joy.

"Good!" thought he; "let us hold firm; he is going to bribe me!"

Before opening the pocket-book, the traveller cast a glance about him: the spot was absolutely deserted; there was not a soul either in the woods or in the valley. The man opened his pocket-book once more and drew from it, not the handful of bills which Thénardier expected, but a simple little paper, which he unfolded and presented fully open to the inn-keeper, saying:—

"You are right; read!"

Thénardier took the paper and read:—

M. Sur M., March 25, 1823

Monsieur Thénardier:—

You will deliver Cosette to this person.

You will be paid for all the little things.

I have the honor to salute you with respect,

Fantine

"You know that signature?" resumed the man.

It certainly was Fantine's signature; Thénardier recognized it.

There was no reply to make; he experienced two violent vexations, the vexation of renouncing the bribery which he had hoped for, and the vexation of being beaten; the man added:—

"You may keep this paper as your receipt."

Thénardier retreated in tolerably good order.

"This signature is fairly well imitated," he growled between his teeth; "however, let it go!"

Then he essayed a desperate effort.

"It is well, sir," he said, "since you are the person, but I must be paid for all those little things. A great deal is owing to me."

The man rose to his feet, filliping the dust from his threadbare sleeve:—

"Monsieur Thénardier, in January last, the mother reckoned that she owed you one hundred and twenty francs. In February, you sent her a bill of five hundred francs; you received three hundred francs at the end of February, and three hundred francs at the beginning of March. Since then nine months have elapsed, at fifteen francs a month, the price agreed upon, which makes one hundred and thirty-five francs. You had received one hundred francs too much; that makes thirty-five still owing you. I have just given you fifteen hundred francs."

Thénardier's sensations were those of the wolf at the moment when he feels himself nipped and seized by the steel jaw of the trap.

"Who is this devil of a man?" he thought.

He did what the wolf does: he shook himself. Audacity had succeeded with him once.

"Monsieur-I-don't-know-your-name," he said resolutely, and this time casting aside all respectful ceremony, "I shall take back Cosette if you do not give me a thousand crowns."

The stranger said tranquilly:—

"Come, Cosette."

He took Cosette by his left hand, and with his right he picked up his cudgel, which was lying on the ground.

Thénardier noted the enormous size of the cudgel and the solitude of the spot.

The man plunged into the forest with the child, leaving the inn-keeper motionless and speechless.

While they were walking away, Thénardier scrutinized his huge shoulders, which were a little rounded, and his great fists.

Then, bringing his eyes back to his own person, they fell upon his feeble arms and his thin hands. "I really must have been exceedingly stupid not to have thought to bring my gun," he said to himself, "since I was going hunting!"

However, the inn-keeper did not give up.

"I want to know where he is going," said he, and he set out to follow them at a distance. Two things were left on his hands, an irony in the shape of the paper signed *Fantine*, and a consolation, the fifteen hundred francs.

The man led Cosette off in the direction of Livry and Bondy. He walked slowly, with drooping head, in an attitude of reflection and sadness. The winter had thinned out the forest, so that Thénardier did not lose them from sight, although he kept at a good distance. The man turned round from time to time, and looked to see if he was being followed. All at once he caught sight of Thénardier. He plunged suddenly into the brushwood with Cosette, where they could both hide themselves. "The deuce!" said Thénardier, and he redoubled his pace.

The thickness of the undergrowth forced him to draw nearer to them. When the man had reached the densest part of the thicket, he wheeled round. It was in vain that Thénardier sought to conceal himself in the branches; he could not prevent the man seeing him. The man cast upon him an uneasy glance, then elevated his head and continued his course. The inn-keeper set out again in pursuit. Thus they continued for two or three hundred paces. All at once the man turned round once more; he saw the inn-keeper. This time he gazed at him with so sombre an air that Thénardier decided that it was "useless" to proceed further. Thénardier retraced his steps.

Number 9,430 Reappears, and Cosette Wins it in the Lottery

Jean Valjean was not dead.

When he fell into the sea, or rather, when he threw himself into it, he was not ironed, as we have seen. He swam under water until he reached a vessel at anchor, to which a boat was moored. He found means of hiding himself in this boat until night. At night he swam off again, and reached the shore a little way from Cape Brun. There, as he did not lack money, he procured clothing. A small country-house in the neighborhood of Balaguier was at that time the dressing-room of escaped convicts,—a lucrative specialty. Then Jean Valjean, like all the sorry fugitives who are seeking to evade the vigilance of the law and social fatality, pursued an obscure and undulating itinerary. He found his first refuge at Pradeaux, near Beausset. Then he directed his course towards Grand-Villard, near Briançon, in the Hautes-Alpes. It was a fumbling and uneasy flight,—a mole's track, whose branchings are untraceable. Later on, some trace of his passage into Ain, in the territory of Civrieux, was discovered; in the Pyrenees, at Accons; at the spot called Grange-de-Doumec, near the market of Chavailles, and in the environs of Perigueux at Brunies, canton of La Chapelle-Gonaguet. He reached Paris. We have just seen him at Montfermeil.

His first care on arriving in Paris had been to buy mourning clothes for a little girl of from seven to eight years of age; then to procure a lodging. That done, he had betaken himself to Montfermeil. It will be remembered that already, during his preceding escape, he had made a mysterious trip thither, or somewhere in that neighborhood, of which the law had gathered an inkling.

However, he was thought to be dead, and this still further increased the obscurity which had gathered about him. At Paris, one of the journals which chronicled the fact fell into his hands. He felt reassured and almost at peace, as though he had really been dead.

On the evening of the day when Jean Valjean rescued Cosette from the claws of the Thénardiers, he returned to Paris. He re-entered it at nightfall, with the child, by way of the Barrier Monceaux. There he entered a cabriolet, which took him to the esplanade of the Observatoire. There he got out, paid the coachman, took Cosette by the hand, and together they directed their steps through the darkness,—through the deserted streets which adjoin the Ourcine and the Glacière, towards the Boulevard de l'Hôpital.

The day had been strange and filled with emotions for Cosette. They had eaten some bread and cheese purchased in isolated taverns, behind hedges; they had changed carriages frequently; they had travelled short distances on foot. She made no complaint, but she was weary, and Jean Valjean perceived it by the way she dragged more and more on his hand as she walked. He took her on his back. Cosette, without letting go of Catherine, laid her head on Jean Valjean's shoulder, and there fell asleep.

BOOK FOURTH
THE GORBEAU HOVEL

I

MASTER GORBEAU

Forty years ago, a rambler who had ventured into that unknown country of the Salpêtrière, and who had mounted to the Barrière d'Italie by way of the boulevard, reached a point where it might be said that Paris disappeared. It was no longer solitude, for there were passers-by; it was not the country, for there were houses and streets; it was not the city, for the streets had ruts like highways, and the grass grew in them; it was not a village, the houses were too lofty. What was it, then? It was an inhabited spot where there was no one; it was a desert place where there was some one; it was a boulevard of the great city, a street of Paris; more wild at night than the forest, more gloomy by day than a cemetery.

It was the old quarter of the Marché-aux-Chevaux.

The rambler, if he risked himself outside the four decrepit walls of this Marché-aux-Chevaux; if he consented even to pass beyond the Rue du Petit-Banquier, after leaving on his right a garden protected by high walls; then a field in which tan-bark mills rose like gigantic beaver huts; then an enclosure encumbered with timber, with a heap of stumps, sawdust, and shavings, on which stood a large dog, barking; then a long, low, utterly dilapidated wall, with a little black door in mourning, laden with mosses, which were covered with flowers in the spring; then, in the most deserted spot, a frightful and decrepit building, on which ran the inscription in large letters: POST NO BILLS,—this daring rambler would have reached little known latitudes at the corner of the Rue des Vignes-Saint-Marcel. There, near a factory, and between two garden walls, there could be seen, at that epoch, a mean building, which, at the first glance, seemed as small as a thatched hovel, and which was, in reality, as large as a cathedral. It presented its side and gable to the public road; hence its apparent diminutiveness. Nearly the whole of the house was hidden. Only the door and one window could be seen.

This hovel was only one story high.

The first detail that struck the observer was, that the door could never have been anything but the door of a hovel, while the window, if it had been carved out of dressed stone instead of being in rough masonry, might have been the lattice of a lordly mansion.

The door was nothing but a collection of worm-eaten planks roughly bound together by cross-beams which resembled roughly hewn logs. It opened directly on a steep staircase of lofty steps, muddy, chalky, plaster-stained, dusty steps, of the same width as itself, which could be seen from the street, running straight up like a ladder and disappearing in the darkness between two walls. The top of the shapeless bay into which this door shut was masked by a narrow scantling in the centre of which a triangular hole had been sawed, which served both as wicket and air-hole when the door was closed. On the inside of the door the figures 52 had been traced with a couple of strokes of a brush dipped in ink, and above the scantling the same hand had daubed the number 50, so that one hesitated. Where was one? Above the door it said, "Number 50"; the inside replied, "no, Number 52." No one knows what dust-colored figures were suspended like draperies from the triangular opening.

The window was large, sufficiently elevated, garnished with Venetian blinds, and with a frame in large square panes; only these large panes were suffering from various wounds, which were both concealed and betrayed by an ingenious paper bandage. And the blinds, dislocated and unpasted, threatened passers-by rather than screened the occupants. The horizontal slats were missing here and there and had been naïvely replaced with boards nailed on perpendicularly; so that what began as a blind ended as a shutter. This door with an unclean, and this window with an honest though dilapidated air, thus beheld on the same house, produced the effect of two incomplete beggars walking side by side, with different miens beneath the same rags, the one having always been a mendicant, and the other having once been a gentleman.

The staircase led to a very vast edifice which resembled a shed which had been converted into a house. This edifice had, for its intestinal tube, a long corridor, on which opened to right and left sorts of compartments of varied dimensions which were inhabitable under stress of circumstances, and rather more like stalls than cells. These chambers received their light from the vague waste grounds in the neighborhood.

All this was dark, disagreeable, wan, melancholy, sepulchral; traversed according as the crevices lay in the roof or in the door, by cold rays or by icy winds. An interesting and picturesque peculiarity of this sort of dwelling is the enormous size of the spiders.

To the left of the entrance door, on the boulevard side, at about the height of a man from the ground, a small window which had been walled up formed a square niche full of stones which the children had thrown there as they passed by.

A portion of this building has recently been demolished. From what still remains of it one can form a judgment as to what it was in former days. As a whole, it was not over a hundred years old. A hundred years is youth in a church and age in a house. It seems as though man's lodging partook of his ephemeral character, and God's house of his eternity.

The postmen called the house Number 50–52; but it was known in the neighborhood as the Gorbeau house.

Let us explain whence this appellation was derived.

Collectors of petty details, who become herbalists of anecdotes, and prick slippery dates into their memories with a pin, know that there was in Paris, during the last century, about 1770, two attorneys at the Châtelet named, one Corbeau (Raven), the other Renard (Fox). The two names had been forestalled by La Fontaine. The opportunity was too fine for the lawyers; they made the most of it. A parody was immediately put in circulation in the galleries of the court-house, in verses that limped a little:—

> *Maître Corbeau, sur un dossier perché,*
> *Tenait dans son bec une saisie exécutoire;*
> *Maître Renard, par l'odeur alléché,*
> *Lui fit à peu près cette histoire:*
> *Hé! bonjour. Etc.*

The two honest practitioners, embarrassed by the jests, and finding the bearing of their heads interfered with by the shouts of laughter which followed them, resolved to get rid of their names, and hit upon the expedient of applying to the king.

Their petition was presented to Louis XV on the same day when the Papal Nuncio, on the one hand, and the Cardinal de la Roche-Aymon on the other, both devoutly kneeling, were each engaged in putting on, in his Majesty's presence, a slipper on the bare feet of Madame du Barry, who had just got out of bed. The king, who was laughing, continued to laugh, passed gayly from the two bishops to the two lawyers, and bestowed on these limbs of the law their former names, or nearly so. By the kings command, Maître Corbeau was permitted to add a tail to his initial letter and to call himself Gorbeau. Maître Renard was less lucky; all he obtained was leave to place a P in front of his R, and to call himself Prenard; so that the second name bore almost as much resemblance as the first.

Now, according to local tradition, this Maître Gorbeau had been the proprietor of the building numbered 50–52 on the Boulevard de l'Hôpital. He was even the author of the monumental window.

Hence the edifice bore the name of the Gorbeau house.

Opposite this house, among the trees of the boulevard, rose a great elm which was three-quarters dead; almost directly facing it opens the Rue de la Barrière des Gobelins, a street then without houses, unpaved, planted with unhealthy trees, which was green or muddy according to the season, and which ended squarely in the exterior wall of Paris. An odor of copperas issued in puffs from the roofs of the neighboring factory.

The barrier was close at hand. In 1823 the city wall was still in existence.

This barrier itself evoked gloomy fancies in the mind. It was the road to Bicêtre. It was through it that, under the Empire and the Restoration, prisoners condemned to death re-entered Paris on the day of their execution. It was there, that, about 1829, was committed that mysterious assassination, called "The assassination of the Fontainebleau barrier," whose authors justice was never able to discover; a melancholy problem which has never been elucidated, a frightful enigma which has never been unriddled. Take a few steps, and you come upon that fatal Rue Croulebarbe, where Ulbach stabbed the goat-girl of Ivry to the sound of thunder, as in the melodramas. A few paces more, and you arrive at the abominable pollarded elms of the Barrière Saint-Jacques, that expedient of the philanthropist to conceal the scaffold, that miserable and shameful Place de Grève of a shop-keeping and bourgeois society, which recoiled before the death penalty, neither daring to abolish it with grandeur, nor to uphold it with authority.

Leaving aside this Place Saint-Jacques, which was, as it were, predestined, and which has always been horrible, probably the most mournful spot on that mournful boulevard, seven and thirty years ago, was the spot which even to-day is so unattractive, where stood the building Number 50–52.

Bourgeois houses only began to spring up there twenty-five years later. The place was unpleasant. In addition to the gloomy thoughts which assailed one there, one was conscious of being between the Salpêtrière, a glimpse of whose dome could be seen, and Bicêtre, whose outskirts one was fairly touching; that is to say, between the madness of women and the madness of men. As far as the eye could see, one could perceive nothing but the abattoirs, the city wall, and the fronts of a few factories, resembling barracks or monasteries; everywhere about stood hovels, rubbish, ancient walls blackened like cerecloths, new white walls like winding-sheets; everywhere parallel rows of trees, buildings erected on a line, flat constructions, long, cold rows, and the melancholy sadness of right angles. Not an unevenness of the ground, not a caprice in the architecture, not a fold. The *ensemble* was glacial, regular, hideous. Nothing oppresses the heart like symmetry. It is because symmetry is ennui, and ennui is at the very foundation of grief. Despair yawns. Something more terrible than a hell where one suffers may be imagined, and that is a hell where one is bored. If such a hell existed, that bit of the Boulevard de l'Hôpital might have formed the entrance to it.

Nevertheless, at nightfall, at the moment when the daylight is vanishing, especially in winter, at the hour when the twilight breeze tears from the elms their last russet leaves, when the darkness is deep and starless, or when the moon and the wind are making openings in the clouds and losing themselves in the shadows, this boulevard suddenly becomes frightful. The black lines sink inwards and are lost in the shades, like morsels of the infinite. The passer-by cannot refrain from recalling the innumerable traditions of the place which are connected with the gibbet. The solitude of this spot, where so many crimes have been committed, had something terrible about it. One almost had a presentiment of meeting with traps in that darkness; all the confused forms of the darkness seemed suspicious, and the long, hollow square, of which one caught a glimpse between each tree, seemed graves: by day it was ugly; in the evening melancholy; by night it was sinister.

In summer, at twilight, one saw, here and there, a few old women seated at the foot of the elm, on benches mouldy with rain. These good old women were fond of begging.

However, this quarter, which had a superannuated rather than an antique air, was tending even then to transformation. Even at that time any one who was desirous of seeing it had to make haste. Each day some detail of the whole effect was disappearing. For the last twenty years the station of the Orleans railway has stood beside the old faubourg and distracted it, as it does to-day. Wherever it is placed on the borders of a capital, a railway station is the death of a suburb and the birth of a city. It seems as though, around these great centres of the movements of a people, the earth, full of germs, trembled and yawned, to engulf the ancient dwellings of men and to allow new ones to spring forth, at the rattle of these powerful machines, at the breath of these monstrous horses of civilization which devour coal and vomit fire. The old houses crumble and new ones rise.

Since the Orleans railway has invaded the region of the Salpêtrière, the ancient, narrow streets which adjoin the moats Saint-Victor and the Jardin des Plantes tremble, as they are violently traversed three or four times each day by those currents of coach fiacres and omnibuses which, in a given time, crowd back the houses to the right and the left; for there are things which are odd when said that are rigorously exact; and just as it is true to say that in large cities the sun makes the southern fronts of houses to vegetate and grow, it is certain that the frequent passage of vehicles enlarges streets. The symptoms of a new life are evident. In this old provincial quarter, in the wildest nooks, the pavement shows itself, the sidewalks begin to crawl and to grow longer, even where there are as yet no pedestrians. One morning,—a memorable morning in July, 1845,—black pots of bitumen were seen smoking there; on that day it might be said that civilization had arrived in the Rue de l'Ourcine, and that Paris had entered the suburb of Saint-Marceau.

II

A Nest for Owl and a Warbler

It was in front of this Gorbeau house that Jean Valjean halted. Like wild birds, he had chosen this desert place to construct his nest.

He fumbled in his waistcoat pocket, drew out a sort of a pass-key, opened the door, entered, closed it again carefully, and ascended the staircase, still carrying Cosette.

At the top of the stairs he drew from his pocket another key, with which he opened another door. The chamber which he entered, and which he closed again instantly, was a kind of moderately spacious attic, furnished with a mattress laid on the floor, a table, and several chairs; a stove in which a fire was burning, and whose embers were visible, stood in one corner. A lantern on the boulevard cast a vague light into this poor room. At the extreme end there was a dressing-room with a folding bed; Jean Valjean carried the child to this bed and laid her down there without waking her.

He struck a match and lighted a candle. All this was prepared beforehand on the table, and, as he had done on the previous evening, he began to scrutinize Cosette's face with a gaze full of ecstasy, in which the expression of kindness and tenderness almost amounted to aberration. The little girl, with that tranquil confidence which belongs only to extreme strength and extreme weakness, had fallen asleep without knowing with whom she was, and continued to sleep without knowing where she was.

Jean Valjean bent down and kissed that child's hand.

Nine months before he had kissed the hand of the mother, who had also just fallen asleep.

The same sad, piercing, religious sentiment filled his heart.

He knelt beside Cosette's bed.

It was broad daylight, and the child still slept. A wan ray of the December sun penetrated the window of the attic and lay upon the ceiling in long threads of light and shade. All at once a heavily laden carrier's cart, which was passing along the boulevard, shook the frail bed, like a clap of thunder, and made it quiver from top to bottom.

"Yes, madame!" cried Cosette, waking with a start, "here I am! here I am!"

And she sprang out of bed, her eyes still half shut with the heaviness of sleep, extending her arms towards the corner of the wall.

"Ah! mon Dieu, my broom!" said she.

She opened her eyes wide now, and beheld the smiling countenance of Jean Valjean.

"Ah! so it is true!" said the child. "Good morning, Monsieur."

Children accept joy and happiness instantly and familiarly, being themselves by nature joy and happiness.

Cosette caught sight of Catherine at the foot of her bed, and took possession of her, and, as she played, she put a hundred questions to Jean Valjean. Where was she? Was Paris very large? Was Madame Thénardier very far away? Was she to go back? etc., etc. All at once she exclaimed, "How pretty it is here!"

It was a frightful hole, but she felt free.

"Must I sweep?" she resumed at last.

"Play!" said Jean Valjean.

The day passed thus. Cosette, without troubling herself to understand anything, was inexpressibly happy with that doll and that kind man.

III

Two Misfortunes Make One Piece of Good Fortune

On the following morning, at daybreak, Jean Valjean was still by Cosette's bedside; he watched there motionless, waiting for her to wake.

Some new thing had come into his soul.

Jean Valjean had never loved anything; for twenty-five years he had been alone in the world. He had never been father, lover, husband, friend. In the prison he had been vicious, gloomy, chaste, ignorant, and shy. The heart of that ex-convict was full of virginity. His sister and his sister's children had left him only a vague and far-off memory which had finally almost completely vanished; he had made every effort to find them, and not having been able to find them, he had forgotten them. Human nature is made thus; the other tender emotions of his youth, if he had ever had any, had fallen into an abyss.

When he saw Cosette, when he had taken possession of her, carried her off, and delivered her, he felt his heart moved within him.

All the passion and affection within him awoke, and rushed towards that child. He approached the bed, where she lay sleeping, and trembled with joy. He suffered all the pangs of a mother, and he knew not what it meant; for that great and singular movement of a heart which begins to love is a very obscure and a very sweet thing.

Poor old man, with a perfectly new heart!

Only, as he was five and fifty, and Cosette eight years of age, all that might have been love in the whole course of his life flowed together into a sort of ineffable light.

It was the second white apparition which he had encountered. The Bishop had caused the dawn of virtue to rise on his horizon; Cosette caused the dawn of love to rise.

The early days passed in this dazzled state.

Cosette, on her side, had also, unknown to herself, become another being, poor little thing! She was so little when her mother left her, that she no longer remembered her. Like all children, who resemble young shoots of the vine, which cling to everything, she had tried to love;

she had not succeeded. All had repulsed her,—the Thénardiers, their children, other children. She had loved the dog, and he had died, after which nothing and nobody would have anything to do with her. It is a sad thing to say, and we have already intimated it, that, at eight years of age, her heart was cold. It was not her fault; it was not the faculty of loving that she lacked; alas! it was the possibility. Thus, from the very first day, all her sentient and thinking powers loved this kind man. She felt that which she had never felt before—a sensation of expansion.

The man no longer produced on her the effect of being old or poor; she thought Jean Valjean handsome, just as she thought the hovel pretty.

These are the effects of the dawn, of childhood, of joy. The novelty of the earth and of life counts for something here. Nothing is so charming as the coloring reflection of happiness on a garret. We all have in our past a delightful garret.

Nature, a difference of fifty years, had set a profound gulf between Jean Valjean and Cosette; destiny filled in this gulf. Destiny suddenly united and wedded with its irresistible power these two uprooted existences, differing in age, alike in sorrow. One, in fact, completed the other. Cosette's instinct sought a father, as Jean Valjean's instinct sought a child. To meet was to find each other. At the mysterious moment when their hands touched, they were welded together. When these two souls perceived each other, they recognized each other as necessary to each other, and embraced each other closely.

Taking the words in their most comprehensive and absolute sense, we may say that, separated from every one by the walls of the tomb, Jean Valjean was the widower, and Cosette was the orphan: this situation caused Jean Valjean to become Cosette's father after a celestial fashion.

And in truth, the mysterious impression produced on Cosette in the depths of the forest of Chelles by the hand of Jean Valjean grasping hers in the dark was not an illusion, but a reality. The entrance of that man into the destiny of that child had been the advent of God.

Moreover, Jean Valjean had chosen his refuge well. There he seemed perfectly secure.

The chamber with a dressing-room, which he occupied with Cosette, was the one whose window opened on the boulevard. This being the only window in the house, no neighbors' glances were to be feared from across the way or at the side.

The ground floor of Number 50–52, a sort of dilapidated penthouse, served as a wagon-house for market-gardeners, and no communication existed between it and the first story. It was separated by the flooring, which had neither traps nor stairs, and which formed the diaphragm of the building, as it were. The first story contained, as we have said, numerous chambers and several attics, only one of which was occupied by the old woman who took charge of Jean Valjean's housekeeping; all the rest was uninhabited.

It was this old woman, ornamented with the name of the *principal lodger*, and in reality intrusted with the functions of portress, who had let him the lodging on Christmas eve. He had represented himself to her as a gentleman of means who had been ruined by Spanish bonds, who was coming there to live with his little daughter. He had paid her six months in advance, and had commissioned the old woman to furnish the chamber and dressing-room, as we have seen. It was this good woman who had lighted the fire in the stove, and prepared everything on the evening of their arrival.

Week followed week; these two beings led a happy life in that hovel.

Cosette laughed, chattered, and sang from daybreak. Children have their morning song as well as birds.

It sometimes happened that Jean Valjean clasped her tiny red hand, all cracked with chilblains, and kissed it. The poor child, who was used to being beaten, did not know the meaning of this, and ran away in confusion.

At times she became serious and stared at her little black gown. Cosette was no longer in rags; she was in mourning. She had emerged from misery, and she was entering into life.

Jean Valjean had undertaken to teach her to read. Sometimes, as he made the child spell, he remembered that it was with the idea of doing evil that he had learned to read in prison. This idea had ended in teaching a child to read. Then the ex-convict smiled with the pensive smile of the angels.

He felt in it a premeditation from on high, the will of some one who was not man, and he became absorbed in reverie. Good thoughts have their abysses as well as evil ones.

To teach Cosette to read, and to let her play, this constituted nearly the whole of Jean Valjean's existence. And then he talked of her mother, and he made her pray.

She called him *father*, and knew no other name for him.

He passed hours in watching her dressing and undressing her doll, and in listening to her prattle. Life, henceforth, appeared to him to be full of interest; men seemed to him good and just; he no longer reproached any one in thought; he saw no reason why he should not live to be a very old man, now that this child loved him. He saw a whole future stretching out before him, illuminated by Cosette as by a charming light. The best of us are not exempt from egotistical thoughts. At times, he reflected with a sort of joy that she would be ugly.

This is only a personal opinion; but, to utter our whole thought, at the point where Jean Valjean had arrived when he began to love Cosette, it is by no means clear to us that he did not need this encouragement in order that he might persevere in well-doing. He had just viewed the malice of men and the misery of society under a new aspect—incomplete aspects, which unfortunately only exhibited one side of the truth, the fate of woman as summed up in Fantine, and public authority as personified in Javert. He had returned to prison, this time for having done right; he had quaffed fresh bitterness; disgust and lassitude were overpowering him; even the memory of the Bishop probably suffered a temporary eclipse, though sure to reappear later on luminous and triumphant; but, after all, that sacred memory was growing dim. Who knows whether Jean Valjean had not been on the eve of growing discouraged and of falling once more? He loved and grew strong again. Alas! he walked with no less indecision than Cosette. He protected her, and she strengthened him. Thanks to him, she could walk through life; thanks to her, he could continue in virtue. He was that child's stay, and she was his prop. Oh, unfathomable and divine mystery of the balances of destiny!

IV

The Remarks of the Principal Tenant

Jean Valjean was prudent enough never to go out by day. Every evening, at twilight, he walked for an hour or two, sometimes alone, often with Cosette, seeking the most deserted side alleys of the boulevard, and entering churches at nightfall. He liked to go to Saint-Médard, which is the nearest church. When he did not take Cosette with him, she remained with the old woman; but the child's delight was to go out with the good man. She preferred an hour with him to all her rapturous *tête-à-têtes* with Catherine. He held her hand as they walked, and said sweet things to her.

It turned out that Cosette was a very gay little person.

The old woman attended to the housekeeping and cooking and went to market.

They lived soberly, always having a little fire, but like people in very moderate circumstances. Jean Valjean had made no alterations in the furniture as it was the first day; he had merely had the glass door leading to Cosette's dressing-room replaced by a solid door.

He still wore his yellow coat, his black breeches, and his old hat. In the street, he was taken for a poor man. It sometimes happened that kind-hearted women turned back to bestow a sou on him. Jean Valjean accepted the sou with a deep bow. It also happened occasionally that he encountered some poor wretch asking alms; then he looked behind him to make sure that no one was observing him, stealthily approached the unfortunate man, put a piece of money into his hand, often a silver coin, and walked rapidly away. This had its disadvantages. He began to be known in the neighborhood under the name of *the beggar who gives alms*.

The old *principal lodger*, a cross-looking creature, who was thoroughly permeated, so far as her neighbors were concerned, with the inquisitiveness peculiar to envious persons, scrutinized Jean Valjean a great deal, without his suspecting the fact. She was a little deaf, which rendered her talkative. There remained to her from her past, two teeth,—one above, the other below,—which she was continually knocking against each other. She had questioned Cosette, who had not been able to tell her anything, since she knew nothing herself except that she had come from Montfermeil. One morning, this spy saw Jean Valjean, with an air which struck the old gossip as peculiar, entering one of the uninhabited compartments of the hovel. She followed him with the step of an old cat, and was able to observe him without being seen, through a crack in the door, which was directly opposite him. Jean Valjean had his back turned towards this door, by way of greater security, no doubt. The old woman saw him fumble in his pocket and draw thence a case, scissors, and thread; then he began to rip the lining of one of the skirts of his coat, and from the opening he took a bit of yellowish paper, which he unfolded. The old woman recognized, with terror, the fact that it was a bank-bill for a thousand francs. It was the second or third only that she had seen in the course of her existence. She fled in alarm.

A moment later, Jean Valjean accosted her, and asked her to go and get this thousand-franc bill changed for him, adding that it was his quarterly income, which he had received the day before. "Where?" thought the old woman. "He did not go out until six o'clock in the evening, and the government bank certainly is not open at that hour." The old woman went to get the bill changed, and mentioned her surmises. That thousand-franc note, commented on and multiplied, produced a vast amount of terrified discussion among the gossips of the Rue des Vignes Saint-Marcel.

A few days later, it chanced that Jean Valjean was sawing some wood, in his shirt-sleeves, in the corridor. The old woman was in the chamber, putting things in order. She was alone. Cosette was occupied in admiring the wood as it was sawed. The old woman caught sight of the coat hanging on a nail, and examined it. The lining had been sewed up again. The good woman felt of it carefully, and thought she observed in the skirts and revers thicknesses of paper. More thousand-franc bank-bills, no doubt!

She also noticed that there were all sorts of things in the pockets. Not only the needles, thread, and scissors which she had seen, but a big pocket-book, a very large knife, and—a suspicious circumstance—several wigs of various colors. Each pocket of this coat had the air of being in a manner provided against unexpected accidents.

Thus the inhabitants of the house reached the last days of winter.

V

A FIVE-FRANC PIECE FALLS ON THE GROUND AND PRODUCES A TUMULT

Near Saint-Médard's church there was a poor man who was in the habit of crouching on the brink of a public well which had been condemned, and on whom Jean Valjean was fond of bestowing charity. He never passed this man without giving him a few sous. Sometimes he spoke to him. Those who envied this mendicant said that he belonged to the police. He was an ex-beadle of seventy-five, who was constantly mumbling his prayers.

One evening, as Jean Valjean was passing by, when he had not Cosette with him, he saw the beggar in his usual place, beneath the lantern which had just been lighted. The man seemed engaged in prayer, according to his custom, and was much bent over. Jean Valjean stepped up to him and placed his customary alms in his hand. The mendicant raised his eyes suddenly, stared intently at Jean Valjean, then dropped his head quickly. This movement was like a flash of lightning. Jean Valjean was seized with a shudder. It seemed to him that he had just caught sight, by the light of the street lantern, not of the placid and beaming visage of the old beadle, but of a well-known and startling face. He experienced the same impression that one would have on finding one's self, all of a sudden, face to face, in the dark, with a tiger. He recoiled, terrified, petrified, daring neither to breathe, to speak, to remain, nor to flee, staring at the beggar who had dropped his head, which was enveloped in a rag, and no longer appeared to know that he was there. At this strange moment, an instinct—possibly the mysterious instinct of self-preservation,—restrained Jean Valjean from uttering a word. The beggar had the same figure, the same rags, the same appearance as he had every day. "Bah!" said Jean Valjean, "I am mad! I am dreaming! Impossible!" And he returned profoundly troubled.

He hardly dared to confess, even to himself, that the face which he thought he had seen was the face of Javert.

That night, on thinking the matter over, he regretted not having questioned the man, in order to force him to raise his head a second time.

On the following day, at nightfall, he went back. The beggar was at his post. "Good day, my good man," said Jean Valjean, resolutely, handing him a sou. The beggar raised his head, and replied in a whining voice, "Thanks, my good sir." It was unmistakably the ex-beadle.

Jean Valjean felt completely reassured. He began to laugh. "How the deuce could I have thought that I saw Javert there?" he thought. "Am I going to lose my eyesight now?" And he thought no more about it.

A few days afterwards,—it might have been at eight o'clock in the evening,—he was in his room, and engaged in making Cosette spell aloud, when he heard the house door open and then shut again. This struck him as singular. The old woman, who was the only inhabitant of the house except himself, always went to bed at nightfall, so that she might not burn out her candles. Jean Valjean made a sign to Cosette to be quiet. He heard some one ascending the stairs. It might possibly be the old woman, who might have fallen ill and have been out to the apothecary's. Jean Valjean listened.

The step was heavy, and sounded like that of a man; but the old woman wore stout shoes, and there is nothing which so strongly resembles the step of a man as that of an old woman. Nevertheless, Jean Valjean blew out his candle.

He had sent Cosette to bed, saying to her in a low voice, "Get into bed very softly"; and as he kissed her brow, the steps paused.

Jean Valjean remained silent, motionless, with his back towards the door, seated on the chair from which he had not stirred, and holding his breath in the dark.

After the expiration of a rather long interval, he turned round, as he heard nothing more, and, as he raised his eyes towards the door of his chamber, he saw a light through the keyhole. This light formed a sort of sinister star in the blackness of the door and the wall. There was evidently some one there, who was holding a candle in his hand and listening.

Several minutes elapsed thus, and the light retreated. But he heard no sound of footsteps, which seemed to indicate that the person who had been listening at the door had removed his shoes.

Jean Valjean threw himself, all dressed as he was, on his bed, and could not close his eyes all night.

At daybreak, just as he was falling into a doze through fatigue, he was awakened by the creaking of a door which opened on some attic at the end of the corridor, then he heard the same masculine footstep which had ascended the stairs on the preceding evening. The step was approaching. He sprang off the bed and applied his eye to the keyhole, which was tolerably large, hoping to see the person who had made his way by night into the house and had listened at his door, as he passed. It was a man, in fact, who passed, this time without pausing, in front of Jean Valjean's chamber. The corridor was too dark to allow of the person's face being distinguished; but when the man reached the staircase, a ray of light from without made it stand out like a silhouette, and Jean Valjean had a complete view of his back. The man was of lofty stature, clad in a long frock-coat, with a cudgel under his arm. The formidable neck and shoulders belonged to Javert.

Jean Valjean might have attempted to catch another glimpse of him through his window opening on the boulevard, but he would have been obliged to open the window: he dared not.

It was evident that this man had entered with a key, and like himself. Who had given him that key? What was the meaning of this?

When the old woman came to do the work, at seven o'clock in the morning, Jean Valjean cast a penetrating glance on her, but he did not question her. The good woman appeared as usual.

As she swept up she remarked to him:—

"Possibly Monsieur may have heard some one come in last night?"

At that age, and on that boulevard, eight o'clock in the evening was the dead of the night.

"That is true, by the way," he replied, in the most natural tone possible. "Who was it?"

"It was a new lodger who has come into the house," said the old woman.

"And what is his name?"

"I don't know exactly; Dumont, or Daumont, or some name of that sort."

"And who is this Monsieur Dumont?"

The old woman gazed at him with her little polecat eyes, and answered:—

"A gentleman of property, like yourself."

Perhaps she had no ulterior meaning. Jean Valjean thought he perceived one.

When the old woman had taken her departure, he did up a hundred francs which he had in a cupboard, into a roll, and put it in his pocket. In spite of all the precautions which he took in this operation so that he might not be heard rattling silver, a hundred-sou piece escaped from his hands and rolled noisily on the floor.

When darkness came on, he descended and carefully scrutinized both sides of the boulevard. He saw no one. The boulevard appeared to be absolutely deserted. It is true that a person can conceal himself behind trees.

He went upstairs again.

"Come." he said to Cosette.

He took her by the hand, and they both went out.

BOOK FIFTH

FOR A BLACK HUNT, A MUTE PACK

I

The Zigzags of Strategy

An observation here becomes necessary, in view of the pages which the reader is about to peruse, and of others which will be met with further on.

The author of this book, who regrets the necessity of mentioning himself, has been absent from Paris for many years. Paris has been transformed since he quitted it. A new city has arisen, which is, after a fashion, unknown to him. There is no need for him to say that he loves Paris: Paris is his mind's natal city. In consequence of demolitions and reconstructions, the Paris of his youth, that Paris which he bore away religiously in his memory, is now a Paris of days gone by. He must be permitted to speak of that Paris as though it still existed. It is possible that when the author conducts his readers to a spot and says, "In such a street there stands such and such a house," neither street nor house will any longer exist in that locality. Readers may verify the facts if they care to take the trouble. For his own part, he is unacquainted with the new Paris, and he writes with the old Paris before his eyes in an illusion which is precious to him. It is a delight to him to dream that there still lingers behind him something of that which he beheld when he was in his own country, and that all has not vanished. So long as you go and come in your native land, you imagine that those streets are a matter of indifference to you; that those windows, those roofs, and those doors are nothing to you; that those walls are strangers to you; that those trees are merely the first encountered haphazard; that those houses, which you do not enter, are useless to you; that the pavements which you tread are merely stones. Later on, when you are no longer there, you perceive that the streets are dear to you; that you miss those roofs, those doors; and that those walls are necessary to you, those trees are well beloved by you; that you entered those houses which you never entered, every day, and that you have left a part of your heart, of your blood, of your soul, in those pavements. All those places which you no longer behold, which you may never behold again, perchance, and whose memory you have cherished, take on a melancholy charm, recur to your mind with the melancholy of an apparition, make the holy land visible to you, and are, so to speak, the very form of France, and you love them; and you call them up as they are, as they were, and you persist in this, and you will submit to no change: for you are attached to the figure of your fatherland as to the face of your mother.

May we, then, be permitted to speak of the past in the present? That said, we beg the reader to take note of it, and we continue.

Jean Valjean instantly quitted the boulevard and plunged into the streets, taking the most intricate lines which he could devise, returning on his track at times, to make sure that he was not being followed.

THIS MANŒUVRE IS PECULIAR TO the hunted stag. On soil where an imprint of the track may be left, this manœuvre possesses, among other advantages, that of deceiving the huntsmen and the dogs, by throwing them on the wrong scent. In venery this is called *false re-imbushment*.

The moon was full that night. Jean Valjean was not sorry for this. The moon, still very close to the horizon, cast great masses of light and shadow in the streets. Jean Valjean could glide along close to the houses on the dark side, and yet keep watch on the light side. He did not, perhaps, take sufficiently into consideration the fact that the dark side escaped him. Still, in the deserted lanes which lie near the Rue Poliveau, he thought he felt certain that no one was following him.

Cosette walked on without asking any questions. The sufferings of the first six years of her life had instilled something passive into her nature. Moreover,—and this is a remark to which we shall frequently have occasion to recur,—she had grown used, without being herself aware of it, to the peculiarities of this good man and to the freaks of destiny. And then she was with him, and she felt safe.

Jean Valjean knew no more where he was going than did Cosette. He trusted in God, as she trusted in him. It seemed as though he also were clinging to the hand of some one greater than himself; he thought he felt a being leading him, though invisible. However, he had no settled idea, no plan, no project. He was not even absolutely sure that it was Javert, and then it might have been Javert, without Javert knowing that he was Jean Valjean. Was not he disguised? Was not he believed to be dead? Still, queer things had been going on for several days. He wanted no more of them. He was determined not to return to the Gorbeau house. Like the wild animal chased from its lair, he was seeking a hole in which he might hide until he could find one where he might dwell.

Jean Valjean described many and varied labyrinths in the Mouffetard quarter, which was already asleep, as though the discipline of the Middle Ages and the yoke of the curfew still existed; he combined in various manners, with cunning strategy, the Rue Censier and the Rue Copeau, the Rue du Battoir-Saint-Victor and the Rue du Puits l'Ermite. There are lodging houses in this locality, but he did not even enter one, finding nothing which suited him. He had no doubt that if any one had chanced to be upon his track, they would have lost it.

As eleven o'clock struck from Saint-Étienne-du-Mont, he was traversing the Rue de Pontoise, in front of the office of the commissary of police, situated at No. 14. A few moments later, the instinct of which we have spoken above made him turn round. At that moment he saw distinctly, thanks to the commissary's lantern, which betrayed them, three men who were following him closely, pass, one after the other, under that lantern, on the dark side of the street. One of the three entered the alley leading to the commissary's house. The one who marched at their head struck him as decidedly suspicious.

"Come, child," he said to Cosette; and he made haste to quit the Rue Pontoise.

He took a circuit, turned into the Passage des Patriarches, which was closed on account of the hour, strode along the Rue de l'Épée-de-Bois and the Rue de l'Arbalète, and plunged into the Rue des Postes.

At that time there was a square formed by the intersection of streets, where the College Rollin stands to-day, and where the Rue Neuve-Sainte-Geneviève turns off.

It is understood, of course, that the Rue Neuve-Sainte-Geneviève is an old street, and that a posting-chaise does not pass through the Rue des Postes once in ten years. In the thirteenth century this Rue des Postes was inhabited by potters, and its real name is Rue des Pots.

The moon cast a livid light into this open space. Jean Valjean went into ambush in a doorway, calculating that if the men were still following him, he could not fail to get a good look at them, as they traversed this illuminated space.

In point of fact, three minutes had not elapsed when the men made their appearance. There were four of them now. All were tall, dressed in long, brown coats, with round hats, and huge cudgels in their hands. Their great stature and their vast fists rendered them no less alarming than did their sinister stride through the darkness. One would have pronounced them four spectres disguised as bourgeois.

They halted in the middle of the space and formed a group, like men in consultation. They had an air of indecision. The one who appeared to be their leader turned round and pointed hastily with his right hand in the direction which Jean Valjean had taken; another seemed to indicate the contrary direction with considerable obstinacy. At the moment when the first man wheeled round, the moon fell full in his face. Jean Valjean recognized Javert perfectly.

II

IT IS LUCKY THAT THE PONT D'AUSTERLITZ BEARS CARRIAGES

Uncertainty was at an end for Jean Valjean: fortunately it still lasted for the men. He took advantage of their hesitation. It was time lost for them, but gained for him. He slipped from under the gate where he had concealed himself, and went down the Rue des Postes, towards the region of the Jardin des Plantes. Cosette was beginning to be tired. He took her in his arms and carried her. There were no passers-by, and the street lanterns had not been lighted on account of there being a moon.

He redoubled his pace.

In a few strides he had reached the Goblet potteries, on the front of which the moonlight rendered distinctly legible the ancient inscription:—

> *De Goblet fils c'est ici la fabrique;*
> *Venez choisir des cruches et des brocs,*
> *Des pots à fleurs, des tuyaux, de la brique.*
> *A tout venant le Cœur vend des Carreaux.*

He left behind him the Rue de la Clef, then the Fountain Saint-Victor, skirted the Jardin des Plantes by the lower streets, and reached the quay. There he turned round. The quay was deserted. The streets were deserted. There was no one behind him. He drew a long breath.

He gained the Pont d'Austerlitz.

Tolls were still collected there at that epoch.

He presented himself at the toll office and handed over a sou.

"It is two sous," said the old soldier in charge of the bridge. "You are carrying a child who can walk. Pay for two."

He paid, vexed that his passage should have aroused remark. Every flight should be an imperceptible slipping away.

A heavy cart was crossing the Seine at the same time as himself, and on its way, like him, to the right bank. This was of use to him. He could traverse the bridge in the shadow of the cart.

Towards the middle of the Bridge, Cosette, whose feet were benumbed, wanted to walk. He set her on the ground and took her hand again.

The bridge once crossed, he perceived some timber-yards on his right. He directed his course thither. In order to reach them, it was necessary to risk himself in a tolerably large unsheltered and illuminated space. He did not hesitate. Those who were on his track had evidently lost the scent, and Jean Valjean believed himself to be out of danger. Hunted, yes; followed, no.

A little street, the Rue du Chemin-Vert-Saint-Antoine, opened out between two timber-yards enclosed in walls. This street was dark and narrow and seemed made expressly for him. Before entering it he cast a glance behind him.

From the point where he stood he could see the whole extent of the Pont d'Austerlitz.

Four shadows were just entering on the bridge.

These shadows had their backs turned to the Jardin des Plantes and were on their way to the right bank.

These four shadows were the four men.

Jean Valjean shuddered like the wild beast which is recaptured.

One hope remained to him; it was, that the men had not, perhaps, stepped on the bridge, and had not caught sight of him while he was crossing the large illuminated space, holding Cosette by the hand.

In that case, by plunging into the little street before him, he might escape, if he could reach the timber-yards, the marshes, the market-gardens, the uninhabited ground which was not built upon.

It seemed to him that he might commit himself to that silent little street. He entered it.

III

To Wit, the Plan of Paris in 1727

Three hundred paces further on, he arrived at a point where the street forked. It separated into two streets, which ran in a slanting line, one to the right, and the other to the left.

Jean Valjean had before him what resembled the two branches of a Y. Which should he choose? He did not hesitate, but took the one on the right.

Why?

Because that to the left ran towards a suburb, that is to say, towards inhabited regions, and the right branch towards the open country, that is to say, towards deserted regions.

However, they no longer walked very fast. Cosette's pace retarded Jean Valjean's.

He took her up and carried her again. Cosette laid her head on the shoulder of the good man and said not a word.

He turned round from time to time and looked behind him. He took care to keep always on the dark side of the street. The street was straight in his rear. The first two or three times that he turned round he saw nothing; the silence was profound, and he continued his march somewhat reassured. All at once, on turning round, he thought he perceived in the portion of the street which he had just passed through, far off in the obscurity, something which was moving.

He rushed forward precipitately rather than walked, hoping to find some side-street, to make his escape through it, and thus to break his scent once more.

He arrived at a wall.

This wall, however, did not absolutely prevent further progress; it was a wall which bordered a transverse street, in which the one he had taken ended.

Here again, he was obliged to come to a decision; should he go to the right or to the left.

He glanced to the right. The fragmentary lane was prolonged between buildings which were either sheds or barns, then ended at a blind alley. The extremity of the cul-de-sac was distinctly visible,—a lofty white wall.

He glanced to the left. On that side the lane was open, and about two hundred paces further on, ran into a street of which it was the affluent. On that side lay safety.

At the moment when Jean Valjean was meditating a turn to the left, in an effort to reach the street which he saw at the end of the lane, he perceived a sort of motionless, black statue at the corner of the lane and the street towards which he was on the point of directing his steps.

It was some one, a man, who had evidently just been posted there, and who was barring the passage and waiting.

Jean Valjean recoiled.

The point of Paris where Jean Valjean found himself, situated between the Faubourg Saint-Antoine and la Râpée, is one of those which recent improvements have transformed from top to bottom,— resulting in disfigurement according to some, and in a transfiguration according to others. The market-gardens, the timber-yards, and the old buildings have been effaced. To-day, there are brand-new, wide streets, arenas, circuses, hippodromes, railway stations, and a prison, Mazas, there; progress, as the reader sees, with its antidote.

Half a century ago, in that ordinary, popular tongue, which is all compounded of traditions, which persists in calling the Institut *les Quatre-Nations*, and the Opera-Comique *Feydeau*, the precise spot whither Jean Valjean had arrived was called *le Petit-Picpus*. The Porte Saint-Jacques, the Porte Paris, the Barrière des Sergents, the Porcherons, la Galiote, les Célestins, les Capucins, le Mail, la Bourbe, l'Arbre de Cracovie, la Petite-Pologne—these are the names of old Paris which survive amid the new. The memory of the populace hovers over these relics of the past.

Le Petit-Picpus, which, moreover, hardly ever had any existence, and never was more than the outline of a quarter, had nearly the monkish aspect of a Spanish town. The roads were not much paved; the streets were not much built up. With the exception of the two or three streets, of which we shall presently speak, all was wall and solitude there. Not a shop, not a vehicle, hardly a candle lighted here and there in the windows; all lights extinguished after ten o'clock. Gardens, convents, timber-yards, marshes; occasional lowly dwellings and great walls as high as the houses.

Such was this quarter in the last century. The Revolution snubbed it soundly. The republican government demolished and cut through it.

Rubbish shoots were established there. Thirty years ago, this quarter was disappearing under the erasing process of new buildings. To-day, it has been utterly blotted out. The Petit-Picpus, of which no existing plan has preserved a trace, is indicated with sufficient clearness in the plan of 1727, published at Paris by Denis Thierry, Rue Saint-Jacques, opposite the Rue du Plâtre; and at Lyons, by Jean Girin, Rue Mercière, at the sign of Prudence. Petit-Picpus had, as we have just mentioned, a Y of streets, formed by the Rue du Chemin-Vert-Saint-Antoine, which spread out in two branches, taking on the left the name of Little Picpus Street, and on the right the name of the Rue Polonceau. The two limbs of the Y were connected at the apex as by a bar; this bar was called Rue Droit-Mur. The Rue Polonceau ended there; Rue Petit-Picpus passed on, and ascended towards the Lenoir market. A person coming from the Seine reached the extremity of the Rue Polonceau, and had on his right the Rue Droit-Mur, turning abruptly at a right angle, in front of him the wall of that street, and on his right a truncated prolongation of the Rue Droit-Mur, which had no issue and was called the Cul-de-Sac Genrot.

It was here that Jean Valjean stood.

As we have just said, on catching sight of that black silhouette standing on guard at the angle of the Rue Droit-Mur and the Rue Petit-Picpus, he recoiled. There could be no doubt of it. That phantom was lying in wait for him.

What was he to do?

The time for retreating was passed. That which he had perceived in movement an instant before, in the distant darkness, was Javert and his squad without a doubt. Javert was probably already at the commencement of the street at whose end Jean Valjean stood. Javert, to all appearances, was acquainted with this little labyrinth, and had taken his precautions by sending one of his men to guard the exit. These surmises, which so closely resembled proofs, whirled suddenly, like a handful of dust caught up by an unexpected gust of wind, through Jean Valjean's mournful brain. He examined the Cul-de-Sac Genrot; there he was cut off. He examined the Rue Petit-Picpus; there stood a sentinel. He saw that black form standing out in relief against the white pavement, illuminated by the moon; to advance was to fall into this man's hands; to retreat was to fling himself into Javert's arms. Jean Valjean felt himself caught, as in a net, which was slowly contracting; he gazed heavenward in despair.

IV

The Gropings of Flight

In order to understand what follows, it is requisite to form an exact idea of the Droit-Mur lane, and, in particular, of the angle which one leaves on the left when one emerges from the Rue Polonceau into this lane. Droit-Mur lane was almost entirely bordered on the right, as far as the Rue Petit-Picpus, by houses of mean aspect; on the left by a solitary building of severe outlines, composed of numerous parts which grew gradually higher by a story or two as they approached the Rue Petit-Picpus side; so that this building, which was very lofty on the Rue Petit-Picpus side, was tolerably low on the side adjoining the Rue Polonceau. There, at the angle of which we have spoken, it descended to such a degree that it consisted of merely a wall. This wall did not abut directly on the street; it formed a deeply retreating niche, concealed by its two corners from two observers who might have been, one in the Rue Polonceau, the other in the Rue Droit-Mur.

Beginning with these angles of the niche, the wall extended along the Rue Polonceau as far as a house which bore the number 49, and along the Rue Droit-Mur, where the fragment was much shorter, as far as the gloomy building which we have mentioned and whose gable it intersected, thus forming another retreating angle in the street. This gable was sombre of aspect; only one window was visible, or, to speak more correctly, two shutters covered with a sheet of zinc and kept constantly closed.

The state of the places of which we are here giving a description is rigorously exact, and will certainly awaken a very precise memory in the mind of old inhabitants of the quarter.

The niche was entirely filled by a thing which resembled a colossal and wretched door; it was a vast, formless assemblage of perpendicular planks, the upper ones being broader than the lower, bound together by long transverse strips of iron. At one side there was a carriage gate of the ordinary dimensions, and which had evidently not been cut more than fifty years previously.

A linden-tree showed its crest above the niche, and the wall was covered with ivy on the side of the Rue Polonceau.

In the imminent peril in which Jean Valjean found himself, this sombre building had about it a solitary and uninhabited look which tempted him. He ran his eyes rapidly over it; he said to himself, that if he could contrive to get inside it, he might save himself. First he conceived an idea, then a hope.

In the central portion of the front of this building, on the Rue Droit-Mur side, there were at all the windows of the different stories ancient cistern pipes of lead. The various branches of the pipes which led from one central pipe to all these little basins sketched out a sort of tree on the front. These ramifications of pipes with their hundred elbows imitated those old leafless vine-stocks which writhe over the fronts of old farm-houses.

This odd espalier, with its branches of lead and iron, was the first thing that struck Jean Valjean. He seated Cosette with her back against a stone post, with an injunction to be silent, and ran to the spot where the conduit touched the pavement. Perhaps there was some way of climbing up by it and entering the house. But the pipe was dilapidated and past service, and hardly hung to its fastenings. Moreover, all the windows of this silent dwelling were grated with heavy iron bars, even the attic windows in the roof. And then, the moon fell full upon that façade, and the man who was watching at the corner of the street would have seen Jean Valjean in the act of climbing. And finally, what was to be done with Cosette? How was she to be drawn up to the top of a three-story house?

He gave up all idea of climbing by means of the drain-pipe, and crawled along the wall to get back into the Rue Polonceau.

When he reached the slant of the wall where he had left Cosette, he noticed that no one could see him there. As we have just explained, he was concealed from all eyes, no matter from which direction they were approaching; besides this, he was in the shadow. Finally, there were two doors; perhaps they might be forced. The wall above which he saw the linden-tree and the ivy evidently abutted on a garden where he could, at least, hide himself, although there were as yet no leaves on the trees, and spend the remainder of the night.

Time was passing; he must act quickly.

He felt over the carriage door, and immediately recognized the fact that it was impracticable outside and in.

He approached the other door with more hope; it was frightfully decrepit; its very immensity rendered it less solid; the planks were rotten; the iron bands—there were only three of them—were rusted. It seemed as though it might be possible to pierce this worm-eaten barrier.

On examining it he found that the door was not a door; it had neither hinges, cross-bars, lock, nor fissure in the middle; the iron bands traversed it from side to side without any break. Through the crevices in the planks he caught a view of unhewn slabs and blocks of stone roughly cemented together, which passers-by might still have seen there ten years ago. He was forced to acknowledge with consternation that this apparent door was simply the wooden decoration of a building against which it was placed. It was easy to tear off a plank; but then, one found one's self face to face with a wall.

V

WHICH WOULD BE IMPOSSIBLE WITH GAS LANTERNS

At that moment a heavy and measured sound began to be audible at some distance. Jean Valjean risked a glance round the corner of the street. Seven or eight soldiers, drawn up in a platoon, had just debouched into the Rue Polonceau. He saw the gleam of their bayonets. They were advancing towards him; these soldiers, at whose head he distinguished Javert's tall figure, advanced slowly and cautiously. They halted frequently; it was plain that they were searching all the nooks of the walls and all the embrasures of the doors and alleys.

This was some patrol that Javert had encountered—there could be no mistake as to this surmise—and whose aid he had demanded.

Javert's two acolytes were marching in their ranks.

At the rate at which they were marching, and in consideration of the halts which they were making, it would take them about a quarter of an hour to reach the spot where Jean Valjean stood. It was a frightful moment. A few minutes only separated Jean Valjean from that terrible precipice which yawned before him for the third time. And the galleys now meant not only the galleys, but Cosette lost to him forever; that is to say, a life resembling the interior of a tomb.

There was but one thing which was possible.

Jean Valjean had this peculiarity, that he carried, as one might say, two beggar's pouches: in one he kept his saintly thoughts; in the other the redoubtable talents of a convict. He rummaged in the one or the other, according to circumstances.

Among his other resources, thanks to his numerous escapes from the prison at Toulon, he was, as it will be remembered, a past master in the incredible art of crawling up without ladder or climbing-irons, by sheer muscular force, by leaning on the nape of his neck, his shoulders, his hips, and his knees, by helping himself on the rare projections of the stone, in the right angle of a wall, as high as the sixth story, if need be; an art which has rendered so celebrated and so alarming that corner of the wall of the Conciergerie of Paris by which Battemolle, condemned to death, made his escape twenty years ago.

Jean Valjean measured with his eyes the wall above which he espied the linden; it was about eighteen feet in height. The angle which it formed with the gable of the large building was filled, at its lower extremity, by a mass of masonry of a triangular shape, probably intended to preserve that too convenient corner from the rubbish of those dirty creatures called the passers-by. This practice of filling up corners of the wall is much in use in Paris.

This mass was about five feet in height; the space above the summit of this mass which it was necessary to climb was not more than fourteen feet.

The wall was surmounted by a flat stone without a coping.

Cosette was the difficulty, for she did not know how to climb a wall. Should he abandon her? Jean Valjean did not once think of that. It was impossible to carry her. A man's whole strength is required to successfully carry out these singular ascents. The least burden would disturb his centre of gravity and pull him downwards.

A rope would have been required; Jean Valjean had none. Where was he to get a rope at midnight, in the Rue Polonceau? Certainly, if Jean Valjean had had a kingdom, he would have given it for a rope at that moment.

All extreme situations have their lightning flashes which sometimes dazzle, sometimes illuminate us.

Jean Valjean's despairing glance fell on the street lantern-post of the blind alley Genrot.

At that epoch there were no gas-jets in the streets of Paris. At nightfall lanterns placed at regular distances were lighted; they were ascended and descended by means of a rope, which traversed the street from side to side, and was adjusted in a groove of the post. The pulley over which this rope ran was fastened underneath the lantern in a little iron box, the key to which was kept by the lamp-lighter, and the rope itself was protected by a metal case.

Jean Valjean, with the energy of a supreme struggle, crossed the street at one bound, entered the blind alley, broke the latch of the little box with the point of his knife, and an instant later he was beside Cosette once more. He had a rope. These gloomy inventors of expedients work rapidly when they are fighting against fatality.

We have already explained that the lanterns had not been lighted that night. The lantern in the Cul-de-Sac Genrot was thus naturally extinct, like the rest; and one could pass directly under it without even noticing that it was no longer in its place.

Nevertheless, the hour, the place, the darkness, Jean Valjean's absorption, his singular gestures, his goings and comings, all had begun to render Cosette uneasy. Any other child than she would have given vent to loud shrieks long before. She contented herself with plucking Jean Valjean by the skirt of his coat. They could hear the sound of the patrol's approach ever more and more distinctly.

"Father," said she, in a very low voice, "I am afraid. Who is coming yonder?"

"Hush!" replied the unhappy man; "it is Madame Thénardier."

Cosette shuddered. He added:—

"Say nothing. Don't interfere with me. If you cry out, if you weep, the Thénardier is lying in wait for you. She is coming to take you back."

Then, without haste, but without making a useless movement, with firm and curt precision, the more remarkable at a moment when the patrol and Javert might come upon him at any moment, he undid his cravat, passed it round Cosette's body under the armpits, taking care that it should not hurt the child, fastened this cravat to one end of the rope, by means of that knot which seafaring men call a "swallow knot," took the other end of the rope in his teeth, pulled off his shoes and stockings, which he threw over the wall, stepped upon the mass of masonry, and began to raise himself in the angle of the wall and the gable with as much solidity and certainty as though he had the rounds of a ladder under his feet and elbows. Half a minute had not elapsed when he was resting on his knees on the wall.

Cosette gazed at him in stupid amazement, without uttering a word. Jean Valjean's injunction, and the name of Madame Thénardier, had chilled her blood.

All at once she heard Jean Valjean's voice crying to her, though in a very low tone:—

"Put your back against the wall."

She obeyed.

"Don't say a word, and don't be alarmed," went on Jean Valjean.

And she felt herself lifted from the ground.

Before she had time to recover herself, she was on the top of the wall.

Jean Valjean grasped her, put her on his back, took her two tiny hands in his large left hand, lay down flat on his stomach and crawled along on top of the wall as far as the cant. As he had guessed, there stood a building whose roof started from the top of the wooden barricade and descended to within a very short distance of the ground, with a gentle slope which grazed the linden-tree. A lucky circumstance, for the wall was much higher on this side than on the street side. Jean Valjean could only see the ground at a great depth below him.

He had just reached the slope of the roof, and had not yet left the crest of the wall, when a violent uproar announced the arrival of the patrol. The thundering voice of Javert was audible:—

"Search the blind alley! The Rue Droit-Mur is guarded! so is the Rue Petit-Picpus. I'll answer for it that he is in the blind alley."

The soldiers rushed into the Genrot alley.

Jean Valjean allowed himself to slide down the roof, still holding fast to Cosette, reached the linden-tree, and leaped to the ground. Whether from terror or courage, Cosette had not breathed a sound, though her hands were a little abraded.

VI

The Beginning of an Enigma

Jean Valjean found himself in a sort of garden which was very vast and of singular aspect; one of those melancholy gardens which seem made to be looked at in winter and at night. This garden was oblong in shape, with an alley of large poplars at the further end, tolerably tall forest trees in the corners, and an unshaded space in the centre, where could be seen a very large, solitary tree, then several fruit-trees, gnarled and bristling like bushes, beds of vegetables, a melon patch, whose glass frames sparkled in the moonlight, and an old well. Here and there stood stone benches which seemed black with moss. The alleys were bordered with gloomy and very erect little shrubs. The grass had half taken possession of them, and a green mould covered the rest.

Jean Valjean had beside him the building whose roof had served him as a means of descent, a pile of fagots, and, behind the fagots, directly against the wall, a stone statue, whose mutilated face was no longer anything more than a shapeless mask which loomed vaguely through the gloom.

The building was a sort of ruin, where dismantled chambers were distinguishable, one of which, much encumbered, seemed to serve as a shed.

The large building of the Rue Droit-Mur, which had a wing on the Rue Petit-Picpus, turned two façades, at right angles, towards this garden. These interior façades were even more tragic than the exterior. All the windows were grated. Not a gleam of light was visible at any one of them. The upper story had scuttles like prisons. One of those façades cast its shadow on the other, which fell over the garden like an immense black pall.

No other house was visible. The bottom of the garden was lost in mist and darkness. Nevertheless, walls could be confusedly made out, which intersected as though there were more cultivated land beyond, and the low roofs of the Rue Polonceau.

Nothing more wild and solitary than this garden could be imagined. There was no one in it, which was quite natural in view of the hour; but it did not seem as though this spot were made for any one to walk in, even in broad daylight.

Jean Valjean's first care had been to get hold of his shoes and put them on again, then to step under the shed with Cosette. A man who is fleeing never thinks himself sufficiently hidden. The child, whose thoughts were still on the Thénardier, shared his instinct for withdrawing from sight as much as possible.

Cosette trembled and pressed close to him. They heard the tumultuous noise of the patrol searching the blind alley and the streets; the blows of their gun-stocks against the stones; Javert's appeals to the police spies whom he had posted, and his imprecations mingled with words which could not be distinguished.

At the expiration of a quarter of an hour it seemed as though that species of stormy roar were becoming more distant. Jean Valjean held his breath.

He had laid his hand lightly on Cosette's mouth.

However, the solitude in which he stood was so strangely calm, that this frightful uproar, close and furious as it was, did not disturb him by so much as the shadow of a misgiving. It seemed as though those walls had been built of the deaf stones of which the Scriptures speak.

All at once, in the midst of this profound calm, a fresh sound arose; a sound as celestial, divine, ineffable, ravishing, as the other had been horrible. It was a hymn which issued from the gloom, a dazzling burst of prayer and harmony in the obscure and alarming silence of the night; women's voices, but voices composed at one and the same time of the pure accents of virgins and the innocent accents of children,—voices which are not of the earth, and which resemble those that the newborn infant still hears, and which the dying man hears already. This song proceeded from the gloomy edifice which towered above the garden. At the moment when the hubbub of demons retreated, one would have said that a choir of angels was approaching through the gloom.

Cosette and Jean Valjean fell on their knees.

They knew not what it was, they knew not where they were; but both of them, the man and the child, the penitent and the innocent, felt that they must kneel.

These voices had this strange characteristic, that they did not prevent the building from seeming to be deserted. It was a supernatural chant in an uninhabited house.

While these voices were singing, Jean Valjean thought of nothing. He no longer beheld the night; he beheld a blue sky. It seemed to him that he felt those wings which we all have within us, unfolding.

The song died away. It may have lasted a long time. Jean Valjean could not have told. Hours of ecstasy are never more than a moment.

All fell silent again. There was no longer anything in the street; there was nothing in the garden. That which had menaced, that which had reassured him,—all had vanished. The breeze swayed a few dry weeds on the crest of the wall, and they gave out a faint, sweet, melancholy sound.

VII

Continuation of the Enigma

The night wind had risen, which indicated that it must be between one and two o'clock in the morning. Poor Cosette said nothing. As she had seated herself beside him and leaned her head against him, Jean Valjean had fancied that she was asleep. He bent down and looked at her. Cosette's eyes were wide open, and her thoughtful air pained Jean Valjean.

She was still trembling.

"Are you sleepy?" said Jean Valjean.

"I am very cold," she replied.

A moment later she resumed:—

"Is she still there?"

"Who?" said Jean Valjean.

"Madame Thénardier."

Jean Valjean had already forgotten the means which he had employed to make Cosette keep silent.

"Ah!" said he, "she is gone. You need fear nothing further."

The child sighed as though a load had been lifted from her breast.

The ground was damp, the shed open on all sides, the breeze grew more keen every instant. The goodman took off his coat and wrapped it round Cosette.

"Are you less cold now?" said he.

"Oh, yes, father."

"Well, wait for me a moment. I will soon be back."

He quitted the ruin and crept along the large building, seeking a better shelter. He came across doors, but they were closed. There were bars at all the windows of the ground floor.

Just after he had turned the inner angle of the edifice, he observed that he was coming to some arched windows, where he perceived a light. He stood on tiptoe and peeped through one of these windows. They all opened on a tolerably vast hall, paved with large flagstones, cut up by arcades and pillars, where only a tiny light and great shadows were visible. The light came from a taper which was burning in one corner. The apartment was deserted, and nothing was stirring in it.

Nevertheless, by dint of gazing intently he thought he perceived on the ground something which appeared to be covered with a winding-sheet, and which resembled a human form. This form was lying face downward, flat on the pavement, with the arms extended in the form of a cross, in the immobility of death. One would have said, judging from a sort of serpent which undulated over the floor, that this sinister form had a rope round its neck.

The whole chamber was bathed in that mist of places which are sparely illuminated, which adds to horror.

Jean Valjean often said afterwards, that, although many funereal spectres had crossed his path in life, he had never beheld anything more blood-curdling and terrible than that enigmatical form accomplishing some inexplicable mystery in that gloomy place, and beheld thus at night. It was alarming to suppose that that thing was perhaps dead; and still more alarming to think that it was perhaps alive.

He had the courage to plaster his face to the glass, and to watch whether the thing would move. In spite of his remaining thus what seemed to him a very long time, the outstretched form made no movement. All at once he felt himself overpowered by an inexpressible terror, and he fled. He began to run towards the shed, not daring to look behind him. It seemed to him, that if he turned his head, he should see that form following him with great strides and waving its arms.

He reached the ruin all out of breath. His knees were giving way beneath him; the perspiration was pouring from him.

Where was he? Who could ever have imagined anything like that sort of sepulchre in the midst of Paris! What was this strange house? An edifice full of nocturnal mystery, calling to souls through the darkness with the voice of angels, and when they came, offering them abruptly that terrible vision; promising to open the radiant portals of heaven, and then opening the horrible gates of the tomb! And it actually was an edifice, a house, which bore a number on the street! It was not a dream! He had to touch the stones to convince himself that such was the fact.

Cold, anxiety, uneasiness, the emotions of the night, had given him a genuine fever, and all these ideas were clashing together in his brain.

He stepped up to Cosette. She was asleep.

VIII

The Enigma Becomes Doubly Mysterious

The child had laid her head on a stone and fallen asleep.

He sat down beside her and began to think. Little by little, as he gazed at her, he grew calm and regained possession of his freedom of mind.

He clearly perceived this truth, the foundation of his life henceforth, that so long as she was there, so long as he had her near him, he should need nothing except for her, he should fear nothing except for her. He was not even conscious that he was very cold, since he had taken off his coat to cover her.

Nevertheless, athwart this reverie into which he had fallen he had heard for some time a peculiar noise. It was like the tinkling of a bell. This sound proceeded from the garden. It could be heard distinctly though faintly. It resembled the faint, vague music produced by the bells of cattle at night in the pastures.

This noise made Valjean turn round.

He looked and saw that there was some one in the garden.

A being resembling a man was walking amid the bell-glasses of the melon beds, rising, stooping, halting, with regular movements, as though he were dragging or spreading out something on the ground. This person appeared to limp.

Jean Valjean shuddered with the continual tremor of the unhappy. For them everything is hostile and suspicious. They distrust the day because it enables people to see them, and the night because it aids in surprising them. A little while before he had shivered because the garden was deserted, and now he shivered because there was some one there.

He fell back from chimerical terrors to real terrors. He said to himself that Javert and the spies had, perhaps, not taken their departure; that they had, no doubt, left people on the watch in the street; that if this man should discover him in the garden, he would cry out for help against thieves and deliver him up. He took the sleeping Cosette gently in his arms and carried her behind a heap of old furniture, which was out of use, in the most remote corner of the shed. Cosette did not stir.

From that point he scrutinized the appearance of the being in the melon patch. The strange thing about it was, that the sound of the bell followed each of this man's movements. When the man approached, the sound approached; when the man retreated, the sound retreated; if he made any hasty gesture, a tremolo accompanied the gesture; when he halted, the sound ceased. It appeared evident that the bell was attached to that man; but what could that signify? Who was this man who had a bell suspended about him like a ram or an ox?

As he put these questions to himself, he touched Cosette's hands. They were icy cold.

"Ah! good God!" he cried.

He spoke to her in a low voice:—

"Cosette!"

She did not open her eyes.

He shook her vigorously.

She did not wake.

"Is she dead?" he said to himself, and sprang to his feet, quivering from head to foot.

The most frightful thoughts rushed pell-mell through his mind. There are moments when hideous surmises assail us like a cohort of furies, and violently force the partitions of our brains. When those we love are in question, our prudence invents every sort of madness. He remembered that sleep in the open air on a cold night may be fatal.

Cosette was pale, and had fallen at full length on the ground at his feet, without a movement.

He listened to her breathing: she still breathed, but with a respiration which seemed to him weak and on the point of extinction.

How was he to warm her back to life? How was he to rouse her? All that was not connected with this vanished from his thoughts. He rushed wildly from the ruin.

It was absolutely necessary that Cosette should be in bed and beside a fire in less than a quarter of an hour.

IX

The Man with the Bell

He walked straight up to the man whom he saw in the garden. He had taken in his hand the roll of silver which was in the pocket of his waistcoat.

The man's head was bent down, and he did not see him approaching. In a few strides Jean Valjean stood beside him.

Jean Valjean accosted him with the cry:—

"One hundred francs!"

The man gave a start and raised his eyes.

"You can earn a hundred francs," went on Jean Valjean, "if you will grant me shelter for this night."

The moon shone full upon Jean Valjean's terrified countenance.

"What! so it is you, Father Madeleine!" said the man.

That name, thus pronounced, at that obscure hour, in that unknown spot, by that strange man, made Jean Valjean start back.

He had expected anything but that. The person who thus addressed him was a bent and lame old man, dressed almost like a peasant, who wore on his left knee a leather knee-cap, whence hung a moderately large bell. His face, which was in the shadow, was not distinguishable.

However, the goodman had removed his cap, and exclaimed, trembling all over:—

"Ah, good God! How come you here, Father Madeleine? Where did you enter? Dieu-Jésus! Did you fall from heaven? There is no trouble about that: if ever you do fall, it will be from there. And what a state you are in! You have no cravat; you have no hat; you have no coat! Do you know, you would have frightened any one who did not know you? No coat! Lord God! Are the saints going mad nowadays? But how did you get in here?"

His words tumbled over each other. The goodman talked with a rustic volubility, in which there was nothing alarming. All this was uttered with a mixture of stupefaction and *naïve* kindliness.

"Who are you? and what house is this?" demanded Jean Valjean.

"Ah! pardieu, this is too much!" exclaimed the old man. "I am the person for whom you got the place here, and this house is the one where you had me placed. What! You don't recognize me?"

"No," said Jean Valjean; "and how happens it that you know me?"

"You saved my life," said the man.

He turned. A ray of moonlight outlined his profile, and Jean Valjean recognized old Fauchelevent.

"Ah!" said Jean Valjean, "so it is you? Yes, I recollect you."

"That is very lucky," said the old man, in a reproachful tone.

"And what are you doing here?" resumed Jean Valjean.

"Why, I am covering my melons, of course!"

In fact, at the moment when Jean Valjean accosted him, old Fauchelevent held in his hand the end of a straw mat which he was occupied in spreading over the melon bed. During the hour or thereabouts that he had been in the garden he had already spread out a number of them. It was this operation which had caused him to execute the peculiar movements observed from the shed by Jean Valjean.

He continued:—

"I said to myself, 'The moon is bright: it is going to freeze. What if I were to put my melons into their greatcoats?' And," he added, looking at Jean Valjean with a broad smile,—"pardieu! you ought to have done the same! But how do you come here?"

Jean Valjean, finding himself known to this man, at least only under the name of Madeleine, thenceforth advanced only with caution. He multiplied his questions. Strange to say, their rôles seemed to be reversed. It was he, the intruder, who interrogated.

"And what is this bell which you wear on your knee?"

"This," replied Fauchelevent, "is so that I may be avoided."

"What! so that you may be avoided?"

Old Fauchelevent winked with an indescribable air.

"Ah, goodness! there are only women in this house—many young girls. It appears that I should be a dangerous person to meet. The bell gives them warning. When I come, they go."

"What house is this?"

"Come, you know well enough."

"But I do not."

"Not when you got me the place here as gardener?"

"Answer me as though I knew nothing."

"Well, then, this is the Petit-Picpus convent."

Memories recurred to Jean Valjean. Chance, that is to say, Providence, had cast him into precisely that convent in the Quartier Saint-Antoine where old Fauchelevent, crippled by the fall from his cart, had been admitted on his recommendation two years previously. He repeated, as though talking to himself:—

"The Petit-Picpus convent."

"Exactly," returned old Fauchelevent. "But to come to the point, how the deuce did you manage to get in here, you, Father Madeleine? No matter if you are a saint; you are a man as well, and no man enters here."

"You certainly are here."

"There is no one but me."

"Still," said Jean Valjean, "I must stay here."

"Ah, good God!" cried Fauchelevent.

Jean Valjean drew near to the old man, and said to him in a grave voice:—

"Father Fauchelevent, I saved your life."

"I was the first to recall it," returned Fauchelevent.

"Well, you can do to-day for me that which I did for you in the olden days."

Fauchelevent took in his aged, trembling, and wrinkled hands Jean Valjean's two robust hands, and stood for several minutes as though incapable of speaking. At length he exclaimed:—

"Oh! that would be a blessing from the good God, if I could make you some little return for that! Save your life! Monsieur le Maire, dispose of the old man!"

A wonderful joy had transfigured this old man. His countenance seemed to emit a ray of light.

"What do you wish me to do?" he resumed.

"That I will explain to you. You have a chamber?"

"I have an isolated hovel yonder, behind the ruins of the old convent, in a corner which no one ever looks into. There are three rooms in it."

The hut was, in fact, so well hidden behind the ruins, and so cleverly arranged to prevent it being seen, that Jean Valjean had not perceived it.

"Good," said Jean Valjean. "Now I am going to ask two things of you."

"What are they, Mr. Mayor?"

"In the first place, you are not to tell any one what you know about me. In the second, you are not to try to find out anything more."

"As you please. I know that you can do nothing that is not honest, that you have always been a man after the good God's heart. And then, moreover, you it was who placed me here. That concerns you. I am at your service."

"That is settled then. Now, come with me. We will go and get the child."

"Ah!" said Fauchelevent, "so there is a child?"

He added not a word further, and followed Jean Valjean as a dog follows his master.

Less than half an hour afterwards Cosette, who had grown rosy again before the flame of a good fire, was lying asleep in the old gardener's bed. Jean Valjean had put on his cravat and coat once more; his hat, which he had flung over the wall, had been found and picked up. While Jean Valjean was putting on his coat, Fauchelevent had removed the bell and kneecap, which now hung on a nail beside a vintage basket that adorned the wall. The two men were warming themselves with their elbows resting on a table upon which Fauchelevent had placed a bit of cheese, black bread, a bottle of wine, and two glasses, and the old man was saying to Jean Valjean, as he laid his hand on the latter's knee: "Ah! Father Madeleine! You did not recognize me immediately; you save people's lives, and then you forget them! That is bad! But they remember you! You are an ingrate!"

X

WHICH EXPLAINS HOW JAVERT GOT ON THE SCENT

The events of which we have just beheld the reverse side, so to speak, had come about in the simplest possible manner.

When Jean Valjean, on the evening of the very day when Javert had arrested him beside Fantine's death-bed, had escaped from the town jail of M. sur M., the police had supposed that he had betaken himself to Paris. Paris is a maelstrom where everything is lost, and everything disappears in this belly of the world, as in the belly of the sea. No forest hides a man as does that crowd. Fugitives of every sort know this. They go to Paris as to an abyss; there are gulfs which save. The police know it also, and it is in Paris that they seek what they have lost elsewhere. They sought the ex-mayor of M. sur M. Javert was summoned to Paris to throw light on their researches. Javert had, in fact, rendered powerful assistance in the recapture of Jean Valjean. Javert's zeal and intelligence on that occasion had been remarked by M. Chabouillet, secretary of the Prefecture under Comte Anglès. M. Chabouillet, who had, moreover, already been Javert's patron, had the inspector of M. sur M. attached to the police force of Paris. There Javert rendered himself useful in divers and, though the word may seem strange for such services, honorable manners.

He no longer thought of Jean Valjean,—the wolf of to-day causes these dogs who are always on the chase to forget the wolf of yesterday,—when, in December, 1823, he read a newspaper, he who never read newspapers; but Javert, a monarchical man, had a desire to know the particulars of the triumphal entry of the "Prince Generalissimo" into Bayonne. Just as he was finishing the article, which interested him; a name, the name of Jean Valjean, attracted his attention at the bottom of a page. The paper announced that the convict Jean Valjean was dead, and published the fact in such formal terms that Javert did not doubt it. He confined himself to the remark, "That's a good entry." Then he threw aside the paper, and thought no more about it.

Some time afterwards, it chanced that a police report was transmitted from the prefecture of the Seine-et-Oise to the prefecture of police in Paris, concerning the abduction of a child, which had taken place, under peculiar circumstances, as it was said, in the commune of Montfermeil. A little girl of seven or eight years of age, the report said, who had been intrusted by her mother to an inn-keeper of that neighborhood, had been stolen by a stranger; this child answered to the name of Cosette, and was the daughter of a girl named Fantine, who had died in the hospital, it was not known where or when.

This report came under Javert's eye and set him to thinking.

The name of Fantine was well known to him. He remembered that Jean Valjean had made him, Javert, burst into laughter, by asking him for a respite of three days, for the purpose of going to fetch that creature's child. He recalled the fact that Jean Valjean had been arrested in Paris at the very moment when he was stepping into the coach for Montfermeil. Some signs had made him suspect at the time that this was the second occasion of his entering that coach, and that he had already, on the previous day, made an excursion to the neighborhood of that village, for he had not been seen in the village itself. What had he been intending to do in that region of Montfermeil? It could not even be surmised. Javert understood it now. Fantine's daughter was there. Jean Valjean was going there in search of her. And now this child had been stolen by a stranger! Who could that stranger be? Could it be Jean Valjean? But Jean Valjean was dead. Javert, without saying anything to anybody, took the coach from the *Pewter Platter*, Cul-de-Sac de la Planchette, and made a trip to Montfermeil.

He expected to find a great deal of light on the subject there; he found a great deal of obscurity.

For the first few days the Thénardiers had chattered in their rage. The disappearance of the Lark had created a sensation in the village. He immediately obtained numerous versions of the story, which ended in the abduction of a child. Hence the police report. But their first vexation having passed off, Thénardier, with his wonderful instinct, had very quickly comprehended that it is never advisable to stir up the prosecutor of the Crown, and that his complaints with regard to the *abduction* of Cosette would have as their first result to fix upon himself, and upon many dark affairs which he had on hand, the glittering eye of justice. The last thing that owls desire is to have a candle brought to them. And in the first place, how explain the fifteen hundred francs which he had received? He turned squarely round, put a gag on his wife's mouth, and feigned astonishment when the *stolen child* was mentioned to him. He understood nothing about it; no doubt he had grumbled for awhile at having that dear little creature "taken from him" so hastily; he should have liked to keep her two or three days longer, out of tenderness; but her "grandfather" had come for her in the most natural way in the world. He added the "grandfather," which produced a good effect. This was the story that Javert hit upon when he arrived at Montfermeil. The grandfather caused Jean Valjean to vanish.

Nevertheless, Javert dropped a few questions, like plummets, into Thénardier's history. "Who was that grandfather? and what was his name?" Thénardier replied with simplicity: "He is a wealthy farmer. I saw his passport. I think his name was M. Guillaume Lambert."

Lambert is a respectable and extremely reassuring name. Thereupon Javert returned to Paris.

"Jean Valjean is certainly dead," said he, "and I am a ninny."

He had again begun to forget this history, when, in the course of March, 1824, he heard of a singular personage who dwelt in the parish of Saint-Médard and who had been surnamed "the mendicant who gives alms." This person, the story ran, was a man of means, whose name no one knew exactly, and who lived alone with a little girl of eight years, who knew nothing about herself, save that she had come from Montfermeil. Montfermeil! that name was always coming up, and it made Javert prick up his ears. An old beggar police spy, an ex-beadle, to whom this person had given alms, added a few more details. This gentleman of property was very shy,—never coming out except in the evening, speaking to no one, except, occasionally to the poor, and never allowing any one to approach him. He wore a horrible old yellow frock-coat, which was worth many millions, being all wadded with bank-bills. This piqued Javert's curiosity in a decided manner. In order to get a close look at this fantastic gentleman without alarming him, he borrowed the beadle's outfit for a day, and the place where the old spy was in the habit of crouching every evening, whining orisons through his nose, and playing the spy under cover of prayer.

"The suspected individual" did indeed approach Javert thus disguised, and bestow alms on him. At that moment Javert raised his head, and the shock which Jean Valjean received on recognizing Javert was equal to the one received by Javert when he thought he recognized Jean Valjean.

However, the darkness might have misled him; Jean Valjean's death was official; Javert cherished very grave doubts; and when in doubt, Javert, the man of scruples, never laid a finger on any one's collar.

He followed his man to the Gorbeau house, and got "the old woman" to talking, which was no difficult matter. The old woman confirmed the fact regarding the coat lined with millions, and narrated to him the episode of the thousand-franc bill. She had seen it! She had handled it! Javert hired a room; that evening he installed himself in it. He came and listened at the mysterious lodger's door, hoping to catch the sound of his voice, but Jean Valjean saw his candle through the key-hole, and foiled the spy by keeping silent.

On the following day Jean Valjean decamped; but the noise made by the fall of the five-franc piece was noticed by the old woman, who, hearing the rattling of coin, suspected that he might be intending to leave, and made haste to warn Javert. At night, when Jean Valjean came out, Javert was waiting for him behind the trees of the boulevard with two men.

Javert had demanded assistance at the Prefecture, but he had not mentioned the name of the individual whom he hoped to seize; that was his secret, and he had kept it for three reasons: in the first place, because the slightest indiscretion might put Jean Valjean on the alert; next, because, to lay hands on an ex-convict who had made his escape and was reputed dead, on a criminal whom justice had formerly classed forever as *among malefactors of the most dangerous sort*, was a magnificent success which the old members of the Parisian police would assuredly not leave to a newcomer like Javert, and he was afraid of being deprived of his convict; and lastly, because Javert, being an artist, had a taste for the unforeseen. He hated those well-heralded successes which are talked of long in advance and have had the bloom brushed off. He preferred to elaborate his masterpieces in the dark and to unveil them suddenly at the last.

Javert had followed Jean Valjean from tree to tree, then from corner to corner of the street, and had not lost sight of him for a single instant; even at the moments when Jean Valjean believed himself to be the most secure Javert's eye had been on him. Why had not Javert arrested Jean Valjean? Because he was still in doubt.

It must be remembered that at that epoch the police was not precisely at its ease; the free press embarrassed it; several arbitrary arrests denounced by the newspapers, had echoed even as far as the Chambers, and had rendered the Prefecture timid. Interference with individual liberty was a grave matter. The police agents were afraid of making a mistake; the prefect laid the blame on them; a mistake meant dismissal. The reader can imagine the effect which this brief paragraph, reproduced by twenty newspapers, would have caused in Paris: "Yesterday, an aged grandfather, with white hair, a respectable and well-to-do gentleman, who was walking with his grandchild, aged eight, was arrested and conducted to the agency of the Prefecture as an escaped convict!"

Let us repeat in addition that Javert had scruples of his own; injunctions of his conscience were added to the injunctions of the prefect. He was really in doubt.

Jean Valjean turned his back on him and walked in the dark.

Sadness, uneasiness, anxiety, depression, this fresh misfortune of being forced to flee by night, to seek a chance refuge in Paris for Cosette and himself, the necessity of regulating his pace to the pace of the child—all this, without his being aware of it, had altered Jean Valjean's walk, and impressed on his bearing such senility, that the police themselves, incarnate in the person of Javert, might, and did in fact, make a mistake. The impossibility of approaching too close, his costume of an *émigré* preceptor, the declaration of Thénardier which made a grandfather of him, and, finally, the belief in his death in prison, added still further to the uncertainty which gathered thick in Javert's mind.

For an instant it occurred to him to make an abrupt demand for his papers; but if the man was not Jean Valjean, and if this man was not a good, honest old fellow living on his income, he was probably some merry blade deeply and cunningly implicated in the obscure web of Parisian misdeeds, some chief of a dangerous band, who gave alms to conceal his other talents, which was an old dodge. He had trusty fellows, accomplices' retreats in case of emergencies, in which he would, no doubt, take refuge. All these turns which he was making through the streets seemed to indicate that he was not a simple and honest man. To arrest him too hastily would be "to kill the hen that laid the golden eggs." Where was the inconvenience in waiting? Javert was very sure that he would not escape.

Thus he proceeded in a tolerably perplexed state of mind, putting to himself a hundred questions about this enigmatical personage.

It was only quite late in the Rue de Pontoise, that, thanks to the brilliant light thrown from a dram-shop, he decidedly recognized Jean Valjean.

There are in this world two beings who give a profound start,—the mother who recovers her child and the tiger who recovers his prey. Javert gave that profound start.

As soon as he had positively recognized Jean Valjean, the formidable convict, he perceived that there were only three of them, and he asked for reinforcements at the police station of the Rue de Pontoise. One puts on gloves before grasping a thorn cudgel.

This delay and the halt at the Carrefour Rollin to consult with his agents came near causing him to lose the trail. He speedily divined, however, that Jean Valjean would want to put the river between his pursuers and himself. He bent his head and reflected like a blood-hound who puts his nose to the ground to make sure that he is on the right scent. Javert, with his powerful rectitude of instinct, went straight to the bridge of Austerlitz. A word with the toll-keeper furnished him with the information which he required: "Have you seen a man with a little girl?" "I made him pay two sous," replied the toll-keeper. Javert reached the bridge in season to see Jean Valjean traverse the small illuminated spot on the other side of the water, leading Cosette by the hand. He saw him enter the Rue du Chemin-Vert-Saint-Antoine; he remembered the Cul-de-Sac Genrot arranged there like a trap, and of the sole exit of the Rue Droit-Mur into the Rue Petit-Picpus. *He made sure of his back burrows*, as huntsmen say; he hastily despatched one of his agents, by a roundabout way, to guard that issue. A patrol which was returning to the Arsenal post having passed him, he made a requisition on it, and caused it to accompany him. In such games soldiers are aces. Moreover, the principle is, that in order to get the best of a wild boar, one must employ the science of venery and plenty of dogs. These combinations having been effected, feeling that Jean Valjean was caught between the blind alley Genrot on the right, his agent on the left, and himself, Javert, in the rear, he took a pinch of snuff.

Then he began the game. He experienced one ecstatic and infernal moment; he allowed his man to go on ahead, knowing that he had him safe, but desirous of postponing the moment of arrest as long as possible, happy at the thought that he was taken and yet at seeing him free, gloating over him with his gaze, with that voluptuousness of the spider which allows the fly to flutter, and of the cat which lets the mouse run. Claws and talons possess a monstrous sensuality,—the obscure movements of the creature imprisoned in their pincers. What a delight this strangling is!

Javert was enjoying himself. The meshes of his net were stoutly knotted. He was sure of success; all he had to do now was to close his hand.

Accompanied as he was, the very idea of resistance was impossible, however vigorous, energetic, and desperate Jean Valjean might be.

Javert advanced slowly, sounding, searching on his way all the nooks of the street like so many pockets of thieves.

When he reached the centre of the web he found the fly no longer there.

His exasperation can be imagined.

He interrogated his sentinel of the Rues Droit-Mur and Petit-Picpus; that agent, who had remained imperturbably at his post, had not seen the man pass.

It sometimes happens that a stag is lost head and horns; that is to say, he escapes although he has the pack on his very heels, and then the oldest huntsmen know not what to say. Duvivier, Ligniville, and Desprez halt short. In a discomfiture of this sort, Artonge exclaims, "It was not a stag, but a sorcerer." Javert would have liked to utter the same cry.

His disappointment bordered for a moment on despair and rage.

It is certain that Napoleon made mistakes during the war with Russia, that Alexander committed blunders in the war in India, that Cæsar made mistakes in the war in Africa, that Cyrus was at fault in the war in Scythia, and that Javert blundered in this campaign against Jean Valjean. He was wrong, perhaps, in hesitating in his recognition of the exconvict. The first glance should have sufficed him. He was wrong in not arresting him purely and simply in the old building; he was wrong in not arresting him when he positively recognized him in the Rue de Pontoise. He was wrong in taking counsel with his auxiliaries in the full light of the moon in the Carrefour Rollin. Advice is certainly useful; it is a good thing to know and to interrogate those of the dogs who deserve confidence; but the hunter cannot be too cautious when he is chasing uneasy animals like the wolf and the convict. Javert, by taking too much thought as to how he should set the bloodhounds of the pack on the trail, alarmed the beast by giving him wind of the dart, and so made him run. Above all, he was wrong in that after he had picked up the scent again on the bridge of Austerlitz, he played that formidable and puerile game of keeping such a man at the end of a thread. He thought himself stronger than he was, and believed that he could play at the game of the mouse and the lion. At the same time, he reckoned himself as too weak, when he judged it necessary to obtain reinforcement. Fatal precaution, waste of precious time! Javert committed all these blunders, and nonetheless was one of the cleverest and most correct spies that ever existed. He was, in the full force of the term, what is called in venery a *knowing dog*. But what is there that is perfect?

Great strategists have their eclipses.

The greatest follies are often composed, like the largest ropes, of a multitude of strands. Take the cable thread by thread, take all the petty determining motives separately, and you can break them one after the other, and you say, "That is all there is of it!" Braid them, twist them together; the result is enormous: it is Attila hesitating between Marcian on the east and Valentinian on the west; it is Hannibal tarrying at Capua; it is Danton falling asleep at Arcis-sur-Aube.

However that may be, even at the moment when he saw that Jean Valjean had escaped him, Javert did not lose his head. Sure that the convict who had broken his ban could not be far off, he established sentinels, he organized traps and ambuscades, and beat the quarter all that night. The first thing he saw was the disorder in the street lantern whose rope had been cut. A precious sign which, however, led him astray, since it caused him to turn all his researches in the direction of the Cul-de-Sac Genrot. In this blind alley there were tolerably low walls which abutted on gardens whose bounds adjoined the immense stretches of waste land. Jean Valjean evidently must have fled in that direction. The fact is, that had he penetrated a little further in the Cul-de-Sac Genrot, he would probably have done so and have been lost. Javert explored these gardens and these waste stretches as though he had been hunting for a needle.

At daybreak he left two intelligent men on the outlook, and returned to the Prefecture of Police, as much ashamed as a police spy who had been captured by a robber might have been.

BOOK SIXTH

LE PETIT-PICPUS

I

Number 62 Rue Petit-Picpus

Nothing, half a century ago, more resembled every other carriage gate than the carriage gate of Number 62 Rue Petit-Picpus. This entrance, which usually stood ajar in the most inviting fashion, permitted a view of two things, neither of which have anything very funereal about them,—a courtyard surrounded by walls hung with vines, and the face of a lounging porter. Above the wall, at the bottom of the court, tall trees were visible. When a ray of sunlight enlivened the courtyard, when a glass of wine cheered up the porter, it was difficult to pass Number 62 Little Picpus Street without carrying away a smiling impression of it. Nevertheless, it was a sombre place of which one had had a glimpse.

The threshold smiled; the house prayed and wept.

If one succeeded in passing the porter, which was not easy,—which was even nearly impossible for every one, for there was an *open sesame!* which it was necessary to know,—if, the porter once passed, one entered a little vestibule on the right, on which opened a staircase shut in between two walls and so narrow that only one person could ascend it at a time, if one did not allow one's self to be alarmed by a daubing of canary yellow, with a dado of chocolate which clothed this staircase, if one ventured to ascend it, one crossed a first landing, then a second, and arrived on the first story at a corridor where the yellow wash and the chocolate-hued plinth pursued one with a peaceable persistency. Staircase and corridor were lighted by two beautiful windows. The corridor took a turn and became dark. If one doubled this cape, one arrived a few paces further on, in front of a door which was all the more mysterious because it was not fastened. If one opened it, one found one's self in a little chamber about six feet square, tiled, well-scrubbed, clean, cold, and hung with nankin paper with green flowers, at fifteen sous the roll. A white, dull light fell from a large window, with tiny panes, on the left, which usurped the whole width of the room. One gazed about, but saw no one; one listened, one heard neither a footstep nor a human murmur. The walls were bare, the chamber was not furnished; there was not even a chair.

One looked again, and beheld on the wall facing the door a quadrangular hole, about a foot square, with a grating of interlacing iron bars, black, knotted, solid, which formed squares—I had almost said meshes—of less than an inch and a half in diagonal length. The little green flowers of the nankin paper ran in a calm and orderly manner to those iron bars, without being startled or thrown into confusion by their funereal contact. Supposing that a living being had been so wonderfully thin as to essay an entrance or an exit through the square hole, this grating would have prevented it. It did not allow the passage of the body, but it did allow the passage of the eyes; that is to say, of the mind. This seems to have occurred to them, for it had been re-enforced by a sheet of tin inserted in the wall a little in the rear, and pierced with a thousand holes more microscopic than the holes of a strainer. At the bottom of this plate, an aperture had been pierced exactly similar to the orifice of a letter box. A bit of tape attached to a bell-wire hung at the right of the grated opening.

If the tape was pulled, a bell rang, and one heard a voice very near at hand, which made one start.

"Who is there?" the voice demanded.

It was a woman's voice, a gentle voice, so gentle that it was mournful.

Here, again, there was a magical word which it was necessary to know. If one did not know it, the voice ceased, the wall became silent once more, as though the terrified obscurity of the sepulchre had been on the other side of it.

If one knew the password, the voice resumed, "Enter on the right."

One then perceived on the right, facing the window, a glass door surmounted by a frame glazed and painted gray. On raising the latch and crossing the threshold, one experienced precisely the same impression as when one enters at the theatre into a grated *baignoire*, before the grating is lowered and the chandelier is lighted. One was, in fact, in a sort of theatre-box, narrow, furnished with two old chairs, and a much-frayed straw matting, sparely illuminated by the vague light from the glass door; a regular box, with its front just of a height to lean upon, bearing a tablet of black wood. This box was grated, only the grating of it was not of gilded wood, as at the opera; it was a monstrous lattice of iron bars, hideously interlaced and riveted to the wall by enormous fastenings which resembled clenched fists.

The first minutes passed; when one's eyes began to grow used to this cellar-like half-twilight, one tried to pass the grating, but got no further than six inches beyond it. There he encountered a barrier of black shutters, re-enforced and fortified with transverse beams of wood painted a gingerbread yellow. These shutters were divided into long, narrow slats, and they masked the entire length of the grating. They were always closed. At the expiration of a few moments one heard a voice proceeding from behind these shutters, and saying:—

"I am here. What do you wish with me?"

It was a beloved, sometimes an adored, voice. No one was visible. Hardly the sound of a breath was audible. It seemed as though it were a spirit which had been evoked, that was speaking to you across the walls of the tomb.

If one chanced to be within certain prescribed and very rare conditions, the slat of one of the shutters opened opposite you; the evoked spirit became an apparition. Behind the grating, behind the shutter, one perceived so far as the grating permitted sight, a head, of which only the mouth and the chin were visible; the rest was covered with a black veil. One caught a glimpse of a black guimpe, and a form that was barely defined, covered with a black shroud. That head spoke with you, but did not look at you and never smiled at you.

The light which came from behind you was adjusted in such a manner that you saw her in the white, and she saw you in the black. This light was symbolical.

Nevertheless, your eyes plunged eagerly through that opening which was made in that place shut off from all glances. A profound vagueness enveloped that form clad in mourning. Your eyes searched that vagueness, and sought to make out the surroundings of the apparition. At the expiration of a very short time you discovered that you could see nothing. What you beheld was night, emptiness, shadows, a wintry mist mingled with a vapor from the tomb, a sort of terrible peace, a silence from which you could gather nothing, not even sighs, a gloom in which you could distinguish nothing, not even phantoms.

What you beheld was the interior of a cloister.

It was the interior of that severe and gloomy edifice which was called the Convent of the Bernardines of the Perpetual Adoration. The box in which you stood was the parlor. The first voice which had addressed you was that of the portress who always sat motionless and silent, on the other side of the wall, near the square opening, screened by the iron grating and the plate with its thousand holes, as by a double visor. The obscurity which bathed the grated box arose from the fact that the parlor, which had a window on the side of the world, had none on the side of the convent. Profane eyes must see nothing of that sacred place.

Nevertheless, there was something beyond that shadow; there was a light; there was life in the midst of that death. Although this was the most strictly walled of all convents, we shall endeavor to make our way into it, and to take the reader in, and to say, without transgressing the proper bounds, things which story-tellers have never seen, and have, therefore, never described.

II

The Obedience of Martin Verga

This convent, which in 1824 had already existed for many a long year in the Rue Petit-Picpus, was a community of Bernardines of the obedience of Martin Verga.

These Bernardines were attached, in consequence, not to Clairvaux, like the Bernardine monks, but to Cîteaux, like the Benedictine monks. In other words, they were the subjects, not of Saint Bernard, but of Saint Benoît.

Any one who has turned over old folios to any extent knows that Martin Verga founded in 1425 a congregation of Bernardines-Benedictines, with Salamanca for the head of the order, and Alcala as the branch establishment.

This congregation had sent out branches throughout all the Catholic countries of Europe.

There is nothing unusual in the Latin Church in these grafts of one order on another. To mention only a single order of Saint-Benoît, which is here in question: there are attached to this order, without counting the obedience of Martin Verga, four congregations,—two in Italy, Mont-Cassin and Sainte-Justine of Padua; two in France, Cluny and Saint-Maur; and nine orders,—Vallombrosa, Granmont, the Célestins, the Camaldules, the Carthusians, the Humiliés, the Olivateurs, the Silvestrins, and lastly, Cîteaux; for Cîteaux itself, a trunk for other orders, is only an offshoot of Saint-Benoît. Cîteaux dates from Saint Robert, Abbé de Molesme, in the diocese of Langres, in 1098. Now it was in 529 that the devil, having retired to the desert of Subiaco—he was old—had he turned hermit?—was chased from the ancient temple of Apollo, where he dwelt, by Saint-Benoît, then aged seventeen.

After the rule of the Carmelites, who go barefoot, wear a bit of willow on their throats, and never sit down, the harshest rule is that of the Bernardines-Benedictines of Martin Verga. They are clothed in black, with a guimpe, which, in accordance with the express command of Saint-Benoît, mounts to the chin. A robe of serge with large sleeves, a large woollen veil, the guimpe which mounts to the chin cut square on the breast, the band which descends over their brow to their eyes,—this is their dress. All is black except the band, which is white. The novices wear the same habit, but all in white. The professed nuns also wear a rosary at their side.

The Bernardines-Benedictines of Martin Verga practise the Perpetual Adoration, like the Benedictines called Ladies of the Holy Sacrament, who, at the beginning of this century, had two houses in Paris,—one at the Temple, the other in the Rue Neuve-Sainte-Geneviève. However, the Bernardines-Benedictines of the Petit-Picpus, of whom we are speaking, were a totally different order from the Ladies of the Holy Sacrament, cloistered in the Rue Neuve-Sainte-Geneviève and at the Temple. There were numerous differences in their rule; there were some in their costume. The Bernardines-Benedictines of the Petit-Picpus wore the black guimpe, and the Benedictines of the Holy Sacrament and of the Rue Neuve-Sainte-Geneviève wore a white one, and had, besides, on their breasts, a Holy Sacrament about three inches long, in silver gilt or gilded copper. The nuns of the Petit-Picpus did not wear this Holy Sacrament. The Perpetual Adoration, which was common to the house of the Petit-Picpus and to the house of the Temple, leaves those two orders perfectly distinct. Their only resemblance lies in this practice of the Ladies of the Holy Sacrament and the Bernardines of Martin Verga, just as there existed a similarity in the study and the glorification of all the mysteries relating to the infancy, the life, and death of Jesus Christ and the Virgin, between the two orders, which were, nevertheless, widely separated, and on occasion even hostile. The Oratory of Italy, established at Florence by Philip de Neri, and the Oratory of France, established by Pierre de Bérulle. The Oratory of France claimed the precedence, since Philip de Neri was only a saint, while Bérulle was a cardinal.

Let us return to the harsh Spanish rule of Martin Verga.

The Bernardines-Benedictines of this obedience fast all the year round, abstain from meat, fast in Lent and on many other days which are peculiar to them, rise from their first sleep, from one to three o'clock in the morning, to read their breviary and chant matins, sleep in all seasons between serge sheets and on straw, make no use of the bath, never light a fire, scourge themselves every Friday, observe the rule of silence, speak to each other only during the recreation hours, which are very brief, and wear drugget chemises for six months in the year, from September 14th, which is the Exaltation of the Holy Cross, until Easter. These six months are a modification: the rule says all the year, but this drugget chemise, intolerable in the heat of summer, produced fevers and nervous spasms. The use of it had to be restricted. Even with this palliation, when the nuns put on this chemise on the 14th of September, they suffer from fever for three or four days. Obedience, poverty, chastity, perseverance in their seclusion,—these are their vows, which the rule greatly aggravates.

The prioress is elected for three years by the mothers, who are called *mères vocales* because they have a voice in the chapter. A prioress can only be re-elected twice, which fixes the longest possible reign of a prioress at nine years.

They never see the officiating priest, who is always hidden from them by a serge curtain nine feet in height. During the sermon, when the preacher is in the chapel, they drop their veils over their faces. They must always speak low, walk with their eyes on the ground and their heads bowed. One man only is allowed to enter the convent,—the archbishop of the diocese.

There is really one other,—the gardener. But he is always an old man, and, in order that he may always be alone in the garden, and that the nuns may be warned to avoid him, a bell is attached to his knee.

Their submission to the prioress is absolute and passive. It is the canonical subjection in the full force of its abnegation. As at the voice of Christ, *ut voci Christi*, at a gesture, at the first sign, *ad nutum, ad primum signum*, immediately, with cheerfulness, with perseverance, with a certain blind obedience, *prompte, hilariter, perseveranter et cæca quadam obedientia*, as the file in the hand of the workman, *quasi limam in manibus fabri*, without power to read or to write without express permission, *legere vel scribere non addiscerit sine expressa superioris licentia*.

Each one of them in turn makes what they call *reparation*. The reparation is the prayer for all the sins, for all the faults, for all the dissensions, for all the violations, for all the iniquities, for all the crimes committed on earth. For the space of twelve consecutive hours, from four o'clock in the afternoon till four o'clock in the morning, or from four o'clock in the morning until four o'clock in the afternoon, the sister who is making *reparation* remains on her knees on the stone before the Holy Sacrament, with hands clasped, a rope around her neck. When her fatigue becomes unendurable, she prostrates herself flat on her face against the earth, with her arms outstretched in the form of a cross; this is her only relief. In this attitude she prays for all the guilty in the universe. This is great to sublimity.

As this act is performed in front of a post on which burns a candle, it is called without distinction, *to make reparation* or *to be at the post*. The nuns even prefer, out of humility, this last expression, which contains an idea of torture and abasement.

To make reparation is a function in which the whole soul is absorbed. The sister at the post would not turn round were a thunderbolt to fall directly behind her.

Besides this, there is always a sister kneeling before the Holy Sacrament. This station lasts an hour. They relieve each other like soldiers on guard. This is the Perpetual Adoration.

The prioresses and the mothers almost always bear names stamped with peculiar solemnity, recalling, not the saints and martyrs, but moments in the life of Jesus Christ: as Mother Nativity, Mother Conception, Mother Presentation, Mother Passion. But the names of saints are not interdicted.

When one sees them, one never sees anything but their mouths.

All their teeth are yellow. No tooth-brush ever entered that convent. Brushing one's teeth is at the top of a ladder at whose bottom is the loss of one's soul.

They never say *my*. They possess nothing of their own, and they must not attach themselves to anything. They call everything *our*; thus: our veil, our chaplet; if they were speaking of their chemise, they would say *our chemise*. Sometimes they grow attached to some petty object,—to a book of hours, a relic, a medal that has been blessed. As soon as they become aware that they are growing attached to this object, they must give it up. They recall the words of Saint Thérèse, to whom a great lady said, as she was on the point of entering her order, "Permit me, mother, to send for a Bible to which I am greatly attached." "Ah, you are attached to something! In that case, do not enter our order!"

Every person whatever is forbidden to shut herself up, to have *a place of her own, a chamber*. They live with their cells open. When they meet, one says, "Blessed and adored be the most Holy Sacrament of the altar!" The other responds, "Forever." The same ceremony when one taps at the other's door. Hardly has she touched the door when a soft voice on the other side is heard to say hastily, "Forever!" Like all practices, this becomes mechanical by force of habit; and one sometimes says *forever* before the other has had time to say the rather long sentence, "Praised and adored be the most Holy Sacrament of the altar."

Among the Visitandines the one who enters says: "Ave Maria," and the one whose cell is entered says, "Gratia plena." It is their way of saying good day, which is in fact full of grace.

At each hour of the day three supplementary strokes sound from the church bell of the convent. At this signal prioress, vocal mothers, professed nuns, lay-sisters, novices, postulants, interrupt what they are saying, what they are doing, or what they are thinking, and all say in unison if it is five o'clock, for instance, "At five o'clock and at all hours praised and adored be the most Holy Sacrament of the altar!" If it is eight o'clock, "At eight o'clock and at all hours!" and so on, according to the hour.

This custom, the object of which is to break the thread of thought and to lead it back constantly to God, exists in many communities; the formula alone varies. Thus at The Infant Jesus they say, "At this hour and at every hour may the love of Jesus kindle my heart!" The Bernardines-Benedictines of Martin Verga, cloistered fifty years ago at Petit-Picpus, chant the offices to a solemn psalmody, a pure Gregorian chant, and always with full voice during the whole course of the office. Everywhere in the missal where an asterisk occurs they pause, and say in a low voice, "Jesus-Marie-Joseph." For the office of the dead they adopt a tone so low that the voices of women can hardly descend to such a depth. The effect produced is striking and tragic.

The nuns of the Petit-Picpus had made a vault under their grand altar for the burial of their community. *The Government*, as they say, does not permit this vault to receive coffins so they leave the convent when they die. This is an affliction to them, and causes them consternation as an infraction of the rules.

They had obtained a mediocre consolation at best,—permission to be interred at a special hour and in a special corner in the ancient Vaugirard cemetery, which was made of land which had formerly belonged to their community.

On Fridays the nuns hear high mass, vespers, and all the offices, as on Sunday. They scrupulously observe in addition all the little festivals unknown to people of the world, of which the Church of France was so prodigal in the olden days, and of which it is still prodigal in Spain and Italy. Their stations in the chapel are interminable. As for the number and duration of their prayers we can convey no better idea of them than by quoting the ingenuous remark of one of them: "The prayers of the postulants are frightful, the prayers of the novices are still worse, and the prayers of the professed nuns are still worse."

Once a week the chapter assembles: the prioress presides; the vocal mothers assist. Each sister kneels in turn on the stones, and confesses aloud, in the presence of all, the faults and sins which she has committed during the week. The vocal mothers consult after each confession and inflict the penance aloud.

Besides this confession in a loud tone, for which all faults in the least serious are reserved, they have for their venial offences what they call the *coulpe*. *To make one's coulpe* means to prostrate one's self flat on one's face during the office in front of the prioress until the latter, who is never called anything but *our mother*, notifies the culprit by a slight tap of her foot against the wood of her stall that she can rise. The *coulpe* or *peccavi*, is made for a very small matter—a broken glass, a torn veil, an involuntary delay of a few seconds at an office, a false note in church, etc.; this suffices, and the *coulpe* is made. The *coulpe* is entirely spontaneous; it is the culpable person herself (the word is etymologically in its place here) who judges herself and inflicts it on herself. On festival days and Sundays four mother precentors intone the offices before a large reading-desk with four places. One day one of the mother precentors intoned a psalm beginning with *Ecce*, and instead of *Ecce* she uttered aloud the three notes *do si sol*; for this piece of absent-mindedness she underwent a *coulpe* which lasted during the whole service: what rendered the fault enormous was the fact that the chapter had laughed.

When a nun is summoned to the parlor, even were it the prioress herself, she drops her veil, as will be remembered, so that only her mouth is visible.

The prioress alone can hold communication with strangers. The others can see only their immediate family, and that very rarely. If, by chance, an outsider presents herself to see a nun, or one whom she has known and loved in the outer world, a regular series of negotiations is required. If it is a woman, the authorization may sometimes be granted; the nun comes, and they talk to her through the shutters, which are opened only for a mother or sister. It is unnecessary to say that permission is always refused to men.

Such is the rule of Saint-Benoît, aggravated by Martin Verga.

These nuns are not gay, rosy, and fresh, as the daughters of other orders often are. They are pale and grave. Between 1825 and 1830 three of them went mad.

III

AUSTERITIES

One is a postulant for two years at least, often for four; a novice for four. It is rare that the definitive vows can be pronounced earlier than the age of twenty-three or twenty-four years. The Bernardines-Benedictines of Martin Verga do not admit widows to their order.

In their cells, they deliver themselves up to many unknown macerations, of which they must never speak.

On the day when a novice makes her profession, she is dressed in her handsomest attire, she is crowned with white roses, her hair is brushed until it shines, and curled. Then she prostrates herself; a great black veil is thrown over her, and the office for the dead is sung. Then the nuns separate into two files; one file passes close to her, saying in plaintive accents, "Our sister is dead"; and the other file responds in a voice of ecstasy, "Our sister is alive in Jesus Christ!"

At the epoch when this story takes place, a boarding-school was attached to the convent—a boarding-school for young girls of noble and mostly wealthy families, among whom could be remarked Mademoiselle de Saint-Aulaire and de Bélissen, and an English girl bearing the illustrious Catholic name of Talbot. These young girls, reared by these nuns between four walls, grew up with a horror of the world and of the age. One of them said to us one day, "The sight of the street pavement made me shudder from head to foot." They were dressed in blue, with a white cap and a Holy Spirit of silver gilt or of copper on their breast. On certain grand festival days, particularly Saint Martha's day, they were permitted, as a high favor and a supreme happiness, to dress themselves as nuns and to carry out the offices and practice of Saint-Benoît for a whole day. In the early days the nuns were in the habit of lending them their black garments. This seemed profane, and the prioress forbade it. Only the novices were permitted to lend. It is remarkable that these performances, tolerated and encouraged, no doubt, in the convent out of a secret spirit of proselytism and in order to give these children a foretaste of the holy habit, were a genuine happiness and a real recreation for the scholars. They simply amused themselves with it. *It was new; it gave them a change.* Candid reasons of childhood, which do not, however, succeed in making us worldlings comprehend the felicity of holding a holy water sprinkler in one's hand and standing for hours together singing hard enough for four in front of a reading-desk.

The pupils conformed, with the exception of the austerities, to all the practices of the convent. There was a certain young woman who entered the world, and who after many years of married life had not succeeded in breaking herself of the habit of saying in great haste whenever any one knocked at her door, "forever!" Like the nuns, the pupils saw their relatives only in the parlor. Their very mothers did not obtain permission to embrace them. The following illustrates to what a degree severity on that point was carried. One day a young girl received a visit from her mother, who was accompanied by a little sister three years of age. The young girl wept, for she wished greatly to embrace her sister. Impossible. She begged that, at least, the child might be permitted to pass her little hand through the bars so that she could kiss it. This was almost indignantly refused.

IV

GAYETIES

Nonetheless, these young girls filled this grave house with charming souvenirs.

At certain hours childhood sparkled in that cloister. The recreation hour struck. A door swung on its hinges. The birds said, "Good; here come the children!" An irruption of youth inundated that garden intersected with a cross like a shroud. Radiant faces, white foreheads, innocent eyes, full of merry light, all sorts of auroras, were scattered about amid these shadows. After the psalmodies, the bells, the peals, and knells and offices, the sound of these little girls burst forth on a sudden more sweetly than the noise of bees. The hive of joy was opened, and each one brought her honey. They played, they called to each other, they formed into groups, they ran about; pretty little white teeth chattered in the corners; the veils superintended the laughs from a distance, shades kept watch of the sunbeams, but what mattered it? Still they beamed and laughed. Those four lugubrious walls had their moment of dazzling brilliancy. They looked on, vaguely blanched with the reflection of so much joy at this sweet swarming of the hives. It was like a shower of roses falling athwart this house of mourning. The young girls frolicked beneath the eyes of the nuns; the gaze of impeccability does not embarrass innocence. Thanks to these children, there was, among so many austere hours, one hour of ingenuousness. The little ones skipped about; the elder ones danced. In this cloister play was mingled with heaven. Nothing is so delightful and so august as all these fresh, expanding young souls. Homer would have come thither to laugh with Perrault; and there was in that black garden, youth, health, noise, cries, giddiness, pleasure, happiness enough to smooth out the wrinkles of all their ancestresses, those of the epic as well as those of the fairy-tale, those of the throne as well as those of the thatched cottage from Hecuba to la Mère-Grand.

In that house more than anywhere else, perhaps, arise those children's sayings which are so graceful and which evoke a smile that is full of thoughtfulness. It was between those four gloomy walls that a child of five years exclaimed one day: "Mother! one of the big girls has just told me that I have only nine years and ten months longer to remain here. What happiness!"

It was here, too, that this memorable dialogue took place:—

A Vocal Mother: Why are you weeping, my child?

The child (aged six): I told Alix that I knew my French history. She says that I do not know it, but I do.

Alix, the big girl (aged nine): No; she does not know it.

The Mother: How is that, my child?

Alix: She told me to open the book at random and to ask her any question in the book, and she would answer it.

"Well?"

"She did not answer it."

"Let us see about it. What did you ask her?"

"I opened the book at random, as she proposed, and I put the first question that I came across."

"And what was the question?"

"It was, 'What happened after that?'"

It was there that that profound remark was made anent a rather greedy paroquet which belonged to a lady boarder:—

"How well bred! it eats the top of the slice of bread and butter just like a person!"

It was on one of the flagstones of this cloister that there was once picked up a confession which had been written out in advance, in order that she might not forget it, by a sinner of seven years:—

"Father, I accuse myself of having been avaricious.

"Father, I accuse myself of having been an adulteress.

"Father, I accuse myself of having raised my eyes to the gentlemen."

It was on one of the turf benches of this garden that a rosy mouth six years of age improvised the following tale, which was listened to by blue eyes aged four and five years:—

"There were three little cocks who owned a country where there were a great many flowers. They plucked the flowers and put them in their pockets. After that they plucked the leaves and put them in their playthings. There was a wolf in that country; there was a great deal of forest; and the wolf was in the forest; and he ate the little cocks."

And this other poem:—

"There came a blow with a stick.

"It was Punchinello who bestowed it on the cat.

"It was not good for her; it hurt her.

"Then a lady put Punchinello in prison."

It was there that a little abandoned child, a foundling whom the convent was bringing up out of charity, uttered this sweet and heart-breaking saying. She heard the others talking of their mothers, and she murmured in her corner:—

"As for me, my mother was not there when I was born!"

There was a stout portress who could always be seen hurrying through the corridors with her bunch of keys, and whose name was Sister Agatha. The *big big girls*—those over ten years of age—called her *Agathocles*.

The refectory, a large apartment of an oblong square form, which received no light except through a vaulted cloister on a level with the garden, was dark and damp, and, as the children say, full of beasts. All the places round about furnished their contingent of insects.

Each of its four corners had received, in the language of the pupils, a special and expressive name. There was Spider corner, Caterpillar corner, Wood-louse corner, and Cricket corner.

Cricket corner was near the kitchen and was highly esteemed. It was not so cold there as elsewhere. From the refectory the names had passed to the boarding-school, and there served as in the old College Mazarin to distinguish four nations. Every pupil belonged to one of these four nations according to the corner of the refectory in which she sat at meals. One day Monseigneur the Archbishop while making his pastoral visit saw a pretty little rosy girl with beautiful golden hair enter the class-room through which he was passing.

He inquired of another pupil, a charming brunette with rosy cheeks, who stood near him:—

"Who is that?"

"She is a spider, Monseigneur."

"Bah! And that one yonder?"

"She is a cricket."

"And that one?"

"She is a caterpillar."

"Really! and yourself?"

"I am a wood-louse, Monseigneur."

Every house of this sort has its own peculiarities. At the beginning of this century Écouen was one of those strict and graceful places where young girls pass their childhood in a shadow that is almost august. At Écouen, in order to take rank in the procession of the Holy Sacrament, a distinction was made between virgins and florists. There were also the "dais" and the "censors,"—the first who held the cords of the dais, and the others who carried incense before the Holy Sacrament. The flowers belonged by right to the florists. Four "virgins" walked in advance. On the morning of that great day it was no rare thing to hear the question put in the dormitory, "Who is a virgin?"

Madame Campan used to quote this saying of a "little one" of seven years, to a "big girl" of sixteen, who took the head of the procession, while she, the little one, remained at the rear, "You are a virgin, but I am not."

V

Distractions

Above the door of the refectory this prayer, which was called the *white Paternoster*, and which possessed the property of bearing people straight to paradise, was inscribed in large black letters:—

"Little white Paternoster, which God made, which God said, which God placed in paradise. In the evening, when I went to bed, I found three angels sitting on my bed, one at the foot, two at the head, the good Virgin Mary in the middle, who told me to lie down without hesitation. The good God is my father, the good Virgin is my mother, the three apostles are my brothers, the three virgins are my sisters. The shirt in which God was born envelopes my body; Saint Margaret's cross is written on my breast. Madame the Virgin was walking through the meadows, weeping for God, when she met M. Saint John. 'Monsieur Saint John, whence come you?' 'I come from *Ave Salus.*' 'You have not seen the good God; where is he?' 'He is on the tree of the Cross, his feet hanging, his hands nailed, a little cap of white thorns on his head.' Whoever shall say this thrice at eventide, thrice in the morning, shall win paradise at the last."

In 1827 this characteristic orison had disappeared from the wall under a triple coating of daubing paint. At the present time it is finally disappearing from the memories of several who were young girls then, and who are old women now.

A large crucifix fastened to the wall completed the decoration of this refectory, whose only door, as we think we have mentioned, opened on the garden. Two narrow tables, each flanked by two wooden benches, formed two long parallel lines from one end to the other of the refectory. The walls were white, the tables were black; these two mourning colors constitute the only variety in convents. The meals were plain, and the food of the children themselves severe. A single dish of meat and vegetables combined, or salt fish—such was their luxury. This meagre fare, which was reserved for the pupils alone, was, nevertheless, an exception. The children ate in silence, under the eye of the mother whose turn it was, who, if a fly took a notion to fly or to hum against the rule, opened and shut a wooden book from time to time. This silence was seasoned with the lives of the saints, read aloud from a little pulpit with a desk, which was situated at the foot of the crucifix. The reader was one of the big girls, in weekly turn. At regular distances, on the bare tables, there were large, varnished bowls in which the pupils washed their own silver cups and knives and forks, and into which they sometimes threw some scrap of tough meat or spoiled fish; this was punished. These bowls were called *ronds d'eau*. The child who broke the silence "made a cross with her tongue." Where? On the ground. She licked the pavement. The dust, that end of all joys, was charged with the chastisement of those poor little rose-leaves which had been guilty of chirping.

There was in the convent a book which has never been printed except as a *unique copy*, and which it is forbidden to read. It is the rule of Saint-Benoît. An arcanum which no profane eye must penetrate. *Nemo regulas, seu constitutiones nostras, externis communicabit.*

The pupils one day succeeded in getting possession of this book, and set to reading it with avidity, a reading which was often interrupted by the fear of being caught, which caused them to close the volume precipitately.

From the great danger thus incurred they derived but a very moderate amount of pleasure. The most "interesting thing" they found were some unintelligible pages about the sins of young boys.

They played in an alley of the garden bordered with a few shabby fruit-trees. In spite of the extreme surveillance and the severity of the punishments administered, when the wind had shaken the trees, they sometimes succeeded in picking up a green apple or a spoiled apricot or an inhabited pear on the sly. I will now cede the privilege of speech to a letter which lies before me, a letter written five and twenty years ago by an old pupil, now Madame la Duchesse de ——, one of the most elegant women in Paris. I quote literally: "One hides one's pear or one's apple as best one may. When one goes upstairs to put the veil on the bed before supper, one stuffs them under one's pillow and at night one eats them in bed, and when one cannot do that, one eats them in the closet." That was one of their greatest luxuries.

Once—it was at the epoch of the visit from the archbishop to the convent—one of the young girls, Mademoiselle Bouchard, who was connected with the Montmorency family, laid a wager that she would ask for a day's leave of absence—an enormity in so austere a community. The wager was accepted, but not one of those who bet believed that she would do it. When the moment came, as the archbishop was passing in front of the pupils, Mademoiselle Bouchard, to the indescribable terror of her companions, stepped out of the ranks, and said, "Monseigneur, a day's leave of absence." Mademoiselle Bouchard was tall, blooming, with the prettiest little rosy face in the world. M. de Quélen smiled and said, "What, my dear child, a day's leave of absence! Three days if you like. I grant you three days." The prioress could do nothing; the archbishop had spoken. Horror of the convent, but joy of the pupil. The effect may be imagined.

This stern cloister was not so well walled off, however, but that the life of the passions of the outside world, drama, and even romance, did not make their way in. To prove this, we will confine ourselves to recording here and to briefly mentioning a real and incontestable fact, which, however, bears no reference in itself to, and is not connected by any thread whatever with the story which we are relating. We mention the fact for the sake of completing the physiognomy of the convent in the reader's mind.

About this time there was in the convent a mysterious person who was not a nun, who was treated with great respect, and who was addressed as *Madame Albertine*. Nothing was known about her, save that she was mad, and that in the world she passed for dead. Beneath this history it was said there lay the arrangements of fortune necessary for a great marriage.

This woman, hardly thirty years of age, of dark complexion and tolerably pretty, had a vague look in her large black eyes. Could she see? There was some doubt about this. She glided rather than walked, she never spoke; it was not quite known whether she breathed. Her nostrils were livid and pinched as after yielding up their last sigh. To touch her hand was like touching snow. She possessed a strange spectral grace. Wherever she entered, people felt cold. One day a sister, on seeing her pass, said to another sister, "She passes for a dead woman." "Perhaps she is one," replied the other.

A hundred tales were told of Madame Albertine. This arose from the eternal curiosity of the pupils. In the chapel there was a gallery called *L'Œil de Bœuf*. It was in this gallery, which had only a circular bay, an *œil de bœuf*, that Madame Albertine listened to the offices. She always occupied it alone because this gallery, being on the level of the first story, the preacher or the officiating priest could be seen, which was interdicted to the nuns. One day the pulpit was occupied by a young priest of high rank, M. Le Duc de Rohan, peer of France, officer of the Red Musketeers in 1815 when he was Prince de Léon, and who died afterward, in 1830, as cardinal and Archbishop of Besançon. It was the first time that M. de Rohan had preached at the Petit-Picpus convent. Madame Albertine usually preserved perfect calmness and complete immobility during the sermons and services. That day, as soon as she caught sight of M. de Rohan, she half rose, and said, in a loud voice, amid the silence of the chapel, "Ah! Auguste!" The whole community turned their heads in amazement, the preacher raised his eyes, but Madame Albertine had relapsed into her immobility. A breath from the outer world, a flash of life, had passed for an instant across that cold and lifeless face and had then vanished, and the mad woman had become a corpse again.

Those two words, however, had set every one in the convent who had the privilege of speech to chattering. How many things were contained in that "Ah! Auguste!" what revelations! M. de Rohan's name really was Auguste. It was evident that Madame Albertine belonged to the very highest society, since she knew M. de Rohan, and that her own rank there was of the highest, since she spoke thus familiarly of so great a lord, and that there existed between them some connection, of relationship, perhaps, but a very close one in any case, since she knew his "pet name."

Two very severe duchesses, Mesdames de Choiseul and de Sérent, often visited the community, whither they penetrated, no doubt, in virtue of the privilege *Magnates mulieres*, and caused great consternation in the boarding-school. When these two old ladies passed by, all the poor young girls trembled and dropped their eyes.

Moreover, M. de Rohan, quite unknown to himself, was an object of attention to the school-girls. At that epoch he had just been made, while waiting for the episcopate, vicar-general of the Archbishop of Paris. It was one of his habits to come tolerably often to celebrate the offices in the chapel of the nuns of the Petit-Picpus. Not one of the young recluses could see him, because of the serge curtain, but he had a sweet and rather shrill voice, which they had come to know and to distinguish. He had been a mousquetaire, and then, he was said to be very coquettish, that his handsome brown hair was very well dressed in a roll around his head, and that he had a broad girdle of magnificent moire, and that his black cassock was of the most elegant cut in the world. He held a great place in all these imaginations of sixteen years.

Not a sound from without made its way into the convent. But there was one year when the sound of a flute penetrated thither. This was an event, and the girls who were at school there at the time still recall it.

It was a flute which was played in the neighborhood. This flute always played the same air, an air which is very far away nowadays,— "My Zétulbé, come reign o'er my soul,"—and it was heard two or three times a day. The young girls passed hours in listening to it, the vocal mothers were upset by it, brains were busy, punishments descended in showers. This lasted for several months. The girls were all more or less in love with the unknown musician. Each one dreamed that she was Zétulbé. The sound of the flute proceeded from the direction of the Rue Droit-Mur; and they would have given anything, compromised everything, attempted anything for the sake of seeing, of catching a glance, if only for a second, of the "young man" who played that flute so deliciously, and who, no doubt, played on all these souls at the same time. There were some who made their escape by a back door, and ascended to the third story on the Rue Droit-Mur side, in order to attempt to catch a glimpse through the gaps. Impossible! One even went so far as to thrust her arm through the grating, and to wave her white handkerchief. Two were still bolder. They found means to climb on a roof, and risked their lives there, and succeeded at last in seeing "the young man." He was an old *émigré* gentleman, blind and penniless, who was playing his flute in his attic, in order to pass the time.

VI

The Little Convent

In this enclosure of the Petit-Picpus there were three perfectly distinct buildings,—the Great Convent, inhabited by the nuns, the Boarding-school, where the scholars were lodged; and lastly, what was called the Little Convent. It was a building with a garden, in which lived all sorts of aged nuns of various orders, the relics of cloisters destroyed in the Revolution; a reunion of all the black, gray, and white medleys of all communities and all possible varieties; what might be called, if such a coupling of words is permissible, a sort of harlequin convent.

When the Empire was established, all these poor old dispersed and exiled women had been accorded permission to come and take shelter under the wings of the Bernardines-Benedictines. The government paid them a small pension, the ladies of the Petit-Picpus received them cordially. It was a singular pell-mell. Each followed her own rule. Sometimes the pupils of the boarding-school were allowed, as a great recreation, to pay them a visit; the result is, that all those young memories have retained among other souvenirs that of Mother Sainte-Bazile, Mother Sainte-Scolastique, and Mother Jacob.

One of these refugees found herself almost at home. She was a nun of Sainte-Aure, the only one of her order who had survived. The ancient convent of the ladies of Sainte-Aure occupied, at the beginning of the eighteenth century, this very house of the Petit-Picpus, which belonged later to the Benedictines of Martin Verga. This holy woman, too poor to wear the magnificent habit of her order, which was a white robe with a scarlet scapulary, had piously put it on a little manikin, which she exhibited with complacency and which she bequeathed to the house at her death. In 1824, only one nun of this order remained; to-day, there remains only a doll.

In addition to these worthy mothers, some old society women had obtained permission of the prioress, like Madame Albertine, to retire into the Little Convent. Among the number were Madame Beaufort d'Hautpoul and Marquise Dufresne. Another was never known in the convent except by the formidable noise which she made when she blew her nose. The pupils called her Madame Vacarmini (hubbub).

About 1820 or 1821, Madame de Genlis, who was at that time editing a little periodical publication called *l'Intrépide*, asked to be allowed to enter the convent of the Petit-Picpus as lady resident. The Duc d'Orléans recommended her. Uproar in the hive; the vocal-mothers were all in a flutter; Madame de Genlis had made romances. But she declared that she was the first to detest them, and then, she had reached her fierce stage of devotion. With the aid of God, and of the Prince, she entered. She departed at the end of six or eight months, alleging as a reason, that there was no shade in the garden. The nuns were delighted. Although very old, she still played the harp, and did it very well.

When she went away she left her mark in her cell. Madame de Genlis was superstitious and a Latinist. These two words furnish a tolerably good profile of her. A few years ago, there were still to be seen, pasted in the inside of a little cupboard in her cell in which she locked up her silverware and her jewels, these five lines in Latin, written with her own hand in red ink on yellow paper, and which, in her opinion, possessed the property of frightening away robbers:—

> *Imparibus meritis pendent tria corpora ramis:*
> *Dismas et Gesmas, media est divina potestas;*
> *Alta petit Dismas, infelix, infima, Gesmas;*
> *Nos et res nostras conservet summa potestas.*
> *Hos versus dicas, ne tu furto tua perdas.*

These verses in sixth century Latin raise the question whether the two thieves of Calvary were named, as is commonly believed, Dismas and Gestas, or Dismas and Gesmas. This orthography might have confounded the pretensions put forward in the last century by the Vicomte de Gestas, of a descent from the wicked thief. However, the useful virtue attached to these verses forms an article of faith in the order of the Hospitallers.

The church of the house, constructed in such a manner as to separate the Great Convent from the Boarding-school like a veritable intrenchment, was, of course, common to the Boarding-school, the Great Convent, and the Little Convent. The public was even admitted by a sort of lazaretto entrance on the street. But all was so arranged, that none of the inhabitants of the cloister could see a face from the outside world. Suppose a church whose choir is grasped in a gigantic hand, and folded in such a manner as to form, not, as in ordinary churches, a prolongation behind the altar, but a sort of hall, or obscure cellar, to the right of the officiating priest; suppose this hall to be shut off by a curtain seven feet in height, of which we have already spoken; in the shadow of that curtain, pile up on wooden stalls the nuns in the choir on the left, the school-girls on the right, the lay-sisters and the novices at the bottom, and you will have some idea of the nuns of the Petit-Picpus assisting at divine service. That cavern, which was called the choir, communicated with the cloister by a lobby. The church was lighted from the garden. When the nuns were present at services where their rule enjoined silence, the public was warned of their presence only by the folding seats of the stalls noisily rising and falling.

VII

SOME SILHOUETTES OF THIS DARKNESS

During the six years which separate 1819 from 1825, the prioress of the Petit-Picpus was Mademoiselle de Blemeur, whose name, in religion, was Mother Innocente. She came of the family of Marguerite de Blemeur, author of *Lives of the Saints of the Order of Saint-Benoît*. She had been re-elected. She was a woman about sixty years of age, short, thick, "singing like a cracked pot," says the letter which we have already quoted; an excellent woman, moreover, and the only merry one in the whole convent, and for that reason adored. She was learned, erudite, wise, competent, curiously proficient in history, crammed with Latin, stuffed with Greek, full of Hebrew, and more of a Benedictine monk than a Benedictine nun.

The sub-prioress was an old Spanish nun, Mother Cineres, who was almost blind.

The most esteemed among the vocal mothers were Mother Sainte-Honorine; the treasurer, Mother Sainte-Gertrude, the chief mistress of the novices; Mother-Saint-Ange, the assistant mistress; Mother Annonciation, the sacristan; Mother Saint-Augustin, the nurse, the only one in the convent who was malicious; then Mother Sainte-Mechtilde (Mademoiselle Gauvain), very young and with a beautiful voice; Mother des Anges (Mademoiselle Drouet), who had been in the convent of the Filles-Dieu, and in the convent du Trésor, between Gisors and Magny; Mother Saint-Joseph (Mademoiselle de Cogolludo), Mother Sainte-Adélaide (Mademoiselle d'Auverney), Mother Miséricorde (Mademoiselle de Cifuentes, who could not resist austerities), Mother Compassion (Mademoiselle de la Miltière, received at the age of sixty in defiance of the rule, and very wealthy); Mother Providence (Mademoiselle de Laudinière), Mother Présentation (Mademoiselle de Siguenza), who was prioress in 1847; and finally, Mother Sainte-Céligne (sister of the sculptor Ceracchi), who went mad; Mother Sainte-Chantal (Mademoiselle de Suzon), who went mad.

There was also, among the prettiest of them, a charming girl of three and twenty, who was from the Isle de Bourbon, a descendant of the

Chevalier Roze, whose name had been Mademoiselle Roze, and who was called Mother Assumption.

Mother Sainte-Mechtilde, intrusted with the singing and the choir, was fond of making use of the pupils in this quarter. She usually took a complete scale of them, that is to say, seven, from ten to sixteen years of age, inclusive, of assorted voices and sizes, whom she made sing standing, drawn up in a line, side by side, according to age, from the smallest to the largest. This presented to the eye, something in the nature of a reed-pipe of young girls, a sort of living Pan-pipe made of angels.

Those of the lay-sisters whom the scholars loved most were Sister Euphrasie, Sister Sainte-Marguérite, Sister Sainte-Marthe, who was in her dotage, and Sister Sainte-Michel, whose long nose made them laugh.

All these women were gentle with the children. The nuns were severe only towards themselves. No fire was lighted except in the school, and the food was choice compared to that in the convent. Moreover, they lavished a thousand cares on their scholars. Only, when a child passed near a nun and addressed her, the nun never replied.

This rule of silence had had this effect, that throughout the whole convent, speech had been withdrawn from human creatures, and bestowed on inanimate objects. Now it was the church-bell which spoke, now it was the gardener's bell. A very sonorous bell, placed beside the portress, and which was audible throughout the house, indicated by its varied peals, which formed a sort of acoustic telegraph, all the actions of material life which were to be performed, and summoned to the parlor, in case of need, such or such an inhabitant of the house. Each person and each thing had its own peal. The prioress had one and one, the sub-prioress one and two. Six-five announced lessons, so that the pupils never said "to go to lessons," but "to go to six-five." Four-four was Madame de Genlis's signal. It was very often heard. "C'est le diable a quatre,"—it's the very deuce—said the uncharitable. Tennine strokes announced a great event. It was the opening of *the door of seclusion*, a frightful sheet of iron bristling with bolts which only turned on its hinges in the presence of the archbishop.

With the exception of the archbishop and the gardener, no man entered the convent, as we have already said. The schoolgirls saw two others: one, the chaplain, the Abbé Banés, old and ugly, whom they were permitted to contemplate in the choir, through a grating; the other the drawing-master, M. Ansiaux, whom the letter, of which we have perused a few lines, calls *M. Anciot*, and describes as *a frightful old hunchback*.

It will be seen that all these men were carefully chosen.

Such was this curious house.

VIII

Post Corda Lapides

After having sketched its moral face, it will not prove unprofitable to point out, in a few words, its material configuration. The reader already has some idea of it.

The convent of the Petit-Picpus-Sainte-Antoine filled almost the whole of the vast trapezium which resulted from the intersection of the Rue Polonceau, the Rue Droit-Mur, the Rue Petit-Picpus, and the unused lane, called Rue Aumarais on old plans. These four streets surrounded this trapezium like a moat. The convent was composed of several buildings and a garden. The principal building, taken in its entirety, was a juxtaposition of hybrid constructions which, viewed from a bird's-eye view, outlined, with considerable exactness, a gibbet laid flat on the ground. The main arm of the gibbet occupied the whole of the fragment of the Rue Droit-Mur comprised between the Rue Petit-Picpus and the Rue Polonceau; the lesser arm was a lofty, gray, severe grated façade which faced the Rue Petit-Picpus; the carriage entrance No. 62 marked its extremity. Towards the centre of this façade was a low, arched door, whitened with dust and ashes, where the spiders wove their webs, and which was open only for an hour or two on Sundays, and on rare occasions, when the coffin of a nun left the convent. This was the public entrance of the church. The elbow of the gibbet was a square hall which was used as the servants' hall, and which the nuns called *the buttery*. In the main arm were the cells of the mothers, the sisters, and the novices. In the lesser arm lay the kitchens, the refectory, backed up by the cloisters and the church. Between the door No. 62 and the corner of the closed Aumarais Lane, was the school, which was not visible from without. The remainder of the trapezium formed the garden, which was much lower than the level of the Rue Polonceau, which caused the walls to be very much higher on the inside than on the outside. The garden, which was slightly arched, had in its centre, on the summit of a hillock, a fine pointed and conical fir-tree, whence ran, as from the peaked boss of a shield, four grand alleys, and, ranged by twos in between the branchings of these, eight small ones, so that, if the enclosure had been circular, the geometrical plan of the alleys would have resembled a cross superposed on a wheel. As the alleys all ended in the very irregular walls of the garden, they were of unequal length. They were bordered with currant bushes. At the bottom, an alley of tall poplars ran from the ruins of the old convent, which was at the angle of the Rue Droit-Mur to the house of the Little Convent, which was at the angle of the Aumarais Lane. In front of the Little Convent was what was called the little garden. To this whole, let the reader add a courtyard, all sorts of varied angles formed by the interior buildings, prison walls, the long black line of roofs which bordered the other side of the Rue Polonceau for its sole perspective and neighborhood, and he will be able to form for himself a complete image of what the house of the Bernardines of the Petit-Picpus was forty years ago. This holy house had been built on the precise site of a famous tennis-ground of the fourteenth to the sixteenth century, which was called the "tennis-ground of the eleven thousand devils."

All these streets, moreover, were more ancient than Paris. These names, Droit-Mur and Aumarais, are very ancient; the streets which bear them are very much more ancient still. Aumarais Lane was called Maugout Lane; the Rue Droit-Mur was called the Rue des Églantiers, for God opened flowers before man cut stones.

A Century Under a Guimpe

Since we are engaged in giving details as to what the convent of the Petit-Picpus was in former times, and since we have ventured to open a window on that discreet retreat, the reader will permit us one other little digression, utterly foreign to this book, but characteristic and useful, since it shows that the cloister even has its original figures.

In the Little Convent there was a centenarian who came from the Abbey of Fontevrault. She had even been in society before the Revolution. She talked a great deal of M. de Miromesnil, Keeper of the Seals under Louis XVI and of a Presidentess Duplat, with whom she had been very intimate. It was her pleasure and her vanity to drag in these names on every pretext. She told wonders of the Abbey of Fontevrault,—that it was like a city, and that there were streets in the monastery.

She talked with a Picard accent which amused the pupils. Every year, she solemnly renewed her vows, and at the moment of taking the oath, she said to the priest, "Monseigneur Saint-François gave it to Monseigneur Saint-Julien, Monseigneur Saint-Julien gave it to Monseigneur Saint-Eusebius, Monseigneur Saint-Eusebius gave it to Monseigneur Saint-Procopius, etc., etc.; and thus I give it to you, father." And the school-girls would begin to laugh, not in their sleeves, but under their veils; charming little stifled laughs which made the vocal mothers frown.

On another occasion, the centenarian was telling stories. She said that *in her youth the Bernardine monks were every whit as good as the mousquetaires*. It was a century which spoke through her, but it was the eighteenth century. She told about the custom of the four wines, which existed before the Revolution in Champagne and Bourgogne. When a great personage, a marshal of France, a prince, a duke, and a peer, traversed a town in Burgundy or Champagne, the city fathers came out to harangue him and presented him with four silver gondolas into which they had poured four different sorts of wine. On the first goblet this inscription could be read, *monkey wine*; on the second, *lion wine*; on the third, *sheep wine*; on the fourth, *hog wine*. These four legends express the four stages descended by the drunkard; the first, intoxication, which enlivens; the second, that which irritates; the third, that which dulls; and the fourth, that which brutalizes.

In a cupboard, under lock and key, she kept a mysterious object of which she thought a great deal. The rule of Fontevrault did not forbid this. She would not show this object to anyone. She shut herself up, which her rule allowed her to do, and hid herself, every time that she desired to contemplate it. If she heard a footstep in the corridor, she closed the cupboard again as hastily as it was possible with her aged hands. As soon as it was mentioned to her, she became silent, she who was so fond of talking. The most curious were baffled by her silence and the most tenacious by her obstinacy. Thus it furnished a subject of comment for all those who were unoccupied or bored in the convent. What could that treasure of the centenarian be, which was so precious and so secret? Some holy book, no doubt? Some unique chaplet? Some authentic relic? They lost themselves in conjectures. When the poor old woman died, they rushed to her cupboard more hastily than was fitting, perhaps, and opened it. They found the object beneath a triple linen cloth, like some consecrated paten. It was a Faenza platter representing little Loves flitting away pursued by apothecary lads armed with enormous syringes. The chase abounds in grimaces and in comical postures. One of the charming little Loves is already fairly spitted. He is resisting, fluttering his tiny wings, and still making an effort to fly, but the dancer is laughing with a satanical air. Moral: Love conquered by the colic. This platter, which is very curious, and which had, possibly, the honor of furnishing Molière with an idea, was still in existence in September, 1845; it was for sale by a bric-à-brac merchant in the Boulevard Beaumarchais.

This good old woman would not receive any visits from outside *because*, said she, the *parlor is too gloomy*.

X

Origin of the Perpetual Adoration

However, this almost sepulchral parlor, of which we have sought to convey an idea, is a purely local trait which is not reproduced with the same severity in other convents. At the convent of the Rue du Temple, in particular, which belonged, in truth, to another order, the black shutters were replaced by brown curtains, and the parlor itself was a salon with a polished wood floor, whose windows were draped in white muslin curtains and whose walls admitted all sorts of frames, a portrait of a Benedictine nun with unveiled face, painted bouquets, and even the head of a Turk.

It is in that garden of the Temple convent, that stood that famous chestnut-tree which was renowned as the finest and the largest in France, and which bore the reputation among the good people of the eighteenth century of being *the father of all the chestnut trees of the realm*.

As we have said, this convent of the Temple was occupied by Benedictines of the Perpetual Adoration, Benedictines quite different from those who depended on Cîteaux. This order of the Perpetual Adoration is not very ancient and does not go back more than two hundred years. In 1649 the holy sacrament was profaned on two occasions a few days apart, in two churches in Paris, at Saint-Sulpice and at Saint-Jean en Grève, a rare and frightful sacrilege which set the whole town in an uproar. M. the Prior and Vicar-General of Saint-Germain des Prés ordered a solemn procession of all his clergy, in which the Pope's Nuncio officiated. But this expiation did not satisfy two sainted women, Madame Courtin, Marquise de Boucs, and the Comtesse de Châteauvieux. This outrage committed on "the most holy sacrament of the altar," though but temporary, would not depart from these holy souls, and it seemed to them that it could only be extenuated by a "Perpetual Adoration" in some female monastery. Both of them, one in 1652, the other in 1653, made donations of notable sums to Mother Catherine de Bar, called of the Holy Sacrament, a Benedictine nun, for the purpose of founding, to this pious end, a monastery of the order of Saint-Benoît; the first permission for this foundation was given to Mother Catherine de Bar by M. de Metz, Abbé of Saint-Germain, "on condition that no woman could be received unless she contributed three hundred livres income, which amounts to six thousand livres, to the principal." After the Abbé of Saint-Germain, the king accorded letters-patent; and all the rest, abbatial charter, and royal letters, was confirmed in 1654 by the Chamber of Accounts and the Parliament.

Such is the origin of the legal consecration of the establishment of the Benedictines of the Perpetual Adoration of the Holy Sacrament at Paris. Their first convent was "a new building" in the Rue Cassette, out of the contributions of Mesdames de Boucs and de Châteauvieux.

This order, as it will be seen, was not to be confounded with the Benedictine nuns of Cîteaux. It mounted back to the Abbé of Saint-Germain des Prés, in the same manner that the ladies of the Sacred Heart go back to the general of the Jesuits, and the sisters of charity to the general of the Lazarists.

It was also totally different from the Bernardines of the Petit-Picpus, whose interior we have just shown. In 1657, Pope Alexander VII had authorized, by a special brief, the Bernardines of the Rue Petit-Picpus, to practise the Perpetual Adoration like the Benedictine nuns of the Holy Sacrament. But the two orders remained distinct nonetheless.

XI

End of the Petit-Picpus

At the beginning of the Restoration, the convent of the Petit-Picpus was in its decay; this forms a part of the general death of the order, which, after the eighteenth century, has been disappearing like all the religious orders. Contemplation is, like prayer, one of humanity's needs; but, like everything which the Revolution touched, it will be transformed, and from being hostile to social progress, it will become favorable to it.

The house of the Petit-Picpus was becoming rapidly depopulated. In 1840, the Little Convent had disappeared, the school had disappeared. There were no longer any old women, nor young girls; the first were dead, the latter had taken their departure. *Volaverunt*.

The rule of the Perpetual Adoration is so rigid in its nature that it alarms, vocations recoil before it, the order receives no recruits. In 1845, it still obtained lay-sisters here and there. But of professed nuns, none at all. Forty years ago, the nuns numbered nearly a hundred; fifteen years ago there were not more than twenty-eight of them. How many are there to-day? In 1847, the prioress was young, a sign that the circle of choice was restricted. She was not forty years old. In proportion as the number diminishes, the fatigue increases, the service of each becomes more painful; the moment could then be seen drawing near when there would be but a dozen bent and aching shoulders to bear the heavy rule of Saint-Benoît. The burden is implacable, and remains the same for the few as for the many. It weighs down, it crushes. Thus they die. At the period when the author of this book still lived in Paris, two died. One was twenty-five years old, the other twenty-three. This latter can say, like Julia Alpinula: *"Hic jaceo. Vixi annos viginti et tres."* It is in consequence of this decay that the convent gave up the education of girls.

We have not felt able to pass before this extraordinary house without entering it, and without introducing the minds which accompany us, and which are listening to our tale, to the profit of some, perchance, of the melancholy history of Jean Valjean. We have penetrated into this community, full of those old practices which seem so novel to-day. It is the closed garden, *hortus conclusus*. We have spoken of this singular place in detail, but with respect, in so far, at least, as detail and respect are compatible. We do not understand all, but we insult nothing. We are equally far removed from the hosanna of Joseph de Maistre, who wound up by anointing the executioner, and from the sneer of Voltaire, who even goes so far as to ridicule the cross.

An illogical act on Voltaire's part, we may remark, by the way; for Voltaire would have defended Jesus as he defended Calas; and even for those who deny superhuman incarnations, what does the crucifix represent? The assassinated sage.

In this nineteenth century, the religious idea is undergoing a crisis. People are unlearning certain things, and they do well, provided that, while unlearning them they learn this: There is no vacuum in the human heart. Certain demolitions take place, and it is well that they do, but on condition that they are followed by reconstructions.

In the meantime, let us study things which are no more. It is necessary to know them, if only for the purpose of avoiding them. The counterfeits of the past assume false names, and gladly call themselves the future. This spectre, this past, is given to falsifying its own passport. Let us inform ourselves of the trap. Let us be on our guard. The past has a visage, superstition, and a mask, hypocrisy. Let us denounce the visage and let us tear off the mask.

As for convents, they present a complex problem,—a question of civilization, which condemns them; a question of liberty, which protects them.

BOOK SEVENTH
PARENTHESIS

I

The Convent as an Abstract Idea

This book is a drama, whose leading personage is the Infinite.
Man is the second.

Such being the case, and a convent having happened to be on our road, it has been our duty to enter it. Why? Because the convent, which is common to the Orient as well as to the Occident, to antiquity as well as to modern times, to paganism, to Buddhism, to Mahometanism, as well as to Christianity, is one of the optical apparatuses applied by man to the Infinite.

This is not the place for enlarging disproportionately on certain ideas; nevertheless, while absolutely maintaining our reserves, our restrictions, and even our indignations, we must say that every time we encounter man in the Infinite, either well or ill understood, we feel ourselves overpowered with respect. There is, in the synagogue, in the mosque, in the pagoda, in the wigwam, a hideous side which we execrate, and a sublime side, which we adore. What a contemplation for the mind, and what endless food for thought, is the reverberation of God upon the human wall!

II

The Convent as an Historical Fact

From the point of view of history, of reason, and of truth, monasticism is condemned. Monasteries, when they abound in a nation, are clogs in its circulation, cumbrous establishments, centres of idleness where centres of labor should exist. Monastic communities are to the great social community what the mistletoe is to the oak, what the wart is to the human body. Their prosperity and their fatness mean the impoverishment of the country. The monastic regime, good at the beginning of civilization, useful in the reduction of the brutal by the spiritual, is bad when peoples have reached their manhood. Moreover, when it becomes relaxed, and when it enters into its period of disorder, it becomes bad for the very reasons which rendered it salutary in its period of purity, because it still continues to set the example.

Claustration has had its day. Cloisters, useful in the early education of modern civilization, have embarrassed its growth, and are injurious to its development. So far as institution and formation with relation to man are concerned, monasteries, which were good in the tenth century, questionable in the fifteenth, are detestable in the nineteenth. The leprosy of monasticism has gnawed nearly to a skeleton two wonderful nations, Italy and Spain; the one the light, the other the splendor of Europe for centuries; and, at the present day, these two illustrious peoples are but just beginning to convalesce, thanks to the healthy and vigorous hygiene of 1789 alone.

The convent—the ancient female convent in particular, such as it still presents itself on the threshold of this century, in Italy, in Austria, in Spain—is one of the most sombre concretions of the Middle Ages. The cloister, that cloister, is the point of intersection of horrors. The Catholic cloister, properly speaking, is wholly filled with the black radiance of death.

The Spanish convent is the most funereal of all. There rise, in obscurity, beneath vaults filled with gloom, beneath domes vague with shadow, massive altars of Babel, as high as cathedrals; there immense white crucifixes hang from chains in the dark; there are extended, all nude on the ebony, great Christs of ivory; more than bleeding,—

bloody; hideous and magnificent, with their elbows displaying the bones, their knee-pans showing their integuments, their wounds showing their flesh, crowned with silver thorns, nailed with nails of gold, with blood drops of rubies on their brows, and diamond tears in their eyes. The diamonds and rubies seem wet, and make veiled beings in the shadow below weep, their sides bruised with the hair shirt and their iron-tipped scourges, their breasts crushed with wicker hurdles, their knees excoriated with prayer; women who think themselves wives, spectres who think themselves seraphim. Do these women think? No. Have they any will? No. Do they love? No. Do they live? No. Their nerves have turned to bone; their bones have turned to stone. Their veil is of woven night. Their breath under their veil resembles the indescribably tragic respiration of death. The abbess, a spectre, sanctifies them and terrifies them. The immaculate one is there, and very fierce. Such are the ancient monasteries of Spain. Liars of terrible devotion, caverns of virgins, ferocious places.

Catholic Spain is more Roman than Rome herself. The Spanish convent was, above all others, the Catholic convent. There was a flavor of the Orient about it. The archbishop, the kislar-aga of heaven, locked up and kept watch over this seraglio of souls reserved for God. The nun was the odalisque, the priest was the eunuch. The fervent were chosen in dreams and possessed Christ. At night, the beautiful, nude young man descended from the cross and became the ecstasy of the cloistered one. Lofty walls guarded the mystic sultana, who had the crucified for her sultan, from all living distraction. A glance on the outer world was infidelity. The *in pace* replaced the leather sack. That which was cast into the sea in the East was thrown into the ground in the West. In both quarters, women wrung their hands; the waves for the first, the grave for the last; here the drowned, there the buried. Monstrous parallel.

To-day the upholders of the past, unable to deny these things, have adopted the expedient of smiling at them. There has come into fashion a strange and easy manner of suppressing the revelations of history, of invalidating the commentaries of philosophy, of eliding all embarrassing facts and all gloomy questions. *A matter for declamations*, say the clever. Declamations, repeat the foolish. Jean-Jacques a declaimer; Diderot a declaimer; Voltaire on Calas, Labarre, and Sirven, declaimers. I know not who has recently discovered that Tacitus was a declaimer, that Nero was a victim, and that pity is decidedly due to "that poor Holofernes."

Facts, however, are awkward things to disconcert, and they are obstinate. The author of this book has seen, with his own eyes, eight leagues distant from Brussels,—there are relics of the Middle Ages there which are attainable for everybody,—at the Abbey of Villers, the hole of the oubliettes, in the middle of the field which was formerly the courtyard of the cloister, and on the banks of the Thil, four stone dungeons, half under ground, half under the water. They were *in pace*. Each of these dungeons has the remains of an iron door, a vault, and a grated opening which, on the outside, is two feet above the level of the river, and on the inside, six feet above the level of the ground. Four feet of river flow past along the outside wall. The ground is always soaked. The occupant of the *in pace* had this wet soil for his bed. In one of these dungeons, there is a fragment of an iron necklet riveted to the wall; in another, there can be seen a square box made of four slabs of granite, too short for a person to lie down in, too low for him to stand upright in. A human being was put inside, with a coverlid of stone on top. This exists. It can be seen. It can be touched. These *in pace*, these dungeons, these iron hinges, these necklets, that lofty peep-hole on a level with the river's current, that box of stone closed with a lid of granite like a tomb, with this difference, that the dead man here was a living being, that soil which is but mud, that vault hole, those oozing walls,—what declaimers!

III

On What Conditions One Can Respect the Past

Monasticism, such as it existed in Spain, and such as it still exists in Thibet, is a sort of phthisis for civilization. It stops life short. It simply depopulates. Claustration, castration. It has been the scourge of Europe. Add to this the violence so often done to the conscience, the forced vocations, feudalism bolstered up by the cloister, the right of the first-born pouring the excess of the family into monasticism, the ferocities of which we have just spoken, the *in pace*, the closed mouths, the walled-up brains, so many unfortunate minds placed in the dungeon of eternal vows, the taking of the habit, the interment of living souls. Add individual tortures to national degradations, and, whoever you may be, you will shudder before the frock and the veil,— those two winding-sheets of human devising. Nevertheless, at certain points and in certain places, in spite of philosophy, in spite of progress, the spirit of the cloister persists in the midst of the nineteenth century, and a singular ascetic recrudescence is, at this moment, astonishing the civilized world. The obstinacy of antiquated institutions in perpetuating themselves resembles the stubbornness of the rancid perfume which should claim our hair, the pretensions of the spoiled fish which should persist in being eaten, the persecution of the child's garment which should insist on clothing the man, the tenderness of corpses which should return to embrace the living.

"Ingrates!" says the garment, "I protected you in inclement weather. Why will you have nothing to do with me?" "I have just come from the deep sea," says the fish. "I have been a rose," says the perfume. "I have loved you," says the corpse. "I have civilized you," says the convent.

To this there is but one reply: "In former days."

To dream of the indefinite prolongation of defunct things, and of the government of men by embalming, to restore dogmas in a bad condition, to regild shrines, to patch up cloisters, to rebless reliquaries, to refurnish superstitions, to revictual fanaticisms, to put new handles on holy water brushes and militarism, to reconstitute monasticism and militarism, to believe in the salvation of society by the multiplication of parasites, to force the past on the present,—this seems strange. Still, there are theorists who hold such theories. These theorists, who are in other respects people of intelligence, have a very simple process; they apply to the past a glazing which they call social order, divine right, morality, family, the respect of elders, antique authority, sacred tradition, legitimacy, religion; and they go about shouting, "Look! take this, honest people." This logic was known to the ancients. The soothsayers practise it. They rubbed a black heifer over with chalk, and said, "She is white, *Bos cretatus*."

As for us, we respect the past here and there, and we spare it, above all, provided that it consents to be dead. If it insists on being alive, we attack it, and we try to kill it.

Superstitions, bigotries, affected devotion, prejudices, those forms, all forms as they are, are tenacious of life; they have teeth and nails in their smoke, and they must be clasped close, body to body, and war must be made on them, and that without truce; for it is one of the fatalities of humanity to be condemned to eternal combat with phantoms. It is difficult to seize darkness by the throat, and to hurl it to the earth.

A convent in France, in the broad daylight of the nineteenth century, is a college of owls facing the light. A cloister, caught in the very act of asceticism, in the very heart of the city of '89 and of 1830 and of 1848, Rome blossoming out in Paris, is an anachronism. In ordinary times, in order to dissolve an anachronism and to cause it to vanish, one has only to make it spell out the date. But we are not in ordinary times.

Let us fight.

Let us fight, but let us make a distinction. The peculiar property of truth is never to commit excesses. What need has it of exaggeration? There is that which it is necessary to destroy, and there is that which it is simply necessary to elucidate and examine. What a force is kindly and serious examination! Let us not apply a flame where only a light is required.

So, given the nineteenth century, we are opposed, as a general proposition, and among all peoples, in Asia as well as in Europe, in India as well as in Turkey, to ascetic claustration. Whoever says cloister, says marsh. Their putrescence is evident, their stagnation is unhealthy, their fermentation infects people with fever, and etiolates them; their multiplication becomes a plague of Egypt. We cannot think without affright of those lands where fakirs, bonzes, santons, Greek monks, marabouts, talapoins, and dervishes multiply even like swarms of vermin.

This said, the religious question remains. This question has certain mysterious, almost formidable sides; may we be permitted to look at it fixedly.

IV

The Convent from the Point of View of Principles

M en unite themselves and dwell in communities. By virtue of what right? By virtue of the right of association.

They shut themselves up at home. By virtue of what right? By virtue of the right which every man has to open or shut his door.

They do not come forth. By virtue of what right? By virtue of the right to go and come, which implies the right to remain at home.

There, at home, what do they do?

They speak in low tones; they drop their eyes; they toil. They renounce the world, towns, sensualities, pleasures, vanities, pride, interests. They are clothed in coarse woollen or coarse linen. Not one of them possesses in his own right anything whatever. On entering there, each one who was rich makes himself poor. What he has, he gives to all. He who was what is called noble, a gentleman and a lord, is the equal of him who was a peasant. The cell is identical for all. All undergo the same tonsure, wear the same frock, eat the same black bread, sleep on the same straw, die on the same ashes. The same sack on their backs, the same rope around their loins. If the decision has been to go barefoot, all go barefoot. There may be a prince among them; that prince is the same shadow as the rest. No titles. Even family names have disappeared. They bear only first names. All are bowed beneath the equality of baptismal names. They have dissolved the carnal family, and constituted in their community a spiritual family. They have no other relatives than all men. They succor the poor, they care for the sick. They elect those whom they obey. They call each other "my brother."

You stop me and exclaim, "But that is the ideal convent!"

It is sufficient that it may be the possible convent, that I should take notice of it.

Thence it results that, in the preceding book, I have spoken of a convent with respectful accents. The Middle Ages cast aside, Asia cast aside, the historical and political question held in reserve, from the purely philosophical point of view, outside the requirements of militant policy, on condition that the monastery shall be absolutely a voluntary matter and shall contain only consenting parties, I shall always consider a cloistered community with a certain attentive, and, in some respects, a deferential gravity.

Wherever there is a community, there is a commune; where there is a commune, there is right. The monastery is the product of the formula: Equality, Fraternity. Oh! how grand is liberty! And what a splendid transfiguration! Liberty suffices to transform the monastery into a republic.

Let us continue.

But these men, or these women who are behind these four walls. They dress themselves in coarse woollen, they are equals, they call each other brothers, that is well; but they do something else?

Yes.

What?

They gaze on the darkness, they kneel, and they clasp their hands.

What does this signify?

V

Prayer

They pray.
    To whom?
To God.

To pray to God,—what is the meaning of these words?

Is there an infinite beyond us? Is that infinite there, inherent, permanent; necessarily substantial, since it is infinite; and because, if it lacked matter it would be bounded; necessarily intelligent, since it is infinite, and because, if it lacked intelligence, it would end there? Does this infinite awaken in us the idea of essence, while we can attribute to ourselves only the idea of existence? In other terms, is it not the absolute, of which we are only the relative?

At the same time that there is an infinite without us, is there not an infinite within us? Are not these two infinites (what an alarming plural!) superposed, the one upon the other? Is not this second infinite, so to speak, subjacent to the first? Is it not the latter's mirror, reflection, echo, an abyss which is concentric with another abyss? Is this second infinity intelligent also? Does it think? Does it love? Does it will? If these two infinities are intelligent, each of them has a will principle, and there is an *I* in the upper infinity as there is an *I* in the lower infinity. The *I* below is the soul; the *I* on high is God.

To place the infinity here below in contact, by the medium of thought, with the infinity on high, is called praying.

Let us take nothing from the human mind; to suppress is bad. We must reform and transform. Certain faculties in man are directed towards the Unknown; thought, reverie, prayer. The Unknown is an ocean. What is conscience? It is the compass of the Unknown. Thought, reverie, prayer,—these are great and mysterious radiations. Let us respect them. Whither go these majestic irradiations of the soul? Into the shadow; that is to say, to the light.

The grandeur of democracy is to disown nothing and to deny nothing of humanity. Close to the right of the man, beside it, at the least, there exists the right of the soul.

To crush fanaticism and to venerate the infinite, such is the law.

Let us not confine ourselves to prostrating ourselves before the tree of creation, and to the contemplation of its branches full of stars. We have a duty to labor over the human soul, to defend the mystery against the miracle, to adore the incomprehensible and reject the absurd, to admit, as an inexplicable fact, only what is necessary, to purify belief, to remove superstitions from above religion; to clear God of caterpillars.

VI

The Absolute Goodness of Prayer

With regard to the modes of prayer, all are good, provided that they are sincere. Turn your book upside down and be in the infinite.

There is, as we know, a philosophy which denies the infinite. There is also a philosophy, pathologically classified, which denies the sun; this philosophy is called blindness.

To erect a sense which we lack into a source of truth, is a fine blind man's self-sufficiency.

The curious thing is the haughty, superior, and compassionate airs which this groping philosophy assumes towards the philosophy which beholds God. One fancies he hears a mole crying, "I pity them with their sun!"

There are, as we know, powerful and illustrious atheists. At bottom, led back to the truth by their very force, they are not absolutely sure that they are atheists; it is with them only a question of definition, and in any case, if they do not believe in God, being great minds, they prove God.

We salute them as philosophers, while inexorably denouncing their philosophy.

Let us go on.

The remarkable thing about it is, also, their facility in paying themselves off with words. A metaphysical school of the North, impregnated to some extent with fog, has fancied that it has worked a revolution in human understanding by replacing the word Force with the word Will.

To say: "the plant wills," instead of: "the plant grows": this would be fecund in results, indeed, if we were to add: "the universe wills." Why? Because it would come to this: the plant wills, therefore it has an I; the universe wills, therefore it has a God.

As for us, who, however, in contradistinction to this school, reject nothing *a priori*, a will in the plant, accepted by this school, appears to us more difficult to admit than a will in the universe denied by it.

To deny the will of the infinite, that is to say, God, is impossible on any other conditions than a denial of the infinite. We have demonstrated this.

The negation of the infinite leads straight to nihilism. Everything becomes "a mental conception."

With nihilism, no discussion is possible; for the nihilist logic doubts the existence of its interlocutor, and is not quite sure that it exists itself.

From its point of view, it is possible that it may be for itself, only "a mental conception."

Only, it does not perceive that all which it has denied it admits in the lump, simply by the utterance of the word, mind.

In short, no way is open to the thought by a philosophy which makes all end in the monosyllable, No.

To No there is only one reply, Yes.

Nihilism has no point.

There is no such thing as nothingness. Zero does not exist. Everything is something. Nothing is nothing.

Man lives by affirmation even more than by bread.

Even to see and to show does not suffice. Philosophy should be an energy; it should have for effort and effect to ameliorate the condition of man. Socrates should enter into Adam and produce Marcus Aurelius; in other words, the man of wisdom should be made to emerge from the man of felicity. Eden should be changed into a Lyceum. Science should be a cordial. To enjoy,—what a sad aim, and what a paltry ambition! The brute enjoys. To offer thought to the thirst of men, to give them all as an elixir the notion of God, to make conscience and science fraternize in them, to render them just by this mysterious confrontation; such is the function of real philosophy. Morality is a blossoming out of truths. Contemplation leads to action. The absolute should be practicable. It is necessary that the ideal should be breathable, drinkable, and eatable to the human mind. It is the ideal which has the right to say: *Take, this is my body, this is my blood*. Wisdom is holy communion. It is on this condition that it ceases to be a sterile love of science and becomes the one and sovereign mode of human rallying, and that philosophy herself is promoted to religion.

Philosophy should not be a corbel erected on mystery to gaze upon it at its ease, without any other result than that of being convenient to curiosity.

For our part, adjourning the development of our thought to another occasion, we will confine ourselves to saying that we neither understand man as a point of departure nor progress as an end, without those two forces which are their two motors: faith and love.

Progress is the goal, the ideal is the type.

What is this ideal? It is God.

Ideal, absolute, perfection, infinity: identical words.

VII

Precautions to be Observed in Blame

History and philosophy have eternal duties, which are, at the same time, simple duties; to combat Caiphas the High-priest, Draco the Lawgiver, Trimalcion the Legislator, Tiberius the Emperor; this is clear, direct, and limpid, and offers no obscurity.

But the right to live apart, even with its inconveniences and its abuses, insists on being stated and taken into account. Cenobitism is a human problem.

When one speaks of convents, those abodes of error, but of innocence, of aberration but of good-will, of ignorance but of devotion, of torture but of martyrdom, it always becomes necessary to say either yes or no.

A convent is a contradiction. Its object, salvation; its means thereto, sacrifice. The convent is supreme egoism having for its result supreme abnegation.

To abdicate with the object of reigning seems to be the device of monasticism.

In the cloister, one suffers in order to enjoy. One draws a bill of exchange on death. One discounts in terrestrial gloom celestial light. In the cloister, hell is accepted in advance as a post obit on paradise.

The taking of the veil or the frock is a suicide paid for with eternity.

It does not seem to us, that on such a subject mockery is permissible. All about it is serious, the good as well as the bad.

The just man frowns, but never smiles with a malicious sneer. We understand wrath, but not malice.

VIII

Faith, Law

A few words more.

We blame the church when she is saturated with intrigues, we despise the spiritual which is harsh toward the temporal; but we everywhere honor the thoughtful man.

We salute the man who kneels.

A faith; this is a necessity for man. Woe to him who believes nothing.

One is not unoccupied because one is absorbed. There is visible labor and invisible labor.

To contemplate is to labor, to think is to act.

Folded arms toil, clasped hands work. A gaze fixed on heaven is a work.

Thales remained motionless for four years. He founded philosophy.

In our opinion, cenobites are not lazy men, and recluses are not idlers.

To meditate on the Shadow is a serious thing.

Without invalidating anything that we have just said, we believe that a perpetual memory of the tomb is proper for the living. On this point, the priest and the philosopher agree. *We must die*. The Abbé de la Trappe replies to Horace.

To mingle with one's life a certain presence of the sepulchre,—this is the law of the sage; and it is the law of the ascetic. In this respect, the ascetic and the sage converge. There is a material growth; we admit it. There is a moral grandeur; we hold to that. Thoughtless and vivacious spirits say:—

"What is the good of those motionless figures on the side of mystery? What purpose do they serve? What do they do?"

Alas! In the presence of the darkness which environs us, and which awaits us, in our ignorance of what the immense dispersion will make of us, we reply: "There is probably no work more divine than that performed by these souls." And we add: "There is probably no work which is more useful."

There certainly must be some who pray constantly for those who never pray at all.

In our opinion the whole question lies in the amount of thought that is mingled with prayer.

Leibnitz praying is grand, Voltaire adoring is fine. *Deo erexit Voltaire*.

We are for religion as against religions.

We are of the number who believe in the wretchedness of orisons, and the sublimity of prayer.

Moreover, at this minute which we are now traversing,—a minute which will not, fortunately, leave its impress on the nineteenth century,—at this hour, when so many men have low brows and souls but little elevated, among so many mortals whose morality consists in enjoyment, and who are busied with the brief and misshapen things of matter, whoever exiles himself seems worthy of veneration to us.

The monastery is a renunciation. Sacrifice wrongly directed is still sacrifice. To mistake a grave error for a duty has a grandeur of its own.

Taken by itself, and ideally, and in order to examine the truth on all sides until all aspects have been impartially exhausted, the monastery, the female convent in particular,—for in our century it is woman who suffers the most, and in this exile of the cloister there is something of protestation,—the female convent has incontestably a certain majesty.

This cloistered existence which is so austere, so depressing, a few of whose features we have just traced, is not life, for it is not liberty; it is not the tomb, for it is not plenitude; it is the strange place whence one beholds, as from the crest of a lofty mountain, on one side the abyss where we are, on the other, the abyss whither we shall go; it is the narrow and misty frontier separating two worlds, illuminated and obscured by both at the same time, where the ray of life which has become enfeebled is mingled with the vague ray of death; it is the half obscurity of the tomb.

We, who do not believe what these women believe, but who, like them, live by faith,—we have never been able to think without a sort of tender and religious terror, without a sort of pity, that is full of envy, of those devoted, trembling and trusting creatures, of these humble and august souls, who dare to dwell on the very brink of the mystery, waiting between the world which is closed and heaven which is not yet open, turned towards the light which one cannot see, possessing the sole happiness of thinking that they know where it is, aspiring towards the gulf, and the unknown, their eyes fixed motionless on the darkness, kneeling, bewildered, stupefied, shuddering, half lifted, at times, by the deep breaths of eternity.

BOOK EIGHTH
CEMETERIES TAKE THAT WHICH IS
COMMITTED THEM

I

WHICH TREATS OF THE MANNER OF ENTERING A CONVENT

It was into this house that Jean Valjean had, as Fauchelevent expressed it, "fallen from the sky."

He had scaled the wall of the garden which formed the angle of the Rue Polonceau. That hymn of the angels which he had heard in the middle of the night, was the nuns chanting matins; that hall, of which he had caught a glimpse in the gloom, was the chapel. That phantom which he had seen stretched on the ground was the sister who was making reparation; that bell, the sound of which had so strangely surprised him, was the gardener's bell attached to the knee of Father Fauchelevent.

Cosette once put to bed, Jean Valjean and Fauchelevent had, as we have already seen, supped on a glass of wine and a bit of cheese before a good, crackling fire; then, the only bed in the hut being occupied by Cosette, each threw himself on a truss of straw.

Before he shut his eyes, Jean Valjean said: "I must remain here henceforth." This remark trotted through Fauchelevent's head all night long.

To tell the truth, neither of them slept.

Jean Valjean, feeling that he was discovered and that Javert was on his scent, understood that he and Cosette were lost if they returned to Paris. Then the new storm which had just burst upon him had stranded him in this cloister. Jean Valjean had, henceforth, but one thought,— to remain there. Now, for an unfortunate man in his position, this convent was both the safest and the most dangerous of places; the most dangerous, because, as no men might enter there, if he were discovered, it was a flagrant offence, and Jean Valjean would find but one step intervening between the convent and prison; the safest, because, if he could manage to get himself accepted there and remain there, who would ever seek him in such a place? To dwell in an impossible place was safety.

On his side, Fauchelevent was cudgelling his brains. He began by declaring to himself that he understood nothing of the matter. How had

M. Madeleine got there, when the walls were what they were? Cloister walls are not to be stepped over. How did he get there with a child? One cannot scale a perpendicular wall with a child in one's arms. Who was that child? Where did they both come from? Since Fauchelevent had lived in the convent, he had heard nothing of M. sur M., and he knew nothing of what had taken place there. Father Madeleine had an air which discouraged questions; and besides, Fauchelevent said to himself: "One does not question a saint." M. Madeleine had preserved all his prestige in Fauchelevent's eyes. Only, from some words which Jean Valjean had let fall, the gardener thought he could draw the inference that M. Madeleine had probably become bankrupt through the hard times, and that he was pursued by his creditors; or that he had compromised himself in some political affair, and was in hiding; which last did not displease Fauchelevent, who, like many of our peasants of the North, had an old fund of Bonapartism about him. While in hiding, M. Madeleine had selected the convent as a refuge, and it was quite simple that he should wish to remain there. But the inexplicable point, to which Fauchelevent returned constantly and over which he wearied his brain, was that M. Madeleine should be there, and that he should have that little girl with him. Fauchelevent saw them, touched them, spoke to them, and still did not believe it possible. The incomprehensible had just made its entrance into Fauchelevent's hut. Fauchelevent groped about amid conjectures, and could see nothing clearly but this: "M. Madeleine saved my life." This certainty alone was sufficient and decided his course. He said to himself: "It is my turn now." He added in his conscience: "M. Madeleine did not stop to deliberate when it was a question of thrusting himself under the cart for the purpose of dragging me out." He made up his mind to save M. Madeleine.

Nevertheless, he put many questions to himself and made himself divers replies: "After what he did for me, would I save him if he were a thief? Just the same. If he were an assassin, would I save him? Just the same. Since he is a saint, shall I save him? Just the same."

But what a problem it was to manage to have him remain in the convent! Fauchelevent did not recoil in the face of this almost chimerical undertaking; this poor peasant of Picardy without any other ladder than his self-devotion, his good will, and a little of that old rustic cunning, on this occasion enlisted in the service of a generous enterprise, undertook to scale the difficulties of the cloister, and the steep escarpments of the rule of Saint-Benoît. Father Fauchelevent was an old man who had been an egoist all his life, and who, towards the end of his days, halt, infirm, with no interest left to him in the world, found it sweet to be grateful, and perceiving a generous action to be performed, flung himself upon it like a man, who at the moment when he is dying, should find close to his hand a glass of good wine which he had never tasted, and should swallow it with avidity. We may add, that the air which he had breathed for many years in this convent had destroyed all personality in him, and had ended by rendering a good action of some kind absolutely necessary to him.

So he took his resolve: to devote himself to M. Madeleine.

We have just called him a *poor peasant of Picardy*. That description is just, but incomplete. At the point of this story which we have now reached, a little of Father Fauchelevent's physiology becomes useful. He was a peasant, but he had been a notary, which added trickery to his cunning, and penetration to his ingenuousness. Having, through various causes, failed in his business, he had descended to the calling of a carter and a laborer. But, in spite of oaths and lashings, which horses seem to require, something of the notary had lingered in him. He had some natural wit; he talked good grammar; he conversed, which is a rare thing in a village; and the other peasants said of him: "He talks almost like a gentleman with a hat." Fauchelevent belonged, in fact, to that species, which the impertinent and flippant vocabulary of the last century qualified as *demi-bourgeois, demi-lout*, and which the metaphors showered by the château upon the thatched cottage ticketed in the pigeon-hole of the plebeian: *rather rustic, rather citified; pepper and salt*. Fauchelevent, though sorely tried and harshly used by fate, worn out, a sort of poor, threadbare old soul, was, nevertheless, an impulsive man, and extremely spontaneous in his actions; a precious quality which prevents one from ever being wicked. His defects and his vices, for he had some, were all superficial; in short, his physiognomy was of the kind which succeeds with an observer. His aged face had none of those disagreeable wrinkles at the top of the forehead, which signify malice or stupidity.

At daybreak, Father Fauchelevent opened his eyes, after having done an enormous deal of thinking, and beheld M. Madeleine seated on his truss of straw, and watching Cosette's slumbers. Fauchelevent sat up and said:—

"Now that you are here, how are you going to contrive to enter?"

This remark summed up the situation and aroused Jean Valjean from his reverie.

The two men took counsel together.

"In the first place," said Fauchelevent, "you will begin by not setting foot outside of this chamber, either you or the child. One step in the garden and we are done for."

"That is true."

"Monsieur Madeleine," resumed Fauchelevent, "you have arrived at a very auspicious moment, I mean to say a very inauspicious moment; one of the ladies is very ill. This will prevent them from looking much in our direction. It seems that she is dying. The prayers of the forty hours are being said. The whole community is in confusion. That occupies them. The one who is on the point of departure is a saint. In fact, we are all saints here; all the difference between them and me is that they say 'our cell,' and that I say 'my cabin.' The prayers for the dying are to be said, and then the prayers for the dead. We shall be at peace here for to-day; but I will not answer for to-morrow."

"Still," observed Jean Valjean, "this cottage is in the niche of the wall, it is hidden by a sort of ruin, there are trees, it is not visible from the convent."

"And I add that the nuns never come near it."

"Well?" said Jean Valjean.

The interrogation mark which accentuated this "well" signified: "it seems to me that one may remain concealed here?" It was to this interrogation point that Fauchelevent responded:—

"There are the little girls."

"What little girls?" asked Jean Valjean.

Just as Fauchelevent opened his mouth to explain the words which he had uttered, a bell emitted one stroke.

"The nun is dead," said he. "There is the knell."

And he made a sign to Jean Valjean to listen.

The bell struck a second time.

"It is the knell, Monsieur Madeleine. The bell will continue to strike once a minute for twenty-four hours, until the body is taken from the church.—You see, they play. At recreation hours it suffices to have a ball roll aside, to send them all hither, in spite of prohibitions, to hunt and rummage for it all about here. Those cherubs are devils."

"Who?" asked Jean Valjean.

"The little girls. You would be very quickly discovered. They would shriek: 'Oh! a man!' There is no danger to-day. There will be no recreation hour. The day will be entirely devoted to prayers. You hear the bell. As I told you, a stroke each minute. It is the death knell."

"I understand, Father Fauchelevent. There are pupils."

And Jean Valjean thought to himself:—

"Here is Cosette's education already provided."

Fauchelevent exclaimed:—

"Pardine! There are little girls indeed! And they would bawl around you! And they would rush off! To be a man here is to have the plague. You see how they fasten a bell to my paw as though I were a wild beast."

Jean Valjean fell into more and more profound thought.—"This convent would be our salvation," he murmured.

Then he raised his voice:—

"Yes, the difficulty is to remain here."

"No," said Fauchelevent, "the difficulty is to get out."

Jean Valjean felt the blood rush back to his heart.

"To get out!"

"Yes, Monsieur Madeleine. In order to return here it is first necessary to get out."

And after waiting until another stroke of the knell had sounded, Fauchelevent went on:—

"You must not be found here in this fashion. Whence come you? For me, you fall from heaven, because I know you; but the nuns require one to enter by the door."

All at once they heard a rather complicated pealing from another bell.

"Ah!" said Fauchelevent, "they are ringing up the vocal mothers. They are going to the chapter. They always hold a chapter when any one dies. She died at daybreak. People generally do die at daybreak. But cannot you get out by the way in which you entered? Come, I do not ask for the sake of questioning you, but how did you get in?"

Jean Valjean turned pale; the very thought of descending again into that terrible street made him shudder. You make your way out of a forest filled with tigers, and once out of it, imagine a friendly counsel that shall advise you to return thither! Jean Valjean pictured to himself the whole police force still engaged in swarming in that quarter, agents on the watch, sentinels everywhere, frightful fists extended towards his collar, Javert at the corner of the intersection of the streets perhaps.

"Impossible!" said he. "Father Fauchelevent, say that I fell from the sky."

"But I believe it, I believe it," retorted Fauchelevent. "You have no need to tell me that. The good God must have taken you in his hand for the purpose of getting a good look at you close to, and then dropped you. Only, he meant to place you in a man's convent; he made a mistake. Come, there goes another peal, that is to order the porter to go and inform the municipality that the dead-doctor is to come here and view a corpse. All that is the ceremony of dying. These good ladies are not at all fond of that visit. A doctor is a man who does not believe in anything. He lifts the veil. Sometimes he lifts something else too. How quickly they have had the doctor summoned this time! What is the matter? Your little one is still asleep. What is her name?"

"Cosette."

"She is your daughter? You are her grandfather, that is?"

"Yes."

"It will be easy enough for her to get out of here. I have my service door which opens on the courtyard. I knock. The porter opens; I have my vintage basket on my back, the child is in it, I go out. Father Fauchelevent goes out with his basket—that is perfectly natural. You will tell the child to keep very quiet. She will be under the cover. I will leave her for whatever time is required with a good old friend, a fruit-seller whom I know in the Rue Chemin-Vert, who is deaf, and who has a little bed. I will shout in the fruit-seller's ear, that she is a niece of mine, and that she is to keep her for me until to-morrow. Then the little one will re-enter with you; for I will contrive to have you re-enter. It must be done. But how will you manage to get out?"

Jean Valjean shook his head.

"No one must see me, the whole point lies there, Father Fauchelevent. Find some means of getting me out in a basket, under cover, like Cosette."

Fauchelevent scratched the lobe of his ear with the middle finger of his left hand, a sign of serious embarrassment.

A third peal created a diversion.

"That is the dead-doctor taking his departure," said Fauchelevent. "He has taken a look and said: 'She is dead, that is well.' When the doctor has signed the passport for paradise, the undertaker's company sends a coffin. If it is a mother, the mothers lay her out; if she is a sister, the sisters lay her out. After which, I nail her up. That forms a part of my gardener's duty. A gardener is a bit of a grave-digger. She is placed in a lower hall of the church which communicates with the street, and into which no man may enter save the doctor of the dead. I don't count the undertaker's men and myself as men. It is in that hall that I nail up the coffin. The undertaker's men come and get it, and whip up, coachman! that's the way one goes to heaven. They fetch a box with nothing in it, they take it away again with something in it. That's what a burial is like. *De profundis*."

A horizontal ray of sunshine lightly touched the face of the sleeping Cosette, who lay with her mouth vaguely open, and had the air of an angel drinking in the light. Jean Valjean had fallen to gazing at her. He was no longer listening to Fauchelevent.

That one is not listened to is no reason for preserving silence. The good old gardener went on tranquilly with his babble:—

"The grave is dug in the Vaugirard cemetery. They declare that they are going to suppress that Vaugirard cemetery. It is an ancient cemetery which is outside the regulations, which has no uniform, and which is going to retire. It is a shame, for it is convenient. I have a friend there, Father Mestienne, the grave-digger. The nuns here possess one privilege, it is to be taken to that cemetery at nightfall. There is a special permission from the Prefecture on their behalf. But how many events have happened since yesterday! Mother Crucifixion is dead, and Father Madeleine—"

"Is buried," said Jean Valjean, smiling sadly.

Fauchelevent caught the word.

"Goodness! if you were here for good, it would be a real burial."

A fourth peal burst out. Fauchelevent hastily detached the belled knee-cap from its nail and buckled it on his knee again.

"This time it is for me. The Mother Prioress wants me. Good, now I am pricking myself on the tongue of my buckle. Monsieur Madeleine, don't stir from here, and wait for me. Something new has come up. If you are hungry, there is wine, bread and cheese."

And he hastened out of the hut, crying: "Coming! coming!"

Jean Valjean watched him hurrying across the garden as fast as his crooked leg would permit, casting a sidelong glance by the way on his melon patch.

Less than ten minutes later, Father Fauchelevent, whose bell put the nuns in his road to flight, tapped gently at a door, and a gentle voice replied: *"Forever! Forever!"* that is to say: *"Enter."*

The door was the one leading to the parlor reserved for seeing the gardener on business. This parlor adjoined the chapter hall. The prioress, seated on the only chair in the parlor, was waiting for Fauchelevent.

II

FAUCHELEVENT IN THE PRESENCE OF A DIFFICULTY

It is the peculiarity of certain persons and certain professions, notably priests and nuns, to wear a grave and agitated air on critical occasions. At the moment when Fauchelevent entered, this double form of preoccupation was imprinted on the countenance of the prioress, who was that wise and charming Mademoiselle de Blemeur, Mother Innocente, who was ordinarily cheerful.

The gardener made a timid bow, and remained at the door of the cell. The prioress, who was telling her beads, raised her eyes and said:—

"Ah! it is you, Father Fauvent."

This abbreviation had been adopted in the convent.

Fauchelevent bowed again.

"Father Fauvent, I have sent for you."

"Here I am, reverend Mother."

"I have something to say to you."

"And so have I," said Fauchelevent with a boldness which caused him inward terror, "I have something to say to the very reverend Mother."

The prioress stared at him.

"Ah! you have a communication to make to me."

"A request."

"Very well, speak."

Goodman Fauchelevent, the ex-notary, belonged to the category of peasants who have assurance. A certain clever ignorance constitutes a force; you do not distrust it, and you are caught by it. Fauchelevent had been a success during the something more than two years which he had passed in the convent. Always solitary and busied about his gardening, he had nothing else to do than to indulge his curiosity. As he was at a distance from all those veiled women passing to and fro, he saw before him only an agitation of shadows. By dint of attention and sharpness he had succeeded in clothing all those phantoms with flesh, and those corpses were alive for him. He was like a deaf man whose sight grows keener, and like a blind man whose hearing becomes more acute. He had applied himself to riddling out the significance of the different peals, and he had succeeded, so that this taciturn and enigmatical cloister possessed no secrets for him; the sphinx babbled all her secrets in his ear. Fauchelevent knew all and concealed all; that constituted his art. The whole convent thought him stupid. A great merit in religion. The vocal mothers made much of Fauchelevent. He was a curious mute. He inspired confidence. Moreover, he was regular, and never went out except for well-demonstrated requirements of the orchard and vegetable garden. This discretion of conduct had inured to his credit. Nonetheless, he had set two men to chattering: the porter, in the convent, and he knew the singularities of their parlor, and the grave-digger, at the cemetery, and he was acquainted with the peculiarities of their sepulture; in this way, he possessed a double light on the subject of these nuns, one as to their life, the other as to their death. But he did not abuse his knowledge. The congregation thought a great deal of him. Old, lame, blind to everything, probably a little deaf into the bargain,— what qualities! They would have found it difficult to replace him.

The goodman, with the assurance of a person who feels that he is appreciated, entered into a rather diffuse and very deep rustic harangue to the reverend prioress. He talked a long time about his age, his infirmities, the surcharge of years counting double for him henceforth, of the increasing demands of his work, of the great size of the garden, of nights which must be passed, like the last, for instance, when he had been obliged to put straw mats over the melon beds, because of the moon, and he wound up as follows: "That he had a brother"— (the prioress made a movement),—"a brother no longer young"—(a second movement on the part of the prioress, but one expressive of reassurance),—"that, if he might be permitted, this brother would come and live with him and help him, that he was an excellent gardener, that the community would receive from him good service, better than his own; that, otherwise, if his brother were not admitted, as he, the elder, felt that his health was broken and that he was insufficient for the work, he should be obliged, greatly to his regret, to go away; and that his brother had a little daughter whom he would bring with him, who might be reared for God in the house, and who might, who knows, become a nun some day."

When he had finished speaking, the prioress stayed the slipping of her rosary between her fingers, and said to him:—

"Could you procure a stout iron bar between now and this evening?"

"For what purpose?"

"To serve as a lever."

"Yes, reverend Mother," replied Fauchelevent.

The prioress, without adding a word, rose and entered the adjoining room, which was the hall of the chapter, and where the vocal mothers were probably assembled. Fauchelevent was left alone.

III

Mother Innocente

About a quarter of an hour elapsed. The prioress returned and seated herself once more on her chair.

The two interlocutors seemed preoccupied. We will present a stenographic report of the dialogue which then ensued, to the best of our ability.

"Father Fauvent!"

"Reverend Mother!"

"Do you know the chapel?"

"I have a little cage there, where I hear the mass and the offices."

"And you have been in the choir in pursuance of your duties?"

"Two or three times."

"There is a stone to be raised."

"Heavy?"

"The slab of the pavement which is at the side of the altar."

"The slab which closes the vault?"

"Yes."

"It would be a good thing to have two men for it."

"Mother Ascension, who is as strong as a man, will help you."

"A woman is never a man."

"We have only a woman here to help you. Each one does what he can. Because Dom Mabillon gives four hundred and seventeen epistles of Saint Bernard, while Merlonus Horstius only gives three hundred and sixty-seven, I do not despise Merlonus Horstius."

"Neither do I."

"Merit consists in working according to one's strength. A cloister is not a dock-yard."

"And a woman is not a man. But my brother is the strong one, though!"

"And can you get a lever?"

"That is the only sort of key that fits that sort of door."

"There is a ring in the stone."

"I will put the lever through it."

"And the stone is so arranged that it swings on a pivot."

"That is good, reverend Mother. I will open the vault."

"And the four Mother Precentors will help you."

"And when the vault is open?"

"It must be closed again."

"Will that be all?"

"No."

"Give me your orders, very reverend Mother."

"Fauvent, we have confidence in you."

"I am here to do anything you wish."

"And to hold your peace about everything!"

"Yes, reverend Mother."

"When the vault is open—"

"I will close it again."

"But before that—"

"What, reverend Mother?"

"Something must be lowered into it."

A silence ensued. The prioress, after a pout of the under lip which resembled hesitation, broke it.

"Father Fauvent!"

"Reverend Mother!"

"You know that a mother died this morning?"

"No."

"Did you not hear the bell?"

"Nothing can be heard at the bottom of the garden."

"Really?"

"I can hardly distinguish my own signal."

"She died at daybreak."

"And then, the wind did not blow in my direction this morning."

"It was Mother Crucifixion. A blessed woman."

The prioress paused, moved her lips, as though in mental prayer, and resumed:—

"Three years ago, Madame de Béthune, a Jansenist, turned orthodox, merely from having seen Mother Crucifixion at prayer."

"Ah! yes, now I hear the knell, reverend Mother."

"The mothers have taken her to the dead-room, which opens on the church."

"I know."

"No other man than you can or must enter that chamber. See to that. A fine sight it would be, to see a man enter the dead-room!"

"More often!"

"Hey?"

"More often!"

"What do you say?"

"I say more often."

"More often than what?"

"Reverend Mother, I did not say more often than what, I said more often."

"I don't understand you. Why do you say more often?"

"In order to speak like you, reverend Mother."

"But I did not say 'more often.'"

At that moment, nine o'clock struck.

"At nine o'clock in the morning and at all hours, praised and adored be the most Holy Sacrament of the altar," said the prioress.

"Amen," said Fauchelevent.

The clock struck opportunely. It cut "more often" short. It is probable, that had it not been for this, the prioress and Fauchelevent would never have unravelled that skein.

Fauchelevent mopped his forehead.

The prioress indulged in another little inward murmur, probably sacred, then raised her voice:—

"In her lifetime, Mother Crucifixion made converts; after her death, she will perform miracles."

"She will!" replied Father Fauchelevent, falling into step, and striving not to flinch again.

"Father Fauvent, the community has been blessed in Mother Crucifixion. No doubt, it is not granted to every one to die, like Cardinal de Bérulle, while saying the holy mass, and to breathe forth their souls to God, while pronouncing these words: *Hanc igitur oblationem.* But without attaining to such happiness, Mother Crucifixion's death was very precious. She retained her consciousness to the very last moment. She spoke to us, then she spoke to the angels. She gave us her last commands. If you had a little more faith, and if you could have been in her cell, she would have cured your leg merely by touching it. She smiled. We felt that she was regaining her life in God. There was something of paradise in that death."

Fauchelevent thought that it was an orison which she was finishing.

"Amen," said he.

"Father Fauvent, what the dead wish must be done."

The prioress took off several beads of her chaplet. Fauchelevent held his peace.

She went on:—

"I have consulted upon this point many ecclesiastics laboring in Our Lord, who occupy themselves in the exercises of the clerical life, and who bear wonderful fruit."

"Reverend Mother, you can hear the knell much better here than in the garden."

"Besides, she is more than a dead woman, she is a saint."

"Like yourself, reverend Mother."

"She slept in her coffin for twenty years, by express permission of our Holy Father, Pius VII.—"

"The one who crowned the Emp—Buonaparte."

For a clever man like Fauchelevent, this allusion was an awkward one. Fortunately, the prioress, completely absorbed in her own thoughts, did not hear it. She continued:—

"Father Fauvent?"

"Reverend Mother?"

"Saint Didorus, Archbishop of Cappadocia, desired that this single word might be inscribed on his tomb: *Acarus*, which signifies, a worm of the earth; this was done. Is this true?"

"Yes, reverend Mother."

"The blessed Mezzocane, Abbot of Aquila, wished to be buried beneath the gallows; this was done."

"That is true."

"Saint Terentius, Bishop of Port, where the mouth of the Tiber empties into the sea, requested that on his tomb might be engraved the sign which was placed on the graves of parricides, in the hope that passers-by would spit on his tomb. This was done. The dead must be obeyed."

"So be it."

"The body of Bernard Guidonis, born in France near Roche-Abeille, was, as he had ordered, and in spite of the king of Castile, borne to the church of the Dominicans in Limoges, although Bernard Guidonis was Bishop of Tuy in Spain. Can the contrary be affirmed?"

"For that matter, no, reverend Mother."

"The fact is attested by Plantavit de la Fosse."

Several beads of the chaplet were told off, still in silence. The prioress resumed:—

"Father Fauvent, Mother Crucifixion will be interred in the coffin in which she has slept for the last twenty years."

"That is just."

"It is a continuation of her slumber."

"So I shall have to nail up that coffin?"

"Yes."

"And we are to reject the undertaker's coffin?"

"Precisely."

"I am at the orders of the very reverend community."

"The four Mother Precentors will assist you."

"In nailing up the coffin? I do not need them."

"No. In lowering the coffin."

"Where?"

"Into the vault."

"What vault?"

"Under the altar."

Fauchelevent started.

"The vault under the altar?"

"Under the altar."

"But—"

"You will have an iron bar."

"Yes, but—"

"You will raise the stone with the bar by means of the ring."

"But—"

"The dead must be obeyed. To be buried in the vault under the altar of the chapel, not to go to profane earth; to remain there in death where she prayed while living; such was the last wish of Mother Crucifixion. She asked it of us; that is to say, commanded us."

"But it is forbidden."

"Forbidden by men, enjoined by God."

"What if it became known?"

"We have confidence in you."

"Oh! I am a stone in your walls."

"The chapter assembled. The vocal mothers, whom I have just consulted again, and who are now deliberating, have decided that Mother Crucifixion shall be buried, according to her wish, in her own coffin, under our altar. Think, Father Fauvent, if she were to work miracles here! What a glory of God for the community! And miracles issue from tombs."

"But, reverend Mother, if the agent of the sanitary commission—"

"Saint Benoît II, in the matter of sepulture, resisted Constantine Pogonatus."

"But the commissary of police—"

"Chonodemaire, one of the seven German kings who entered among the Gauls under the Empire of Constantius, expressly recognized the right of nuns to be buried in religion, that is to say, beneath the altar."

"But the inspector from the Prefecture—"

"The world is nothing in the presence of the cross. Martin, the eleventh general of the Carthusians, gave to his order this device: *Stat crux dum volvitur orbis*."

"Amen," said Fauchelevent, who imperturbably extricated himself in this manner from the dilemma, whenever he heard Latin.

Any audience suffices for a person who has held his peace too long. On the day when the rhetorician Gymnastoras left his prison, bearing in his body many dilemmas and numerous syllogisms which had struck in, he halted in front of the first tree which he came to, harangued it and made very great efforts to convince it. The prioress, who was usually subjected to the barrier of silence, and whose reservoir was overfull, rose and exclaimed with the loquacity of a dam which has broken away:—

"I have on my right Benoît and on my left Bernard. Who was Bernard? The first abbot of Clairvaux. Fontaines in Burgundy is a country that is blest because it gave him birth. His father was named Técelin, and his mother Alèthe. He began at Cîteaux, to end in Clairvaux; he was ordained abbot by the bishop of Châlon-sur-Saône, Guillaume de Champeaux; he had seven hundred novices, and founded a hundred and sixty monasteries; he overthrew Abeilard at the council of Sens in 1140, and Pierre de Bruys and Henry his disciple, and another sort of erring spirits who were called the Apostolics; he confounded Arnauld de Brescia, darted lightning at the monk Raoul, the murderer of the Jews, dominated the council of Reims in 1148, caused the condemnation of Gilbert de Poréa, Bishop of Poitiers, caused the condemnation of Éon de l'Étoile, arranged the disputes of princes, enlightened King Louis the Young, advised Pope Eugene III, regulated the Temple, preached the crusade, performed two hundred and fifty miracles during his lifetime, and as many as thirty-nine in one day. Who was Benoît? He was the patriarch of Mont-Cassin; he was the second founder of the Sainteté Claustrale, he was the Basil of the West. His order has produced forty popes, two hundred cardinals, fifty patriarchs, sixteen hundred archbishops, four thousand six hundred bishops, four emperors, twelve empresses, forty-six kings, forty-one queens, three thousand six hundred canonized saints, and has been in existence for fourteen hundred years. On one side Saint Bernard, on the other the agent of the sanitary department! On one side Saint Benoît, on the other the inspector of public ways! The state, the road commissioners, the public undertaker, regulations, the administration, what do we know of all that? There is not a chance passer-by who would not be indignant to see how we are treated. We have not even the right to give our dust to Jesus Christ! Your sanitary department is a revolutionary invention. God subordinated to the commissary of police; such is the age. Silence, Fauvent!"

Fauchelevent was but ill at ease under this shower bath. The prioress continued:—

"No one doubts the right of the monastery to sepulture. Only fanatics and those in error deny it. We live in times of terrible confusion. We do not know that which it is necessary to know, and we know that which we should ignore. We are ignorant and impious. In this age there exist people who do not distinguish between the very great Saint Bernard and the Saint Bernard denominated of the poor Catholics, a certain good ecclesiastic who lived in the thirteenth century. Others are so blasphemous as to compare the scaffold of Louis XVI to the cross of Jesus Christ. Louis XVI was merely a king. Let us beware of God! There is no longer just nor unjust. The name of Voltaire is known, but not the name of César de Bus. Nevertheless, César de Bus is a man of blessed memory, and Voltaire one of unblessed memory. The last arch-bishop, the Cardinal de Périgord, did not even know that Charles de Gondren succeeded to Berulle, and François Bourgoin to Gondren, and Jean-François Senault to Bourgoin, and Father Sainte-Marthe to Jean-François Senault. The name of Father Coton is known, not because he was one of the three who urged the foundation of the Oratorie, but because he furnished Henri IV, the Huguenot king, with the material for an oath. That which pleases people of the world in Saint François de Sales, is that he cheated at play. And then, religion is attacked. Why? Because there have been bad priests, because Sagittaire, Bishop of Gap, was the brother of Salone, Bishop of Embrun, and because both of them followed Mommol. What has that to do with the question? Does that prevent Martin de Tours from being a saint, and giving half of his cloak to a beggar? They persecute the saints. They shut their eyes to the truth. Darkness is the rule. The most ferocious beasts are beasts which are blind. No one thinks of hell as a reality. Oh! how wicked people are! By order of the king signifies to-day, by order of the revolution. One no longer knows what is due to the living or to the dead. A holy death is prohibited. Burial is a civil matter. This is horrible. Saint Leo II wrote two special letters, one to Pierre Notaire, the other to the king of the Visigoths, for the purpose of combating and rejecting, in questions touching the dead, the authority of the exarch and the supremacy of the Emperor. Gauthier, Bishop of Châlons, held his own in this matter against Otho, Duke of Burgundy. The ancient magistracy agreed with him. In former times we had voices in the chapter, even on matters of the day. The Abbot of Cîteaux, the general of the order, was councillor by right of birth to the parliament of Burgundy. We do what we please with our dead. Is not the body of Saint Benoît himself in France, in the abbey of Fleury, called Saint Benoît-sur-Loire, although he died in Italy at Mont-Cassin, on Saturday, the 21st of the month of March, of the year 543? All this is incontestable. I abhor psalm-singers, I hate priors, I execrate heretics, but I should detest yet more any one who should maintain the contrary. One has only to read Arnoul Wion, Gabriel Bucelin, Trithemus, Maurolics, and Dom Luc d'Achery."

The prioress took breath, then turned to Fauchelevent.

"Is it settled, Father Fauvent?"

"It is settled, reverend Mother."

"We may depend on you?"

"I will obey."

"That is well."

"I am entirely devoted to the convent."

"That is understood. You will close the coffin. The sisters will carry it to the chapel. The office for the dead will then be said. Then we shall return to the cloister. Between eleven o'clock and midnight, you will come with your iron bar. All will be done in the most profound secrecy. There will be in the chapel only the four Mother Precentors, Mother Ascension and yourself."

"And the sister at the post?"

"She will not turn round."

"But she will hear."

"She will not listen. Besides, what the cloister knows the world learns not."

A pause ensued. The prioress went on:—

"You will remove your bell. It is not necessary that the sister at the post should perceive your presence."

"Reverend Mother?"

"What, Father Fauvent?"

"Has the doctor for the dead paid his visit?"

"He will pay it at four o'clock to-day. The peal which orders the doctor for the dead to be summoned has already been rung. But you do not understand any of the peals?"

"I pay no attention to any but my own."

"That is well, Father Fauvent."

"Reverend Mother, a lever at least six feet long will be required."

"Where will you obtain it?"

"Where gratings are not lacking, iron bars are not lacking. I have my heap of old iron at the bottom of the garden."

"About three-quarters of an hour before midnight; do not forget."

"Reverend Mother?"

"What?"

"If you were ever to have any other jobs of this sort, my brother is the strong man for you. A perfect Turk!"

"You will do it as speedily as possible."

"I cannot work very fast. I am infirm; that is why I require an assistant. I limp."

"To limp is no sin, and perhaps it is a blessing. The Emperor Henry II, who combated Antipope Gregory and re-established Benoît VIII, has two surnames, the Saint and the Lame."

"Two surtouts are a good thing," murmured Fauchelevent, who really was a little hard of hearing.

"Now that I think of it, Father Fauvent, let us give a whole hour to it. That is not too much. Be near the principal altar, with your iron bar, at eleven o'clock. The office begins at midnight. Everything must have been completed a good quarter of an hour before that."

"I will do anything to prove my zeal towards the community. These are my orders. I am to nail up the coffin. At eleven o'clock exactly, I am to be in the chapel. The Mother Precentors will be there. Mother Ascension will be there. Two men would be better. However, never mind! I shall have my lever. We will open the vault, we will lower the coffin, and we will close the vault again. After which, there will be no trace of anything. The government will have no suspicion. Thus all has been arranged, reverend Mother?"

"No!"

"What else remains?"

"The empty coffin remains."

This produced a pause. Fauchelevent meditated. The prioress meditated.

"What is to be done with that coffin, Father Fauvent?"

"It will be given to the earth."

"Empty?"

Another silence. Fauchelevent made, with his left hand, that sort of a gesture which dismisses a troublesome subject.

"Reverend Mother, I am the one who is to nail up the coffin in the basement of the church, and no one can enter there but myself, and I will cover the coffin with the pall."

"Yes, but the bearers, when they place it in the hearse and lower it into the grave, will be sure to feel that there is nothing in it."

"Ah! the de—!" exclaimed Fauchelevent.

The prioress began to make the sign of the cross, and looked fixedly at the gardener. The *vil* stuck fast in his throat.

He made haste to improvise an expedient to make her forget the oath.

"I will put earth in the coffin, reverend Mother. That will produce the effect of a corpse."

"You are right. Earth, that is the same thing as man. So you will manage the empty coffin?"

"I will make that my special business."

The prioress's face, up to that moment troubled and clouded, grew serene once more. She made the sign of a superior dismissing an inferior to him. Fauchelevent went towards the door. As he was on the point of passing out, the prioress raised her voice gently:—

"I am pleased with you, Father Fauvent; bring your brother to me tomorrow, after the burial, and tell him to fetch his daughter."

IV

In which Jean Valjean has Quite the Air of Having Read Austin Castillejo

The strides of a lame man are like the ogling glances of a one-eyed man; they do not reach their goal very promptly. Moreover, Fauchelevent was in a dilemma. He took nearly a quarter of an hour to return to his cottage in the garden. Cosette had waked up. Jean Valjean had placed her near the fire. At the moment when Fauchelevent entered, Jean Valjean was pointing out to her the vintner's basket on the wall, and saying to her, "Listen attentively to me, my little Cosette. We must go away from this house, but we shall return to it, and we shall be very happy here. The good man who lives here is going to carry you off on his back in that. You will wait for me at a lady's house. I shall come to fetch you. Obey, and say nothing, above all things, unless you want Madame Thénardier to get you again!"

Cosette nodded gravely.

Jean Valjean turned round at the noise made by Fauchelevent opening the door.

"Well?"

"Everything is arranged, and nothing is," said Fauchelevent. "I have permission to bring you in; but before bringing you in you must be got out. That's where the difficulty lies. It is easy enough with the child."

"You will carry her out?"

"And she will hold her tongue?"

"I answer for that."

"But you, Father Madeleine?"

And, after a silence, fraught with anxiety, Fauchelevent exclaimed:—

"Why, get out as you came in!"

Jean Valjean, as in the first instance, contented himself with saying, "Impossible."

Fauchelevent grumbled, more to himself than to Jean Valjean:—

"There is another thing which bothers me. I have said that I would put earth in it. When I come to think it over, the earth instead of the corpse will not seem like the real thing, it won't do, it will get displaced, it will move about. The men will bear it. You understand, Father Madeleine, the government will notice it."

Jean Valjean stared him straight in the eye and thought that he was raving.

Fauchelevent went on:—

"How the de—uce are you going to get out? It must all be done by to-morrow morning. It is to-morrow that I am to bring you in. The prioress expects you."

Then he explained to Jean Valjean that this was his recompense for a service which he, Fauchelevent, was to render to the community. That it fell among his duties to take part in their burials, that he nailed up the coffins and helped the grave-digger at the cemetery. That the nun who had died that morning had requested to be buried in the coffin which had served her for a bed, and interred in the vault under the altar of the chapel. That the police regulations forbade this, but that she was one of those dead to whom nothing is refused. That the prioress and the vocal mothers intended to fulfil the wish of the deceased. That it was so much the worse for the government. That he, Fauchelevent, was to nail up the coffin in the cell, raise the stone in the chapel, and lower the corpse into the vault. And that, by way of thanks, the prioress was to admit his brother to the house as a gardener, and his niece as a pupil. That his brother was M. Madeleine, and that his niece was Cosette. That the prioress had told him to bring his brother on the following evening, after the counterfeit interment in the cemetery. But that he could not bring M. Madeleine in from the outside if M. Madeleine was not outside. That that was the first problem. And then, that there was another: the empty coffin.

"What is that empty coffin?" asked Jean Valjean.

Fauchelevent replied:—

"The coffin of the administration."

"What coffin? What administration?"

"A nun dies. The municipal doctor comes and says, 'A nun has died.' The government sends a coffin. The next day it sends a hearse and undertaker's men to get the coffin and carry it to the cemetery. The undertaker's men will come and lift the coffin; there will be nothing in it."

"Put something in it."

"A corpse? I have none."

"No."

"What then?"

"A living person."

"What person?"

"Me!" said Jean Valjean.

Fauchelevent, who was seated, sprang up as though a bomb had burst under his chair.

"You!"

"Why not?"

Jean Valjean gave way to one of those rare smiles which lighted up his face like a flash from heaven in the winter.

"You know, Fauchelevent, what you have said: 'Mother Crucifixion is dead.' and I add: 'and Father Madeleine is buried.'"

"Ah! good, you can laugh, you are not speaking seriously."

"Very seriously, I must get out of this place."

"Certainly."

"I have told you to find a basket, and a cover for me also."

"Well?"

"The basket will be of pine, and the cover a black cloth."

"In the first place, it will be a white cloth. Nuns are buried in white."

"Let it be a white cloth, then."

"You are not like other men, Father Madeleine."

To behold such devices, which are nothing else than the savage and daring inventions of the galleys, spring forth from the peaceable things which surrounded him, and mingle with what he called the "petty course of life in the convent," caused Fauchelevent as much amazement as a gull fishing in the gutter of the Rue Saint-Denis would inspire in a passer-by.

Jean Valjean went on:—

"The problem is to get out of here without being seen. This offers the means. But give me some information, in the first place. How is it managed? Where is this coffin?"

"The empty one?"

"Yes."

"Downstairs, in what is called the dead-room. It stands on two trestles, under the pall."

"How long is the coffin?"

"Six feet."

"What is this dead-room?"

"It is a chamber on the ground floor which has a grated window opening on the garden, which is closed on the outside by a shutter, and two doors; one leads into the convent, the other into the church."

"What church?"

"The church in the street, the church which any one can enter."

"Have you the keys to those two doors?"

"No; I have the key to the door which communicates with the convent; the porter has the key to the door which communicates with the church."

"When does the porter open that door?"

"Only to allow the undertaker's men to enter, when they come to get the coffin. When the coffin has been taken out, the door is closed again."

"Who nails up the coffin?"

"I do."

"Who spreads the pall over it?"

"I do."

"Are you alone?"

"Not another man, except the police doctor, can enter the dead-room. That is even written on the wall."

"Could you hide me in that room to-night when every one is asleep?"

"No. But I could hide you in a small, dark nook which opens on the dead-room, where I keep my tools to use for burials, and of which I have the key."

"At what time will the hearse come for the coffin to-morrow?"

"About three o'clock in the afternoon. The burial will take place at the Vaugirard cemetery a little before nightfall. It is not very near."

"I will remain concealed in your tool-closet all night and all the morning. And how about food? I shall be hungry."

"I will bring you something."

"You can come and nail me up in the coffin at two o'clock."

Fauchelevent recoiled and cracked his finger-joints.

"But that is impossible!"

"Bah! Impossible to take a hammer and drive some nails in a plank?"

What seemed unprecedented to Fauchelevent was, we repeat, a simple matter to Jean Valjean. Jean Valjean had been in worse straits than this. Any man who has been a prisoner understands how to contract himself to fit the diameter of the escape. The prisoner is subject to flight as the sick man is subject to a crisis which saves or kills him. An escape is a cure. What does not a man undergo for the sake of a cure? To have himself nailed up in a case and carried off like a bale of goods, to live for a long time in a box, to find air where there is none, to economize his breath for hours, to know how to stifle without dying—this was one of Jean Valjean's gloomy talents.

Moreover, a coffin containing a living being,—that convict's expedient,—is also an imperial expedient. If we are to credit the monk Austin Castillejo, this was the means employed by Charles the Fifth, desirous of seeing the Plombes for the last time after his abdication.

He had her brought into and carried out of the monastery of Saint-Yuste in this manner.

Fauchelevent, who had recovered himself a little, exclaimed:—

"But how will you manage to breathe?"

"I will breathe."

"In that box! The mere thought of it suffocates me."

"You surely must have a gimlet, you will make a few holes here and there, around my mouth, and you will nail the top plank on loosely."

"Good! And what if you should happen to cough or to sneeze?"

"A man who is making his escape does not cough or sneeze."

And Jean Valjean added:—

"Father Fauchelevent, we must come to a decision: I must either be caught here, or accept this escape through the hearse."

Every one has noticed the taste which cats have for pausing and lounging between the two leaves of a half-shut door. Who is there who has not said to a cat, "Do come in!" There are men who, when an incident stands half-open before them, have the same tendency to halt in indecision between two resolutions, at the risk of getting crushed through the abrupt closing of the adventure by fate. The over-prudent, cats as they are, and because they are cats, sometimes incur more danger than the audacious. Fauchelevent was of this hesitating nature. But Jean Valjean's coolness prevailed over him in spite of himself. He grumbled:—

"Well, since there is no other means."

Jean Valjean resumed:—

"The only thing which troubles me is what will take place at the cemetery."

"That is the very point that is not troublesome," exclaimed Fauchelevent. "If you are sure of coming out of the coffin all right, I am sure of getting you out of the grave. The grave-digger is a drunkard, and a friend of mine. He is Father Mestienne. An old fellow of the old school. The grave-digger puts the corpses in the grave, and I put the grave-digger in my pocket. I will tell you what will take place. They will arrive a little before dusk, three-quarters of an hour before the gates of the cemetery are closed. The hearse will drive directly up to the grave. I shall follow; that is my business. I shall have a hammer, a chisel, and some pincers in my pocket. The hearse halts, the undertaker's men knot a rope around your coffin and lower you down. The priest says the prayers, makes the sign of the cross, sprinkles the holy water, and takes his departure. I am left alone with Father Mestienne. He is my friend, I tell you. One of two things will happen, he will either be sober, or he will not be sober. If he is not drunk, I shall say to him: 'Come and drink a bout while the *Bon Coing* (the Good Quince) is open.' I carry him off, I get him drunk,—it does not take long to make Father Mestienne drunk, he always has the beginning of it about him,—I lay him under the table, I take his card, so that I can get into the cemetery again, and I return without him. Then you have no longer any one but me to deal with. If he is drunk, I shall say to him: 'Be off; I will do your work for you.' Off he goes, and I drag you out of the hole."

Jean Valjean held out his hand, and Fauchelevent precipitated himself upon it with the touching effusion of a peasant.

"That is settled, Father Fauchelevent. All will go well."

"Provided nothing goes wrong," thought Fauchelevent. "In that case, it would be terrible."

V

IT IS NOT NECESSARY TO BE DRUNK IN ORDER TO BE IMMORTAL

On the following day, as the sun was declining, the very rare passers-by on the Boulevard du Maine pulled off their hats to an old-fashioned hearse, ornamented with skulls, cross-bones, and tears. This hearse contained a coffin covered with a white cloth over which spread a large black cross, like a huge corpse with drooping arms. A mourning-coach, in which could be seen a priest in his surplice, and a choir boy in his red cap, followed. Two undertaker's men in gray uniforms trimmed with black walked on the right and the left of the hearse. Behind it came an old man in the garments of a laborer, who limped along. The procession was going in the direction of the Vaugirard cemetery.

The handle of a hammer, the blade of a cold chisel, and the antennæ of a pair of pincers were visible, protruding from the man's pocket.

The Vaugirard cemetery formed an exception among the cemeteries of Paris. It had its peculiar usages, just as it had its carriage entrance and its house door, which old people in the quarter, who clung tenaciously to ancient words, still called the *porte cavalière* and the *porte piétonne*. The Bernardines-Benedictines of the Rue Petit-Picpus had obtained permission, as we have already stated, to be buried there in a corner apart, and at night, the plot of land having formerly belonged to their community. The grave-diggers being thus bound to service in the evening in summer and at night in winter, in this cemetery, they were subjected to a special discipline. The gates of the Paris cemeteries closed, at that epoch, at sundown, and this being a municipal regulation, the Vaugirard cemetery was bound by it like the rest. The carriage gate and the house door were two contiguous grated gates, adjoining a pavilion built by the architect Perronet, and inhabited by the door-keeper of the cemetery. These gates, therefore, swung inexorably on their hinges at the instant when the sun disappeared behind the dome of the Invalides. If any grave-digger were delayed after that moment in the cemetery, there was but one way for him to get out—his grave-digger's card furnished by the department of public funerals. A sort of letter-box was constructed in the porter's window. The grave-digger dropped his card into this box, the porter heard it fall, pulled the rope, and the small door opened. If the man had not his card, he mentioned his name, the porter, who was sometimes in bed and asleep, rose, came out and identified the man, and opened the gate with his key; the grave-digger stepped out, but had to pay a fine of fifteen francs.

This cemetery, with its peculiarities outside the regulations, embarrassed the symmetry of the administration. It was suppressed a little later than 1830. The cemetery of Mont-Parnasse, called the Eastern cemetery, succeeded to it, and inherited that famous dram-shop next to the Vaugirard cemetery, which was surmounted by a quince painted on a board, and which formed an angle, one side on the drinkers' tables, and the other on the tombs, with this sign: *Au Bon Coing*.

The Vaugirard cemetery was what may be called a faded cemetery. It was falling into disuse. Dampness was invading it, the flowers were deserting it. The bourgeois did not care much about being buried in the Vaugirard; it hinted at poverty. Père-Lachaise if you please! to be buried in Père-Lachaise is equivalent to having furniture of mahogany. It is recognized as elegant. The Vaugirard cemetery was a venerable enclosure, planted like an old-fashioned French garden. Straight alleys, box, thuya-trees, holly, ancient tombs beneath aged cypress-trees, and very tall grass. In the evening it was tragic there. There were very lugubrious lines about it.

The sun had not yet set when the hearse with the white pall and the black cross entered the avenue of the Vaugirard cemetery. The lame man who followed it was no other than Fauchelevent.

The interment of Mother Crucifixion in the vault under the altar, the exit of Cosette, the introduction of Jean Valjean to the dead-room,—all had been executed without difficulty, and there had been no hitch.

Let us remark in passing, that the burial of Mother Crucifixion under the altar of the convent is a perfectly venial offence in our sight. It is one of the faults which resemble a duty. The nuns had committed it, not only without difficulty, but even with the applause of their own consciences. In the cloister, what is called the "government" is only an intermeddling with authority, an interference which is always questionable. In the first place, the rule; as for the code, we shall see. Make as many laws as you please, men; but keep them for yourselves. The tribute to Cæsar is never anything but the remnants of the tribute to God. A prince is nothing in the presence of a principle.

Fauchelevent limped along behind the hearse in a very contented frame of mind. His twin plots, the one with the nuns, the one for the convent, the other against it, the other with M. Madeleine, had succeeded, to all appearance. Jean Valjean's composure was one of those powerful tranquillities which are contagious. Fauchelevent no longer felt doubtful as to his success.

What remained to be done was a mere nothing. Within the last two years, he had made good Father Mestienne, a chubby-cheeked person, drunk at least ten times. He played with Father Mestienne. He did what he liked with him. He made him dance according to his whim. Mestienne's head adjusted itself to the cap of Fauchelevent's will. Fauchelevent's confidence was perfect.

At the moment when the convoy entered the avenue leading to the cemetery, Fauchelevent glanced cheerfully at the hearse, and said half aloud, as he rubbed his big hands:—

"Here's a fine farce!"

All at once the hearse halted; it had reached the gate. The permission for interment must be exhibited. The undertaker's man addressed himself to the porter of the cemetery. During this colloquy, which always is productive of a delay of from one to two minutes, some one, a stranger, came and placed himself behind the hearse, beside Fauchelevent. He was a sort of laboring man, who wore a waistcoat with large pockets and carried a mattock under his arm.

Fauchelevent surveyed this stranger.

"Who are you?" he demanded.

"The man replied:—

"The grave-digger."

If a man could survive the blow of a cannon-ball full in the breast, he would make the same face that Fauchelevent made.

"The grave-digger?"

"Yes."

"You?"

"I."

"Father Mestienne is the grave-digger."

"He was."

"What! He was?"

"He is dead."

Fauchelevent had expected anything but this, that a grave-digger could die. It is true, nevertheless, that grave-diggers do die themselves.

By dint of excavating graves for other people, one hollows out one's own.

Fauchelevent stood there with his mouth wide open. He had hardly the strength to stammer:—

"But it is not possible!"

"It is so."

"But," he persisted feebly, "Father Mestienne is the grave-digger."

"After Napoleon, Louis XVIII. After Mestienne, Gribier. Peasant, my name is Gribier."

Fauchelevent, who was deadly pale, stared at this Gribier.

He was a tall, thin, livid, utterly funereal man. He had the air of an unsuccessful doctor who had turned grave-digger.

Fauchelevent burst out laughing.

"Ah!" said he, "what queer things do happen! Father Mestienne is dead, but long live little Father Lenoir! Do you know who little Father Lenoir is? He is a jug of red wine. It is a jug of Surêne, morbigou! of real Paris Surêne? Ah! So old Mestienne is dead! I am sorry for it; he was a jolly fellow. But you are a jolly fellow, too. Are you not, comrade? We'll go and have a drink together presently."

The man replied:—

"I have been a student. I passed my fourth examination. I never drink."

The hearse had set out again, and was rolling up the grand alley of the cemetery.

Fauchelevent had slackened his pace. He limped more out of anxiety than from infirmity.

The grave-digger walked on in front of him.

Fauchelevent passed the unexpected Gribier once more in review.

He was one of those men who, though very young, have the air of age, and who, though slender, are extremely strong.

"Comrade!" cried Fauchelevent.

The man turned round.

"I am the convent grave-digger."

"My colleague," said the man.

Fauchelevent, who was illiterate but very sharp, understood that he had to deal with a formidable species of man, with a fine talker. He muttered:

"So Father Mestienne is dead."

The man replied:—

"Completely. The good God consulted his note-book which shows when the time is up. It was Father Mestienne's turn. Father Mestienne died."

Fauchelevent repeated mechanically: "The good God—"

"The good God," said the man authoritatively. "According to the philosophers, the Eternal Father; according to the Jacobins, the Supreme Being."

"Shall we not make each other's acquaintance?" stammered Fauchelevent.

"It is made. You are a peasant, I am a Parisian."

"People do not know each other until they have drunk together. He who empties his glass empties his heart. You must come and have a drink with me. Such a thing cannot be refused."

"Business first."

Fauchelevent thought: "I am lost."

They were only a few turns of the wheel distant from the small alley leading to the nuns' corner.

The grave-digger resumed:—

"Peasant, I have seven small children who must be fed. As they must eat, I cannot drink."

And he added, with the satisfaction of a serious man who is turning a phrase well:—

"Their hunger is the enemy of my thirst."

The hearse skirted a clump of cypress-trees, quitted the grand alley, turned into a narrow one, entered the waste land, and plunged into a thicket. This indicated the immediate proximity of the place of sepulture. Fauchelevent slackened his pace, but he could not detain the hearse. Fortunately, the soil, which was light and wet with the winter rains, clogged the wheels and retarded its speed.

He approached the grave-digger.

"They have such a nice little Argenteuil wine," murmured Fauchelevent.

"Villager," retorted the man, "I ought not be a grave-digger. My father was a porter at the Prytaneum (Town-Hall). He destined me for literature. But he had reverses. He had losses on 'change. I was obliged to renounce the profession of author. But I am still a public writer."

"So you are not a grave-digger, then?" returned Fauchelevent, clutching at this branch, feeble as it was.

"The one does not hinder the other. I cumulate."

Fauchelevent did not understand this last word.

"Come have a drink," said he.

Here a remark becomes necessary. Fauchelevent, whatever his anguish, offered a drink, but he did not explain himself on one point; who was to pay? Generally, Fauchelevent offered and Father Mestienne paid. An offer of a drink was the evident result of the novel situation created by the new grave-digger, and it was necessary to make this offer, but the old gardener left the proverbial quarter of an hour named after Rabelais in the dark, and that not unintentionally. As for himself, Fauchelevent did not wish to pay, troubled as he was.

The grave-digger went on with a superior smile:—

"One must eat. I have accepted Father Mestienne's reversion. One gets to be a philosopher when one has nearly completed his classes. To the labor of the hand I join the labor of the arm. I have my scrivener's stall in the market of the Rue de Sèvres. You know? the Umbrella Market. All the cooks of the Red Cross apply to me. I scribble their declarations of love to the raw soldiers. In the morning I write love letters; in the evening I dig graves. Such is life, rustic."

The hearse was still advancing. Fauchelevent, uneasy to the last degree, was gazing about him on all sides. Great drops of perspiration trickled down from his brow.

"But," continued the grave-digger, "a man cannot serve two mistresses. I must choose between the pen and the mattock. The mattock is ruining my hand."

The hearse halted.

The choir boy alighted from the mourning-coach, then the priest.

One of the small front wheels of the hearse had run up a little on a pile of earth, beyond which an open grave was visible.

"What a farce this is!" repeated Fauchelevent in consternation.

VI

BETWEEN FOUR PLANKS

Who was in the coffin? The reader knows. Jean Valjean.

Jean Valjean had arranged things so that he could exist there, and he could almost breathe.

It is a strange thing to what a degree security of conscience confers security of the rest. Every combination thought out by Jean Valjean had been progressing, and progressing favorably, since the preceding day. He, like Fauchelevent, counted on Father Mestienne. He had no doubt as to the end. Never was there a more critical situation, never more complete composure.

The four planks of the coffin breathe out a kind of terrible peace. It seemed as though something of the repose of the dead entered into Jean Valjean's tranquillity.

From the depths of that coffin he had been able to follow, and he had followed, all the phases of the terrible drama which he was playing with death.

Shortly after Fauchelevent had finished nailing on the upper plank, Jean Valjean had felt himself carried out, then driven off. He knew, from the diminution in the jolting, when they left the pavements and reached the earth road. He had divined, from a dull noise, that they were crossing the bridge of Austerlitz. At the first halt, he had understood that they were entering the cemetery; at the second halt, he said to himself:—

"Here is the grave."

Suddenly, he felt hands seize the coffin, then a harsh grating against the planks; he explained it to himself as the rope which was being fastened round the casket in order to lower it into the cavity.

Then he experienced a giddiness.

The undertaker's man and the grave-digger had probably allowed the coffin to lose its balance, and had lowered the head before the foot. He recovered himself fully when he felt himself horizontal and motionless. He had just touched the bottom.

He had a certain sensation of cold.

A voice rose above him, glacial and solemn. He heard Latin words, which he did not understand, pass over him, so slowly that he was able to catch them one by one:—

"Qui dormiunt in terræ pulvere, evigilabunt; alii in vitam æternam, et alii in approbrium, ut videant semper."

A child's voice said:—

"De profundis."

The grave voice began again:—

"Requiem æternam dona ei, Domine."

The child's voice responded:—

"Et lux perpetua luceat ei."

He heard something like the gentle patter of several drops of rain on the plank which covered him. It was probably the holy water.

He thought: "This will be over soon now. Patience for a little while longer. The priest will take his departure. Fauchelevent will take Mestienne off to drink. I shall be left. Then Fauchelevent will return alone, and I shall get out. That will be the work of a good hour."

The grave voice resumed

"Requiescat in pace."

And the child's voice said:—

"Amen."

Jean Valjean strained his ears, and heard something like retreating footsteps.

"There, they are going now," thought he. "I am alone."

All at once, he heard over his head a sound which seemed to him to be a clap of thunder.

It was a shovelful of earth falling on the coffin.

A second shovelful fell.

One of the holes through which he breathed had just been stopped up.

A third shovelful of earth fell.

Then a fourth.

There are things which are too strong for the strongest man. Jean Valjean lost consciousness.

VII

In which will be Found the Origin of the Saying: Don't Lose the Card

This is what had taken place above the coffin in which lay Jean Valjean.

When the hearse had driven off, when the priest and the choir boy had entered the carriage again and taken their departure, Fauchelevent, who had not taken his eyes from the grave-digger, saw the latter bend over and grasp his shovel, which was sticking upright in the heap of dirt.

Then Fauchelevent took a supreme resolve.

He placed himself between the grave and the grave-digger, crossed his arms and said:—

"I am the one to pay!"

The grave-digger stared at him in amazement, and replied:—

"What's that, peasant?"

Fauchelevent repeated:—

"I am the one who pays!"

"What?"

"For the wine."

"What wine?"

"That Argenteuil wine."

"Where is the Argenteuil?"

"At the *Bon Coing*."

"Go to the devil!" said the grave-digger.

And he flung a shovelful of earth on the coffin.

The coffin gave back a hollow sound. Fauchelevent felt himself stagger and on the point of falling headlong into the grave himself. He shouted in a voice in which the strangling sound of the death rattle began to mingle:—

"Comrade! Before the *Bon Coing* is shut!"

The grave-digger took some more earth on his shovel. Fauchelevent continued.

"I will pay."

And he seized the man's arm.

"Listen to me, comrade. I am the convent grave-digger, I have come to help you. It is a business which can be performed at night. Let us begin, then, by going for a drink."

And as he spoke, and clung to this desperate insistence, this melancholy reflection occurred to him: "And if he drinks, will he get drunk?"

"Provincial," said the man, "if you positively insist upon it, I consent. We will drink. After work, never before."

And he flourished his shovel briskly. Fauchelevent held him back.

"It is Argenteuil wine, at six."

"Oh, come," said the grave-digger, "you are a bell-ringer. Ding dong, ding dong, that's all you know how to say. Go hang yourself."

And he threw in a second shovelful.

Fauchelevent had reached a point where he no longer knew what he was saying.

"Come along and drink," he cried, "since it is I who pays the bill."

"When we have put the child to bed," said the grave-digger.

He flung in a third shovelful.

Then he thrust his shovel into the earth and added:—

"It's cold to-night, you see, and the corpse would shriek out after us if we were to plant her there without a coverlet."

At that moment, as he loaded his shovel, the grave-digger bent over, and the pocket of his waistcoat gaped. Fauchelevent's wild gaze fell mechanically into that pocket, and there it stopped.

The sun was not yet hidden behind the horizon; there was still light enough to enable him to distinguish something white at the bottom of that yawning pocket.

The sum total of lightning that the eye of a Picard peasant can contain, traversed Fauchelevent's pupils. An idea had just occurred to him.

He thrust his hand into the pocket from behind, without the grave-digger, who was wholly absorbed in his shovelful of earth, observing it, and pulled out the white object which lay at the bottom of it.

The man sent a fourth shovelful tumbling into the grave.

Just as he turned round to get the fifth, Fauchelevent looked calmly at him and said:—

"By the way, you new man, have you your card?"

The grave-digger paused.

"What card?"

"The sun is on the point of setting."

"That's good, it is going to put on its nightcap."

"The gate of the cemetery will close immediately."

"Well, what then?"

"Have you your card?"

"Ah! my card?" said the grave-digger.

And he fumbled in his pocket.

Having searched one pocket, he proceeded to search the other. He passed on to his fobs, explored the first, returned to the second.

"Why, no," said he, "I have not my card. I must have forgotten it."

"Fifteen francs fine," said Fauchelevent.

The grave-digger turned green. Green is the pallor of livid people.

"Ah! Jésus-mon-Dieu-bancroche-à-bas-la-lune!" he exclaimed. "Fifteen francs fine!"

"Three pieces of a hundred sous," said Fauchelevent.

The grave-digger dropped his shovel.

Fauchelevent's turn had come.

"Ah, come now, conscript," said Fauchelevent, "none of this despair. There is no question of committing suicide and benefiting the grave. Fifteen francs is fifteen francs, and besides, you may not be able to pay it. I am an old hand, you are a new one. I know all the ropes and the devices. I will give you some friendly advice. One thing is clear, the sun is on the point of setting, it is touching the dome now, the cemetery will be closed in five minutes more."

"That is true," replied the man.

"Five minutes more and you will not have time to fill the grave, it is as hollow as the devil, this grave, and to reach the gate in season to pass it before it is shut."

"That is true."

"In that case, a fine of fifteen francs."

"Fifteen francs."

"But you have time. Where do you live?"

"A couple of steps from the barrier, a quarter of an hour from here. No. 87 Rue de Vaugirard."

"You have just time to get out by taking to your heels at your best speed."

"That is exactly so."

"Once outside the gate, you gallop home, you get your card, you return, the cemetery porter admits you. As you have your card, there will be nothing to pay. And you will bury your corpse. I'll watch it for you in the meantime, so that it shall not run away."

"I am indebted to you for my life, peasant."

"Decamp!" said Fauchelevent.

The grave-digger, overwhelmed with gratitude, shook his hand and set off on a run.

When the man had disappeared in the thicket, Fauchelevent listened until he heard his footsteps die away in the distance, then he leaned over the grave, and said in a low tone:—

"Father Madeleine!"

There was no reply.

Fauchelevent was seized with a shudder. He tumbled rather than climbed into the grave, flung himself on the head of the coffin and cried:—

"Are you there?"

Silence in the coffin.

Fauchelevent, hardly able to draw his breath for trembling, seized his cold chisel and his hammer, and pried up the coffin lid.

Jean Valjean's face appeared in the twilight; it was pale and his eyes were closed.

Fauchelevent's hair rose upright on his head, he sprang to his feet, then fell back against the side of the grave, ready to swoon on the coffin. He stared at Jean Valjean.

Jean Valjean lay there pallid and motionless.

Fauchelevent murmured in a voice as faint as a sigh:—

"He is dead!"

And, drawing himself up, and folding his arms with such violence that his clenched fists came in contact with his shoulders, he cried:—

"And this is the way I save his life!"

Then the poor man fell to sobbing. He soliloquized the while, for it is an error to suppose that the soliloquy is unnatural. Powerful emotion often talks aloud.

"It is Father Mestienne's fault. Why did that fool die? What need was there for him to give up the ghost at the very moment when no one was expecting it? It is he who has killed M. Madeleine. Father Madeleine! He is in the coffin. It is quite handy. All is over. Now, is there any sense in these things? Ah! my God! he is dead! Well! and his little girl, what am I to do with her? What will the fruit-seller say? The idea of its being possible for a man like that to die like this!

When I think how he put himself under that cart! Father Madeleine! Father Madeleine! Pardine! He was suffocated, I said so. He wouldn't believe me. Well! Here's a pretty trick to play! He is dead, that good man, the very best man out of all the good God's good folks! And his little girl! Ah! In the first place, I won't go back there myself. I shall stay here. After having done such a thing as that! What's the use of being two old men, if we are two old fools! But, in the first place, how did he manage to enter the convent? That was the beginning of it all. One should not do such things. Father Madeleine! Father Madeleine! Father Madeleine! Madeleine! Monsieur Madeleine! Monsieur le Maire! He does not hear me. Now get out of this scrape if you can!"

And he tore his hair.

A grating sound became audible through the trees in the distance. It was the cemetery gate closing.

Fauchelevent bent over Jean Valjean, and all at once he bounded back and recoiled so far as the limits of a grave permit.

Jean Valjean's eyes were open and gazing at him.

To see a corpse is alarming, to behold a resurrection is almost as much so. Fauchelevent became like stone, pale, haggard, overwhelmed by all these excesses of emotion, not knowing whether he had to do with a living man or a dead one, and staring at Jean Valjean, who was gazing at him.

"I FELL ASLEEP," SAID JEAN Valjean.

And he raised himself to a sitting posture.

Fauchelevent fell on his knees.

"Just, good Virgin! How you frightened me!"

Then he sprang to his feet and cried:—

"Thanks, Father Madeleine!"

Jean Valjean had merely fainted. The fresh air had revived him.

Joy is the ebb of terror. Fauchelevent found almost as much difficulty in recovering himself as Jean Valjean had.

"So you are not dead! Oh! How wise you are! I called you so much that you came back. When I saw your eyes shut, I said: 'Good! there he is, stifled,' I should have gone raving mad, mad enough for a strait jacket. They would have put me in Bicêtre. What do you suppose I should have done if you had been dead? And your little girl? There's that fruit-seller,—she would never have understood it! The child is thrust into your arms, and then—the grandfather is dead! What a story! good saints of paradise, what a tale! Ah! you are alive, that's the best of it!"

"I am cold," said Jean Valjean.

This remark recalled Fauchelevent thoroughly to reality, and there was pressing need of it. The souls of these two men were troubled even when they had recovered themselves, although they did not realize it, and there was about them something uncanny, which was the sinister bewilderment inspired by the place.

"Let us get out of here quickly," exclaimed Fauchelevent.

He fumbled in his pocket, and pulled out a gourd with which he had provided himself.

"But first, take a drop," said he.

The flask finished what the fresh air had begun, Jean Valjean swallowed a mouthful of brandy, and regained full possession of his faculties.

He got out of the coffin, and helped Fauchelevent to nail on the lid again.

Three minutes later they were out of the grave.

Moreover, Fauchelevent was perfectly composed. He took his time. The cemetery was closed. The arrival of the grave-digger Gribier was not to be apprehended. That "conscript" was at home busily engaged in looking for his card, and at some difficulty in finding it in his lodgings, since it was in Fauchelevent's pocket. Without a card, he could not get back into the cemetery.

Fauchelevent took the shovel, and Jean Valjean the pick-axe, and together they buried the empty coffin.

When the grave was full, Fauchelevent said to Jean Valjean:—

"Let us go. I will keep the shovel; do you carry off the mattock."

Night was falling.

Jean Valjean experienced some difficulty in moving and in walking. He had stiffened himself in that coffin, and had become a little like a corpse. The rigidity of death had seized upon him between those four planks. He had, in a manner, to thaw out, from the tomb.

"You are benumbed," said Fauchelevent. "It is a pity that I have a game leg, for otherwise we might step out briskly."

"Bah!" replied Jean Valjean, "four paces will put life into my legs once more."

They set off by the alleys through which the hearse had passed. On arriving before the closed gate and the porter's pavilion Fauchelevent, who held the grave-digger's card in his hand, dropped it into the box, the porter pulled the rope, the gate opened, and they went out.

"How well everything is going!" said Fauchelevent; "what a capital idea that was of yours, Father Madeleine!"

They passed the Vaugirard barrier in the simplest manner in the world. In the neighborhood of the cemetery, a shovel and pick are equal to two passports.

The Rue Vaugirard was deserted.

"Father Madeleine," said Fauchelevent as they went along, and raising his eyes to the houses, "Your eyes are better than mine. Show me No. 87."

"Here it is," said Jean Valjean.

"There is no one in the street," said Fauchelevent. "Give me your mattock and wait a couple of minutes for me."

Fauchelevent entered No. 87, ascended to the very top, guided by the instinct which always leads the poor man to the garret, and knocked in the dark, at the door of an attic.

A voice replied: "Come in."

It was Gribier's voice.

Fauchelevent opened the door. The grave-digger's dwelling was, like all such wretched habitations, an unfurnished and encumbered garret. A packing-case—a coffin, perhaps—took the place of a commode, a butter-pot served for a drinking-fountain, a straw mattress served for a bed, the floor served instead of tables and chairs. In a corner, on a tattered fragment which had been a piece of an old carpet, a thin woman and a number of children were piled in a heap. The whole of this poverty-stricken interior bore traces of having been overturned. One would have said that there had been an earthquake "for one." The covers were displaced, the rags scattered about, the jug broken, the mother had been crying, the children had probably been beaten; traces of a vigorous and ill-tempered search. It was plain that the grave-digger had made a desperate search for his card, and had made everybody in the garret, from the jug to his wife, responsible for its loss. He wore an air of desperation.

But Fauchelevent was in too great a hurry to terminate this adventure to take any notice of this sad side of his success.

He entered and said:—

"I have brought you back your shovel and pick."

Gribier gazed at him in stupefaction.

"Is it you, peasant?"

"And to-morrow morning you will find your card with the porter of the cemetery."

And he laid the shovel and mattock on the floor.

"What is the meaning of this?" demanded Gribier.

"The meaning of it is, that you dropped your card out of your pocket, that I found it on the ground after you were gone, that I have buried the corpse, that I have filled the grave, that I have done your work, that the porter will return your card to you, and that you will not have to pay fifteen francs. There you have it, conscript."

"Thanks, villager!" exclaimed Gribier, radiant. "The next time I will pay for the drinks."

VIII

A Successful Interrogatory

An hour later, in the darkness of night, two men and a child presented themselves at No. 62 Rue Petit-Picpus. The elder of the men lifted the knocker and rapped.

They were Fauchelevent, Jean Valjean, and Cosette.

The two old men had gone to fetch Cosette from the fruiterer's in the Rue du Chemin-Vert, where Fauchelevent had deposited her on the preceding day. Cosette had passed these twenty-four hours trembling silently and understanding nothing. She trembled to such a degree that she wept. She had neither eaten nor slept. The worthy fruit-seller had plied her with a hundred questions, without obtaining any other reply than a melancholy and unvarying gaze. Cosette had betrayed nothing of what she had seen and heard during the last two days. She divined that they were passing through a crisis. She was deeply conscious that it was necessary to "be good." Who has not experienced the sovereign power of those two words, pronounced with a certain accent in the ear of a terrified little being: *Say nothing!* Fear is mute. Moreover, no one guards a secret like a child.

But when, at the expiration of these lugubrious twenty-four hours, she beheld Jean Valjean again, she gave vent to such a cry of joy, that any thoughtful person who had chanced to hear that cry, would have guessed that it issued from an abyss.

Fauchelevent belonged to the convent and knew the pass-words. All the doors opened.

Thus was solved the double and alarming problem of how to get out and how to get in.

The porter, who had received his instructions, opened the little servant's door which connected the courtyard with the garden, and which could still be seen from the street twenty years ago, in the wall at the bottom of the court, which faced the carriage entrance.

The porter admitted all three of them through this door, and from that point they reached the inner, reserved parlor where Fauchelevent, on the preceding day, had received his orders from the prioress.

The prioress, rosary in hand, was waiting for them. A vocal mother, with her veil lowered, stood beside her.

A discreet candle lighted, one might almost say, made a show of lighting the parlor.

The prioress passed Jean Valjean in review. There is nothing which examines like a downcast eye.

Then she questioned him:—

"You are the brother?"

"Yes, reverend Mother," replied Fauchelevent.

"What is your name?"

Fauchelevent replied:—

"Ultime Fauchelevent."

He really had had a brother named Ultime, who was dead.

"Where do you come from?"

Fauchelevent replied:—

"From Picquigny, near Amiens."

"What is your age?"

Fauchelevent replied:—

"Fifty."

"What is your profession?"

Fauchelevent replied:—

"Gardener."

"Are you a good Christian?"

Fauchelevent replied:—

"Every one is in the family."

"Is this your little girl?"

Fauchelevent replied:—

"Yes, reverend Mother."

"You are her father?"

Fauchelevent replied:—

"Her grandfather."

The vocal mother said to the prioress in a low voice

"He answers well."

Jean Valjean had not uttered a single word.

The prioress looked attentively at Cosette, and said half aloud to the vocal mother:—

"She will grow up ugly."

The two mothers consulted for a few moments in very low tones in the corner of the parlor, then the prioress turned round and said:—

"Father Fauvent, you will get another knee-cap with a bell. Two will be required now."

On the following day, therefore, two bells were audible in the garden, and the nuns could not resist the temptation to raise the corner of their veils. At the extreme end of the garden, under the trees, two men, Fauvent and another man, were visible as they dug side by side. An enormous event. Their silence was broken to the extent of saying to each other: "He is an assistant gardener."

The vocal mothers added: "He is a brother of Father Fauvent."

Jean Valjean was, in fact, regularly installed; he had his belled knee-cap; henceforth he was official. His name was Ultime Fauchelevent.

The most powerful determining cause of his admission had been the prioress's observation upon Cosette: "She will grow up ugly."

The prioress, that pronounced prognosticator, immediately took a fancy to Cosette and gave her a place in the school as a charity pupil.

There is nothing that is not strictly logical about this.

It is in vain that mirrors are banished from the convent, women are conscious of their faces; now, girls who are conscious of their beauty do not easily become nuns; the vocation being voluntary in inverse proportion to their good looks, more is to be hoped from the ugly than from the pretty. Hence a lively taste for plain girls.

The whole of this adventure increased the importance of good, old Fauchelevent; he won a triple success; in the eyes of Jean Valjean, whom he had saved and sheltered; in those of grave-digger Gribier, who said to himself: "He spared me that fine"; with the convent, which, being enabled, thanks to him, to retain the coffin of Mother Crucifixion under the altar, eluded Cæsar and satisfied God. There was a coffin containing a body in the Petit-Picpus, and a coffin without a body in the Vaugirard cemetery, public order had no doubt been deeply disturbed thereby, but no one was aware of it.

As for the convent, its gratitude to Fauchelevent was very great. Fauchelevent became the best of servitors and the most precious of gardeners. Upon the occasion of the archbishop's next visit, the prioress recounted the affair to his Grace, making something of a confession at the same time, and yet boasting of her deed. On leaving the convent, the archbishop mentioned it with approval, and in a whisper to M. de Latil, Monsieur's confessor, afterwards Archbishop of Reims and Cardinal. This admiration for Fauchelevent became widespread, for it made its way to Rome. We have seen a note addressed by the then reigning Pope, Leo XII, to one of his relatives, a Monsignor in the Nuncio's establishment in Paris, and bearing, like himself, the name of Della Genga; it contained these lines: "It appears that there is in a convent in Paris an excellent gardener, who is also a holy man, named Fauvent." Nothing of this triumph reached Fauchelevent in his hut; he went on grafting, weeding, and covering up his melon beds, without in the least suspecting his excellences and his sanctity. Neither did he suspect his glory, any more than a Durham or Surrey bull whose portrait is published in the *London Illustrated News*, with this inscription: "Bull which carried off the prize at the Cattle Show."

IX

CLOISTERED

C osette continued to hold her tongue in the convent.

It was quite natural that Cosette should think herself Jean Valjean's daughter. Moreover, as she knew nothing, she could say nothing, and then, she would not have said anything in any case. As we have just observed, nothing trains children to silence like unhappiness. Cosette had suffered so much, that she feared everything, even to speak or to breathe. A single word had so often brought down an avalanche upon her. She had hardly begun to regain her confidence since she had been with Jean Valjean. She speedily became accustomed to the convent. Only she regretted Catherine, but she dared not say so. Once, however, she did say to Jean Valjean: "Father, if I had known, I would have brought her away with me."

Cosette had been obliged, on becoming a scholar in the convent, to don the garb of the pupils of the house. Jean Valjean succeeded in getting them to restore to him the garments which she laid aside. This was the same mourning suit which he had made her put on when she had quitted the Thénardiers' inn. It was not very threadbare even now. Jean Valjean locked up these garments, plus the stockings and the shoes, with a quantity of camphor and all the aromatics in which convents abound, in a little valise which he found means of procuring. He set this valise on a chair near his bed, and he always carried the key about his person. "Father," Cosette asked him one day, "what is there in that box which smells so good?"

Father Fauchelevent received other recompense for his good action, in addition to the glory which we just mentioned, and of which he knew nothing; in the first place it made him happy; next, he had much less work, since it was shared. Lastly, as he was very fond of snuff, he found the presence of M. Madeleine an advantage, in that he used three times as much as he had done previously, and that in an infinitely more luxurious manner, seeing that M. Madeleine paid for it.

The nuns did not adopt the name of Ultime; they called Jean Valjean *the other Fauvent*.

If these holy women had possessed anything of Javert's glance, they would eventually have noticed that when there was any errand to be done outside in the behalf of the garden, it was always the elder Fauchelevent, the old, the infirm, the lame man, who went, and never the other; but whether it is that eyes constantly fixed on God know not how to spy, or whether they were, by preference, occupied in keeping watch on each other, they paid no heed to this.

Moreover, it was well for Jean Valjean that he kept close and did not stir out. Javert watched the quarter for more than a month.

This convent was for Jean Valjean like an island surrounded by gulfs. Henceforth, those four walls constituted his world. He saw enough of the sky there to enable him to preserve his serenity, and Cosette enough to remain happy.

A very sweet life began for him.

He inhabited the old hut at the end of the garden, in company with Fauchelevent. This hovel, built of old rubbish, which was still in existence in 1845, was composed, as the reader already knows, of three chambers, all of which were utterly bare and had nothing beyond the walls. The principal one had been given up, by force, for Jean Valjean had opposed it in vain, to M. Madeleine, by Father Fauchelevent. The walls of this chamber had for ornament, in addition to the two nails whereon to hang the knee-cap and the basket, a Royalist bank-note of '93, applied to the wall over the chimney-piece, and of which the following is an exact facsimile:—

This specimen of Vendean paper money had been nailed to the wall by the preceding gardener, an old Chouan, who had died in the convent, and whose place Fauchelevent had taken.

Jean Valjean worked in the garden every day and made himself very useful. He had formerly been a pruner of trees, and he gladly found himself a gardener once more. It will be remembered that he knew all sorts of secrets and receipts for agriculture. He turned these to advantage. Almost all the trees in the orchard were ungrafted, and wild. He budded them and made them produce excellent fruit.

Cosette had permission to pass an hour with him every day. As the sisters were melancholy and he was kind, the child made comparisons and adored him. At the appointed hour she flew to the hut. When she entered the lowly cabin, she filled it with paradise. Jean Valjean blossomed out and felt his happiness increase with the happiness which he afforded Cosette. The joy which we inspire has this charming property, that, far from growing meagre, like all reflections, it returns to us more radiant than ever. At recreation hours, Jean Valjean watched her running and playing in the distance, and he distinguished her laugh from that of the rest.

For Cosette laughed now.

Cosette's face had even undergone a change, to a certain extent. The gloom had disappeared from it. A smile is the same as sunshine; it banishes winter from the human countenance.

Recreation over, when Cosette went into the house again, Jean Valjean gazed at the windows of her class-room, and at night he rose to look at the windows of her dormitory.

God has his own ways, moreover; the convent contributed, like Cosette, to uphold and complete the Bishop's work in Jean Valjean. It is certain that virtue adjoins pride on one side. A bridge built by the devil exists there. Jean Valjean had been, unconsciously, perhaps, tolerably near that side and that bridge, when Providence cast his lot in the convent of the Petit-Picpus; so long as he had compared himself only to the Bishop, he had regarded himself as unworthy and had remained humble; but for some time past he had been comparing himself to men in general, and pride was beginning to spring up. Who knows? He might have ended by returning very gradually to hatred.

The convent stopped him on that downward path.

This was the second place of captivity which he had seen. In his youth, in what had been for him the beginning of his life, and later on, quite recently again, he had beheld another,—a frightful place, a terrible place, whose severities had always appeared to him the iniquity of justice, and the crime of the law. Now, after the galleys, he saw the cloister; and when he meditated how he had formed a part of the galleys, and that he now, so to speak, was a spectator of the cloister, he confronted the two in his own mind with anxiety.

Sometimes he crossed his arms and leaned on his hoe, and slowly descended the endless spirals of reverie.

He recalled his former companions: how wretched they were; they rose at dawn, and toiled until night; hardly were they permitted to sleep; they lay on camp beds, where nothing was tolerated but mattresses two inches thick, in rooms which were heated only in the very harshest months of the year; they were clothed in frightful red blouses; they were allowed, as a great favor, linen trousers in the hottest weather, and a woollen carter's blouse on their backs when it was very cold; they drank no wine, and ate no meat, except when they went on "fatigue duty." They lived nameless, designated only by numbers, and converted, after a manner, into ciphers themselves, with downcast eyes, with lowered voices, with shorn heads, beneath the cudgel and in disgrace.

Then his mind reverted to the beings whom he had under his eyes.

These beings also lived with shorn heads, with downcast eyes, with lowered voices, not in disgrace, but amid the scoffs of the world, not with their backs bruised with the cudgel, but with their shoulders lacerated with their discipline. Their names, also, had vanished from among men; they no longer existed except under austere appellations. They never ate meat and they never drank wine; they often remained until evening without food; they were attired, not in a red blouse, but in a black shroud, of woollen, which was heavy in summer and thin in winter, without the power to add or subtract anything from it; without having even, according to the season, the resource of the linen garment or the woollen cloak; and for six months in the year they wore serge chemises which gave them fever. They dwelt, not in rooms warmed only during rigorous cold, but in cells where no fire was ever lighted; they slept, not on mattresses two inches thick, but on straw. And finally, they were not even allowed their sleep; every night, after a day of toil, they were obliged, in the weariness of their first slumber, at the moment when they were falling sound asleep and beginning to get warm, to rouse themselves, to rise and to go and pray in an ice-cold and gloomy chapel, with their knees on the stones.

On certain days each of these beings in turn had to remain for twelve successive hours in a kneeling posture, or prostrate, with face upon the pavement, and arms outstretched in the form of a cross.

The others were men; these were women.

What had those men done? They had stolen, violated, pillaged, murdered, assassinated. They were bandits, counterfeiters, poisoners, incendiaries, murderers, parricides. What had these women done? They had done nothing whatever.

On the one hand, highway robbery, fraud, deceit, violence, sensuality, homicide, all sorts of sacrilege, every variety of crime; on the other, one thing only, innocence.

Perfect innocence, almost caught up into heaven in a mysterious assumption, attached to the earth by virtue, already possessing something of heaven through holiness.

On the one hand, confidences over crimes, which are exchanged in whispers; on the other, the confession of faults made aloud. And what crimes! And what faults!

On the one hand, miasms; on the other, an ineffable perfume. On the one hand, a moral pest, guarded from sight, penned up under the range of cannon, and literally devouring its plague-stricken victims; on the other, the chaste flame of all souls on the same hearth. There, darkness; here, the shadow; but a shadow filled with gleams of light, and of gleams full of radiance.

Two strongholds of slavery; but in the first, deliverance possible, a legal limit always in sight, and then, escape. In the second, perpetuity; the sole hope, at the distant extremity of the future, that faint light of liberty which men call death.

In the first, men are bound only with chains; in the other, chained by faith.

What flowed from the first? An immense curse, the gnashing of teeth, hatred, desperate viciousness, a cry of rage against human society, a sarcasm against heaven.

What results flowed from the second? Blessings and love.

And in these two places, so similar yet so unlike, these two species of beings who were so very unlike, were undergoing the same work, expiation.

Jean Valjean understood thoroughly the expiation of the former; that personal expiation, the expiation for one's self. But he did not understand that of these last, that of creatures without reproach and without stain, and he trembled as he asked himself: The expiation of what? What expiation?

A voice within his conscience replied: "The most divine of human generosities, the expiation for others."

Here all personal theory is withheld; we are only the narrator; we place ourselves at Jean Valjean's point of view, and we translate his impressions.

Before his eyes he had the sublime summit of abnegation, the highest possible pitch of virtue; the innocence which pardons men their faults, and which expiates in their stead; servitude submitted to, torture accepted, punishment claimed by souls which have not sinned, for the sake of sparing it to souls which have fallen; the love of humanity swallowed up in the love of God, but even there preserving its distinct and mediatorial character; sweet and feeble beings possessing the misery of those who are punished and the smile of those who are recompensed.

And he remembered that he had dared to murmur!

Often, in the middle of the night, he rose to listen to the grateful song of those innocent creatures weighed down with severities, and the blood ran cold in his veins at the thought that those who were justly chastised raised their voices heavenward only in blasphemy, and that he, wretch that he was, had shaken his fist at God.

There was one striking thing which caused him to meditate deeply, like a warning whisper from Providence itself: the scaling of that wall, the passing of those barriers, the adventure accepted even at the risk of death, the painful and difficult ascent, all those efforts even, which he had made to escape from that other place of expiation, he had made in order to gain entrance into this one. Was this a symbol of his destiny? This house was a prison likewise and bore a melancholy resemblance to that other one whence he had fled, and yet he had never conceived an idea of anything similar.

Again he beheld gratings, bolts, iron bars—to guard whom? Angels.

These lofty walls which he had seen around tigers, he now beheld once more around lambs.

This was a place of expiation, and not of punishment; and yet, it was still more austere, more gloomy, and more pitiless than the other.

These virgins were even more heavily burdened than the convicts. A cold, harsh wind, that wind which had chilled his youth, traversed the barred and padlocked grating of the vultures; a still harsher and more biting breeze blew in the cage of these doves.

Why?

When he thought on these things, all that was within him was lost in amazement before this mystery of sublimity.

In these meditations, his pride vanished. He scrutinized his own heart in all manner of ways; he felt his pettiness, and many a time he wept. All that had entered into his life for the last six months had led him back towards the Bishop's holy injunctions; Cosette through love, the convent through humility.

Sometimes at eventide, in the twilight, at an hour when the garden was deserted, he could be seen on his knees in the middle of the walk which skirted the chapel, in front of the window through which he had gazed on the night of his arrival, and turned towards the spot where, as he knew, the sister was making reparation, prostrated in prayer. Thus he prayed as he knelt before the sister.

It seemed as though he dared not kneel directly before God.

Everything that surrounded him, that peaceful garden, those fragrant flowers, those children who uttered joyous cries, those grave and simple women, that silent cloister, slowly permeated him, and little by little, his soul became compounded of silence like the cloister, of perfume like the flowers, of simplicity like the women, of joy like the children. And then he reflected that these had been two houses of God which had received him in succession at two critical moments in his life: the first, when all doors were closed and when human society rejected him; the second, at a moment when human society had again set out in pursuit of him, and when the galleys were again yawning; and that, had it not been for the first, he should have relapsed into crime, and had it not been for the second, into torment.

His whole heart melted in gratitude, and he loved more and more.

Many years passed in this manner; Cosette was growing up.

A Note About the Author

Victor Hugo (1802–1885) was a French writer and prominent figure during Europe's Romantic movement. As a child, he traveled across the continent due to his father's position in the Napoleonic army. As a young man, he studied law although his passion was always literature. In 1819, Hugo created *Conservateur Littéraire*, a periodical that featured works from up-and-coming writers. A few years later he published a collection of poems *Odes et Poésies Diverses* followed by the novel *Han d'Islande* in 1825. Hugo has an extensive catalog, yet he's best known for the classics *The Hunchback of Notre-Dame* (1831) and *Les Misérables* (1862).

A Note from the Publisher

Spanning many genres, from non-fiction essays to literature classics to children's books and lyric poetry, Mint Edition books showcase the master works of our time in a modern new package. The text is freshly typeset, is clean and easy to read, and features a new note about the author in each volume. Many books also include exclusive new introductory material. Every book boasts a striking new cover, which makes it as appropriate for collecting as it is for gift giving. Mint Edition books are only printed when a reader orders them, so natural resources are not wasted. We're proud that our books are never manufactured in excess and exist only in the exact quantity they need to be read and enjoyed.

bookfinity™

Discover more of your favorite classics with Bookfinity™.

- Track your reading with custom book lists.
- Get great book recommendations for your personalized Reader Type.
- Add reviews for your favorite books.
- AND MUCH MORE!

Visit **bookfinity.com** and take the fun Reader Type quiz to get started.

Enjoy our classic and modern companion pairings!

Classic & Modern